I0525692

Dead 'til Dawn

By Gerald Dean Rice
Kindle Press Edition
Copyright 2017 Melted Brain Books

Kindle Press Edition, License Notes
This eBook is licensed for your personal enjoyment only. This eBook may not be re-sold or given away to other people. If you would like to share this book with another person, please purchase an additional copy for each recipient. If you're reading this book and did not purchase it, or it was not purchased for your use only, then please return to Kindle.com and purchase your own copy. Thank you for respecting the hard work of this author.

Dead 'til Dawn © 2017
Written by Gerald Dean Rice. All rights reserved.
This book is a work of fiction. Any resemblance to
persons, places or events is purely coincidental and
unintended. All rights reserved. No part of this
publication may be reproduced or transmitted by any
means, electronic, mechanical or written, without
express permission from the author.

Other titles available on Kindle...
Vamp-Hire
Fleshbags
The Zombie Show
The Ghost Toucher
30 Minute Plan
The Best Night of the Year
Tales from an Apartment

Dedication

Metaphorically speaking, this is the greatest book you're going to read all year. Maybe even in the last few years. Or ever. That being said—okay, *written*, if you want to be picky—this book is dedicated to someone who is truly deserving. Someone who was there at any time of day, someone who was there in sickness and health, someone who listened to my ideas no matter how off-the-wall. I don't need to stress this person's importance because there literally would be no me had this person not come into my life and showed me such wondrous things and taken me down such astounding paths of thought. This person's influence goes without saying; every spoken sentence is a line of poetry, every idea making the world just a tad brighter. This one's dedicated to me. I'm actually sort of touched. Nobody has ever dedicated a book to me before. I'll cherish this.

Dead 'til Dawn

Gerald Dean Rice

Prologue

Friday

Gary was dead, and Jim was on his way. He lay there, waiting for the end of his life, listening to the retreating footsteps of his killers and reflecting on how exactly he'd gotten here, on the dirty floor of some quack scientist's laboratory.

"Is this linoleum?" Jim may or may not have said aloud. He didn't think he could have, but then again, what did he know? Dead people didn't write books, and he seriously doubted that those people who had clinically died could be trusted. Seriously, if you couldn't trust the eyewitness account of someone who was drunk, how could you trust the account of someone whose brain was oxygen-deprived for a long period of time?

Wait, where was he again? Oh yeah, how had he gotten on this floor? Jim dialed back his memory to this morning. He'd gotten up at 6:15 a.m. like he did every morning. Mel, his fiancée, was already up, and he had a sneaking sensation she'd been exercising. The scent of her was playing in the air like a golden dewdrop. Jim loathed physical exertion, but through cajoling and the promising and delivering of sex, she'd gotten him to drop two dozen pounds or so.

He'd gone to work and dealt with an employee who'd been making the work environment uncomfortable. She was a lesbian—not that her sexuality was the issue, but she liked to talk about her latest conquests and detail exactly what she'd done to them. Maybe her sexuality had been an issue, and Jim had covered the company by explaining to all the employees that talking about their sex lives could be interpreted as sexual harassment.

After work he'd run into Gary. In hindsight, he should have literally run into Gary. Maybe then they wouldn't both be lying on the floor dying. Jim sighed. Oh well, it had been a good life. And by *good* he meant decent. And *decent* was just the word you used in place of *awful* when you really didn't want to open up and say it out loud, but just pass through the pleasantries to slug through the day.

It had been . . . a life. He could leave it at that.

Chapter 1

"I call this one BTTF," Dr. Knochenmus said. Gary had said everyone called him Dr. K for short, and he seemed cool enough, especially considering the giant fatty he'd just put to his lips to partake of.

"Buttfa?" Gary asked, a big smile on his face as he waited his turn. Jim wasn't sure exactly how he'd gotten here. He remembered his friend sitting on the hood of his Fiesta as he'd left work, like a scene out of some eighties movie, arms folded across his chest. That probably had more to do with the cold and his complete lack of a jacket than anything else. Jim remembered them getting in his car, and the rest had been like a vague fog clouding his memory until somehow they had wound up here.

Wherever here was. Gary had a knack for talking him into things.

Gary finished a long spliff before passing it to him. It slid so easily into Jim's hand, he remembered the feel, the smell, and was seconds away from taking a puff when he asked, "So why is it called B . . ."

"Back to the Future," the "doctor" finished for him. "Because it takes you back in time, man. You see your whole life flash before your eyes." The much older man nodded and smiled as if that particular sensation would be enjoyable to everybody. Not that Jim's childhood had been the worst, but he didn't feel like taking this particular trip down memory lane. He handed the joint back to the doctor.

"No, thanks."

"No, thanks? Who is this man, man? G, you said he was cool." The doctor was looking at Gary with half a scowl. Gary gave Jim a sideward glance, a look of disappointment on his face.

"He *is* cool." Gary slid the joint from the doctor's hand. "He's just under stress at work. Right, Jim?"

"No. Actually, everything at work is going pretty good." That made both Gary and the doctor frown.

"If this is your best friend, then your best friend is a total square."

Jim didn't know if he was supposed to take offense at such an ancient insult and stayed silent. The doctor continued staring at him.

"Give me that." Dr. K snatched the joint back from Gary. He took a long hit, held it, then leveled his gaze on Gary. "You didn't bring Five-O to my operation, did you?" Dr. K was easily thirty years older than them, skinny, and looked like he had never been in a fight in his life, but the look in his eyes told Jim he could be dangerous.

"No, man." Gary laughed nervously. "I told you, he's my best friend. I've known him since second grade. He's in AA." That last part seemed really tacked on to Jim's ears, a lie that could be spotted a mile off, but the doctor's expression brightened.

"Aw, geez, why didn't you tell me that?" He slapped Gary's shoulder and stubbed the joint out on the table, blowing the smoke high over his head and waving at it with a free hand. "Uh, congratulations," he said, dropping the doobie in his pocket and grabbing Jim's hand for a stiff, awkward shake. The three of them all looked at one another, no one knowing what to say.

"Come with me," Dr. K said. "I want to show you something." This was just how Jim wanted to spend his Friday night. Oh no, not at home with his beautiful fiancée for wingding and movie night; it was much more engaging here with Gary and Dr. Weed. He was going to have to think of a better one than that later.

All that sarcasm swimming around in his head, and yet Jim still went with them. Dr. K led them out of the office and past several lab stations, all littered with various types of equipment. Everything after a beaker and Bunsen burner was beyond Jim's ability to identify, leaving him to ponder at the various colored liquids and lab equipment he saw.

At the back of this room were thick plastic curtains. Dr. K parted them, leading Gary and Jim through. It was freezing in here, and Jim found it hard to believe that just a yellowed, translucent curtain could keep all the cold air in this space. Curls of refrigerated mist poured from vents overhead.

"You guys want to see something really cool?" Dr. K was beaming at them, puffs of white smoke coming out of his mouth with each word, seemingly unaware how cold it was in here. Jim looked around and saw tall racks with small labeled vials in small, foam-cushioned holders. Dr. K picked up a cup that had steam drifting out of the top, and Jim wondered how it could be hot still. Then he noticed the cup itself. It looked like it was ceramic, some shade of orange, and the handle didn't appear to be connected to the cup in any way. Jim looked where it should have touched at the top and at the bottom, wondering if there was some sort of clear plastic.

"Do you like my cup?"

"Yeah," Jim said. "How do you do that? Magnets?"

"Nope. Force fields. This cup is all ceramic." He took a big sip and set it back down. "Anyway, here's the thing I wanted you to see." Dr. K sat in an armless office chair and picked up a beat-up blue and white cooler sitting in another office chair in front of a draft table. He set it in his lap, sitting back and drumming his fingers on the sides. Jim thought he hadn't looked any more like a mad scientist than in that moment.

"So . . ." Gary began, "what's in the cooler?" Dr. K slowly turned in his chair and settled his eyes on him.

"The future and end of all war. Want a hit?"

"Hell, yeah," Gary said. Dr. K flashed his yellowed, crooked teeth and sat forward. He slid the top back, and steam from the dry ice inside drifted out and poured over the sides.

"Is that stuff safe?" Jim asked.

"Of course it's safe," Dr. K said. "I invented it!" Jim took a step backward and watched as the doctor reached inside and pulled out a small semitranslucent brown container. "It actually doesn't need to be refrigerated at all. It just looks cooler. I'm gonna present it to my customers tonight."

"On a Friday night?" Jim made a face. "Shouldn't you do that during normal business hours?" He began to wonder about the "doctor's" credentials. His lab was on 7 Mile on the east side, the building looked abandoned, and he was meeting with "customers" after six o'clock. "What did you invent for your customer?" he asked, standing securely behind Gary.

"An antideath pill." Dr. K's face beamed.

"And you're just gonna let us have some of it?"

"I made extra. Besides, how much fun can it be if you can't share it with friends?"

"Puff-puff-give, big bro," Gary said, taking the small container from Dr. K. He began wrestling with the top, twisting to no avail. After a minute, he looked at Jim and held it up.

"Jim, for the assist?"

Jim eyed the container in his friend's hand. He didn't want to touch it. More than ever, he really did not want to be here. But he'd never made a habit out of saying no to his best friend and squirmed at the thought of doing so now. Jim took the container and unscrewed it.

Nestled inside were five black pills about the size of bullets atop a bed of cotton.

"These aren't suppositories, are they?" he asked, trying to make a joke.

Dr. K's face screwed up in disgust, and he took the pills back. "For a period of forty-eight hours after you swallow this pill, you are effectively dead. Just like Jesus!"

"Jesus?" Gary asked. "What do you mean?"

"Jesus was crucified on a Friday and rose on a Sunday."

"I know my Bible. Jesus was dead for three days. Luke 24, verse 7."

Dr. K looked at Gary with a wary look. "How many days between Friday and Sunday? Count on your fingers."

Gary held up a hand and began to count. "Friday . . . Saturday . . . Sunday. Three."

"You don't count Friday. From Friday to Saturday is one day. And from Saturday to Sunday is two days." Dr. K held up his hand with a peace sign. "*Two.*"

"Yeah, but Friday is one whole day. Saturday is one whole day. Sunday is one whole day. One plus one plus one is three."

"No. You don't count the days. You count *between* the days. One plus one is two. *Two.* Besides, it's not like he was crucified at midnight Friday and rose at 11:59 Sunday."

"Yeah, but if I'm Friday, you're Saturday, and Jim is Sunday, then there's three of us. That makes three days."

"Yes, but you're counting the days wrong. Today is Friday. In twenty-four hours it will be Saturday. In forty-eight hours it will be Sunday." Jim was watching the exchange between his best friend and the crazy doctor. Dr. K looked at him. "Help a brother out here?"

"My name is Paul. That's between y'all."

"Never mind." Dr. K waved him off. "The pill works for forty-eight hours. Then you come back to life."

"So he'd be just a corpse for two days?" Jim asked. "What fun is that?"

"No. You would have full cognitive and motor function. Your nervous system would shut down, and autonomic function would cease."

"Autonomic function?"

"That means you'd stop breathing," Jim said.

"Among other things." Dr. K nodded. "Your heart would stop, your bowels, your breathing. You would have to blink intentionally."

"Cool." Gary nodded.

"No, that is not cool," Jim said. "Look, Dr. K, thanks, but *we're* not interested."

Something in the doctor's lab coat pocket beeped. He had opened his mouth to say something, but looked in his pocket and pulled out what looked like a hybrid between a walkie-talkie and a cell phone.

"Hello?" The man listened a moment, nodded, then said, "I'll be right there."

Dr. K looked at them and said, "My customers are particularly early." He held up a finger as he left the room. "Stay right there. I'll be right back." He came back immediately and grabbed the cooler, closing the lid. Then he was gone again.

"All right, I'd say this place has to have some sort of rear exit. I suggest we find it," Jim said.

Gary looked at him. "Why are you in such a rush to leave? Dr. K's cool; he wants us to try his antideath pill." Gary held up the container. "He forgot this."

Jim rolled his eyes. "Okay, on the off chance he isn't goofing on us, what do you think the odds are that an *anti death* pill works?" Jim stressed the words "anti death" for effect. "This guy's a quack, a snake oil salesman. The only legit drug he has in the whole place is probably weed."

"What happened to you, man? You used to be the boldest of us all."

"Is that why you brought me here? Because you thought I was so bold I'd be dumb enough to take unknown drugs off a complete stranger?"

"Nah, man. He's not a complete stranger. I vouch for him. Like I vouched for you. That used to be enough."

"Yeah, it used to be. Back when I didn't mind getting kicked out of school or getting sent to boot camp. I grew up, Gary. Just because you vouch for him doesn't make him legit. Do you know what compounds are in those pills?" Jim pointed to the open container the doctor had left in the room with them.

"No."

"Do you know that you *won't* drop dead the second you pop one of those in your mouth? Do you *know*?"

"No. I don't know."

"And do you know if this doctor actually went to an accredited university and attained an actual PhD in any of the sciences?"

Gary's mouth was a grim line. "Okay, Matlock, I get the picture."

"No, you don't. If he came back in here with more drugs, you would happily take them. What do you know about this guy? Where did you meet him?"

"He redid some siding on my dad's house."

Jim barked out a laugh. "So the scientist you would take drugs from also works on houses on the side?"

"He found him on Angie's list."

Jim narrowed his eyes at his friend. "Are you doing this on purpose?"

"Doing what?"

"Being dumb. Is this intentional? Are you looking for me to be the voice of reason? You asked what happened to me, but what happened to you? How are you this naïve?"

"Wait a minute. Stop. I brought you here because you're my best friend. Dr. K is a good friend of mine too. However we met. And no, I don't know everything about him, but I trust him. We've hung out. Like you and I used to. I miss you, man. And I thought it would be cool for us to just get out and do something together. Ever since you and Mel—"

"Are you going to start *that* again? Leave my fiancée out of it. She has nothing to do with why we don't hang out."

"Right. Because you are *so* into dog shows."

"This again? This again?" Jim growled and shook his fists in the air. "You know, when you're in a relationship with someone you care about, sometimes you do things you don't necessarily want to do. It's called compromise. She does it for me. And another thing, when was the last time you—"

Jim was cut off by the sound of a gunshot. They both looked in the direction of the plastic curtains, and when he looked at his friend again, they were both clinching each other's shirts.

Chapter 2

"That was a gunshot," Gary whispered as if Jim didn't know that. "A Beretta M9." Okay, that he didn't know.

"How do *you* know that?"

Instead of answering, Gary pulled him down until they were both crouching.

"Whoever it is, they're coming this way." Jim couldn't hear anything except the constant hum of fluorescent lights in the other room and the insistent hammering of his heart. He tried to look through the plastic curtains, but they were only clear enough to let light through so he could see generalized, globular shapes, not gun-toting psychopaths.

He looked around for something to defend himself with. Maybe he could use the chair. Gary would probably be no help; he'd never been good with thinking on his feet in school. It was up to Jim to save them now.

"Where the hell are you going?" he asked as Gary duckwalked to the curtains and peered out.

After about thirty seconds Gary pulled his head back and looked at Jim. "Two guys in weird robes, at least one armed."

And? Jim wanted to say. He wasn't foolish enough to think they hadn't just killed Dr. K, and neither was he about to go charging out there to get his own head blown off.

Gary duckwalked back and reached for the container.

Jim reflexively snatched it away. "Now is not the time to get high."

"Give those to me." Gary made a gimme gesture with his fingers.

Jim decided this would be his last stand. If he had never stood up to his friend before, now was the perfect time. He wasn't going to let his last moments be lost in a drug-induced stupor. They would face the end together and do it sober.

"No."

Gary got up on his knees, crawled over to Jim, and with his pointed index finger, poked him somewhere in the chest. The pain was explosive and paralyzing, and Jim yipped as his friend plucked the container from his grasp, reached inside, and took out a black pill, popping it in his mouth without a second thought. He tossed his head back and dry-swallowed before reaching in and taking out another.

"Now you."

"N-n-no," he managed to say through gritted teeth.

"Look, I'm only doing this because I love you." Gary reached toward Jim's face, the pill pinched between thumb and forefinger. Even though his chest throbbed, Jim intentionally turned his head at the last moment, swinging his face back in an attempt to knock the pill from Gary's fingers. The maneuver worked, sending the pill skittering beneath some sort of skinny black machine. Gary reached after it, cursed, then fished out another from the container.

"Hold still," he said, palming the top of Jim's head, holding another pill.

"No. I don't want that!" Jim was screaming and didn't care. They were going to die, and he wanted it to be on his terms. He tried to get a hand up, but Gary pinned it down with his knee. More pain; this time he felt like his forearm would break Gary leaned so hard on it. "No!" Jim howled and closed his mouth too late as Gary shoved the pill between his lips.

He kept his teeth clenched, pushing the pill away with his mouth. Jim had managed to kick over both swivel chairs, enough noise to surely bring the gunmen. He could feel the pill begin to mix with his saliva, a warm, metallic taste seeping between his teeth.

Then Gary leaned off him.

"Whoa," he said, staring at Jim. He stood, turned, and dived through the plastic curtains. Immediately someone began shooting, at least some of the bullets striking the threshold and curtains themselves, making them part and billow.

"Gary, no!" Jim said, his pain forgotten as he got to his feet. They were killing his best friend, and he had to stop them. He stood and charged through, seeing one robed man staring down at Gary's prone body, the other looking at him as he was sliding another clip into the gun. He pulled back on the slide thingy, and Jim roared as he charged him, arms raised like a rabid gorilla, intent on smashing the man's head in even if he did shoot.

The man danced back a few steps, firing in Jim's direction. Vials and beakers exploded around him, and Jim tripped over his feet, landing hard on his face. He tried to get up, but he found he couldn't move his arms or legs. He blinked as something warm began to spread beneath him.

This is it, he thought. *This is what dying feels like.*

Chapter 3

Jim's vision fuzzed over, but he never lost consciousness. He didn't feel like he was dying, merely waiting. For what he didn't know. Maybe a guy in a black robe with a scythe, maybe an angel, maybe he wasn't supposed to go anywhere and he'd just remain here, in his own dead body, like that episode of the *Twilight Zone*. Wait, that was the *Twilight Zone*, wasn't it? Maybe one of those knockoffs, he couldn't be sure, but it was a good one. The dude was all, "Don't cut me open, bro—I'm not dead!" and "Look at my finger! Look at my finger! I can wiggle my finger!"

Gary saw that one too. Me, him, and what's-her-name . . .

Jim continued cycling through random thoughts as he waited for his mind to spin down and shut off. He had to be dying because nothing hurt. If he were just badly wounded, he'd be writhing in agony. No, he had to be dying. He just hoped he'd be presentable enough for an open casket. Something he could float over, and as his mother stood before his body, he could wag a finger and say, "See? I told you!" although what he'd told her in particular escaped him at the moment.

Jim had been lying on the floor dead for maybe ten minutes when he decided to stop waiting and get up. He'd begun drumming his fingers on the floor and finally popped his head up on his chin and looked around. Gary was sitting up, looking at him, a blank expression on his face.

"Hey," his friend said.

"Hey," he said back. Gary didn't look right, which made sense considering he was dead too. He sort of wavered like old monitors did after you hit the degauss button, except in extremely slow motion. Then Jim realized it wasn't just Gary; it was everything around them.

Maybe heaven was a laboratory.

"So what now?" he asked.

"I don't know." Gary went back to staring at his hand, turning it back and forth as if trying to remember which side was which. "Maybe we stay here awhile, get high."

"You already did that when you were living. Do you want to spend the rest of your afterlife high too?"

"You don't? Hey, we're dead. It's not like drugs will kill us."

Either that was a solid argument, or Jim was still a little lightheaded from dying. "How do we get out of here? I mean, this is in heaven, isn't it?"

"Heaven? You think we're that kind of dead?" Gary laughed. "You think *you* would go to heaven?"

"Yeah. I'm a good person. I don't steal. I don't take anything that doesn't belong to me. I put money in the kettle for the Salvation Army around Christmas."

"There's a lot of good people in hell." Gary shook his head, and Jim could imagine the thoughts going through his dead brain. Gary had been raised in large part by his grandparents, and his grandfather—well, his stepgrandfather—had been the pastor of their church. Even though he was nonpracticing, Gary could run theological circles around most Christians.

"You think I'm going to hell?"

"Well, I don't *know* that you're going to hell." He mumbled something Jim couldn't hear.

"What was that? Gary, did you just mumble a Bible verse?"

"I . . . no . . . yeah."

"Which one?"

"And again I say unto you, it is easier for a camel to go through the eye of a needle, than for a rich man to enter into the Kingdom of God."

"But I'm not rich."

"Parables, my man. Parables."

Jim let it go. No, he didn't.

"Gary, say I'm not going to hell!"

"Fine." Gary shrugged. "You're not going to hell."

"What do you mean not 'that kind of dead'?" he asked after a moment.

"Dr. K's pills. They worked."

"What do you mean they worked? The guy's a quack!"

"A quack that saved your life."

"After you put it in danger!"

Gary held out his arms, and for the first time Jim noticed the three bullet holes strafing his body from just about his hip to the upper corner of his chest in a diagonal line.

"Oh my God. Gary, you've been shot!"

"Well, yeah. They shot you too, right?"

"That's right. They did." Jim sat up and patted himself down like he was looking for his keys, then he got into a crouch, looking around for the man who had shot them.

"Don't worry about it. They're gone."

"What do you mean 'don't worry about it'? They tried to kill us!"

"And here we are not dead."

"Well, not for lack of trying."

"Right. Because Dr. K's pills worked."

"Would you stop? You sound like Jack the Giant Slayer, talking about magic beans."

"Then you agree I'm right then. Jack's mother didn't believe him, but he did really have magic beans."

"That's not my point. You sound like an insane person."

"So what? The two aren't mutually exclusive. I'm right even if I do sound crazy. Just look at me, I have three bullet holes in my body, and I'm not even *bleeding*. How boss is that?" Gary said it like he thought that was cool, making Jim worry for his sanity even more. He didn't know what the answer was, but Jim was sure magical, deathproof pills were not the answer. When he checked himself over thoroughly, not finding any gunshots, he realized he wasn't dead after all.

"I'm not shot."

Gary sat up straighter and focused on him. "What do you mean?"

"I mean they must have missed me. I'm not shot at all."

"Let me see." Gary pushed off the floor and crawled over. He put his hands through Jim's hair, yanking and pulling for some reason.

"Ow!"

Gary's prodding really hadn't hurt, but he was rough. He continued pinching and prodding and poking until he got down to Jim's knees.

"You aren't shot. I guess you bit the dick."

"I know."

"Then why did you fall down?"

"Because I tripped."

"So you played dead. Smart."

There was a hint of sarcasm to that last word that Jim resented. He did actually run out in a display of solidarity. His intention had been to either save his best friend's life or die along with him in the process. But something about him not being wounded at all and just lying there came off as cowardly. That burned just as much as Gary's suspicion that he had done that very thing.

"Hey, I could have been shot." Gary didn't say anything. Jim was embarrassed he was actually trying to defend himself and decided to move on. "So what do we do now? I have the feeling calling the police probably isn't the best idea."

Gary nodded. "There's enough weed in this building to send us to prison for the rest of our natural lives. I say we get out of here and maybe call the cops from a pay phone."

"Pay phone? When was the last time you saw one of those?"

Gary shrugged. "Gotta be one somewhere." They helped each other up, and Jim was surprised at how weak he felt on his feet. They held onto one another, walking back the way they'd come. Jim felt pretty certain the gunmen were gone but felt a growing sense of dread at the prospect of coming across Dr. K's dead body.

"Gary?"

"Yeah, I know, Jim. If you want to close your eyes—"

"No—no. I'll be fine. Just . . . hold my hand tighter?"

"Sure, J."

Gary hadn't called him that since they were twelve, after his grandfather had died. Throughout his childhood, Jim's parents had had a habit of separating and leaving him with his father's father while they sorted things out. Jim had spent probably a total of two years with him and had grown very close to his Oldpa and had been rocked to his core to find him dead when he'd come home from school one day. Gary had lived more than a mile away, but Jim had run to his friend's house, crying all the way.

"I want to go to Dr. K's office," Gary said.

"Why?" Jim sounded a little whinier than he would have liked.

"Notes. Anything that'll tell us more about how that pill works."

"I told you, that pill is crap. Don't waste time—"

Gary let go of his hands and walked into Dr. K's open office. Jim stood and watched as he rifled through papers that had already been spilled from drawers, stepping over mismatched metal cabinets that had been pulled down. One had a big dent in it, and Jim wondered if that had already been there or if one of the gunmen had kicked it.

He didn't remember hearing anything like that, but maybe he'd passed out on the floor.

Jim went over those few moments after he'd tripped. The man in the robe who'd actually held the gun had fired on him several times, obviously missing with each shot. There hadn't been anything in his path, but somehow Jim had tripped. Maybe he'd gotten his feet tangled, although he recalled making long, running strides, so they should have been far apart. He wanted to go back to look for anything that may have been dropped on the floor, but couldn't stand the thought of going backward. He would have to settle his curiosity with just his memory.

Gary came out of Dr. K's office, a satisfied look on his face.

"Did you find it?"

"Yeah. A whole baggie." Gary held up a gallon-size Ziploc bag filled with pot.

"What about the papers?"

"Oh yeah!" Gary ducked back into the office and came back with a booklet of rolling papers.

"No, not that. The . . . the documents . . . about the pills!"

Gary turned and looked back in the office. "I can't find anything in there. That office is a mess." He walked ahead. Jim tried to mount an argument but found it impossible to both not believe the pills had actually held active ingredients of any kind and yell at Gary for not finding any information on said pills. He caught up just as they reached the front door.

"Okay, your car's still there," Gary said.

"Good—let's go!"

"Hold it. Something isn't right."

"You said it yourself, they're gone."

"Yeah. And so is Dr. K's body. If they killed him even."

"So what does that have to do with my car?"

"They could have booby-trapped it. You know anybody with a tow truck you can trust?"

"No. Why?"

"Because we can't call the police if your car is still out there."

"Oh yeah."

"I'm gonna go out. You stay here until I give the all clear."

Jim wanted to say "wait," but Gary had the door open and was in the middle of a tuck–n-roll before he could speak.

Chapter 4

Gary came to his feet and rolled sideways, squarely into the floodlight in front of the building. Then he dived, disappearing on the other side of Jim's Fiesta. Gary burst from behind the car in a sprint, zigzagging across the small parking lot before leaping over the fence into a line of hedges.

Jim waited for five minutes, looking out the small window. He was still unsure about outside, but felt an increasing amount of unease until he had to get out. He tried tuck-n-rolling like he'd seen Gary do, but managed to smash his forehead on the asphalt. It hadn't hurt much—at all, actually—which he thought made sense considering it only trickled a little bit of blood. He followed Gary's circuitous route, going around his car, and ran a Z across the parking lot before climbing the fence and falling headfirst into the bushes.

Gary was sitting a few feet away, holding a foil wrapper filled with what looked like a rotten taco and eating hungrily from it.

"Gary," Jim whispered loudly, "I thought you were going to give me the high sign when it was okay."

"I never said that," his friend said around a mouthful.

"Yeah, you did. You said you were going to tell me when it was clear."

Gary took another bite, then shook his head. After he'd finished whatever it was he was eating, he said, "I told you I'd give the all clear."

"Yeah."

"Well, when I made it out of the parking lot, that was me telling you. What was I supposed to do, walk all the way back and get you?"

For the second time, Jim found himself speechless. His friend had been the one to be brave while he had stayed back. He wasn't really in a position to complain.

"Are you eating garbage?"

Gary shook his head, his mouth stuffed.

"Where did you get that from?"

"Over there in that big food bin." He thumbed over his shoulder, and Jim looked. The only thing he saw next to the liquor store was a dumpster.

"Food bin? Do you mean that dumpster?"

Gary turned.

"No, it's not—oh my God, I'm eating *garbage*!" He hurled the foil-wrapped garbage, a rotten tomato falling out and adhering to his hand. Gary looked and shook it off. "I don't know why I did that. It just smelled so . . . . *good*."

"Maybe it was that pill."

Gary's eyes rolled up to him.

"I hope not. You better hope too."

"Why? I didn't swallow that pill."

"My man, when I was shoving it in your mouth, it . . . melted. I'd bet the effects are transmittable through mucous membranes."

Jim was impressed. Gary was smart, but in an I-really-don't-want-to-apply-myself kind of way. If a teacher could trick him into learning something, he could be impressive. He'd gotten a 30 on the ACT back in high school, while Jim had only gotten a 27. Clearly, he was the smarter of the two somehow, but only displayed it on the rarest of occasions.

"Hey, what's that on your pants?"

Jim looked down. The sun had just set, and he couldn't see that well. "What?"

"It's a big dark spot like you pissed yourself."

"I don't know what it is. Maybe when I fell I spilled one of those beakers on my clothes."

Gary gave him a look. "I didn't see any broken glass."

"Well, I didn't piss myself. Okay?" Although Jim wasn't so sure about that.

"Let me smell."

"No!"

"Come on. Let me sniff. I'm not going to tell anybody. I didn't tell anybody when you did it in second grade."

"I had a urinary tract infection in second grade. That wasn't my fault, and you would've been a jerk if you'd told anyone. And you're not sniffing my crotch."

"Well, I didn't." Gary mumbled something.

"What was that?"

Gary sighed. "I said men can't get urinary tract infections."

"I had one, dammit!"

"I'm not saying you didn't have a *something*." Gary held his hands up as if to ward Jim off. "Just not a UTI. Ladies get those."

Jim glowered at him, forcibly holding back a flood of words. Somebody had told on him in second grade. He'd carefully kept his crouch hidden until almost the end of class before the whole class seemingly turned on him in unison and began laughing.

Someone had told, and Jim had never forgotten his vow to find out who.

"I can't believe I was eating garbage," Gary said, looking at his hand. "I need to find a restroom so I can wash my hands."

"There's a Lightning Burger around the corner." Jim's voice was clipped as he still brooded over his childhood humiliation. That had stuck with him for years. They walked, looking around for the two gunmen or anything suspicious.

The farther away from Dr. K's building they got, the more he relaxed. They pushed through the outer doors of the Lightning Burger and pushed out of the vestibule.

"Go get the key," Gary said, pausing by the trash receptacle. Jim wanted to ask what was up but saw the look on Gary's face, like he was trying to remain incognito.

Good call, he thought. Two guys bellying up to the counter probably would look suspicious. Especially considering one of them had three bullet holes in his shirt.

Jim still hadn't wrapped his head around that one. Gary should be writhing in agony or dead, but instead he was hungry enough to eat garbage and was talking and walking. His gunshot wounds weren't even bleeding. Maybe there *was* something to this pill of Dr. K's.

No. That wasn't it. Couldn't be. Maybe Gary was in shock. Maybe the shots had only grazed him. Maybe they'd been pellets. The most important thing right now was to keep calm—

"Jim! Hey, Jim!"

He looked back at Gary.

"Can you hurry it up? I'm about to lick my fingers here."

"Right." Jim nodded, stepping past several people to get to the counter.

"Get to the back of the line!" a deep voice boomed. Jim looked up at a man who had to have been at least seven feet tall and almost as wide. His tightly knotted fist hung at his side almost level with Jim's face. Jim was in a hurry, though, and didn't have time for this.

"Yes, sir!" Jim said and marched to the rear.

He stood behind a young woman with thick, copper braids down to her waist, standing next to a stout, iron-haired woman he guessed was her grandmother. The seven-footer was two places ahead, mumbling loudly about how people didn't know they place and how he was bound to get arrested for stomping a mudhole in a motherfucker.

Jim tried to make himself as small as possible, feeling the big man's eyes on him even though he wasn't looking. The two women turned back and looked at him, examining him like he had been sentenced to die.

"You okay, sweetie?" the grandmother asked. "You look sick." That was about what he felt like, or at least what he thought he felt like. Jim had never been a fighter, the prospect always terrifying him. To be afraid of a confrontation had always been his natural reaction, although when he examined his actual feelings, he realized he wasn't afraid.

"Yes, ma'am. I'm fine." He nodded at the woman and her cute granddaughter. Jim wondered how a man could talk to a woman when her grandmother or mother was present. It probably couldn't be done, which was just as well. He had a fiancée, and he was perfectly happy with Mel.

Mel! In all this craziness, he hadn't thought about calling her. She would be at home now, wondering where he was. He'd left his cell phone in his car, though. Jim made up his mind to go back to his car as soon as Gary had washed his hands. That was as much for his own benefit as Gary's. Mel hated a messy car, and a garbage smell would send her through the roof.

With his newfound lack of fear, he stepped out of line and sauntered up to the counter.

"Man!" Jim didn't bother looking at the giant as he smiled at the woman behind the counter, helping another customer. Either the big guy would start something or he wouldn't. Jim felt a strange confidence that he could handle whatever came up.

"Excuse me. May I have the restroom key?"

The woman continued order-taking as if he hadn't spoken, and Jim loudly cleared his throat.

"May I have the restroom key, please?" She took the patron's money and rolled her eyes toward him.

"You have to buy something to use the restroom."

"Then make me a chocolate shake," he said. "I gotta go real bad."

The cashier handed back change, and Jim felt a mighty hand fall on his shoulder.

"I told you to get to the end of the line. Yo McNuggets been canceled." Jim wanted to point out that McNuggets were from McDonald's. Lightning Burger had Chicken Sparks. Sure, the name wasn't clever, but they had a theme going on—Thunder Shakes, Flash Fries, Cyclone Burgers . . .

"Sure would've been easier if you just gave me that key." Jim looked at the cashier and winked before turning to the big man. "I suppose you already had your rabies vaccination?"

"Huh?" The man reluctantly pulled his hand back.

"I mean, if you just go around punching random strangers who could have God knows what, then you must have had a rabies vaccination. Probably all those other ones too. Because I have rabies. Do you want my rabies?"

Jim hadn't seen himself in a mirror, but he figured he must look awful, especially after the old lady had asked if he was sick.

The man studied him, an unreadable look on his face. Then he slugged Jim.

Surprisingly, it didn't hurt. In truth, it had seemed like a half-hearted punch, like the big man had changed his mind midswing. Something that felt like jelly spurted out of Jim's nostrils as his head snapped back. Jim slumped against the counter but didn't go down. Several people gasped, and instead of hitting him again, the giant took a step back, raising both arms in a half-offensive posture.

"What?" Jim asked. When nobody responded he took a step toward the big man, curious as to what should happen next.

The next punch was wild, a hook that still came fast, but Jim saw it coming and stepped inside, catching the meat of his opponent's forearm on the side of his head. Jim didn't know why, but he reached up, grabbing the guy's arm, and took a big bite. The man screamed, shaking Jim off and throwing himself backward.

The big man said something so fast it sounded like he was speaking in tongues. Rather than engaging further in the fight, he turned and ran for the exit. Gary was still leaning against the trash can and stuck a foot out right as the big man reached the door, and the man's upper body propelled through, palms first. He smacked into the glass, taking the whole square out. His thighs caught on the grab bar, his forward momentum continuing as he somersaulted and landed on his head.

But the big man was not out. He scrabbled to his feet, taking a moment to look into the restaurant proper, his expression terrified, before shoving the outer door open so violently the glass shattered against the side of the building as he escaped.

Nobody else had moved. Gary looked back at Jim, stood up straight, and began a slow clap. When no one joined him, he stopped and said, "Not the right time?"

Jim looked back at the cashier. She held a key up on a long piece of flat wood. "The cops are coming," she said flatly.

"Eventually," Gary said, yanking the key from her hand. He looked beyond the young woman and waved to somebody in the back. "Hey, Kelsey!" A petite blonde standing by the fry-o-lator sheepishly held up a hand and wiggled her fingers. Gary grabbed Jim under the arm and hustled him toward the restroom door.

"We gotta get ourselves presentable." Gary turned on the faucet as soon as they entered the restroom. He shuffled Jim to the sink and locked the door behind them. Jim held his hands under the water and looked at his reflection. The man staring back at him didn't seem to meet his eyes, as if his reflection had somewhat of a will of its own and wasn't bound to his actions. His curly hair was flat-looking, his skin grayish, his nose severely broken. His lips peeled back, and he bared his teeth. They looked normal, but his gums were ashen. Jim realized he was thirsty and dipped his head to his cupped hands, splashing water into his mouth. The water tasted awful, but it lubricated his cheeks and tongue so he didn't have cottonmouth.

"I think we're dead," Jim said after a long moment. He reached up with one hand and snapped his nose back in place. As expected, no pain.

"No shit, homie." Gary shouldered him aside, his shirt already off. He prodded at each of the three bullet holes strafing him diagonally from hip to chest. The wounds looked impossibly deep and singed black. Gary poked at the one in the center of his chest, and watery brown fluid trickled out.

"What is that?" Jim asked.

"Blood. Or at least it used to be." Gary began opening and closing his mouth and turning his head from side to side.

"What are you doing?"

"I can't blink."

"So, what are you doing?"

"I'm working my muscles so rigor mortis doesn't set in." He stepped back from the sink and straightened his legs before touching his toes. His back popped several times, and he stood up, reaching for the ceiling with one hand and then the other.

"I don't get it. What does that have to do with your eyelids?"

"Rigor mortis starts with your eyelids, jaw, and neck. I didn't think we'd get it because we're only kind of dead. But if I can't blink, then the rest of my body might go stiff. I'm hoping if I stretch, it'll keep rigor at bay or prevent it altogether."

"Right." Jim began stretching as well. "What are you gonna do about those bullet holes?"

"Nothing. Well, maybe I'll put a Band-Aid on them or something."

"But that's short-term. Eventually this pill is supposed to wear off, and then what?"

"I'm not sure. Maybe we can ask Dr. K's wife."

"Dr. K has a wife?" Jim seized Gary by the shoulders. "We should get over there right now. Where does he live?"

Gary shrugged. "Maybe we can look her up in the Yellow Pages?"

"The White Pages."

"Uh-huh. That's what I said."

It never ceased to amaze Jim how brilliant Gary was sometimes and then completely unaware most other times.

"Okay, get your shirt back on. I say we go back to my car. We have to chance it."

Gary nodded.

"Hold up. Let me do this first." Gary stood in front of the mirror again, put his fingers to either side of the bullet hole in his chest, and squeezed. A second later a bullet popped out like a giant zit, plunking and rolling around in the sink. Gary snatched it out, pocketed it, and turned for the door.

"You handled yourself pretty well," Gary said to Jim. "With that big guy."

"Why didn't you help me? That guy was a giant."

"I wanted to see you do it. I bailed you out of a lot of jams when we were kids. I wanted you to do yourself proud."

"Uh-huh." Jim wanted to call his friend a coward, but he did feel oddly proud of how he had carried himself. Manly. Who was he kidding? He could be proud and bust balls. "Chickenshit."

The restaurant had all but been abandoned by customers, the cashier standing behind the counter. Gary tossed her the key. As they headed back to his car, Jim found himself wondering how he was going to explain this to his fiancée.

They made it back to the car. Jim was feeling careless and strode right up to it, pressing the button on his key fob and unlocking the door. He slid in and started the engine. No boom.

Gary looked at him from about twenty feet away, eyebrows raised. When the car continued not to explode, he walked over and got in.

Jim reversed and peeled out of the parking lot. In minutes they were back on I-75, and he had his cell in his hand.

"You know it's really not safe for you to drive and talk," Gary said. Jim eyed him and put the phone on speaker before resting it on his thigh.

Mel normally picked up by the second ring, so by the third he began to worry. He took a deep breath, imagining her sweet scent filling his nose. When it went to voice mail, he really began to worry.

"I'm sure it's fine," Gary said. It probably was, but the way he said it sounded like he meant something else.

"What do you mean by tha—hey honey, it's me, Jim. Just calling to let you know I got caught up, but I'm on my way home now. I'll see you soon?"

He disconnected the call. "Now what do you mean by that?" He sounded angrier than he really was with good reason: this was a conversation he had needed to have with his best friend for a long time. When things had turned serious between him and Mel, Gary had gotten weird. He started getting possessive and showing up at the apartment at all times of the night. That kind of stuff had been cool when he was single, but Mel's sleep got disturbed really easily, and she had to get up for work early a lot of times.

"I don't mean anything. Forget it." Gary's tone was flat.

"No—no. You meant something. Express yourself."

Gary looked at him and smiled. "I think everything is wonderful and perfect. We're going to go home and find your girlfriend totally clothed and not in bed getting long-dicked."

"Mel isn't like that." Jim bristled but kept his composure. "She wouldn't cheat on me. And why would she move in with me if she wasn't serious? Why would she agree to marry me?"

Gary and Jim had chanced upon his well-endowed downstairs neighbor when he had knocked on Jim's door to actually ask to borrow a cup of sugar. When Gary had answered, he'd been greeted by a tall, onyx-skinned man, who was chiseled from his eyebrows down, wearing nothing but a yellow silk robe. He'd let the man in while Jim fished around for the sugar. He poured some into a Tupperware container while Gary had chatted with him, and at some point the silk robe, which came to midthigh, had slipped open, revealing stainless steel abs and a girthy penis that could have had its own femur bone.

The man hadn't seemed to notice, and not more than three minutes after he was gone with the sugar, the ecstatic moans of a woman could be heard through the floor.

It had gone on for four hours.

"Mel isn't like that. She *loves* me." Jim hated the way his tone come off whiny, but he had to finally get this point out. "Why are you always competing?"

"I'm not competing." Gary looked shocked. "I'm your bro. I care about who you're with."

"You never gave Mel a chance."

"That's because she's a horrible human being. And an alleged slut."

"She is not a horrible human being. And you're the one doing all the alleging."

"Not true. All the guys she bangs say so too."

Jim narrowed his eyes. "She is *not* a slut."

"I didn't say she was. Did I say she eats more cylindrical meat than Kobayashi? Or that she's had more guys behind her than the first person in line for *Star Wars*? Or—"

"How about those Tigers?" Jim slapped his palm on the dashboard. Jim didn't actually want to talk about the Tigers. That was their signal that a subject had become too hot and needed to be changed.

They were both silent a few minutes before Gary said, "So we have to figure out what happens when this pill runs its course."

Jim was surprised. Gary had actually brought up a subject that mattered.

Jim said, "I'd say we have to find Dr. K's wife and see if she has notes of some kind."

"And tell her her husband is dead."

Jim hadn't thought about that. That made him uncomfortable. Death had never been a subject he felt was in his wheelhouse of conversation. To actually tell someone her husband had been murdered wasn't going to be an easy talk.

Jim almost would prefer to go back to talking about Deepdick and Mel.

"First things first. I want to get back home and check on Mel. And get cleaned up too. I stink."

"Yeah, you do stink."

"Like you don't?"

"No. I do not have the capacity to excrete the commensurate oils that would generate an offense to the olfactory sense." Gary turned his head from side to side while scissoring his hands through the air in front of him like a robot.

"If only there was a way to harness your stupid for *good*." Jim shook his head.

They pulled into Jim's apartment complex, and he parked in his carport. It was an open apartment building, all units accessible from outside, and Jim looked from his second-floor window facing the lot to the window on the first floor. Deepdick's light was on, and he was home.

Jim tried not to think about him or more specifically "it" and what "it" should not be doing to his fiancée at this or any other moment.

"You want me to wait here?" Gary asked, examining his fingernails.

"No. It's fine if you come in." His friend gave him a wry smile, and they climbed out of the car together. Jim wasn't about to admit even to himself that there was a possibility Mel could be with his neighbor right now and Jim just might need help fighting him. No. Mel was good. Mel was faithful. Mel was true.

He crossed his fingers just the same.

Fall was only a few days old, and the air had rapidly chilled with the sunset. Jim felt the cold, but it didn't settle into his bones the way it normally would have. He had to shake out his legs, and Gary's back crackled like bubble wrap as he stretched. They both began walking toward the building, noticeably stiffer.

"We look like zombies," Gary said. Jim thought he'd gotten his normal gate back until they reached the stairs. One knee didn't want to bend, and he had to grab the railings and hop his way up the first flight of stairs. By the second flight, his knee had loosened, making the stairs more manageable.

Getting the key into the lock was a whole other story. Jim had to flex his fingers continuously for five minutes before he barely had enough dexterity to find his apartment key.

Once they were inside, Gary made a show of sniffing the air.

Jim's broken nose had gotten progressively worse to the point he could no longer smell anything, including his own stinky body. "What is it?" he asked. Jim resisted the urge to go into a Lassie routine.

"Sex. I smell sex."

"Come on . . ."

"No, I'm serious. Somebody been fuckin'. It's thick too. Like he got all the way to the back."

Jim quickly made his way to the bedroom and threw open the door. Gary was right behind him, and they both saw the empty bed together. The sheets were tousled, which was odd considering he had made the bed with Mel before leaving.

"Is that normal?" Gary asked.

"No." Jim approached. He touched the sheets. They were cool, but the window was open.

"Like somebody heard us coming and jumped out the window."

"Stop it, already. We can see the window from the parking lot."

"Yeah. And whoever was here leapt out when they heard the key hit the door."

"If anybody was in here. If *Mel* was in here, she would have just come out the bedroom door. She lives here. Even if she were with somebody in here, he could have jumped out while she stalled us at the door. That would make the most sense. So we must have forgotten to make the bed."

"*And* opened the window? C'mon, J. You hate your bedroom window being open. You couldn't have slept. If you'd gotten hot, you would've turned on the air-conditioning or something."

That was true.

"Hm. Maybe Mel came back home for something?"

"Some*thing*?" Gary nodded vigorously.

"Stop it. I suppose someone could have broken into the apartment." He began rooting through his dresser drawers and checking the TV stand for his CDs and Xbox. After about three minutes of roaming the apartment, he met Gary in the little hall outside his bedroom.

"Nothing's missing." Now he was concerned. The two things that could have happened in his apartment didn't exactly fit. He called Mel's cell again. After a few rings, it went to voice mail again. He left her another message, trying not to sound worried, his anxiety rising by the second.

"What are you gonna do?"

"I don't know. I need to use the bathroom."

"Good idea."

Jim brushed past Gary and shut the door.

"Sometimes I do my best thinking when I'm blowing out the old colon," Gary added.

Jim stared at himself in the mirror. He didn't look dead exactly. He looked more exhausted. Severely exhausted. His reflection still had that quality to it like the eyes didn't exactly meet his, but he noticed more of a twinkle in them than before. They were less dull, more present. His skin looked a bit fresher too. He prodded at his nose, turning his head from side to side as he examined it. It looked stuffed.

Jim leaned over the sink, pressed a nostril closed with one finger, and blew. Nothing came out, but something was definitely up there. He did it twice more, and the third time thick, reddish green mucous blasted out into the sink. He felt immediate relief, although imbalanced, like the other nostril was still full. He repeated on the other side, and once everything felt clear, he turned on the hot water.

He had to splash it around for a good minute for the stuff to loosen up enough to rinse down and then looked at his face in the mirror again. That fresh look seemed to have spread out from the center of his face, and now his eyes looked a lot brighter. His mouth didn't seem to have that pinched-down frown to it, and when he forced his mouth into a smile, his dimples appeared.

Ah, those award-winning dimples that had melted many a heart when he was a child. Jim was pretty sure they had done 90 percent of the work in bringing him and Mel together.

"What the hell happened?" He wondered if the effects of the pill were wearing off. If so, great for him, but then his thoughts turned to Gary. The pill wearing off might mean something entirely different for him, with three bullet holes in his body. Would he die?

Jim felt a cramp and realized he really did have to take a dump. He quickly sat on the toilet and felt *everything* come out. The awful smell told him that particular sense had returned, and he had to courtesy flush twice before his body finally felt empty.

He looked over at the tub, longing for a shower more than ever, but couldn't justify taking the time. He was growing more worried for Mel by the second on top of his and Gary's situation. Jim flushed one last time before zipping up and washing his hands.

He joined Gary in the small nook area off the kitchen. His friend had a carton of chocolate ice cream, half a pack of raw bacon, orange juice, and an apple. Gary was chewing with a concerned look on his face.

"What's wrong?" Jim asked.

"The food. It doesn't taste right."

'This from the guy who was eating garbage about an hour ago."

"I'm serious. Has this stuff been here long?"

"No. Mel and I just went shopping two days ago."

Gary shook his head, spooned out one last scoop of ice cream, and slapped the carton back on the table.

"Taste it. This stuff is disgusting."

"Well, after that rousing endorsement . . ." Jim picked up the ice cream and hesitated. It had been a lot of years since he and Gary had eaten after one another. There was a time when he wouldn't have thought twice about it, but that had passed after he'd seen Gary kiss Topeka Davis. Topeka was the skankiest girl in school, and the rumor floating around was that she had had the clap twice. And there his best friend was sucking face with her.

Hell, he was dead. Gary's cooties were the least of his worries. Jim ate a spoonful, grimaced, and it was all he could do to keep from spitting it out. He didn't know how to describe it. It tasted like he'd remembered chocolate ice cream tasting, but it was wrong somehow. Not spoiled, but upside down somehow. The bitter of the chocolate was too full, the sweet too syrupy and tinny.

He nodded and set the carton of ice cream back on the table. Then he went to the closet by the front door.

"What are you doing?" Gary asked. Jim pushed around boxes on the floor until he found a copy of the White Pages hiding in the corner. As fastidious as Mel was, it was a miracle the book was still here. "What's that?"

"Phone book. I'm going to look up Dr. K's wife."

"Why didn't you just Google her on your phone?"

Jim felt his minor sense of accomplishment deflate. This copy of the White Pages was two years old. It was doubtful the doctor's info would be there, but he was invested now.

Jim fished his cell phone out of his jacket pocket, surprised at the return of his fingers' dexterity. If he couldn't find her in the White Pages, then he'd ask Siri. He looked at Gary's hands, clawlike, the digits seemingly glued together.

"You okay?" Jim asked.

"Never better."

There was nothing Jim could've done about it at that moment no matter what Gary said. "How do you spell Dr. K's name?"

"I don't know. I don't think I ever asked what his first name is."

"You don't know his first name? He's a friend of yours, and you don't know his first name?"

"No. What's my middle name?"

"Peyton. After your mother's favorite book."

"Oh. That would be *one* acceptable answer."

"Your parents were not going to name you Shandling."

"Hey, you don't know that. If my mother were around right now, I guarantee you I'd be Gary Shandling Tate." They'd had this conversation many times before. Gary's mother had died in childbirth, and because of their mutual love of Gary Shandling, Gary was convinced his mother had wanted to give him the comedian's name. Jim had gone so far as to ask Gary's father, a man who had been way too permissive with his son's upbringing, and he'd said the plan had always been for her to pick the first name and him to pick the middle. Peyton had been Gary's grandmother's maiden name, and no one knew exactly where Gary came from.

"Whatever." Jim went back to the White Pages. "How in the world do you spell Knochenmus?"

"Phonetically, I hope. It's a German name, so I would guess it begins with 'K-N.' Maybe it's like 'knock.' like with a door. but a 'C-H' instead of a 'C-K.' Think that might be a good start?"

"Uh, yeah. I think I can fill in the rest." Jim turned to the K's and began combing through until he found a Knochenmus, Doris, and a Knochenmus, Gay.

"Gay," he said and smirked. He called that number first, and it was answered on the first ring.

"Hello?" came the reedy voice.

"Mrs. Knochenmus?"

"Yes?"

"My name is Jim. My friend Gary is friends with your husband, Dr. Knochenmus."

Dammit, he should have said Dr. K!

"Oh, really? And who is your friend?"

"Gary. Gary Tate." Gary perked up at the mention of his name.

"Benny talks about Gary all the time." He'd found her! Things just might be looking up. "He sells the good shit."

"Yes, his shit is definitely fantastic. Um, listen, Mrs. Knochenmus, I was wondering if we could come by and see you. We had a few questions about your husband's research."

"What's happened?" She sounded more alert. "Is Benny all right?"

"Ma'am, we'd like to speak with you if we could."

"Are you the police?"

"No—no. We're friends with your husband. We just want to talk—"

"Where is Benny?"

"I . . . we . . . don't know." It was as honest an answer as he was capable of at the moment.

"I don't think I can—"

Jim missed the rest because Gary snatched the cell out of his hand.

"Hey, Mrs. K, it's Gary. Yeah. Yeah. No. He's dead. Okay." He took the phone away from his ear and handed it back. That went downhill in a hurry.

"Did you have to tell her like that? Over the phone?" Jim was hoping to do it in person—actually, he was hoping she'd learn it by osmosis. Gary had handled it, though.

"You were beating around the bush, and she deserves to know."

"And now what?"

"I thought the plan was to go see her."

"How are we gonna do that? She hung up on you."

"Yeah. After she gave me her address."

"Serious? Let's go before she changes her mind."

"Wait." Gary held up a hand. "We need to get cleaned up. We stink. Besides, she said not to come for another two hours."

"You're right."

Gary headed for the bathroom, stripping off his clothes. He was naked by the time he got to the door, leaving Jim to hurriedly clean up his mess. He didn't want Mel to see the apartment in disarray in case she got back while he was gone.

He kicked all the clothes into a pile by the bathroom door and began clearing the table. The ice cream went into the sink, and he tossed the carton in the garbage. It had been at least a day since he'd thrown out the garbage, and something inside the can smelled good.

Jim ignored it, going back to the rest of the food on the table. It all smelled terrible, and he hated the thought of putting everything back in the fridge, so he thought it was best to just throw it all away.

There it was again.

He wanted to dig it out, but that was disgusting. He'd never eaten out of the garbage in his life. Except for when they'd ordered pizzas from the Little Caesars behind Gary's apartment when they were twelve. They'd waited for the pizzas to be thrown away when they weren't picked up an hour later, then climbed in the dumpster and taken them out. But that had been totally different.

When his stomach growled loudly, Jim's hands moved with a will of their own. He reached in, wedging aside the items he had just thrown away. When he felt his hands smoosh into something soft and warm, he grabbed it and pulled it out. It was the French toast he had been making for breakfast. Jim had everything set and was about to put it in the pan when the bowl fumbled out of his hands, and he dropped the whole works on the floor.

Jim just stared at the soggy bread in his hands. It looked grotesque, but smelled wonderful. Maybe he should take a bite just for curiosity's sake. Like a scientist would. He brought it up to his mouth, imagining his salivary glands filling his mouth had they actually worked still.

"No. This is just too gross. Put it back. Put it back and wash your hands." Jim managed to set the bread on top of the trash, and his stomach groaned in protest.

Just as he was reaching in to take it out again, the bathroom door opened. Gary came out completely naked, drying his hair with a towel. "All right, you're up."

Jim jumped back a little too quickly, attracting Gary's eye. He came over as Jim stuffed everything in the bag down and tied a knot in it. Jim washed his hands, grabbed the bag, and set it outside.

"I'm going to be quick," he said. "If Mel calls before I get out, holler."

"Why not take it in there with you?"

"Because Mel says—because it's bad for your phone. Moisture gets in and—"

"—messes up the resale value. I know."

Jim headed for the shower, not as bold as Gary, waiting until he was securely locked in the bathroom before he began removing his clothes. Naked was never an easy option for him. Maybe that was because his parents had walked in on him completely naked during his first sexual experience—and he later found his father dead without a stitch of clothing on. Now that he thought about it, finding men in his family dead was like a thing with him. His father, grandfather, and an uncle who'd been mysteriously crushed in the alley behind his home. He hadn't been run over by a car; rather, something had folded his arms and legs behind him and compressed him into a two-foot cubic square. It had been ruled accidental, but that had never set right to a ten-year-old Jim. Whether it was murder was an entirely different story, but no way had it not been done on purpose.

Jim wondered what family member would stumble upon his corpse in a few days. He allowed his mind to wallow in despair a moment, thinking there was no real hope for his and Gary's situation and the pills would run their course and they would simply expire—or whoever had killed Dr. K would catch up to them and finish what they had started.

He quickly soaped his body, not bothering with shampoo, dragging the bar through his hair until he had an all-over lather. Jim closed his eyes and stepped under the showerhead, the water pelting his scalp.

The water had just begun seeping in, a chill Jim hadn't been aware of subtly fading. He knew he should get out of here, but he just needed a moment for himself. If he died because he had taken an extra thirty seconds, then so be it.

Something flashed behind his eyes. Jim jerked, and a second later came another flash. It had looked like a lightning strike, but he was certain it was just a product of his imagination. Then his imagination got really weird. Something began fading into view. At first Jim took it for television static, but the longer he looked, the sharper the image got, and the more horrified he became.

It was rotten brown meat, filled with thousands upon thousands of squirming maggots. He assumed it was just a visual imagination, but then came the sound of chewing.

Jim's eyes snapped open, and he saw he was lying on the floor of the tub. He got up, turned off the water, and got out. He noticed Mel's towel was gone and realized Gary had been using it. Nothing to be done about it now. He grabbed his own and began drying himself off.

Gary had left a change of clothes for him on the sink. Jim was surprised to see his friend had done something actually considerate. Thinking of others or doing things to save time weren't things typically found in Gary's wheelhouse.

Jim put on the jeans, wondering how far back in his closet Gary had dug to find these. Over the last year or so since he'd been with Mel, Jim had lost weight, going from a size thirty-eight in the waist to a thirty-four. One thing his fiancé was not was a cook. Surprisingly, the pants were only slightly loose. He wondered if his deadish body was bloating. Jim didn't bother with deodorant, figuring once he started to stink again, the perfumey scent of Degree would only make him smell worse.

He put on his shirt and tousled his curly hair. It was still a mess, but that wasn't unusual. Jim came out of the bathroom to see Gary in the living room wearing another pair of Jim's fat jeans and a faded T-shirt. The TV was on, but he was watching Jim. He began a slow clap, but the look on Jim's face must have stopped him.

Gary was a little taller, but they were generally the same size. The pile of clothes Gary had stripped off remained by the bathroom door, including the underwear. But that meant—

"Hey, compadre, you ready to go?" Gary asked.

"Those are my clothes."

"Yeah, my stuff was gross."

"And my underwear?"

"I can't go commando anymore. The monster needs a cage."

Jim shuddered, but decided to let it go, his dream or vision in the shower temporarily forgotten. They left the apartment and Jim locked it after them, snatching up the trash bag and hustling down the stairs to the parking lot.

"I heard you shave a little off the top."

Jim narrowed his eyes, then realized what Gary meant.

"I wasn't masturbating. I fell."

"Shit, don't make it sound so clinical. That's why you're supposed to sit down when you do it. Good for the prostate. That's what I do when I'm in the shower."

"Wait—in my shower?" Jim turned to him as they reached the dumpster and he tossed the bag in. "Did you—"

"Beat it like I was Michael Jackson? Hells yes. Please refer to said monster comment above. Hey, is the whole being dead thing supposed to make you horny? 'Cause I have had a serious case of deadwood. I even have another one in the chamber already!"

"Please . . . stop." The realization that Jim had just been lying in Gary's spooge hit him. Millions of tadpole Garys (Garies?) squirming all over his body. Gary went on for another moment while Jim did his best to mentally scour his body. He knew Gary's . . . *remnants* had more than likely been rinsed down the drain, but he couldn't help but feel like things were *attached* to him.

They opened their car doors, neither of them noticing the man approaching them even when he pulled out his gun.

"All I'm saying is if you cranked it more often, you wouldn't be as needy," Gary said.

"I am not needy," Jim replied. "I have a . . . a . . . very satisfying . . . an intimate relationship . . . with Mel."

"Okay, so you fuck her. She let you put it in her ass?"

Jim felt his face flush. He opened his mouth, but the approaching man spoke first.

"Excuse me," the man said, holding up his gun. Gary and Jim looked, and both took a reflexive step back. He cleared his throat. "Excuse me. I'm sorry, but I need your car." They looked at each other, dumbfounded, then back to him. It wasn't so much the gun; after this toilet flush of a day, a carjacking fit right in. He was holding a toddler in his other arm, though.

Jim was sensing Gary holding back like a racing stallion having its reins pulled. Hopefully he wasn't about to do something stupid because bullets wouldn't kill him.

"Uh, sure, buddy," Jim said, trying to sound calm. The man kept wavering between him and Gary standing on either side of the Fiesta. "You don't have to do this, y'know. We can give you a ride."

The man made a face, hitched the sliding child back up, then refocused his aim on Jim. "No. I appreciate the offer, but no. I need the car."

"We don't have a car seat, though," Gary said. "She looks about three? The minimum age is eight." He glanced over at the minivan parked next to them. "Hey, this guy has two car seats." He nodded toward the building. "Go jack him; he's in 3C."

The gun shook so violently in his hand Jim was certain he was about to shoot.

"I don't have time to argue. I need *your* car, and I need it now. Give me the keys right now, or I'll shoot your friend."

Jim noted how nervous he was and how determined he sounded. The man was scared of something and sweating profusely despite the coolness of the fall evening. His daughter was calm and quiet, smooshing her father's cheeks between her pudgy hands as he conducted his unpleasant business.

"Okay," Jim said, slowly extending his hand. "Whatever it is, we can help. We wouldn't mind. Right, Gary? We're going through a thing right now too, and we were just about to—"

The gun went off. The driver-side mirror exploded, a couple of shards clipping Jim's arm. He yelped and spun around, more from reflex than anything.

"I don't care about your fucking lovers' quarrel. Just gimme the keys!"

"Daddy, bad word," the little girl said and slapped him.

"I'm sorry, baby."

Jim tossed the keys, and they landed about a foot away from the man.

"Now how are you going to get them?" Gary asked, a dare in his tone. The man let his daughter slip off his leg, and she bent neatly, one hand high up in the air as she plucked them off the ground. "Oh," Gary said.

"Turn around, both of you. Walk over on the grass, get on your knees, and lace your ankles." They did as they were told as he spoke softly to the little girl, telling her to get in and sit still. "I'm sorry about what I said before.

Maybe if you make a conscious effort to say something nice to one another . . . He's got nice eyes. Maybe say something about them every now and then. It might seem like work at first, but you can make a habit of it with a little work. I'll return your car if I can."

With that, the door shut, and the engine turned on. Jim stayed put, still half-convinced the man might shoot them. As he heard the car reverse and then rapidly pull away, he felt Gary's eyes on him.

"Do you think my eyes are nice?" Gary asked.

"What makes you think he was talking to me?" Jim asked.

Chapter 5

"They're gone." Fyukis nodded, as close to frustration or any other emotion as he'd been in over thirty years. Tim and Ed looked at him expectantly, like puppies waiting for their master to throw them a bone. Well, he wasn't about to praise them this time; they had screwed up.

They were supposed to kill the doctor *after* they had the Bloom, not blow him away as soon as he said he didn't have it. They'd determined after the fact that the man had simply meant he didn't have it on his person and began a systematic search of the small building. When they'd walked into the laboratory area, a second man had charged out of a back room. Once again, Tim had proved too quick with that gun of his and had shot him to death, losing yet another opportunity to question someone who could've answered a simple enough question.

Then a third man had come out, and Tim had shot him too. If it weren't for the bulk of evidence proving how incredibly stupid the two of them were, Fyukis might have suspected they had stolen the Bloom for themselves. That in and of itself made no sense, considering the Adjacent were the sole reason the pills had been manufactured, and there was one for each of them. But greed had a way of corrupting the most honorable of purposes at times, and it wouldn't have surprised him had it been true.

So here they were, back at Dr. Knochenmus's lab, Fyukis personally leading the search. Tim and Ed had taken the doctor's body and put it in the trunk of their vehicle to bring to him, as if that somehow made sense. They would stay here all night if need be to find those pills. Gunshots in this part of the city were beyond common, and it was highly unlikely the police would show up in a timely fashion if at all. The two in the rear of the building must have been lab assistants, and maybe they had been holding onto the Adjacent's property for some reason. But the two other bodies were gone.

"You two idiots are too stupid to even kill right," Fyukis had wanted to say, but had instead limited his comments to the obvious.

"They're gone."

"Yes, Brother Fyukis," Tim and Ed said in unison, their bulbous heads nodding. There was blood on the floor, though not much, and a distant, yet not unpleasing, smell. Fyukis got on his knees and began to sniff. After a moment he determined it was the blood itself he was smelling. He dipped his head and took a deep whiff of the largest spot. The Testimony had described everything about the Bloom, but that could never be the same as being in its presence. Fyukis had studied the Testimony for decades, and if anyone had an idea of how the words would translate into the physical plane, it would be he.

He dipped his tongue, touching the crimson black spot with the tip. It burned, and he leapt back, cried out in pain, then bowed his head, prostrate before the dried blood. That definitely had a tinge of the Bloom, which meant someone had consumed it. Fyukis looked around anew. There definitely should be a body. The Testimony had foretold that whoever consumed the Bloom would have death everlasting. No one could have ingested it and simply walked away. There had to be another explanation.

"You said they came out of that room, the ones you shot?" Fyukis pointed, and Tim nodded. "Quickly then. We must search there."

They walked to the back of the room and passed through the plastic curtains. The tiny room was disheveled, chairs overturned. There was a container that had rolled to the wall. Fyukis bent to pick it up and examined inside. There were four empty slots that could have held pills roughly the size and shape of the specifications they had given the doctor to produce the Bloom.

So his plan had been to short them all along. The Adjacent were legion in spirit, but only five on the physical plane. Maybe Tim and Ed had been right to shoot him. He wouldn't tell them that, though. That would only embolden them to do something even dumber at some later point.

Why did the Adjacent have to be five? Fyukis sighed. The thought of being linked into eternity with these two was almost disheartening.

So the two assistants had absconded with pills meant for them. But how had they survived being shot to death? This deserved a good deal of pondering. Not now, though. They were too close, and whatever had happened here, the Bloom couldn't be allowed to slip through their fingers.

"You there." He snapped his fingers, the man's name momentarily slipping his mind. "Ed. You said you went through his office?" The man nodded. "Go through it again; see if you can find any paperwork on his employees. W-2s, tax papers, disciplinary files, anything of the sort."

"We were given the impression he was a solo operation. That was why he was selected."

"And you also shot him to death because he lied to us. Perhaps he decided not to tell us about two part-time employees during our selection process."

"Yes, Brother. Right away." Ed left the small room, leaving Fyukis with Tim. This was the idiot who had carried the gun against his express orders. The intention all along had been to kill the doctor and anyone else he had been connected to, but *after* they had gotten their product. They could not risk the formula being reduplicated and falling into the wrong hands. Falling into any other hands for that matter. The pills were a holy sacrament of the Adjacent, the ingredients and subsequent combination coming from the pages of the Testimony itself. Fyukis had no idea what their effect would be on the physiology of a normal human being, but it would have been an abomination in Brother's eyes.

Then he thought of the spot of blood on the floor and the scent of the Bloom in it. Could they have ingested it? Could life be sustained once the Bloom had been consumed by a normal human being?

He pictured Tim shooting the second and then the third. Blood was spattered in one place only. Had they missed the other, and he'd simply played dead? That must have been so. The second one had been killed, and the third one had taken away his body. To what purpose he couldn't have guessed. Perhaps they had experienced the power of the Bloom and had intended to keep it for themselves all along. Something about the events that had transpired here didn't quite fit in his mind. He was missing something.

It hit him. The second man had come out here and then been shot, leaving his blood on the floor. That meant he had been alive. Fyukis had known that the Bloom would kill whoever consumed it who was found undeserving. But he wasn't too familiar with that section of the Testimony. Perhaps he would need to read those verses again and in more depth. It looked as though he was due for some pondering, after all. A great deal, in fact.

The two men searched in silence for the next ten minutes. Tim continually would come back to the container, as if the pills had crawled back inside. Frustrated, Fyukis decided to attempt to re-create the two men's last seconds in this room. The second had come charging out, which left the third in here. No doubt with the remainder of the Bloom, considering they had to have been aware of its value to attempt to steal it. But then the third had come charging out as well. Perhaps they had both consumed the Bloom and it had driven them mad.

But if they believed the Bloom would bestow some otherworldly power upon them, would they not have taken it at the same time? If it had driven them mad, would they not have charged out of the room at the same time? No, madness was not what it had caused. Perhaps they had believed their cause righteous, and the second had willingly sacrificed himself to protect the other so he could do something with the Bloom. Buried it, destroyed it, given it to another?

He paused. What if . . . what if the Bloom somehow allowed them to survive death? That the man Tim had shot had gotten up and walked out under his own power? There would have been no point to the third man dragging him away, and Tim had described the three shots as being center mass. Even had he not died immediately, he would not have gone far. And there had been no blood trail leading to the door.

Fyukis got down on his hands and knees, bowing his head low and pondering right then. There were a great many things he did not understand, things that had not yet been revealed to him. If it were Brother's will that this be true, then so be it. He opened his eyes and stared momentarily at the floor. Fyukis turned his head slightly to the right and saw something small and black. He didn't reach for it immediately, not certain if what he was seeing was real. He had experienced on several occasions something dematerializing even as he put his hands on it.

The pill appeared solid and remained after several seconds. Slowly he reached for it, dragging it out from underneath some sort of machine. He held it tightly in his fist, taking another moment to ponder before opening his hand.

He sat on the floor, crossing his legs, and just held it. The Bloom was real, and he was holding a portion of it. All thoughts of the two lab assistants who may or may not have been dead left his mind. Fyukis realized for the very first time that he was pondering with his eyes open. The Bloom crowded out all other thought, filling his vision. He did not hear, feel, or smell anything else.

After a period of sitting, he came to his senses. Tim and Ed were standing a few feet away, staring at him. He should keep the Bloom to himself. There were more than likely several ways to do it in the Testimony. All he had to do was go home, lock himself in his room, and ponder and read until he had divined it.

That would have been the easiest path, but that would not honor the vow he had made to Brother or the others. Fyukis held up his hand and opened it for the other two to see.

"The Bloom," Ed said, and they both fell to their hands and knees, heads hung low.

Yes, even these two idiots deserved salvation.

Chapter 6

They had been walking for little more than an hour in silence. Gary had fired up a joint, hit it, then tossed it away in disgust half an hour ago. Now he lit another, took another spliff, then offered it to Jim.

Jim shook his head. "I don't do that anymore."

Gary pinched the joint between the tip of his middle finger and the pad of his thumb and flicked it away.

"Being dead sucks," he said.

"So this isn't all that you thought it was cracked up to be?" Jim asked.

His friend finally let go of his breath, smoke clouding over his head momentarily. "No. I thought death was gonna be the ultimate high, y'know?"

"Did you think about how you were going to come down from it?"

"Yeah . . . no."

"And you didn't think about reeling me into this? I have a girlfriend!"

"Fiancée. I know."

"What were you thinking? Anything at all?"

"I was thinking I wanted to have one last run with my best friend before you left me."

Jim felt his gut clench. "I'm not going anywhere."

Gary waved him off. "You know what I mean. You and Mel . . . you guys have your own thing going. There's been nothing but less and less Gary time."

"There's been no Gary time? No Gary time?" Jim realized he was flummoxed for an actual response. "You've done nothing but antagonize Mel. Why would she want to be around you?"

"It's not her I needed to be around."

"We're a package deal. If you can't handle that, it's not my fault. And that's the other thing: all the cheating comments—they need to stop. I need you to admit she's never cheated on me."

"Not that I know of."

"Gary, *damn*!"

"Look, I'm telling you the truth. I have never seen her *cheat* on you."

Jim noted he had stressed the word "cheat."

"What the hell is that supposed to mean?"

"Nothing. I saw . . . nothing."

It certainly didn't sound like nothing. But for the sake of their dwindling friendship, Jim let it go. He felt his anger on the verge of eruption, and he sensed a long night ahead of them.

Gary made some sort of choked sound, and Jim's heart began to break a little. As much as he'd ignored it, that still didn't change the fact there was a chasm between them, and it was growing. He didn't know how to fix it, though, feeling like he was caught in a tide, being washed farther and farther out to sea and away from the man who'd been his best friend since he was seven.

"Oh my God," Gary said, and Jim felt himself choke up. He reached out to grasp Gary's shoulder. "Do you smell that? It stinks!"

A moment later a heavy stench wafted over him. Jim breathed it in, and to say it was awful would fall short of describing the assault on his olfactory sense.

"What crawled up in you and died?" Jim asked before starting a coughing fit. He was certain that if his life were not already in a state of suspension, he would have keeled over right then. Gary let go of another, this time a high-pitched sound like a trumpet.

He waved his hands in the air, shouting, "It's sticking to me! It's sticking to me!" He gagged and Jim gagged too, and before he knew it, they both were laughing.

Jim let go a couple of times too, the two scents mixing into something truly toxic. This invoked more peals of laughter and gagging until they were lying in the right-of-way next to the street.

"What are we going to do?" Jim asked.

"We're going to die, that's what we're going to do. But I'm okay with that because I get to do it with my best friend."

"Well, I'm not okay with that. I don't want to die—be dead. Whatever. There has to be a way out of this. Did Mrs. K say how long she's going to be home?"

"She didn't say one way or the other. I assume she's expecting us soon."

Gary sat up and looked around.

"Hey, I know a place." Gary got up and began staggering, stiff-legged, across the street.

"Know what place?" Jim said, following as quickly as his stiffened body would allow.

"Where we can get a ride. It's at this party not far from here."

"Party?" Jim asked, knowing his best friend was well on his way to being distracted.

Chapter 7

By the time they reached the house, Jim had figured out where they were going. Wayne Wesley had been a high school associate of theirs, not someone they disliked exactly, but not someone either man would have described as a friend. Wayne Wesley was a nerd, and anyone desiring a vital social life during those crucial four years was wise to avoid crossing him.

They had been lucky only in that they had not gone out of their way to be cruel to Wayne Wesley, and on rare occasions when it was socially acceptable to talk to him, they had. And as reward for those paltry few conversations, Wayne Wesley had spared Jim and Gary the fate of so many jocks, cheerleaders, weed dealers, partyers, and other cool kids.

While the upper echelon of their graduating class and the one that had come before it spent their respective senior years solidifying epic runs that would be as quickly forgotten as the tossing of a mortarboard, Wayne Wesley had been building a blackmail list that would last for many years after. Every bully who had ever slapped his books out of his hands or taken his lunch and eaten it right in front of him or pantsed him in front of a pretty girl had been brought low. Every girl who had ever laughed at him or beaten him up or summarily dismissed him as not even existing had been leveraged. Now that these were people who had girded themselves against the cold of the real world, they were made all the more chilly for provoking Wayne Wesley.

It didn't matter if they had gone on to graduate magna cum laude from Ivy League universities or become captains of industry or superstar athletes. Even if senior year had been the crest of their lives and they were working minimum-wage jobs in the same city they'd all grown up in, Wayne Wesley held not a drop of mercy for any of them.

Gary had claimed to have seen the book he'd kept on them, but Jim had always doubted that. Despite his loyalty, Gary had a big mouth, and it could be taken for fact that if he were told something in secret, the number of people who also knew increased exponentially by the hour.

There was a giant of a man standing on the porch of Wayne Wesley's house. Jim recognized him, but couldn't place his name. He probably had played football, but his physique had mostly likely softened and enlarged since high school.

Jim followed Gary up the stairs.

"What up, G-man? J?" He gave them both fist bumps with a massive paw, and Jim was mildly embarrassed that he couldn't respond in kind with a nickname.

"Mad Dog!" Gary shouted, pulling him in for a half hug. Between the two of them, Gary was by far the one to be considered a social butterfly. He always made friends, no matter what social class. "What's happening, Max Damage?"

"Just out here maintainin', you know what I'm sayin'?"

"I heard, I heard."

"What's going on, Max?" Jim said, mistakenly believing it was safe to follow suit and address him by the name Gary had. The man turned small wet eyes on him that looked like the irises had bled brown into the whites. He gave Jim a sour face.

"Nothin'," he said, devoid of the good humor he'd had a second ago. Mad Dog or Max continued giving Jim a flat-eyed stare until they were completely past one another, Jim feeling awkward the entire way.

"What the hell just happened there?" Jim asked.

"You mean you completely making an ass of yourself, calling Mitchell by the wrong name?"

"Yeah, but you called him Max too."

"No." Gary waggled a finger at him as they stepped out of the vestibule and into the great room. A pretty woman who looked semifamiliar and then very familiar when Jim saw her from behind, walked by, giving them a finger wave. "I called him Max Damage. I also called him Mad Dog. The initials are MD, just like master debater, which he was considered as back in high school."

"Master debater? That guy didn't play football?"

"Shame on you, Jim. Just because the guy's big automatically means he had to have played sports?"

Jim was a little shamed. He probably had known back then that MD had been on the debate team, but he could barely remember what extracurricular activities he'd been in at any point in his life. He might've been on the police athletic league when he was a tween, but Jim wasn't entirely sure.

He made a mental note to apologize on their way out. The two of them made their rounds, saying hello to several people, Gary remembering everyone's names, while Jim could only recall a few.

As they moved through the house, they kept coming closer to the source of music and then retreating from it. Jim spotted no speakers and guessed they must've been built into the walls. The song currently playing was by some Swedish band he could never remember the name of. It was something about trusting in gold—at least that's what it sounded like—and no matter how hard he tried to find the name of the song, he always struck out.

Just about everyone Jim saw was holding a red cup. He realized his profound thirst and ran a dry tongue over his chapped lips. He looked around for a punch bowl or a beer keg just before stepping into the kitchen, where two skinny blondes stood on either side of an island.

"You do it, Sara," one young woman said.

"No, you go first." Sara shook her head. As Jim and Gary stepped around her, Jim saw the two women were standing around a small mound of cocaine. Wayne Wesley sat against the sink, his arms folded across his narrow chest.

He looked exactly the same as he had in high school. He had the same mousy brown hair cut into the same eighties hairstyle. He still had a petite, trim figure and soulless black eyes.

"Wayne Wesley, what's up?" Jim said. He wanted to get his greeting in before Gary this time to show that he remembered who someone was. Gary was oddly silent, and Jim glanced his way to see his friend staring at something on the island. There was a small white mound of powder. Gary had casually used cocaine, but Jim would not have described him as an addict prior to now. The look on his face, though, was that of a hungry man looking at food for the first time in a long time.

He elbowed the blonde who wasn't Sara aside and said, "Hey, watch this," and slammed his face into the powder. Gary snorted long and loud and then began going over smaller drifts of powder that he had created in his wake. After a good thirty seconds, it was all gone.

"Holy shit," the other four people in the room said.

"Gary, that was baby powder, man," Wayne Wesley said. "That's gotta burn!"

"Huh? Yeah." Gary pinched his nose and shut his eyes. "Ow. Man." But Jim could tell it was a fake job and found himself hoping nobody else noticed.

"Get him some water. Oh my gosh." The two blondes were standing shoulder to shoulder, and Jim couldn't tell which one was Sara. They didn't look anything alike in the face, but there was something between them that was very similar.

It could have been their vacuous blue eyes, but Jim couldn't be sure.

One of them turned to the sink and tore off a sheet of paper towel before wetting it and handing it to Gary. He made a sufficient enough show of howling in pain as he wiped his face. Jim helped, getting his ears and some spots along his jawline that he had missed. Then Jim saw how foggy his eyes appeared.

"Let's get your eyes under the tap," Jim said, escorting his friend. Gary nodded, allowing himself to be led. Jim made a show of splashing water in his face and getting Gary's eyeballs wet enough to rinse the grainy film of baby powder off them. Neither man had the ability to tear up, and Jim thought the others would ask questions if they saw Gary's dry eyeballs.

Jim tore off another paper towel and handed it to Gary to pat his face dry.

"You've always been hard-core," Wayne Wesley said, giving Gary a wry smile.

"You know me," Gary said, sounding a little crestfallen. "Always hard-core."

"You know Blake is looking for you." He said it like a statement of fact.

"Blake, huh?"

Blake Baker was the only person Jim knew of who outwardly disliked Gary. Sure, there were other people who didn't care for him, but he had such a gregarious and fun personality that mostly everyone else would have thought something was wrong with you if you didn't like Gary.

That was only part of the reason Blake didn't like— no, hated—Gary. In Gary's defense, Blake didn't like anyone and was more than likely a sociopath. It mostly had to do with the fact Gary had unintentionally gouged out Blake's left eye.

It was a long story that involved scissors and running. Needless to say, had Gary not shoved the scissors away from himself at a critical moment, they would have wound up in Gary's chest instead of Blake's eye socket. Also in Gary's defense, he'd tried to be helpful. Amid

Blake's screams, he'd commanded Gary to pull them out despite Gary's suggestion that doing so might do even more damage.

Blake had pulled on the handle several times but had been unable to extricate them from his skull. Finally Gary had relented, wrapped his hands around them, and tugged like he was unsheathing Excalibur from a stone. Out came the scissors and Blake's eyeball, flopping onto his cheek, still connected to stringy veins running out of a gaping hole in his face.

Wayne Wesley nodded, an evil smirk on his face. "His van's outside in back."

Gary sighed. Since the eyeball incident, Gary had been in no rush to encounter him again. Not that Jim's best friend was afraid—he seemingly lacked the gene for fear—but as he admitted one drunken night, he was running out of excuses not to fight Blake.

They were grown men, and Jim realized Blake's hatred had to run deep for him to still be carrying this grudge more than a decade later.

Gary shrugged.

Jim saw the look in his eye and knew there were wheels already turning.

"Hey, Jim," he said, waving at him absentmindedly, "ask him about the thing." Then Gary left them to join a group of good-looking people sitting on and around a couch by a lit fireplace.

Maybe Gary didn't have something up his sleeve after all.

It took a moment after Jim had turned to Wayne Wesley to decipher what Gary was requesting him to ask. The shorter man waited patiently, glancing over at Gary as he easily inserted himself into the conversation, and everyone immediately laughed at something he said.

"Wayne, could I ask you something?"

The short man's head slowly cranked to face Jim. "Depends," he said.

"On what?" Jim asked hesitantly.

"On if I can ask you something first."

Jim's stomach dropped. Wayne Wesley was in the information business. Jim didn't know how, but he was certain the man had acquired everything around them through squeezing other people one way or another. It was a very ornate home, smallish, but in an affluent section of town.

"Yeah," Jim said as noncommittally as possible.

Wayne Wesley stepped closer, definitely inside Jim's personal space.

"Shirley Pickover. Did you have sex with her?" He narrowed his eyes at Jim as if examining him already for telltale signs of a truthful answer.

Jim had. In eleventh grade. "What?" he asked, stalling while he mentally scrutinized how a truthful answer might be used against him at a later date. He turned to the table beside them and grabbed a plastic cup filled with what looked like fruit punch but smelled like about a half dozen kinds of alcohol mixed together. He downed it and remembered to make a sour face. Jim had no sense of taste, or rather, a deeply diminished one.

Jim looked over at his friend and saw he was currently coaxing a wide-eyed brunette into swallowing whole a particularly long snack tray carrot. Gary had self-taught a minor enough amount of hypnosis that he could coach someone out of a natural gag reflex. He'd also learned the reverse. He'd tried it on Jim, and even now, if Jim thought about something that was in his mouth for too long—like his toothbrush—he would dry-heave.

"Jim?" Wayne said.

"Yeah. A long time ago."

Jim waited for the trap to spring. Instead, Wayne Wesley folded his arms. It had been high school. Jim hadn't known Mel then. Shirley had been the second girl he'd been with. Mel was the third. And Shirley got engaged their senior year.

Shit. She had married that guy. The one she'd been dating senior year. Jim remembered hearing about that a few years ago. Had she told him she was a virgin? Jim hadn't considered how his answer might be used against her, hoping his answer was just a link in a much longer chain.

Jim opened his mouth to say something and closed it. Going down this road with Wayne Wesley was a bad idea.

"Thanks," the other man said, giving Jim's shoulder a squeeze. "Sheesh, you been working out? Your arm is as hard as a rock!"

Jim didn't respond, not sure if speaking at all was an option. He dropped his eyes from Wayne Wesley's and headed toward Gary.

"Jim?" Wayne Wesley said, and he turned. The man cocked an eyebrow. "Didn't you want to ask me something?"

"Oh. Uh, yeah. My car, um, broke down, and Gary and I were hoping you could drop us off somewhere."

"Aw shit, man, say no more. Just let me know when you're ready to ride. Just throw me a couple bucks for gas, cool?"

"Cool."

Jim felt his tension unwinding the farther he moved away from Wayne Wesley and was leaning in to whisper in Gary's ear when somebody from across the room screamed Gary's name.

They both looked up.

It was Blake Baker.

"Shit," they both said.

Chapter 8

"Okay, so what's it going to take to make this even finally?" Gary asked after the third punch to his gut.

"Shut up!" Blake said again, giving him a right cross to the face. Jim knew the blows weren't hurting his best friend, but they were still painful to watch. He knew he should jump in and felt like he'd almost worked up the nerve when Wayne Wesley sidled up to the big man and tapped him on the shoulder.

"Hey, BB, this is my house."

"Shut up!" Blake said and looked at him. Jim could see the color drain from his face and his body stiffen. He wondered what in the hell Wayne Wesley could have had on him of all people. "I—"

Wayne Wesley put up a dismissive hand.

"Just . . . take this outside."

Blake sneered, putting his face as close to Gary's as heterosexually possible for a homophobe like him.

"Me and you," he said. "Outside."

He dragged Gary through the small crowd of people in his path, crossing the threshold into the kitchen, where the back door was. Gary didn't struggle but had a look of mild annoyance on his face. Everyone looked at one another and then at the two of them.

"Fight," a bald-headed guy said.

A hawkish-looking brunette smiled and repeated, "Fight."

A chant quickly began. Jim looked at Wayne Wesley.

"But you said you'd give us a ride."

"And I will," Wayne Wesley said. "As soon as those two have finally gotten this out of their system."

"*Their* system?" Jim asked. "Come on, Gary isn't the one with the problem. Blake is a crazy person." Jim made sure to whisper the last two words.

Wayne Wesley's face darkened. "He's also my cousin."

"Oh. I didn't know that." Jim regretted his words, but was angry enough not to take them back. He turned on his heel and followed the small group outside.

He figured at some point Blake was going to have to let go of Gary. If only so he could get into a proper throwing stance to hit Gary even harder. Jim guessed that was when Gary would run.

When he stepped onto the small back porch, he found the opposite was true. The two men faced each other with about fifteen feet of space between them. About a dozen people were surrounding them outside, with a steady trickle coming outside to join in.

The chants of "fight—fight—fight" were steadily getting louder. Jim wanted to run out with Gary, but held back. They were staring each other down, Blake shaking his head and twisting his upper body like he was limbering up.

Blake had taken off his jacket, exposing well-muscled arms and chest and a trim waist. He looked mostly the same as he had in high school, maybe with twenty pounds of added mass, but none of it fat.

"So, what do you want to do, Blake?" Gary asked.

The other man's good eye zeroed in on him, fury blazing in it.

"I want to tear off your head and shit down your neck."

"Okay. Anything else?"

"I'm gonna put my foot so far up your ass you're gonna sneeze Nike."

"All right. And then?" Gary sounded like a waiter taking an order.

"I'm gonna beat you like my dick—no, wait. Beat you like a . . . like a . . ." Blake trailed off, trying to catch the thread of what he'd been trying to say.

"Gonna beat me like I stole something?"

"Yeah!" Blake pointed at him. "That's it."

"Any other clichés?"

"No. Shut the fuck up!"

"All right. Let's do it." Gary took off his jacket too. "And this time, we're done. Deal?"

"Not by a long shot. We're not done until I'm standing over your dead body."

Gary shrugged.

"Ready to kiss your ass goodbye?"

Gary made a move that could have been a nod. He stood there as Blake stalked over to him. Blake cocked back a fist and swatted Gary down like a fly.

"Get up, you pussy. I'm not done with you by a damn sight."

Gary was very still.

"I said get up!" Blake kicked him. Gary still didn't move.

The chanting ceased, and people began drawing closer. Jim stepped off the porch.

"All right, I'll come to you if that's how you want it."

"Blake, hold on!" Jim said. He pried Gary's shirt out of his fist. Gary's staring eyes were a million miles away. Panicked, Jim felt for a pulse, and when he felt nothing, laid Gary on the ground and began pumping on his chest.

"He's not breathing," Jim said, a quaver in his voice. "Dammit, he isn't *breathing*."

"Wait. What?" Blake took a step backward. "Hey, I only hit him once. I didn't do all that. He must've had an underlying health condition or some shit."

"Somebody call 911," someone said.

Jim ignored everyone, concentrating on saving his friend's life. This was just so stupid and unnecessary. Gary had gotten out of fights with Blake before. Why didn't he do it this time?

"Fuck that. No!" And there was a slapping sound before a cell phone landed two feet away from Jim in the grass. He saw Blake's feet turn as the big man ran, and a moment later, an engine started and wheels peeled rubber.

Jim began compressing on his friend's chest again as the small crowd closed in on him.

"Dammit, Gary, don't do this. Don't be dead."

If he'd had tear ducts that worked, Jim might have cried.

He went on pumping on Gary's chest for another two minutes before a few people gradually pulled him away. Jim felt numb—well, apart from physiological numbness— as his mind spun, trying to figure out what he was to do next. Gary's brother . . . his father . . . what would he say to them? Would they blame him?

He stared at his hands, the last part of him that had touched Gary. *Gary's body.*

Oh God.

Jim was halfway descended into his despair when he heard someone shout, "Bravo! Brav-*fucking*-o!"

All these bastards at Wayne Wesley's party had to have been drunk or high, and of course they'd do something idiotic like cheer a man dying.

Someone seized Jim firmly by the wrist, and before he could snatch his hand away, he was unceremoniously yanked to his feet.

He was about to yell at the person who had so rudely interrupted his grieving when he saw that person was Gary. Jim's best friend took a deep bow, still holding onto his wrist and pulling Jim with him. Shocked, Jim allowed himself to be pulled, and they stepped forward together. Jim saw that Gary had even added the flourish of crossing one foot in front of the other and spreading his free arm wide.

"What in the hell?" he mouthed at Gary. But his friend had eyes only for the crowd, a big grin on his face. Jim snatched his hand away as Gary took another bow, even deeper this time. Their small audience clapped furiously for over a minute straight.

Chapter 9

The crowd of people followed them back in the house, cheering them with each step. Jim noted a few people apologizing profusely on the phone and asking for emergency services not to be sent. He breathed a small sigh of relief—the last thing they needed was an EMS worker insisting on taking Gary's or his pulse.

Jim kicked himself for not realizing what his friend was up to sooner. Of course Gary appeared dead—he technically was. It just had never crossed his mind in the heat of the moment that Gary had just laid down and not moved. Jim had tried playing dead on several occasions growing up, but his eyes always had stung and he'd blinked, or there was a telltale sign of his chest expanding and contracting just the tiniest bit as he breathed. Jim still doubted he could do it even now, and he'd been absolutely convinced that Gary was gone.

Gary got another ovation, and though it appeared as if they were clapping for Jim too, he didn't really feel like he was a part of it. He'd honestly thought his friend was dead, and his reaction hadn't been pretend. But to save face, he went along, smiling and nodding to people as he passed by. Someone slapped a cup of beer in Jim's hand, and he had guzzled it before he'd even given it a thought. His stomach did something, although Jim wasn't sure what.

Wayne Wesley sidled up to him, a beaming smile on his face.

"That was awesome, man. I mean, it's going to be a long while before Blake lives this one down."

"Yeah, speaking of Blake," Jim said, his agitation rising from being jostled and punched in the arm by people as they came near, "you think we can get that ride?"

Wayne Wesley's face dropped. "Oh, man," he said and slapped his forehead. "Blake has my van." Jim knew that meant the vehicle was actually Blake's, but that Wayne Wesley made the man run all his errands or chauffeur for him. "I can try to get him back if you want."

"No." Jim did not want to deal with him again tonight if he didn't need to. This was going to be the ultimate humiliation for Blake, and he much preferred for Gary and he to steer clear of him for as long as possible. "I guess we'll try to find another way."

As soon as they were back in the living room, Jim saw someone had poured out a mountain of cocaine on a silver tray on the coffee table.

Gary fell in front of the table, one hand feebly rising and clawing at the air. "Leave me here," he said weakly.

Chapter 10

They finally bummed a ride from a hyperactive woman named Nance, who had the attention span of a gnat. She was a flurry of questions, but never paused long enough for either of them to answer. Wayne Wesley had suggested a beer run, and she'd agreed while they went along for the ride. Gary was certain he could convince her to drop them close to Dr. K's apartment, but so far he wasn't able to get a word in edgewise.

"I think I wanna shave my head next summer," she said, her eyes darting around the road. "You guys think that would be a good look for me? Everybody's doing it— maybe I could just do one side and see. I have to get a skirt. Hey, are either of you guys Scottish? I think you'd look totally hot in one of those kilts. My friend Kelsey dated a guy who wore a kilt. He wasn't Scottish, though. I think he had a yeast infection on his balls or something. That's completely *gor*, but it's the truth so I'm not apologizing."

"Excuse me—" Gary said, holding up a finger, but she rolled on.

"I think I need to stop by my dispensary to refill my medical marijuana prescription. I have glaucoma or something like that, but I just know I'm smoking wayyy too much for my own good. You think too much weed can give you cancer? Is there a weed cancer?"

"I—" Jim said.

"No, they would have totally told us by now. Remember all those commercials they used to show about the negative effects of weed? Like the one where the guy just sits in his mother's basement and he's thirty-five, or that other one where the guy's sister gets raped by his best friend—"

"Frying pan—" Gary said. Jim punched him in the arm for not trying to ask for a drop-off.

"*Oh yeah!* This is your brain on drugs? No, you haven't seen my brain on drugs 'cause I get *turnt up!*" She rolled down the window and yelled, neglecting to roll it back up. The air blew in Jim's eyes, drying them out again.

"You guys want to get some cheeseburgers? Either of you want to fuck? I could do you both at the same time if you want."

Gary and Jim glanced at each other. Before they could answer, she continued on to some other subject and had touched on several before they stopped at a Rite-Aid.

Gary began climbing out of the car, and Jim grabbed his arm.

"Where are you going?"

"We need makeup," he said. "We look horrible." Gary pulled down the visor mirror and turned it so Jim could see himself from the backseat. He wouldn't have said he looked like a zombie, per se, but it definitely wasn't a flattering look.

They went ahead of Nance, who had forgotten her keys were in the ignition of her still-running car. She had continued talking despite Jim and Gary not being with her, and then she sat back down in her car.

"You think she's safe to be alone?" Gary asked.

"Well, she's made it this far," Jim said, meaning she'd reached adulthood rather than meaning the ride she had just given them. Gary nodded and went inside. Jim was right on his heels when he saw Nance throw the car in reverse and back out of the parking spot, all while looking at something in the passenger seat next to her and talking on her cell phone.

"Damn," Gary said. "And we never got to double-team her."

Chapter 11

They spent the next ten minutes routing through the makeup display, trying to find concealer that matched their respective skin tones.

"Wait a minute," Jim said. "We look like two walking corpses. Sure, that worked for the party we just came from, but we're probably going to get funny looks from the cashier, especially if we have makeup that only adds to a corpselike appearance."

Gary nodded. "Good point. Okay, so let's pick out makeup that matches what our skin used to look like."

They both began to scan through the different colors and shades. Jim found himself constantly looking over at Gary's face, trying to picture what his pallor had been just a few short hours ago.

"Wait a minute," Jim said, holding up a finger. "I'll be right back." He left Gary there, poring over the makeup, while he went in search of an employee. He spotted a short blonde, plain-faced and acne-riddled. No, she wouldn't do. Jim went down a few more aisles, looking in both directions until he found an olive-skinned woman with thick arched eyebrows and dark red lipstick. Her hair was cut into a neat bob, curling about her ears and forehead. If he weren't with Mel, he might think . . . no, who was he kidding? His fiancée was some sort of weird anomaly. Except for her, hot women never looked at him. Mel was hotter than this woman, but Jim still wouldn't have a chance with her.

"Excuse me," he said.

She stopped restocking, turned a brilliantly white smile on him, and said, "Can I help you find something?" He didn't know the accent, but it was sexy. It raised her attractiveness up a couple of notches, and Jim felt instant guilt about it. Here was this woman doing her job when some guy was judging her by her looks.

Jim cleared his throat. "I need a little help with some makeup." She made a face, but her smile didn't waver. "My friend and I are headed to a party . . . Well, it would be easier if I could just show you." Jim pointed back the way he'd come, and the woman put down the box she'd had in her hand and followed him.

They found Gary sitting on the floor amid a pile of different makeup colors, holding two of them up to the light.

"See, what we are doing is kind of a nouveau riche thing where we dress up as zombies trying to look like living people." Jim had no idea what nouveau riche meant, and he hoped she didn't either.

"You got the zombie thing pretty much down pat," the woman said.

Gary put down the two bottles and stared at the woman.

"Right?" Jim gave her his best smile, mentally crossing his fingers that she really was buying this.

"Well, almost."

She stepped in front of Gary and stooped. The woman quickly gathered a couple of items and came back to Jim, opening and applying things to his face. After five minutes, she spun a carousel display around until the mirror faced Jim.

"You're amazing," Gary said.

Jim couldn't really tell that much of a difference. If anything, he looked a little less shiny.

"I think I have an idea what you're going for," the woman said. "But I'm sure you guys are going to want pictures, and with what you had on, you would not have been photogenic. I put a nice solid base on so you don't look washed out in pictures." She turned back to the makeup and began plucking out several colors. "The trick is not using just one color. You have to blend." She began swiping on more makeup, and when Jim looked at himself in the mirror again, he thought he looked very much how he remembered.

"You *are* amazing," he said, putting one hand to his cheek.

"Thank you. I can do your friend if you want, unless you think you've got it."

"Please do me," Gary said.

Chapter 12

Jim quickly learned the woman's enthusiasm had more to do with a sale than an actual passion for makeup. Gary had no cash, as usual, and Jim had resorted to putting one hundred twenty-seven dollars and thirty-seven cents worth of makeup and a Peppermint Patty on his Discover card.

That wasn't what was bumming him out, though. Jim would have gladly charged triple that amount if he didn't have to face what he'd realized as the cashier had rung them up.

Gary took a bite out of the patty and promptly wretched before tossing it away as they stepped outside. They walked across the parking lot to the sidewalk and stopped. Jim looked, with a tremendous amount of dread, west.

"We still need a ride," he said.

"I guess we could walk. Probably take us three hours. Or we could get a cab."

"No. Pretty sure I just maxed out my credit card in there." Jim took a deep breath and let it out.

Gary looked around, and when he smiled, Jim knew he knew where they were.

"Oh no. Don't say it." The words sounded disingenuous coming off Gary's lips. "You don't really mean—"

"Yeah. Let's go see my mom."

Chapter 13

Gary knew how Jim felt about his mother. It wasn't hate . . . exactly. He definitely loved her, but that was more of a genetically programmed thing. Just like the salmon swam back to the pond of their birth to spawn and die, he annually returned to his mother's home, praying he would drop dead before she opened the door. At least he had the element of surprise this time, rather than coming on his birthday.

"Why do you think you come every year for your birthday, do you think?" Gary asked.

"I'm not sure." Jim thought a moment. "I guess because despite the pain and awkwardness, it's still easier than not showing up and getting *the* phone call."

Since moving out after he'd turned eighteen, Jim had missed exactly two visits at his mother's house for his birthday, both of which had resulted in a painfully humiliating, debilitating, boiling down of a guilt-ridden conversation in which she detailed the circumstances behind the seventeen-plus hours of labor and the subsequent near-death experience she had endured to lovingly shove him out of her body.

He was taking pleasure from the notion that he hadn't called ahead. His mother hated phone calls after 7:00 p.m. and absolutely did not see visitors after eight. But her door was always open to family, and he knew she wouldn't refuse him.

He'd been living in his apartment for the last four years, only a few blocks away from her house the next town over. Had they been close, he would have expected little casual annoyances like the occasional drop-in for no reason at all, requests for him to do outdoor chores such as mowing the lawn, or mutually borrowing items from each other's homes.

It didn't take them long to reach her house. They'd been walking in that direction from the start. Jim stared at Gary before they turned onto her walkway. He had not been around his mother and his best friend at the same time in over a decade. On that occasion he'd just returned from summer camp, where he'd been a counselor to earn a little extra cash before going to college, and there was a weird energy between Gary and his mother.

Jim had ignored it, eventually forgetting all about it as the years had pressed on, but now it came back to him.

"So, what was the deal between you and my mother?"

Gary smiled sheepishly, his eyes lowering to the ground. "Your mother is a very special lady, Jim." He put his hand on Jim's shoulder in a way that made him want to slug him. He may not have liked her very much, but dammit, she was *his* mother, and he felt possessive of her in a way he couldn't explain.

Jim seized his friend by the shirt. "No shit right now. What did you do to my mom?"

Gary's eyebrows went up, and he smiled. "Relax. I helped her move some furniture one summer, and we smoked some after."

"Smoked some—" Jim's eyebrows narrowed. If he didn't know Gary as well as he did, he might think smoking was a double entendre of some kind. Hell, it just might be.

He'd never seen his mother smoke anything stronger than a cigar and found Gary's words hard to believe. But that was much easier to swallow than the awful alternative. "That's it?"

"Come on, man. Why would I lie to you about that? If I'd railed your mom, I'd totally tell you all about it."

The truth of Gary's words stung, and Jim released him. There were a great many "conquests" Jim had heard tale of, and getting his mother in the sack would be the crown jewel for Gary. Jim had to admit his mother, even in her midfifties now, was a looker, and Gary had always been very open about his abundant lust for her since he was a preteen.

"Just keep the monster in the cage this time, okay?"

"But I'm not wearing—"

"You know what I mean."

Gary nodded, and they turned up the walkway. The house was old, but very well kept. Jim had lived here only briefly. After his father had died, he'd gone to stay with other relatives while his mother "recovered." His parents had been separated at the time, and by the time Jim had come to stay with her, he was a junior in high school.

The grass was cut painfully short and lined with perennials to either side of the walkway. Tall arborvitae obscured the front face of the house except for the stairs, which Jim knew allowed her to look out while preventing others from looking in. The house itself was painted ash gray, trimmed in white, and he guessed that color would have to go next year. She rotated her entire exterior color scheme every four years, which meant the flowers and bushes would have to go, and the house would be coated in some entirely different scheme, probably Prussian blue or Farrow & Ball Citron. His mother had picked her color schemes several years in advance, and how in the world they had become committed to his memory, he had no idea.

The porch light was on, as always when it was dark outside. Jim took a deep breath, fear coursing through him much more than it had when he had faced off with the giant. He rang the doorbell, steeling himself for her to pop out of the door like a jack-in-the-box.

Gary was uncharacteristically sedate, one hand clasping the other, rocking back and forth. He had a passive smile on his face, giving him the look of an undertaker. Jim wanted to change everything about him in that instant. While Jim looked very little like his father had, Gary had all his father's classic features, which was probably why his mother found him attractive and frequently flirted back.

He rang the doorbell again and looked at Gary, still rocking back and forth and still being himself somehow despite how strange he was coming off in this moment. He heard shuffling inside, and a moment later, a hazel green eye peered at them from behind a curtain on the other side of the glass door.

"Hey, Ma." Jim held up a hand and wiggled his fingers at her. The eye narrowed and disappeared behind the curtain. That was probably the closest he'd seen his mother come to emoting in at least the last eight years.

Several minutes passed with them standing on the porch. Gary shrugged and reached for the doorbell, and Jim slapped his hand away.

"No. If you do that, she wins."

"Wins what?" He looked confused.

"Trust me. We have to set the stage from the start, or this could go belly-up."

"I don't know what the hell you're talking about. Your mom is a sweet lady. Why are you always trying to make her out like some kind of monster?"

"You didn't grow up with her. You wouldn't understand."

"If she was standing, I wouldn't mind being under."

Jim gave Gary a look. Before he could say anything more, the door unlocked. It swung inward, and there Carol Butcher-Reeve stood, all five feet two inches of her. She had a dusting of eyeshadow, lightly rouged cheeks, and glistening lips. She had on a champagne-colored sleeping gown that uplifted and contained her wealth of cleavage while highlighting her slender waist and curvy hips. Currently she wore what looked like her own hair for a change in a cut that was short on the sides and back and almost medium length up top, with frosty-blonde ends.

"Boys!" she exclaimed as if shouting to the neighborhood that she had guests. She had a rich, womanly tenored voice that tended to be soothing even when she was meting out the harshest of criticisms. "How are you this evening?"

Jim's mother blocked the threshold of her home with her petite frame. Jim made no move, awaiting her eventual invite. He would not ask; that was what she wanted.

"Carol!" Gary bent for a brief hug and kiss on the cheek. "Mind if we come in?"

Dammit, Gary!

"Oh, come on," she said, taking a step back and waving them inside. "I'll cut a wedge of pumpkin pie for you."

"You know my favorite." Gary hated pumpkin pie. But he always liked it when Jim's mother was offering.

Jim followed them inside, noting the nauseating chemistry going on between the two. He felt like the ball was in her court now, and they would have to play her game. It grated on him, although Gary seemed either completely unaware or was more than happy to oblige.

The house smelled wonderful. Jim shut the door behind them and looked around at the various changes she'd made.

"Nice wainscoting," Gary said.

Jim had to admit it was. The walls were a shade of cream, the wainscoting a powdery red that broke up the otherwise blank walls in this room nicely. There was an extrawide fireplace in the far wall with a picture of her and his father above the mantel. Incredibly soft-looking couches surrounded a coffee table a few feet away, and a baby grand piano was at an adjacent wall. Jim subconsciously rubbed his knuckles, shuddering at the years of lessons he'd spent at the thing under the tutelage of his mother and the woman he affectionately came to know as Genghis Mary. His mother also had a Christmas tree up in the corner even though Halloween hadn't even come yet.

"Getting started early on Christmas?" Jim asked.

She laughed. "My dear, that isn't a Christmas tree. It's a Pettlier."

Jim was just about to call BS when Gary said, "Are you serious?" He rushed over to it and began looking the tree up and down. "It's gorgeous!" He raised his hands and turned to her. "May I?"

"Gently." She nodded. Gary began feeling the tree. It was odd to see him be so . . . tender. It was almost surreal watching him stroke the boughs, fingers gentling across the pine needles. If they were even called pine needles.

Jim looked back and forth between his friend and his mother, feeling like he was losing an ally. This was going to be hard. Probably impossible. He might as well just turn around and walk out the front door.

Finally Gary turned away from the tree. "How about that pie?"

"If you're ready for it."

"You know I like it hot. With whipped cream."

"I know *exactly* how you like it."

Their chemistry was as sexy as a documentary on metaphilia. Jim charged into the kitchen, stomping his feet as he went.

"What's the matter with Jim?" she asked from behind him.

"Not sure. Something with Mel; he hasn't been able to get hold of her since work."

"Oh no," his mother said as they followed him into the kitchen, arm in arm. Jim plunked down on one of the low-backed barstools in the breakfast nook. She went to the refrigerator and took out a large pumpkin pie that hadn't had any slices cut out of it yet. She and Jim hated pumpkin pie. The only people he knew who actually liked it were Gary and his father. His mother took out a crazy-looking pie knife with a blade wide enough to sever limbs and deftly cut out a wide wedge, gently taking it out with a fork and knife and placing it on a saucer. After thirty seconds in the microwave, homemade cream topped the pie, also something his mother never ate, and she set it next to the head of the table.

Gary sat down, taking up the utensil, slicing off a huge chunk, and forking it into his mouth. "Carol, your pie is always the best," he said, his mouth full. It was especially disgusting, considering that if he was experiencing the same revulsion from food as Jim, then Gary was eating what was tantamount to garbage. He had no idea how Gary was managing it, but his friend continued, smacking his lips and moaning with feigned pleasure with each bite.

When he was finally done, he set the fork down and sat back, patting his stomach. Jim half expected Gary to kiss his fingertips and fan them out before him, exclaiming *"C'est magnifique"'* His mother's eyes were wide, as if she had gained pleasure from him eating, and she rested a hand on Gary's wrist. She opened her mouth as if to speak and then looked over at Jim, as if noticing him for the first time.

"I'm sorry, Jimmy. Did you want something too? I've got some chocolate ice cream in the freezer, I think."

Something rolled over in the pit of him, and it was all he could do to hold still.

"No, thank you."

She looked from him to Gary and then back. "So what brings you here tonight?" His mother was playing direct. Usually there was at least a twenty-minute span of innocuous conversation before someone began to hint at the crux of what had brought them together.

"Hey, is that Pettlier thing a real thing, or are you just goofing?" Jim asked.

His mother and Gary both looked at him like an alien.

"Carol, could I apologize for disturbing you again?" Gary finally said. He let his eyes trail down her figure, gesturing to her with one hand. "You look absolutely amazing. If I didn't know better, I'd think you were Jim's younger sister."

Aw, come on. That was too corny.

His mother's laugh leapt out of her like a flock of birds surprised from a tree. Many, many men had come on to her with much better lines—executive vice presidents, professional athletes, CEOs, models—and she'd barely registered their presence. She'd always seemed immune to compliments, even from him and his father, and for her to reduce herself to a giggling mess over Gary's malformed attempt at being complimentary was . . . offensive.

Jim wondered why it bothered him.

When she finally had returned to a calmer demeanor, she was gripping Gary's hand tightly. Jim didn't like him holding her hand like that and felt like throwing a punch at somebody.

"You know, Carol, we're kind of in a bind. Mel and Jim got engaged a few months ago, and she's kind of been hinting that she isn't satisfied with the ring he got her. She left enough clues around for him to figure out what she really wanted, and he found it at this jeweler over in Southfield. He's holding it for Jim, but he's got to get it tonight."

His mother put her free hand to her mouth, one eyebrow raised in intrigue. "Let me guess, the ring isn't exactly in his budget, and he needs you to negotiate."

"Exactly," Gary said, smiling wide.

"That's so great of you, Gary." Jim's mother looked at Jim. "What a great friend you have, Jimmy." He nodded, having no idea what words would best fit this situation. "What brings you here, though?"

Gary looked at her, a sheepish grin on his face. "I . . . don't have a car, and Jim's just broke down. We need to get there before nine."

She looked up at the clock on the microwave. "It's eight fifty now. You'll never make it."

"I already spoke to the jeweler. He says he won't wait a minute past nine thirty."

"You need to borrow my car?"

Oh my god, Gary is a genius.

Jim's anger, frustration, and confusion melted in an instant.

Gary held his hand out, fingers spread as if waiting for the keys. "If we could impose. I mean, we wouldn't need it for more than an hour?" He looked at Jim. "Hour and a half?"

"Maybe two." Jim hunkered over the table.

"I *love* Mel," Jim's mother said, the implication hitting Jim's ears as, "I love Mel. Not Jim," and he felt fouled again. "Of course." She looked at Jim, and her expression was as straightforward as he'd ever seen. She typically had an air about her as if nothing in life should be taken seriously. "Of course," she said to him too.

His mother got up and walked to the back of the kitchen, opening the door to the laundry room that connected to the garage. Jim hated that she kept her keys there, but she'd always acquiesced to his request to keep them in her bedroom with her, only to return them to the hook on the wall in there. She came back, detaching the car key and fob from the rest, and handed them to Gary.

"Why don't you go warm her up?"

Gary's eyebrows went up. "Thank you." He wrapped his hand over hers before taking the key. They pecked on the lips, and it was all Jim could do not to leap on one of them and go punchy. "You have a fantastic night, Carol."

"I just did."

Jim found himself making mocking faces at their conversation behind Gary and his mother's backs.

Gary went into the garage, and a moment later came the growl of the garage door winding up. Jim stood to go, prepared to give his mother the obligatory hug and kiss.

Her eyes turned to two scrutinous slits.

"What is wrong with you?"

"What?"

"*You*. You—you—you." She tapped his chest with her index finger with each word. "You look sick. What happened?"

"I'm not sure . . . I don't know what you're talking about." At first he mistook her scornful tone for anger and there was some of that, but at its base her voice was filled with concern.

She was actually worried about him.

Jim couldn't remember the last time that had happened and wondered if she was angry because he'd done something to make himself sick or something had made him sick and her fear had turned to anger. He had no doubt that if someone had done something to him that her response would be swift and violent. He had seen it happen more than once. His mind almost drifted to that poor, poor principal who'd made the mistake of suspending Jim . . .

She pinned him to the wall with one sharp fingernail.

"Look, Ma. I don't know what to tell you. I'm in the middle of a thing I can't talk about right now. It's a no . . . talky thingy."

Her eyes narrowed even more. "Do you need my help? Should I come with you?"

"No! No—no. I don't think we need that kind of help. Thank you, Ma, but no."

She stood back from him, a warning finger in the air. "Don't shut me out, Jim. Don't wait until it's too late. Your father did that. I hate that."

Jim felt chilled from her words. She really was worried. She had no idea what he was into and how deep, but here she was, ready to stick her neck out.

"What do you mean about Dad?" he asked. It was nearly impossible to get his mother to speak about his father since his suicide. Now was his chance, and he was going for it.

She shook her head. "Your father had been depressed off and on for years. It was what drove me most crazy about him and the reason I stuck with him so long. I didn't want to lose him; I didn't want you to lose him."

It was the first time he could recall his mother speaking about anything in such a sober manner. It made him think there was a chance they could build a bridge to each other, that they could have an actual functional mother-son relationship.

"I have to go check on my trolley orchid," she said, laying her head on his chest and hugging him.

"Okay," he said. "Can you promise me we can continue this conversation later?"

"As long as you promise me you'll come back so we can have the conversation."

"I guarantee you I'm coming back."

She nodded and wiped her eye. Was that a tear? It gave him hope. Jim smiled at his mother before turning for the door.

"You sure you can't check on that orchid later? It's dark outside."

"It has to be done. Goodbye, son."

"Bye, Ma."

Chapter 14

"What took you so long?" Gary asked as they pulled out of the driveway.

"We had a little chat." Jim was looking out the window, trying to spot his mother coming outside.

"What are you doing?"

"I'm looking for my mom. She said she had to check on an orchid."

"Orchid? I didn't see any orchid. What kind?"

"A trolley orchid?"

Gary yanked the wheel over, leapt out of the car, and began vomiting violently. Then he dropped trou and began doing the same thing from the other end. Jim marveled as mushed pumpkin pie came out of him like soft-serve ice cream. After a minute he wiped his mouth and returned, making weird coughing sounds.

"You okay?"

Gary went on, and after a moment Jim realized his friend was laughing.

"What's so funny?"

"Your mom. I saw all the signs, but I just didn't put it together." He shook his head. "I just did."

Jim stared at him. Gary eventually stared back.

"Don't you get it? She's got a man in there."

"No, she doesn't." Jim had never reconciled the notion that his mother had had sex with anyone before or after his father, and the thought of it now made him deeply uncomfortable. In his mind, she wasn't a sexual human being with desires and needs she wanted to have met. She was his mother, and any sexual contact came at his father's insistence, and then only to conceive Jim. In his mind, they'd had sex perhaps a half dozen times or so.

"You didn't see how the piped pillows were all disarranged on the couch, the flokati rug was turned horizontal instead of vertical, the smell of leather, sandalwood, and a little bit of sweat?" Jim hadn't understood half the words in his question, but remained silent. "I thought at first she might have been getting freaky by her lonesome, but you sealed it—your mother is about to get her back broken!"

"Shut the fuck up."

"Hey, I'm sorry. I'm sooo sorry." Gary broke into peals of laughter again.

After about three minutes, he was composed enough to drive. It didn't take long to get to Mrs. K's home, a high-rise apartment in Southfield around the corner from city hall. Gary found a parking spot, foregoing the connected parking structure for a strip mall with a TGI Friday's.

"We have to be careful," Gary said. "Those guys killed Dr. K; they might not have gotten what they are looking for. Or maybe they did, and they want to tie up some loose ends."

"Okay. Let me give her a call to let her know we are here."

Gary grabbed his hand. "No. Don't do that. If they are in her apartment, you'll be letting them know."

Jim nodded. That made total sense. They crossed the street, weaving around the small amount of cross traffic.

"I doubt we can just walk up to her apartment and knock on the door," Jim said. "We're going to have to tip our hand at some point. Maybe we can use some kind of code word to see if it's really safe."

Gary just looked at him.

"What? I'm trying to come up with something here at least."

Gary passed the entrance of the building, and Jim followed without a word. A man was walking a little dog, and a woman in a belly shirt stood idle, mock smoking a cigarette in one of those long, thin cigarette holders.

"I'm starved!" Gary said too loudly. "You want sliders? I want sliders."

"Sure?" Jim said, not sure what was going on. He noticed there was a Granny's on the corner across the street. Gary was heading in that direction, and he realized he hadn't eaten there since the last time he had gotten high. Granny's was like a greasier, dirtier version of Waffle House. He remembered it because it was the day before he'd met Mel.

Chapter 15

Jim caught up with Gary but was cut off before he could speak. "You know, tomorrow night Eddie is going to be downtown, throwing one of those pop-up parties."

"For real?" Jim only cared because they'd gone to high school with the mononymous "Eddie," whose only claim to celebrity was roaming the Earth and putting on massive parties that were set up and torn down in a single night. Edward Keach had been a tall, gangly, quiet kid who had no enemies and probably a handful of friends. He'd thrown one party after graduation, and instead of orientation at Eastern, he'd turned into *the* party man.

For the last twelve years, he'd been throwing parties around the world for celebrities, children of prime ministers, athletes, and maybe even a dictator or two. When not doing that, he would plan pop-up parties that could happen in any city at any time of year. His website and Twitter account sprinkled clues people could follow, and shows like *Extra* even had a segment dedicated to speculation as to where the next party was going to be.

Eddie didn't invite just anyone to his parties. He selected from the millions of people who had queued up to his website, and even those were from a select few who had been granted access to create a login and thus leave a message with their e-mail.

He selected from the local celebrity pool and also international stars, who were more than glad to drop everything and fly across the world to attend. Athletes, politicians, musicians, and champions of industry were all well stocked at an Eddie party, no matter where it was held.

"It's supposed to be tomorrow. We should crash."

"Yeah, but we kind of have this whole being dead thing going on." Even though Jim was the voice of reason, he still felt a pang of regret that they wouldn't be able to go. He imagined walking arm in arm with Mel right up to Eddie and introducing her to the kid he'd once seen vomit pizza out of his nose. "What was up outside?"

"Couldn't be sure, but I think someone is watching the outside."

"Where?" Jim hadn't seen anything.

"Three people. The blonde with the really long hair, the dog walker, and the homeless guy."

"What homeless guy?"

"The one behind the bushes in front of the building."

"The other two looked normal to me."

"They might be; I can't tell for sure. I figured we'd wait here, and in a few minutes if they're still around, we'd know something is up."

They sat at the counter that seemingly wound through the whole restaurant. A pretty waitress with a heavy amount of makeup and blonde hair pulled into a loose ponytail came over with a notepad.

"What can I get you handsome gentlemen tonight?" That got Gary's attention. Anytime a woman was complimentary, he tended to interpret it as sexual desire.

"A piece of paper with your phone number on it would be nice," he said. She flashed him a disarming smile and laughed appreciably.

It was already too awkward for Jim, and he jumped in. "Two coffees for now? And we're going to look over the menu."

"Sure thing." She turned her big smile on Jim, and there seemed to be a thank you in her eyes. She quickly left, disappearing into the kitchen.

He figured a change of subject would get Gary's mind off the waitress. "So, what's the deal with Mel? I mean, you two used to get along. And don't give me that she's-cheating-on-me nonsense. You have to know I know that isn't true."

"Okay, you got me. I don't know that she's cheating on you. I haven't seen that with my own eyes."

"Then what's the deal? Just give it to me straight. Exactly what is your problem with her?"

Gary shifted on his stool. He couldn't meet Jim's eyes, which meant a lot coming from the person who hadn't shown fear of anything so far as Jim could remember.

"Look, it's okay. Whatever it is, you can tell me. I might get mad, I might fly off the handle, but I love you, man. I know I haven't said it before, Gary. But I mean it. I love you like you're my brother." Jim clasped one of Gary's hands between his two. "I love you. You *are* my brother."

Gary steeled himself and gave a slight nod. He took a deep breath and let it out slowly. "I saw her kill a guy."

Jim tossed his hand away.

"Come on. I'm trying to have a moment with you. I want to connect with you, Jim said.

Just then the waitress brought over their coffees, her smile at half-mast.

"I'll just give you two a couple more minutes."

"No, wait. This is my best friend. We're just trying to talk something through. I have a girlfriend. A fiancée. I have a fiancée who's a woman with a naturally formed vagina—"

The waitress nodded. "That's great. Whatever you want to do." She turned around and left before Jim could say anything more.

"Great," Gary said. "Now she won't give either of us her number." He rolled his eyes at Jim. "So, Mel's vagina is naturally formed?"

If Jim had had running blood in his veins, his cheeks would have been red. It was his turn to not meet Gary's eyes.

"I'm just looking for a straightforward answer, Gary. You don't have to make stuff up."

"I'm not, though." Gary took Jim's hand and wrapped it lovingly in his. He waved the waitress over, and she came reluctantly.

"I want to apologize for my J-bear. He gets so shy around people. Hasn't even told his mom about us."

"I totally get it." The waitress smiled again. "My brother is totally gay. He's always checking out guys, y'know? But he just won't admit it."

"Well, sweetie, all you can do is love him through it until he's ready to love himself."

"Wow," she said thoughtfully. "That's really sweet. Thanks."

"We'll take one of those number fours, mkay?"

"Be right out with that." She disappeared into the kitchen again.

"What the hell are you doing?"

"Relieving the tension. You were awkward, she was awkward—we weren't going to get quality service until this was resolved."

"But she thinks we're gay." It wasn't the gay part that bothered Jim the most. It was the sexually active part. Jim felt most comfortable when he was perceived as asexual. He wasn't the type who liked to flaunt his manliness. He didn't wear tight clothes, shirts that showed off his muscles, or cologne. All those things struck him as something someone would do who was trying to attract the opposite sex.

It was a wonder that he found Mel, and in truth, that probably had more to do with her than him. Mel had a very up-front manner about her. She tended to lock onto a target and not yield until she'd acquired it. She'd somehow made him comfortable enough in his skin so that he didn't mind being "seen" by other people when they were together. That was why he knew she wouldn't ever cheat on him. It would have destroyed everything she had created.

"So what?" Gary said. "It's not like it's the worst thing that's happened to you today."

Jim considered his point. Someone he'd probably never see again thought something about him.

"Yeah. So what?" Jim shrugged, adjusting to his new perspective. They sat in silence until the waitress came with their food. Jim didn't intend to eat anything, but he made a show of picking up one of the sliders and taking a nibble.

It was delicious. He took another bite, then stuffed the whole thing in his mouth, chewing hungrily. Gary, a curious look on his face, joined in. They both tore into the six little burgers, not pausing until they were completely gone. The fries remained untouched.

"Now what do you mean you saw Mel kill a guy? Is that one of your euphemisms for something?"

"It's a euphemism for I saw her aim a muzzle-loaded .45 and knock out the back of a guy's skull with it. And before you go on about how I'm lying, really think about it: why would I lie about something like that? What purpose does it serve me to call the love of your life a murderer?"

"You're kidding, right? You'd say anything to get us to break up."

"Okay, point taken. If I were going to make something up, though, why something so easy to disprove? I bet you don't have a .45 in your apartment."

"We have a gun." Jim had no idea what kind.

"I bet it was her idea to get it. No, wait. I bet it was *your* idea, but it somehow came to you after she moved in."

"Yeah, so what?"

Gary shook his head like Jim just didn't get it. "Other than where she's from and what she allegedly does for a living, how much do you know about her?"

"She's from Colorado, and her parents are dead. She was an only child."

"What an awesome cover story. No family to account for, no 'back home' to visit."

"Cover story? A cover story for what?"

"Some wetwork-type shit. That's right, I think your girlfriend is an assassin or a hit man—*woman*. The reason I haven't checked her background is because they can trace that kind of stuff back to me, and I don't want to get shot in the face."

Poor Gary. All that weed had made him paranoid.

"Oh, and before you write me off as a nutjob, consider this—she has a menial job as a junior accountant, yet she has a locked cell phone that's provided by the company. Why?"

"It's her work phone; I don't care." Jim shrugged.

"Does she leave the room when she gets an after-hours call? Does she have to work into the early hours of the morning?"

"Yeah. Especially during tax season."

"Hm. I may have made a left turn at a pivotal moment. To be continued on this."

They went to the cash register, and Jim paid, a lot more relieved with the conversation than he knew Gary had hoped. It was his weed paranoia flaring up—another reason he was glad to have given the stuff up.

Outside, Jim followed Gary's lead again. He had absolutely no experience with anything clandestine, and his friend appeared to know at least something. They walked the half block back to the apartment building, passing the entrance again. They went around the corner, and Gary stopped.

"Okay, so that guy with the dog is definitely staking out the place."

"But he wouldn't know that we don't live there."

"We'll look suspicious, though, when we don't have a key."

"Right." Jim hadn't thought of that. Gary took out his wallet and fished around until he took out what looked at first like a black credit card. He removed it from its sleeve, and Jim saw it had no logo, numbers, or name on it. One long edge looked to be serrated, and he had a strong suspicion the other was sharp as a blade. A short end had a notch in it, and what looked to be a bottle opener was on the other end.

"Where did you get that thing?"

"I made it. Found the specs on the Internet."

"Ever used it before?"

Gary shrugged. Instead of heading back to the front entrance, he continued walking down the street until they had reached the alley. He kept his head down, and Jim did the same, watching his back and giving him a good ten-foot lead. Gary glanced briefly up as they passed the rear service entrance. He must have been dissatisfied with what he saw because he continued walking.

Once they reached the other end of the alley, he stopped.

"What's wrong?"

"Camera on the service door. Can't risk it."

"Well, we're going to have to risk something. You sure we can't just call her?"

"That may be our best bet." Gary took out his cell phone. Jim noted it was the exact same model as his. "What's her number?"

Jim gave it to him, and a moment later he was calling.

"Hello?" Mrs. K said.

"Oh, thank God you picked up. Hey, this is Gary. Is there any way you can come meet me? My car broke down."

"Oh! Well, I'm not sure. Where are you?"

"Not far, just too far away to walk. I'm in Berkeley on Twelve mile. I'm at a gas station, and there's a bar or restaurant a couple blocks away. Maybe we could meet there?"

Silence for a long moment, then, "I don't think so. Are you sure you can't make it here?"

"It'll take me a little while. Maybe I can bum a ride or something. Are you sure this won't be too late? I could always come back tomorrow."

"No—no. You can come now. I'll be up all night."

"Okay. Maybe I can be there in an hour or an hour and a half."

"All right. You be safe."

The line went dead.

"Somebody's in there with her."

"So we call the police."

Gary shook his head. "I doubt she'd be alive by the time they got to her apartment."

"So what do we—"

Gary walked away from him, quickly rounding the corner and then rounding the next to the front of the building. He found the man walking his dog, snatched the leash out of his hand, and gave him a shove.

"Hey!" the man said, and Gary decked him. He went down, clutching at his face.

"Gary!" Jim rushed over the last few feet. He stopped short of kneeling to help the man, remembering what Gary had said.

"How many up there?" Gary asked.

"I don't know what you're talking about!" came the man's muffled reply as he held a hand over his nose and mouth.

"Tell me, or the dog gets it." Gary picked the dog up by the scruff and lifted it above his head.

"Please, no!" The man immediately rolled onto his knees, ignoring his nose. "Please don't hurt my dog. I'll give you whatever you want."

"I want to know how many people are up there with her. What have they done with her?" He gave the tiny dog, which didn't seem to be much more than a puff of hair, the smallest shake.

"Okay! Okay!" The man held his hands up, crying as if asking for mercy from the Lord. "There are four of them."

"Have they done anything to her yet?"

The man shuddered, doubled over on his knees while hugging himself. He nodded, a trail of thick saliva draping over his pooched bottom lip.

"They probably . . ." he began and took a hitching breath. His voice was far away. "They probably took turns getting oral. Maybe some light slapping and choking. Then she probably jumped right in with some . . . some . . . DP."

"DP? What the hell are you talking about?" Jim asked.

"That's double penetration. Traditionally, one in the front and one in the back, but they could both just as easily be in the poop chute," Gary said.

Jim looked at him. "Gary!"

"Yeah. Ew. She's gotta be like sixty years old. That has to be hard for her to take in."

"Sixty?" The man on his knees looked confused. "My wife isn't sixty."

"*Your* wife?" Jim asked.

He nodded. "Aren't you guys from cuckoldmyhusband.com too? She said she wanted two more around eleven."

"N—" Jim began.

"Yes. Yes, we are," Gary said. "So why don't you open the door for us?"

The man nodded like a child and climbed to his feet. He was taller than both of them by half a head and was three hundred pounds of flab. He was probably the type who had peaked in high school, and it had been all downhill from there.

"Why did you think my wife was sixty?"

Gary's eyes went wide. "Shut the fuck up!" He pulled his hand back like he was about to slap him, and the man flinched. "Open this door 'fore I bitch slap you."

The man hustled to the door and opened it.

"Key, bitch!"

"You don't need it. It's already open."

"Bitch, I said gimme the key!"

The man held his keys out, and Gary took them.

"Could I have my dog?"

Jim glared at the man as he passed by, trying to look in character as he jive stepped or whatever he was doing with his gait. Gary took the leash off the dog and lofted it to the sidewalk.

"Fetch," he said as the little canine took off and the man ran after.

"Cocaine! C'mere, Cocaine! Oh, sweet baby!" the man said as he waddled in pursuit.

They walked down the hall to the elevators.

"Six dicks?" Gary asked.

"Damn," Jim said.

Chapter 16

The plan was for one of them to go one floor above Mrs. K's, find a window, climb outside, and rappel into her apartment. That way they would have the element of surprise over whoever was inside. The other person would be waiting for the sound of breaking glass to kick in the front door. Gary guessed no more than four people were inside by virtue of the size of the apartments. That meant two apiece. Jim had no idea how he could know that. That woman had six other people in her apartment.

After convincing Gary they didn't have time to check out the cuckholded husband's apartment, they went their separate ways. Gary got off on Mrs. K's floor, while Jim continued up. The quiet was unsettling as he got off the elevator. The halls were painted off-white, with sconces every half dozen feet or so giving the entire floor a soft look. Jim walked, thankful for the soft carpet underfoot keeping his footfalls silent. Not that that was necessary. Whoever was in Mrs. K's apartment had no idea who he was, and had they seen him, would not have known he didn't belong there. Just like he wouldn't have known about them.

He passed by two heavyset Asian women with short, black hair. The one with glasses eyed him up and down, saying nothing. Jim tried to give a reassuring I-belong-here smile and wondered if they would call the police.

He wasn't afraid for once, though. He'd been in a few scraps, unavoidable where he grew up, but he'd been scared during every single one whether he won or lost.

The only thing that worried him here was falling eight stories. Jim had no idea if the fall would kill him or not in his current state. The scariest notion of all would be surviving and being nothing but a quadriplegic mess or a brain in a jar.

He came to a window at the end of the hall and tugged at it. It rose half an inch and stuck. Jim examined all four corners of the window, examining it for where it had caught. The thing looked as though it had been painted several times, and he noticed tiny tendrils of paint at the edges that had to have come from the window being forced open. He spent a couple of minutes peeling soft, excess paint off the windowpane until he could slide it up enough to get his head through. Jim peeked out.

The person looking up at him was a surprise.

Chapter 17

The man gave him a come-down-here wave.

Jim frowned.

"The hell I will," he said and stood. He turned around and saw a man staring at him who was almost as wide as the hallway.

He may have been one of the men who shot at him and Gary. Jim couldn't be sure given the intensity of the situation. He gestured to Jim with his index finger and folded his arms.

Jim slumped his shoulders. It was one thing to take a guy out when he didn't expect you; it was another thing entirely when he had the drop on you.

"Which way?" he asked, walking ahead of the man down the hall.

"Elevator." The man had a voice as deep as a well. Jim pushed the up button and was shoved against the wall. "Funny business."

He was relatively certain the man meant *no* funny business and thought his clipped speech meant he wasn't kept around for his brains. Or his looks. The guy was hideous. He had a face like a bouquet of hemorrhoids. Jim would have to be careful with how he tested him.

The man thumbed the down button, and they let the first elevator pass as it was going up.

"See anybody, play nice. Or somebody gets hurt."

"Original. I like that in a villain." When the man didn't respond, Jim was certain he was being delivered to someone. Probably whoever was in Mrs. K's apartment.

A second elevator came, and they got on. Luckily or unluckily, they were alone and got off one floor down. Jim was herded to the right, the man's sausage fingers prodding him in the back. The man finally clasped a hand on him that felt like it could easily crush his collarbone, and they stopped.

This was her apartment. But Gary wasn't there. Jim felt a flutter of hope and restrained himself from looking around. Any moment now his best friend would pop out from somewhere and rescue him.

A fist that looked as hard as a stone rapped on the door three times, and then the man stepped back.

"It's open," somebody called from inside. The man prodded Jim in the back, and he opened the door. The first thing Jim noticed when he stepped inside was the overwhelmingly prevalent smell of weed. This was definitely the right place.

It was thick and heavy in the air, like stepping into a big, warm coat made of marijuana smoke and buttoning up. It was saturating him and everything he had on.

The room itself was plainly furnished, a brown couch in the center of the room behind a glass coffee table. There was an old television on a small table in a corner, and a big window in the far wall, with cream curtains drawn.

A man was on all fours by the window, his head down like he'd been throwing up. He looked up at Jim, gray eyes like old diamonds twinkling in his head.

"Hello," the man said. It wasn't the voice of the person who'd told them to enter.

"Hey," Jim said, not knowing what to expect, but hoping Gary would still come leaping out of the shadows.

"Bring the other." He didn't break eye contact with Jim, but someone in the next room moved. Another big man came in, dragging a hands-tied Gary with him.

"Wassup?"

"Gary!" Jim realized he had no right to be, but he was disappointed. He'd been captured just the same, but that left no means of rescue unless Mrs. K was hiding somewhere.

The man on his hands and knees slowly stood, brushing imaginary lint off his suit. It almost matched the curtains, Jim noted. He was a little shorter than Jim, very slender, bronze-skinned, with hands that looked like they'd never seen a day of manual labor. He looked manufactured.

"I won't waste your time, gentlemen. You have an item that belongs to us." He reached into his suit jacket and pulled out a black pill pinched between his index finger and thumb. "There should have been five of these, but the empty container I'm supposing this used to be in only had four slots. Which means you meant to cheat us from the start, and then you decided to keep them all to yourselves."

"I . . . we don't know anything about that," Jim said.

The man's eyebrows raised. "Ah. So neither of you consumed the Bloom?" Jim's eyes bugged, and he realized he had given them away. "That is what I thought. I'm curious, was it one or both of you?" Jim's eyes bugged again.

Dammit, eyes!

The man nodded. "Allow me to introduce myself. I am Sebastian Fyukis. We are Adjacent."

"Adjacent to what?" Gary asked.

"No, you don't understand. We are . . . Adjacent. You know, like you would say you're Christian."

"How did you know I'm Christian?"

"I don't know you're Christian."

"You just said I was."

"I meant that only as an example."

"Then you should've said that. You should've said, 'We are Parallel, just as others call themselves Christian.'"

"Adjacent. We are Adjacent. Not Parallel. Those guys are weirdos."

"Point taken," Gary said. "Adjacent to what now?"

"I don't know if I feel like telling you now."

"Come on."

"No."

"Don't be like that. Please?"

Fyukis folded his arms.

"Would a sorry help?" Gary said.

"Maybe."

"Well then in the best interest of us all getting along, I'm sorry. Okay?"

"Okay," Fyukis said. He looked around the room as if not knowing where to start. Gary had thrown off his rhythm, something Jim was very familiar with.

"Bring the crone!"

A raven-haired woman walked in the room with her arm wrapped around the thin shoulders of a sixtyish woman. She had to be Mrs. K. The two women were about the same height, although the older woman was slightly stooped at the shoulder.

"You must know that you are infinitely more valuable to me than this person. Please know that I will not hesitate to hurt her." He looked back and forth between Gary and Jim.

"Okay," Jim said. "We get it. So what next?"

The unreserved recklessness that had been slowly unleashing in Jim suddenly choked off. There was someone he was being made to feel responsible for, and the feeling was unpleasant, like a pebble in his shoe.

"The lie would be that you give me the Bloom, and I let you all live. You have to have figured by now that that is not a possibility."

"No, we didn't. We have every hope that we will walk out of this totally unscathed." Gary smiled.

Fyukis nodded to his man standing next to Gary. This man was leaner than the one Jim had come in with, but taller. They had both exchanged their robes for street clothes, and the taller man's forearms rippled with ropy muscle.

He grasped the neck of Gary's shirt and tore it open, exposing Gary's torso down to his navel. The man stepped aside so everyone could see the three bullet holes.

"You're going to pay for that." Gary looked at Jim. "I always wanted to say that. Oh my gosh, I always wanted to say, 'I always wanted to say that'!"

"Are you in any pain?" Fyukis asked.

"Agony. Why don't you come suck my cock and take my mind off it?"

"Vile." The man pulled a disgusted face.

"He . . . smells," the taller man said.

"You bet I do. I got three bullet holes in me. Is somebody calling a doctor? Better yet, take me to the hospital. I could drop dead any minute."

"I know, Tim. That's the Bloom you smell. It has saturated his blood."

"I'm surprised you can smell anything past the weed," Jim said.

Mrs. K looked sheepish. "I thought they were the cops," she said. "I was burning the evidence."

"Don't worry, Mrs. K," Gary said. "We'll have you out of here in a little bit."

"I don't know how you expect to get anything back," Jim said. "We swallowed those pills hours ago."

"We can shit in his hand. I got one almost charged up if you can wait five minutes."

Fyukis smirked. "The Bloom cannot be digested. It is not filtered by liver, thinned in blood, broken down into baser parts by small and large intestine. If the Bloom is in you and you are alive, then it is only a matter of time before it leaves you and you are no longer alive."

"The Bloom," Jim said. "Gary, do you remember eating any flowers? I don't."

"Uh-uh."

"I get it. You believe that your false bravado will somehow save you at the last moment. That your bravery in the very face of death will somehow betray our cowardice or some other flaw for you to exploit and effect an escape."

"Kinda," Gary said.

"Tim, decapitate him."

The tall man slid out a long knife with a wide blade. Maybe it was a machete—Jim wasn't sure.

"Oh." That was the extent to which Gary acknowledged the weapon in the man's hand. "Aren't you going to tell us what this is all about? I'm sure cutting my head off isn't going to get your flower back. Who's the other person? The woman back there." Gary nodded toward the room the two women had come out of.

Fyukis lifted one eyebrow. "Mr. Gary, how very astute of you." He turned toward the door. "Mary, if you would come in here, please."

A moment later a tall, thin woman came into the room. Jim immediately recognized her as the woman outside in the belly shirt. She'd been gone when they came back, but of course that meant she was already up here.

With whatever that thing in her hands was.

It was an ornately designed box, carved out of some sort of dark wood, or perhaps it was stained. The two sides Jim could see had what appeared to be legless, coily dragons with their tongues flicked out.

"What is that, Pandora's box?" Gary asked. "I knew it! You guys are Pandorans."

Fyukis didn't react, taking Gary's comment for the distraction it had been meant to be. Jim watched with waxing interest. Something bad was in there, and it was meant for them.

"Hold it, big guy," Jim said. Tim had the knife to Gary's throat and was about to begin sawing. "If he really wanted you to saw my friend's head off, then he wouldn't be interested in getting this Bloom thing back."

Tim looked at Fyukis. The other man gave a slight shake of his head.

"What do you mean?" Fyukis asked.

"If my guess is right, the Bloom has some sort of religious importance to you. You had Dr. K whip it up in his lab, and you intended to use it for some sort of ceremony. Right?"

Fyukis nodded.

"Well, as far as you know, we *are* the Bloom now. I'm imagining that this compound is rare, hasn't been on Earth in a long time, or is completely new. Which means you don't entirely know how it works. You may have already irrevocably damaged it by shooting my friend, and after you killed Dr. K—"

"My Benny?" Mrs. K said. Damn, he'd forgotten all about her. At least he'd avoided the initial awkward part. "He's . . . dead?"

"After Dr. K's untimely demise, you don't have anyone on hand who can produce more for you. Sorry," Jim said, looking at the new widow. He was doing a lot of guessing and hoped he'd struck at least a couple of notes.

"As I said," Fyukis said, "the Testimony states that the Bloom cannot be digested. It can only be held for a brief period of time. Two days."

"You mean three days," Gary said.

"No. Two. Like when Jesus rose from the dead after two days."

"Jesus rose after *three* days," Gary said vehemently. "Three."

"No. Two." Fyukis counted off on his fingers. "Saturday . . . Sunday."

"You have to count Friday, though. You can't skip Friday."

"No. Friday was the day he died. One day after is Saturday. One day after that is Sunday. One plus one is two."

"Okay, I'm Friday, Jim is Saturday, you're Sunday. One plus one plus one is three."

"That's not how that works. You count between the days."

"You can't count between days. What comes between Friday and Saturday?"

"One day."

"How many days are Friday and Saturday?"

"Two."

"And Sunday makes three!"

"Tim, hit him."

The tall man reared back and smashed Gary's face with a massive fist. Gary's head snapped back, and he stumbled back a few steps but kept his feet.

"Ohhh, two days," Gary said.

"There are several mistruths in your Christian Bible," Fyukis said. "One of which is that God is your father." Gary made an angry, confused face but said nothing. "This mistruth is simply a continuation of the same one perpetuated in the Torah. God is not your father, but rather your brother."

"What?"

"The Adjacent are the holders of the True Word as revealed to the Ancestor. He passed it along to me before rejoining Brother by his side."

"I'm sensing a lot of capitalized words here," Jim said.

"I have carried the Testimony for seventy-five years, collecting brothers and sisters into the Congregation along the way."

"Are there more of you?"

"No." Fyukis smiled. "Our number is small, intentionally so. See, in your Father's house there may have been many apartments, but we intend to sit with Brother in His room for alway."

"A lot of capitalized words," Gary said. "Blasphemer."

"So you're saying you're what, a hundred or so years old?" Jim asked.

"I am one hundred and ten. When the Ancient found me when I was thirty-five, he bestowed the Testimony upon me and the knowledge to understand it."

"Where is this book?" Gary said. "I'd like to piss on it."

"Ah, a doubter." Fyukis walked closer and began to pace in front of Gary. "I'm sure you are familiar with John 3:16? 'For He so loved the world that he gave his only begotten son' and blah blah blah. I submit to you that this is wrong and not just intentionally wrong. It is wrong with a purpose. There is a significance to the numbers 3 and 1 and 6, in that order, and in their sum total."

"You didn't provide any evidence it's wrong." Gary scowled.

"Of course I didn't. I need to provide evidence that something that is unprovable is incorrect? The Testimony is not faith. It is knowledge."

"So you lean to your own understanding?"

"No. My brother's. When the Adjacent partakes of the Bloom, only then shall we be transcendent over death and join Him in His room."

"That room is in somebody's basement."

Fyukis smiled broadly. "Perhaps. But we shall be together."

"If you're so knowledgeable, who created your brother?"

He shrugged. "I don't know. And neither does Brother. The point is once we are together, we may explore that answer for ourselves. Let me ask you a question—who created God?"

"God."

"So your creator created himself? Is that not a nonsensical answer? The Adjacent acknowledge that there was one who came before. But that entity has never set foot in this universe. No one knows that entity. Including you."

"Oh, I'm going to pray for you. So *hard*."

"Feel free in the little time you have left. Your simple death will be as forgotten as the grains of sand on a beach."

"So let me get this straight," Jim said. "This Bloom thing, you guys want it so you can all commit suicide?"

"I support you killing yourself," Gary said, nodding. "That's a good idea."

"If you need to oversimplify it, yes. We will kill ourselves using the Bloom and rejoin Brother."

"Who gets all your stuff?" Gary asked.

"You said rejoin," Jim said. "Does that mean you were already with him?

"Either by will or by some other force—we cannot say—but in the beginning there was one spirit, a Holy Spirit. It created the heavens and the earth. At some point the spirit was cleaved in two. The smaller portion settled over the earth and was perceived as dust. The larger portion breathed upon the earth, attempting to blow the dust off its surface. But the dust became life, each granule taking human form."

"That sounds stupid," Gary said.

"No dumber than a God who gathered the dust of the earth and breathed life into it to create one lone person. Brother fostered this new life, encouraged its growth. But He immediately saw the torn nature of mankind. He began coaxing the spirit away from many of these violent ones, slowly over time coalescing it into a few bodies." Fyukis raised his hands, gesturing to the people around the room.

"What, the five of you?" Jim asked. "Sorry, I have to agree with Gary on this one."

"Jim, from across the room, air five," Gary said.

"Received. Say hello to the Heaven's Gaters on the way out."

"And your name rhymes with mucous."

Fyukis's face reddened. "Fiel, do it." The tall woman stepped forward, smiling broadly. Jim noted she was pretty, beautiful even, but overly so. Like she wasn't real. She threw open the top of the box in front of Gary. He flinched and shielded himself, and Jim cried out.

For a long moment, everyone was still. The big man behind Jim had his hands locked on him, and Jim eventually sagged in his grip.

"I don't think your little box worked," Mrs. K said. Before Fyukis could respond, Gary snatched the knife away from Tim and plunged it into the crotch of Fyukis's pants. He shoved him into the window by the throat, the glass cracking.

"I cannot die by any conventional means. The Adjacent are perimortal. Plunge your knife into me. I will not die, and the others will pull you to pieces. We will have the Bloom—all of it—one way or another." Fyukis's voice was high and constrained, his eyes wide.

"Then I guess you're okay not making the trip to see your big bro intact." Gary gave the handle of the knife a slight twitch, and Fyukis's eyes went wide. "Way I see it, it'll be even. Three boys and three girls."

"No!" Fyukis waved Tim back, and the big one who'd been holding Jim. "Stay back!" The black-haired woman remained mute by the old woman's side, while the tall blonde seemed keenly interested. She'd retained her look of constant amusement as if nothing had changed.

"I'm a Jedi," Gary said, his eyes big. "Want to see me use the Force?" He inched the knife upward. "All the blasphemous motherfuckers shall leave the room."

"Everybody get out!" Fyukis shouted. "Now!" Everyone hesitated, and Gary twitched the knife again. "Now!"

The big man by the door turned around and walked out first. He was followed closely by the one named Tim, then the brunette, and lastly the tall blonde Fyukis had called Fiel. Jim did his best to commit the two names to memory. He was certain they would be seeing them again. Probably as soon as they left the apartment.

Before she left, Fiel turned around and said, "You're all going to die. Soon." She smiled widely and almost skipped out the door.

"Now, what are we going to do with you?" Gary asked.

"If you believe you can kill me, do it." Fyukis flashed a daring smile. "I have lived more than a hundred years. The spirit dwells within me, and I will return."

"So you believe death is only a layover?" Jim asked.

Fyukis's eyes turned on him. He licked his lips. Jim noted there was a certain degree of bravado in the man, but he was nervous. "You won't have long," he said. "One way or another, my people will get to me. They're probably waiting outside the door. If you harm me—"

"You'll just do all the stuff to us you were planning on doing anyway," Gary said.

"So it appears we are at a stalemate."

"Not exactly. You're alive. Jim, I think it's time we called 911 and reported two murders. Make sure you give a real good description of our friend here."

Jim narrowed his eyes, not sure where Gary was going.

"Trust me." He looked at Mrs. K and asked, "Do you have any rope?"

"I'm sure I have some in a closet."

"Tie her up, Jim."

"I don't get it," Jim said. "Why?"

"It's a surefire way to throw suspicion off her when the police come and discover us dead. The others will clear out, and Fyukis here will be arrested."

The man didn't appear to have a reaction. Jim decided to toss in an explanation just to be sure. And to twist the knife a little.

"That Bloom of yours had an effect on us you probably didn't anticipate. We don't respirate or have a pulse. As far as anyone can tell, we're dead."

Fyukis looked at Jim. "There's a problem with your thinking," he said.

"Oh yeah?" Gary asked, giving the knife's edge one more jab into his crotch. Fyukis grimaced. He managed to return to a blank expression.

"I won't tell you a thing. You'll see for yourself."

Jim pulled out his cell and dialed 911. A moment later the call was placed, and the operator told him that a vehicle would be dispatched immediately. Mrs. K returned with the rope, and Jim did his best to tie her hands.

"Put her in the bathroom," Gary said. Jim followed her to the bathroom and shut the door behind her. The three of them waited in silence until they heard footsteps coming down the hall.

"You lose," Gary said before tossing the knife and slumping onto the floor. Jim looked at him, shrugged, and did the same. He felt Fyukis looking down at them, but Jim had fallen so that he was looking at Gary, who had the worst death rictus on his face.

"You gotta stop," Jim said. "You're gonna make me laugh."

Someone pounded on the door, and that was when Gary did some sort of death gurgle, loud enough that they had to have heard.

"Southfield Police, we're coming inside!" There was a pounding at the door.

"No, you lose," Fyukis said. A moment later, Jim heard glass shatter and felt a cool breeze coming from outside.

"Dih he yust yucking yump out the window?" Gary said without closing his mouth.

"Uh-huh."

"*Yastard.*"

Chapter 18

Fyukis had no doubt Brother would protect him. At the same time, though, he experienced a few long seconds of weightless terror.

When he finally hit the ground, the pain was beyond description. At impact he either fainted or his mind blanked out, and he experienced several seconds of white before returning to his senses.

His shattered body echoed the impact over and over, thankfully diminishing with each pass. Then came the agony of his body knitting itself together again. It felt like the opposite, like someone was carving out sections of him. The entire process probably took less than a minute, but time was a dimension of agony until he'd been pieced together again.

Fyukis tried to stand, fell, and vomited.

"Hurry." He looked up and saw Fiel sitting in her purple Cabriolet, the top down. "It won't be long before the authorities arrive." He stumbled toward the car, feeling a sensation like seasickness. His hearing was tinny and he was seeing double, but a moment later he was in the passenger seat.

"Thank Brother I am alive," he said after his jaw relocated.

"Yes," she said. "Thank Brother." There was something about her tone he didn't like, but at this very moment, he couldn't concentrate on it.

"Where are the others?"

"Everyone went home when the police arrived. I could call them, let them know you're safe." There it was again, just a pinch of sarcasm to her tone. Fyukis filed it away for later. He wasn't the leader of the Adjacent—they were all equals; however, there was definite disrespect in how she was speaking to him.

"Take me home, please." He had been injured before in his many years, but never this badly. Well, maybe that one time in Gary. Fyukis shuddered even now from that brief recollection. Internal things were still fixing themselves, smaller parts of him. He could feel his gorge rising again and mentally forced it back.

Today had been a disaster. They had lost the Bloom, found it, and lost it again. His confidence was nil, and he had no hope for finding it again. Those two were lost in the wind, he was certain.

"There has to be a way. There has to be."

"There is a way," she said. "It's in the Testimony. I know you'll find it."

Fiel's strength in the knowledge amazed him. Barely two years with the Adjacent, and she was unshakable. Although she was as naive as Tim and Ed were dumb, she was a buoy for him in his moment of low.

He had no idea how to find those two. Gary and Jim their names were. He opened his eyes.

"Drive back around."

"What do you mean? The police—"

"I said drive back around. I have to see something."

By the time they parked in the lot across the street from the apartment building, there was a circus outside. A half dozen police cars and two ambulances were parked haphazardly in the street, lights flashing. People were milling about, although a few officers were ushering them back as another made a yellow-taped hodgepodge semicircle using the crest of police cruisers as posts.

The police were leading the old woman out in handcuffs, a precautionary measure for sure, until they figured out for themselves what had happened.

"This is perfect," Fyukis said. He could feel Fiel's violet eyes on him, and he turned to her. Such adoration in that gaze. He would never take advantage of such an innocent creature as she. "They're still up there."

"Yes." She said it like he'd only made a statement of fact. Fiel didn't understand, but beyond what she was missing, he understood something greater. The Bloom, taken by a normal human being, had a profound, yet contradictory, effect. It killed the person who ingested it, while infusing that person with a kind of unlife. The one called Gary had been fatally shot three times, and yet there he had been, walking and talking.

Mouthing off was more like it, though. He should have let Tim cut his head off. At the very least, cut out his tongue. He wondered if that would have had a negative effect on the Bloom in his body. And the Living Water, why hadn't that worked? It should have taken the Bloom out of him, but it had simply remained in the box.

The Living Water was the most direct method Brother had for interacting with the Adjacent. It could heal wounds or kill. It could show them messages in its depths—it should have done *something*. But it had been useless.

That meant something, although what Fyukis had no idea just yet. He would consult the Testimony before long. He was exhausted but had a great deal of work to do before allowing himself rest.

If everything went as he planned, though, very shortly he might never have need of sleep again.

"We need to get to the medical examiner's office. Call the others. My cell phone is broken."

"They will be looking for you."

"I know. That's why we will hit them sooner rather than later, capture them, and figure out how to retrieve the Bloom from them. The Testimony will hold the answer."

"But you said the container had only held four pills. What about the fifth?"

"Brother will find a way. He has only given success. The failures have been ours."

Chapter 19

Saturday

"We need to talk about it," Gary said.

"Not right now, okay?" Jim said.

"It's not like we're going anywhere."

"And we won't if you don't help get us out of here."

Jim imagined his calf and foot were cramping. That wasn't possible, but the idea gave him comfort. It was a reminder of something that happened to him on occasion when he was alive. The last few hours had given him time to contemplate.

It had been difficult at first with police officers and detectives stepping around and over him. He kept wanting to move, expecting his body to twitch or to blink and it kept not happening. It was disturbing how well he was capable of playing dead.

The easy answer for why he was in the situation was Gary. But that was just an easy answer. Not the right one. Gary hadn't forced his way into Jim's car, and he hadn't forced him to drive to Dr. K's laboratory. Sure, Gary had forced him to take that stupid pill, but under the circumstances, knowing what it did, Gary was reasonably trying to save some semblance of his life.

But dammit, they'd missed him. And so far as Jim could tell, his only injury in those crucial few moments had been a stubbed toe. As much as it burned him to know how the situation had actually turned out, he knew it wasn't fair to blame Gary for making him take that pill. Besides, he had so much more to blame Gary for.

And it wasn't just about going to the lab. Gary had gotten him into trouble many times over the years. From luring him into the gym locker room to smoke weed, to stealing snacks from the corner liquor store when they didn't have cash and getting caught, and just about every situation he could think of, Gary had been a huge negative influence.

Sure, Gary had never forced him to do anything. Jim had always had the right to say no, and occasionally he had. But because of the insecurity he had grown up with, Jim, most times, didn't know how to refuse his friend. He had never been trained to stand up for himself, had never been forced to fight his own battles. Jim had had two bullies throughout his school career, and both times Gary had put a stop to them.

When they were in second grade, a much larger boy had been picking on him for weeks. Jim knew it was only a matter of time before it turned into a full-blown pummeling, and one afternoon on his walk home from school, Tory Green had finally caught up to him.

Tory looked like he was perhaps on his third go-round in second grade, as he was almost a full head taller than Jim. It began with a few playful slaps—playful for Tory, at least—before he smashed Jim's nose with a meaty fist.

The boy hadn't said anything to Jim up until this point, leaving him to assume he was going to be beaten to death without a word being said to him.

Jim had blanked out, but came to from repeated kicks to his ribs. Then the blows had stopped.

"What do you want, homo?"

Jim had just assumed the boy had been talking to him and opened his mouth to answer. Nothing but a dry croak came out, which almost sounded like a question itself. Then came a thick whipping sound through the air, like a big branch, and a crunch.

Tory Green howled in agony until two more swings silenced him. When Jim dared to open his eyes and look at what had happened, he saw a skinny boy, not much bigger than him, holding a branch as thick as one of his thighs, standing a few feet away from Tory.

That had been how he and Gary had met.

From then until he'd wound up where ever this place was had been a long, crazy trip with Gary, and Jim felt ready to get off.

"I can't do this anymore," Jim said.

"What, you stuck? It can't be rigor mortis—that would've passed hours ago."

"No. With you. I can't do this with you anymore."

"What the hell does that mean?"

"It's not you. Literally, it's me. I have allowed myself to get in these situations. It's got to stop. I have to get off."

"You said 'get off.'"

Jim sighed heavily.

"Gary, I can't be friends with you anymore."

"Is this about Mel? Look, I'm telling you the truth. I—"

"No, it isn't about Mel. It's all of it. Can't imagine what my life would be like, where I'd be, if you hadn't dominated so much of it."

"Tory Green would probably still be beating the shit out of you."

"Or maybe I would have grown a pair and stood up to him."

"Eh."

Jim wanted to scream and batter his way out of his body bag. Just like everything in his life that he had allowed to restrain and crush him, this bag was a physical metaphor of how he had lived his life.

He vowed right now that that would happen no more.

"Hold on a second. Be quiet." Jim screamed one last time. "Somebody's coming!" That got Gary to be quiet. A moment later, he heard footsteps, clear and hard, with just a small amount of grit between shoe and floor. If he'd had a heartbeat, it would have been racing right now.

They were locked in here, and despite his best efforts, there was no way to escape. If this was one of those Adjacent people, then it was over.

The footsteps came nearer and stopped. There was a beep then a click and then a gentle, whooshing as a door opened and the room pressurized. Jim wanted to scream again, for it to finally be over with as he tried fishing a finger into the body bag's zipper to open it from the inside.

He felt the person approach, a woman by the sweet smell of perfume cutting through the foul-tinted air. He went limp, eyes open. Jim didn't want to see the end coming, but he couldn't stand the thought of not seeing it.

A beautiful, olive-skinned woman with her hair pulled back, wearing a pair of black, wire-rim glasses, stared at him after unzipping his bag. He had never seen her before, but she looked familiar somehow.

"Jim?"

He blinked reflexively, and her face relaxed. She stepped back as he sat up, watching him as he swung his legs out and hopped onto the floor. Jim's body felt heavy and light at the same time, like an hourglass that had just been turned over. In the back of his mind, he knew that was the dead blood inside his body turned into sludge slowly settling to his feet.

"You know me?"

"My father sent me."

"Your father?"

"Yeah." She looked annoyed. And not at all surprised to be talking to two corpses. "Dr. Knochenmus is my father."

Something inside a body bag on the other side of the room began tossing around violently. Gary. A moment later she had unzipped him too.

"Dr. K is alive?" Gary said.

Chapter 20

"Do you want to call him?" Tim asked.

"It's *your* trunk," Ed said.

The two big men stood behind the car, staring at the spot in the trunk where a dead body was supposed to have been.

Chapter 21

Dr. Knochenmus's daughter said, "Not exactly. He had a contingency plan for this. My mother called."

The dark-haired woman was holding a bag filled with Jim's belongings. He took it from her and tore it open. These were his clothes, but not the ones he'd been wearing. Gary's cell phone clattered to the floor, and Jim picked it up. It was the same model as his, and he reflexively swiped the screen and saw an icon stating he'd had several missed calls from Mel.

"Wuzzit?" he said, not understanding what he was seeing. He unlocked the phone with his own password and saw this actually was his phone. He'd seen earlier that Gary had the same model, but assumed it was coincidence.

"Gary, why do you have my phone?"

"Uh, it's not what it looks like?"

Dr. K's daughter had another bag, and he tore that open, rooting through the contents until he came to the other cell. Jim unlocked it and saw all the same apps he knew he had. He went to his call log and saw multiple calls made to Mel. But when he opened the details on one of the calls, Jim saw it was the wrong number.

He'd never actually called her at all.

Jim looked at the other cell phone, his real cell phone. He checked the call log and saw there were twelve voice-mail messages. All this time he'd been worrying that something had happened to her. That—*dammit*—she had been cheating on him.

"Gary, you son of a bitch."

"Okay, now I know it probably looks bad. But before I say anything, can you tell me exactly what it is you just found out?"

"You had my cell phone this whole time!"

"Yes?"

"And you let me think—God only knows all the things I was thinking. How could you?"

"Um, should I give you a minute?" Dr. K's daughter asked. "I'm only mounting this rescue effort at the risk of my career and possible freedom."

"If you don't mind," Gary said from the top shelf.

"No. It's fine. Let's get him out, and then we can both be out of your hair," Jim said.

They helped Gary down, and Jim saw he was naked, which made him realize he was naked. In front of a woman.

"So are those your underwear or mine?" Gary pointed, and Jim looked down to see his erect penis and the remnants of a pair of boxers hanging off it.

"I have other clothes for you," the woman said as Jim hurriedly covered himself with the scraps of clothes that had been cut off his body not long before.

"It's fine. I'm fine." Jim could feel Gary's eyes on him and refused to look back.

"I'm Kenya, by the way." She took a step closer to Jim. "Amazing."

He could deal with compliments. He'd even tolerated being called handsome a time or two, but the word "amazing" made his empty cheeks want to flush with some of that blood that was in his feet.

"Can we get out of here? I mean, can we just walk out?" Jim asked.

Kenya handed them both jackets. Jim slid his on and zipped it up before taking the baseball cap she was holding.

"There's some information you need. Plus, I'd like to get you past security without someone thinking I snuck two guys in here."

"Anything freaky like that ever happen in here?" Gary asked.

She looked at him like he'd spoken in another language.

"Take these IDs, and once we're in the atrium, you can take them off and go about your business." Kenya handed them badges on lanyards for two people who looked nothing like them. Jim made a face before putting it on. "Don't worry, we'll be walking too fast for anyone to get a good look. They'll suspect you're legit. Are you both . . . able to walk?"

"We can walk fine," Jim said.

"We can do a lot of things fine. Half of us are pretty damn good at it," Gary said.

She ignored him again and turned to Jim. "I have to ask—what symptoms have you experienced since you took those pills?"

Jim wasn't sure how much he should say.

"You mean other than being a cold slab of meat?" Gary said.

"I mean cognitive function. Behavioral changes. Anything like that?"

Gary paused and scratched his head. "No."

"It's not just your bodies that are dying. Your minds are too. Synaptic function is decreasing. You may become confused, disoriented. You may . . . crave certain things."

"Like what?" they both asked.

"Nonconventional foods. And, um . . . living flesh."

"No," Jim said horrified. "Nothing like that."

"Just garbage." Gary smiled sheepishly. "I believe in full disclosure when I'm courting a woman." Jim didn't confess that he'd almost eaten out of his trash at home. "Jim bit a guy."

"I did, but I was only defending myself. The guy was trying to fight me."

Kenya nodded and made a face like she was making some scientific calculation. He did notice that she took a small step away from both of them.

"I've read over all his research. Studied some of the lab mice."

"Does the effect of these pills wear off?" Jim asked.

"Yes. After approximately forty-eight hours."

"So, not the amount of time it took Jesus to rise from the dead?" Gary asked.

"What? No, forty-eight hours from when you ingested the pill. So if it was yesterday evening, it'll wear off Sunday evening."

Jim saw Gary's wheels turning, trying to make an argument for how that was three days.

"So after that, everything goes back to normal, right?" Gary asked. "Heart starts beating again, and all the effects of this pill reverse."

"Um, yes."

Jim noticed the uncertainty of her voice, and so did Gary.

"Doc, that doesn't sound like a rousing endorsement. Can we drop the other shoe already?" Gary asked.

"Well, you have three gunshot wounds, one of which at least would have been fatal. If you'd been shot in the foot or maybe the arm, so long as an artery hadn't been severed, it would be treatable."

"So I got shot in the chest? People survive gunshots all the time to the chest. 50 Cent was shot like eight times. I'm like 19 Cent if you're rounding."

"I'm sorry to say, but 50 Cent wasn't shot directly in the heart. When that pill wears off, it will be the same for you as anyone else who's been shot in the heart. You'll die again, but for good."

"Damn, I gotta say your bedside manner is terrible."

"I'm sorry. There's nothing we can really do for you. Before my father—*Dr. Knochenmus*—made those pills, he experimented extensively on lab mice, subjecting them to just about every possible situation. In every case when they were inflicted with a nonbrain fatal wound, they carried on with physiomental function until the effects wore off. Then they expired."

"Nonbrain?" Jim asked. "So what happens if someone smashes my head open with a tire iron?"

"You will die right then. There's nothing to continue brain function if there's no brain."

"What's the point of this fucking pill?" Gary asked. "I thought it was supposed to have some cool military application, but this shit sucks."

"The formula was supplied to him by people who wanted it for another purpose."

"Yeah, we know all about them. They think the pill will help them commit suicide."

"I don't know about that application." She made a face.

"Speaking of which . . ." Gary began pawing through the shelves of corpses. He stood on a shelf and peeked in a few bags.

"What are you doing?" Kenya asked.

"I'm looking for a guy. About six feet tall, well groomed, flat as a pancake. You seen him? He should've come in right behind us."

She shook her head. "Nobody like that came in last night. Why?"

Gary grimaced. "I was afraid of that. I think . . . I think those guys might have been the real deal, Jim."

"Don't talk to me. I'm pissed at you. We're not friends."

"Jim, we don't have time for this. Those guys aren't going to stop until they get what's inside us."

"And all I have to do is hole up somewhere they can't find me until this shit passes out of my system. Then I could mail it across country and tell them to go fetch."

"But I can't run. Jim, I'm gonna die."

"That's not my fault." Jim felt like a shit as the words came out of his mouth, but he dug his heels in. This really was a problem of Gary's own creation. Jim couldn't help what he'd already done to himself.

Except that had never been his best friend's attitude toward him. No matter what the problem was or whose fault it was, Gary had always jumped in on Jim's side with both feet. It didn't just feel like he was bailing on Gary; he really was.

"I don't . . . I can't help that."

"I see." Gary sounded far off and robotic. "Well, we need to get back to Dr. K's apartment. Karen needs her car back."

Jim had completely forgotten about that. And his promise to his mother. He had a fiancée too, whom he needed to call, by the way.

"Can we go now?" he asked, putting his cell phone to his ear as he called Mel's number.

Chapter 22

The Adjacent were were all present. Fyukis wanted no chances taken. They advanced on the Oakland County Medical Examiner's building fully armed. Those two held the key to the Bloom, what little they had of it, and if the Adjacent were all going to ascend, Fyukis had to have what was inside them.

The problem was even if they could get the Bloom from these two, that left only a total of three pills. Obviously Dr. K wasn't as dead as they had thought, which meant he had a part of it too. If they could get that back, that left a total of four parts. Still short by one. But if they could get the pill Dr. K had taken back, that meant they would have Dr. K. Either he had hidden it, or they would have to make him make another.

Again he pondered the possibility of making it work with only four. He had been combing through the Testimony since yesterday, exploring whether or not that was something that could have been done. Whereas his original thought had been no, everything he was reading was telling him definitely no. There had to be five. And all would go, or none would go.

They spread out just before the entrance doors, Tim and Fiel circling around to the rear of the building to cover any emergency exits, and he and Ed would go through the front door. Mary hung back, pretending to smoke a cigarette. There was something about that woman that made her hard to notice. No doubt Gary and Jim had seen her, but he doubted they would recognize her. On two separate occasions, Fyukis had had to take a moment to realize at whom he was looking when by coincidence he'd run into her at a grocery store and the mall.

The office opened at 8:00 a.m. It was now 7:50. He intended to get through these doors and into that autopsy room. He had no desire to kill, but recognized it as an extreme possibility. They could let nothing stand in the way of their ascension. It was their destiny to be with Brother.

"Follow my lead," he said. "If you can."

Fyukis began furiously banging on the glass. It might have been easier to break in the building two hours ago when no one was here, but it turned out that Mary knew the building had security twenty-four hours a day, seven days a week. He kept banging at the glass for a minute straight until he saw a figure from inside begin to approach.

Fyukis didn't know if he had roused this man from sleep, but his droopy, red-rimmed eyes were a clue.

"We don't open 'til eight," the man said without opening the door. "You gotta wait outside."

"Thank you. Thank you," Fyukis mouthed and put his hand on the door handle.

"No—no. I said you have to wait *outside* until eight. I can't let you in until the doctors are here."

Fyukis had no doubt the doctors were already here and that this man would stand on ceremony until the official opening time.

Fyukis gave the door a tug, and when it didn't open, he looked up at the security guard, affixing a hangdog expression on his face.

"Sir, stop pulling on my door. We're not open yet."

"Yes—yes, open. I would like to come in." He smiled again, a little less forcefully, giving the guard the impression he was sad, but still hopeful. Fyukis wasn't sure what the accent was he was doing, but he could see he was having the desired effect. The guard looked frustrated and annoyed, and the way Fyukis had beat on the door to get him to come out to begin with had to have told him they weren't just going to go away.

The security guard's eyes traveled over him and then Ed. He pursed his lips, and Fyukis could see his wheels turning. He sighed.

"Sorry. I can't let you in."

The glass door exploded, and the security guard was yanked off his feet and outside. The man was bloody and not just from sharp edges of glass. There was a hole in his significant gut that began spouting blood like a water fountain. For a few seconds, at least.

"Your lead was a dead-end," Ed said, taking a moment to wipe his bloody fist on the dying man's shirt. He rose as the guard clutched at his robes, grip already weakening.

Ed cut an imposing figure in his robes. Fyukis almost wished he had worn his. Even though he hadn't figured out every piece of this puzzle, he could sense the end of this long journey coming. Brother would make a way where they saw none. He had seen it too many times before, particularly last night, to doubt it.

They stepped through the door after Ed cleared the shards of glass. Fyukis didn't particularly care for killing. Too often that involved physical contact, but he found he didn't really mind that the security guard was dead.

Now they would have to move quickly, and he texted the others to get in the building by any means possible. Tim had acquired a layout of the building they had committed to memory, and Fyukis and Ed advanced toward the autopsy room. Either the doctors and other staff had not heard the commotion at the door, or they really weren't here.

When a bespectacled young woman in a lab coat stepped into the hall they were in, Starbucks in hand, Ed shot her in the head. He had affixed a suppression device to the end of his gun, and it had made a noise like someone taking a loud spit. She fell to the floor, the cup splashing open, and the coffee mixed with the spreading pool of blood. Fyukis had flinched, not knowing the shot was coming. He wouldn't be able to drink a cup of decaf until he'd gotten that image out of his head.

Ed stepped in front of him and put a hand to Fyukis's chest. This sort of thing was definitely not his expertise, and he allowed the much bigger man to step to the fore to handle the situation. He peeked into the room ahead of them. Fyukis guessed it was the break room from the sliver he could see of it. Ed stepped in front of the threshold, two guns in hand, and began shooting.

It was over in seconds, but the loud eruption of the other gun firing made Fyukis flinch again. Ed about-faced, locked eyes with him, turned back, and aimed again.

"No!" Fyukis said, ducking and raising his arms. Ed fired again, and someone grunted. Fyukis turned to see a heavyset man hit the floor. They both turned at the sound of several more gunshots from the other end of the hall. A young, skinny man with a cloud of brown hair came around the corner, running straight at them. He didn't seem to have seen them, half looking behind him. Fyukis hadn't seen Ed put his guns away, and the big man caught the other man in a one-armed hug. The man's eyes went big, the cloud of hair settling over half of his face. Ed spun away from him a large, bloody knife in hand, and blood exploded out of the man, spraying the lower half of Fyukis's cream suit.

A moment later Tim and Fiel joined them. The two large men nodded at one another.

"The autopsy room is this way," Tim said.

Fiel's eyes were as wide as Fyukis guessed his were.

"So much death," she said and took a deep breath. The two big men proceeded down the hall, and she followed them. Fyukis shuffled after, feeling like a little boy following an older sibling.

They entered the autopsy room. It had a half dozen tables, all empty, and looked a lot cleaner than he expected. He was expecting something a lot grizzlier—skin hung over a clothesline, limbs strewn about the room. Aside from the antiseptic smell, the tables with the drains on one end, and a few big motorized saws, there wasn't anything to indicate what this room was used for.

They didn't even have those . . . morgue drawer things like in the movies. Fyukis supposed the big metal door at the back of the room must've been some sort of walk-in cooler where they stored their dead. He mentally crossed his fingers that that door didn't have a means of being opened from the inside.

Ed stood back from the door about five feet while Tim approached the handle. Fyukis was amazed how the two men tended to communicate without words.

Tim opened the door, and Ed swept left and right. They went inside, each taking a side. Fiel watched, and Fyukis noted the keen note of excitement on her face. They'd both just been witness to mass murder, but she looked like she was waiting in line for a new ride at Cedar Point. In the brief time she had been with the Adjacent, he had tried to get to know her and every time had come away feeling like she was still a stranger.

She turned her wide blue eyes on him, and for a moment Fyukis felt like he was being drawn in. Like he was about to be devoured. The cooler was deep enough that he lost sight of the two men for a moment before they came back out, dragging two bodies apiece with them.

"Not sure if they're in there," Tim said.

"Brought these. Thought they looked close." Ed's eyes were locked on Fyukis's, searching for approval.

Fyukis felt obligated to check even though he doubted any of these were the two they were looking for. They ruled out the first corpse, which was heavily inked, including what looked like a dragon on its cheek. The next one was bald. The third he actually had to remove the plastic covering to examine. It only had two bullet holes in its chest, but that didn't mean it couldn't have been the other one. Jim, his name had been.

But the problem with all these was that they were really dead. Those two hadn't been; they'd only pretended in an attempt to get him arrested. Fyukis kicked the corpse and then stepped on its chest.

It let out a moan, and he leapt back.

"Is it . . . alive?" His voice had more quaver than he would've liked.

Tim stepped forward and shot it once in the forehead. "Probably not."

Fiel removed the plastic shrouding the last one. She sat with it and cradled it as gently as a mother with her child. She stroked the face, looking it over as if she had known the person in life.

"Well?" Fyukis said. "Is it him?"

"No," she said without looking at him. "They are not here." She opened one of its half-lidded eyes fully and gazed into it. Fyukis thought he was going to be sick. "I feel them. Or rather, I feel their absence. I know where they are because I feel the hole where they should be."

"What are you saying?"

"They are with Mary. They have her now."

"No!" he shouted. "We have to stop them. Everything's going wrong!"

"Wait," Tim said. "It's the Testimony. It's speaking through her."

"What are you talking about, you idiot? They're getting away!"

"And she sees where they are going. Brother is strong within her."

This was the most verbose Tim had ever been. Fyukis felt his words burn. That couldn't have been true. For decades he'd listened and rarely had heard a peep from Brother. The Ancient had taught him well, fine-tuned him to listen through pondering and studying the Testimony. He realized he was jealous that Fiel was hearing Brother when she had been within the Adjacent for such a short time, whereas he'd been within since before her mother had been born. He was in the knowledge more than any of them.

Chapter 23

It had been Gary's idea to hang back and wait for them to come. They saw the four of them exit the Chrysler Town and Country, leaving the last person behind. Fyukis was with one of the big ones, heading for the front door, while the other big one and the creepy-eyed woman walked around to the back of the building. After a little bit of convincing, Kenya had agreed to play decoy, approaching the vehicle to ask for directions. Gary had finally gotten to use his little card thing, jimmying open the passenger door while the woman inside was distracted.

By the time she realized what was happening, it was too late, but that didn't stop her from putting up a hell of a good fight. She pepper-sprayed Gary, which would have been a good move if it weren't for the fact he had no active pain receptors. He cringed on instinct, hesitating long enough for her to begin batting his head with a seven-inch metal rod on the end of her key chain.

Gary got his hands up, and immediately there was a crunch as she smashed one of his fingers. He seized her by the jacket and yanked. He managed to pull her across the passenger seat and onto the ground, and she kicked him in the solar plexus. Again, it was a good move and would have had the desired, paralyzing effect if it had actually hurt and he needed to breathe. Jim assisted by trying to grab her legs, and she twisted her body while Gary still held the jacket, a foot landing squarely in Jim's crotch. Jim seized her by the ankle and pulled, stretching her leg so she wasn't able to kick him again.

"What the hell do we do?" Jim asked.

"I don't know. I've never actually kidnapped anyone before." Jim could see her slipping an arm out of her jacket, and Gary wrapped the whole thing over her head. "Do you have any chloroform?"

Kenya was nearby, a concerned look on her face. No doubt she was thinking this looked exactly like what it was—two men attempting to force a woman into a situation she wanted no part of. She pulled something out of her purse, and a second later Jim felt her go stiff, then limp.

Kenya put the Taser back and bent neatly to check the woman's pulse. Jim realized then that the woman hadn't made a sound.

"Let's get her inside," Gary said.

"We're taking their car?" Jim said.

"Yeah." Gary smiled. "That way they don't have a ride to chase us."

"I could take my car," Kenya said.

"And I could ride with her," Jim said.

"And who's going to keep the Tasmanian devil tame when she wakes up on I-94?"

Jim found that thinking hard to argue with. He helped Gary load her in and got in behind her.

"Hey, baby," Gary said to Kenya. "I appreciate you helping us out and all." He had produced a toothpick from somewhere and was now rolling it around in his mouth as he spoke. "I understand if you're a little too scared to join up. You can meet me at my place sometime tonight. I could fill you in—"

"Save your breath," Kenya said. "You smell like a corpse anyway."

Gary made a show of sniffing his armpits. He made a face.

"Me and Jim just took a shower not more than a few hours ago."

"Uh, not . . . together," Jim said.

"Please don't misunderstand," Kenya said. "I'm coming with you. I'm just taking my own car. You're a valuable scientific interest, and I mean to dog you, collecting every piece of data as I see fit, until you have expressed those pills."

"You can collect my data anytime."

"I'm not interested in sleeping with you."

"You'd deny a dying man his last request?"

"There's no valuable scientific data in *that*. On second thought, though, I will ride with you." She climbed into the passenger side, and Gary got behind the wheel.

As they were pulling out of the lot, Gary said, "Did you hear something? It sounded like popping."

Jim and Kenya both said no, and they kept on their way.

Chapter 24

"Guys, before we go another mile, I need a coffee and a bagel, or I'm liable to kill someone," Kenya said.

"Come to think of it, I'm kind of hungry too. What about you, Jim?"

"Still not speaking to you, but yes, I'm hungry."

"Interesting," the doctor said. "Are you craving anything in particular?"

"I don't think so," Jim said. He felt his stomach grumble. Then an intense squeeze of pain. It didn't feel like any hunger he'd ever had before. They hadn't eaten anything since the sliders at Granny's. Jim looked at the unconscious woman lying on the floor of the minivan. Would he try to eat her? Would that be a bad thing? Would he know it was a bad thing if he were about to take a bite of her?

To get his mind off eating, he took out his cell phone and called Mel. She picked up on the fourth ring. That was odd; she was normally no more than a three-ring person.

"Hullo?" a male voice said. He sounded sleepy or high, and there was a weird yet familiar noise in the background.

"I'm sorry, I must have the wrong number."

"Naw, man. You tryin' to call Mel?"

"Yes . . ." Jim said hesitantly.

"She's here, man . . . somewhere." There was noise on the line, and the man grunted. "Hold on, I think she's in the shower. Lemme check."

Let me check? What the fuck?

He listened as the man moved around. Eventually came the sound of running water.

"Hey, there's a guy on the phone."

"Who is it?" Jim heard his fiancée say.

"I don't know. Who dis?" he asked Jim.

"I'm her fiancé," Jim said.

"Jim? Aw, man, pleasure speaking to you. This is—"

Jim ended the call.

"We have to go to my apartment. Right now."

Chapter 25

Jim had given the briefest of explanations of what had transpired during his conversation with the "other man," as he'd been mechanically referring to him. Jim wasn't really talking to Gary or even Kenya; rather, he was recounting pieces of the conversation, giving the other man a nasally, whiny voice and responding with statements he'd never actually said. Like threatening to tear out his throat and eat it in front of him, or to boil his balls in a fine stew, or to roast his eyeballs in his skull, or to skin him a piece at a time and consume his crisped flesh like potato chips.

"Man, all that sounds delicious," Gary said.

Kenya looked between them, her eyes wide.

"Sorry," Jim said. "I don't know what I'm saying. I'm just so . . . angry."

"I'm sorry," Gary said. There wasn't a hint of sarcasm or some sort of biting statement immediately after. This was one of those rare moments, like Halley's Comet, when Gary was absolutely serious and without ulterior motive. As angry as he was with his former best friend, Jim appreciated it.

They pulled into the apartment complex, the woman still asleep thanks to several more jolts from Kenya's Taser. Jim was out of the minivan before Gary had come to a complete stop.

He ran up the stairs to his apartment door, fumbling for his keys. His cell had rung several times on the drive here, but he had refused to answer it. He wanted to see what was happening with his own eyes.

Jim couldn't believe it. Gary had been right about Mel. What excuse could she give him about some man walking in on her in the shower? He was still sorting through his keys when the door was flung inward and Mel snatched him into a bear hug.

"Oh my God, I was so worried!" she said into his ear. "Where were you?"

"I should ask you the same thing," he said, his tone a lot cooler than he expected. "I had to run an errand with Gary. But after, I came home and you were gone."

"I know. And I'm sorry about that." She pulled back and fixed her eyes on him. "Why didn't you call me, though? I tried to call you, but you never picked up your phone."

Jim felt he had to defend Gary a little bit here, all things considered. "Service. I called you several times and couldn't get through. I stopped by later, and you weren't here. Where were you?"

Her eyes dropped, and she half smiled. It was a look that said she wasn't happy about what she was about to say, which meant he wasn't happy about what she was about to say.

Jim looked at her for the first time since coming in. Damn, Mel looked good. Smelled really good too. Like flowers. No matter what else was going on, that was true. Even now. For a moment he almost wanted to drop the whole thing. She was more beautiful than any woman he deserved. She was almost as tall as him, thin but curvy, and her long black hair hung in thick wet curls around her face.

She found his hand. "Your hand is cold! Are you okay?"

"I'm fine." He felt his body steeling, as if preparing for a blow.

"I need to talk to you. There's something you should know before we go any further." It sounded like the preamble to a breakup, and it was all he could do not to pull his hand away. Jim let her lead him into the apartment, toward their bedroom. Either that other guy was still here and she was looking to do something freaky, which he definitely was not down with, or he was gone and she was going to pretend like he'd never been there at all.

"Chad? Are you dressed?" Mel asked.

Jim tensed. That answered that question. Only thing left to do now was to see how far this thing went. He didn't want to; Jim would have preferred to turn around and run right out. But he had gone through too much over the last twelve hours, things that had actually been dangerous. His heart being ripped out of his body now was just a formality.

They stepped into the bedroom, and Jim saw a long, athletically built man with hair really long and curly like Mel's. She definitely didn't have a type if she was into this guy. Jim looked absolutely nothing like him.

If anything, he looked like her.

Chad was stripped down to a pair of boxers and had a soft cast on his lower leg, with his toes peeking out.

"Jim, this is my brother."

Jim was ready to call BS on whatever she said, and this caught him totally by surprise. What came out of his mouth was a car crash of syllables that sounded like, "Boowhargh?"

"Hey, bro." Chad smiled broadly and gave him a lazy salute, with wiggly fingers on the end. Jim did a double take between the siblings, finally settling on her.

"Are you two—"

"Twins? Yes." Mel nodded furiously, her smile turning nervous. "Excuse us, C."

"Doddle-la," it sounded like he said.

She almost dragged Jim into the living room and hugged him tight.

"I'm sorry," she said. He knew why she was apologizing. Mel had told him she was an only child and that her parents had died in a car crash in Oregon. She held both his hands tightly in hers, and for the first time since Jim had known her, she looked worried.

"Mel, I don't care that you have a brother. I mean, it's great you do, but you didn't have to lie to me about it."

"I know, I know. It's stupid. I just thought I needed a fresh start. That's why I came to Michigan; I needed someplace nobody knew me. Please don't be mad."

He stroked her face and saw how pale his hand was. Jim quickly buried it in her hair.

"I'm not mad; I'm relieved." Jim felt the tension flood out of him, his shoulders unhitching. "Gary's been going on and on about how you're cheating, and then he went really over the top and said he saw you shoot somebody—"

"When was this?" she asked a little too quickly. Something in her tone set off alarms in the back of Jim's mind.

"What does it matter? It's not true. You're not cheating on me, and you're not a killer, right?"

"Right." Again, right answer all wrong. He could see she was tense, and he leaned in for a hug. He kissed her neck, and she went pliant in his arms. Not responsive; more like clay that had gone from cold to warmish.

"Mel, what's wrong?" He leaned back and looked at her. For just a moment, but long enough, he saw. Mel was gone. And then she was back.

She smiled, and it was as normal a smile as he'd ever seen from her. To quote the old clichéd expression, she wouldn't have said shit if she'd had a mouthful of it.

Jim leaned close again. He hugged her once more, rubbing his body into hers. Mel hated being dirty and despised getting anything on her, especially right after a shower. She'd trained her body so that she used the toilet before a shower every morning. Like clockwork. Jim knew he smelled, but when he pulled back and looked at her again, she still had the relaxed, easygoing smile that was typical of her.

This was very wrong.

"What is going on, Mel?"

"What do you mean?"

Jim narrowed his eyes. "You. You're acting so normal."

"Why wouldn't I be normal? Is there something wrong with that?" She laughed nervously.

"Yeah. I stink. I smell like a wet dumpster, and you don't seem to mind."

"Jim, I'm just happy to see you're home."

"No. It's something else. That guy in there—is he really your brother?"

She nodded.

He quickly went over their conversation in his head. Chad was her brother. That felt true, although their brother/sister bond seemed a little weird. He smelled, but she was ignoring that to make peace.

Jim locked eyes with her. They watched each other for several seconds.

"Mel, it's not true, is it?"

Her face worked. "Can we . . . can we not do this right now?"

He stepped back. "Mel. No." Jim felt like he was looking at a stranger.

"Jim, wait. I can explain."

"I don't know if I want to hear it. Will I be implicated after the fact? Called to testify?"

"No. Nothing like that. It's not like that."

"What do you mean, it's not like that? My best friend had been terrified to tell me what he saw you do. He hid my cell phone from me so I couldn't talk to you. He tried to make me believe you were cheating because he thought it would be easier for me to believe. And you know what? He's right! I still can't believe it. I ended a twenty-plus-year relationship for you. I gave up *weed* for you."

Mel had been reeling the entire time he'd been speaking, but Jim registered it when she'd gotten her mental footing again. He'd been pacing back and forth as he'd been speaking.

"Jim, stop talking."

He shut up. Mel used the same tone she'd always put on when she was about to get her way. It was the kind of voice that was not subject to debate or negotiation; only absolute obedience was acceptable.

"You could be in danger." She was whispering for some reason. Mel swarmed closer, planting her hand on the wall behind him and blocking him with her body. Jim had no choice but to meet her eyes. "I need you to tell me when this was, where this was, and why he was there."

Jim managed a half smile and a cough of a laugh. "I could be in danger? That's a laugh."

He shoved her hand away, probably a little rougher than he intended, but so be it. This was over; there was no way he could be with a murderer. Jim stalked toward the door.

"Everything cool out here, M?" He turned back and saw Chad, bad leg half lifted off the floor, holding onto the wall for support. Jim noticed one hand conspicuously out of sight behind his back.

"Him too?" Jim said, circling back toward the kitchen. Mel followed him, talking in that serious monotone, but he was too upset to hear a word. She tried to put her hands on him, and he managed to shrug her off without actually touching her back. He stood in front of the sink, stooped, and opened the cabinet doors. There was the small garbage can, and he dug in with two hands, fishing out something that squished like cookie dough in one hand and a brick of dry Ramen noodles in the other.

Jim didn't even look as he began to eat. It was simultaneously tasteless and delicious as the sliders at Granny's, and he eyed Mel, who had reared back in disgust, mouth open as she watched him head to the door.

"Jim . . . *baby*." She didn't move, watching him as he fumbled with the doorknob with two greasy fingers. He dropped the mushy stuff on the floor and shrugged. It came out of the garbage; it wasn't like adding a few additional germs was going to hurt him. He picked up as much as could with one scoop and tore off a mouth-stuffing piece.

"Gabai, Mao," he said and was out the door.

Chapter 26

Jim thought he could feel her eyes on him from the window, but he didn't dare turn around. Let it burn her as much as it burned him. If there were a God, it would have been raining right now so he could pretend he did have tears and could cry. Jim swallowed what was in his mouth, stumbling back to the minivan. He didn't notice Kenya holding the Taser tightly in her hand or the way Gary completely avoided looking at him. Jim figured the best thing for him to do right now was to avoid the pain.

"So where to next, guys?" he asked and licked his fingers.

"Our silent friend woke up. Kenya and I tried to have a little conversation with her. She's a rock. Or a mute. Not sure, but she didn't tell us anything."

Jim looked down as they pulled out of the apartment complex. The woman had been hogtied with some twine and was lying on her side. Her face was a sweaty mess, her neat black hair plastered to her head.

"I went a little extracurricular on her," Kenya said. "We were listening to WJR, and there's a story about a shooting at the ME's office. Apparently we left just in time to miss it."

"Anybody hurt?" Jim knew it was a stupid question as soon as it left his mouth.

"There. Was. A. Shooting." Kenya stared at Jim.

"Three confirmed dead. Not sure how many injured," Gary said.

"So do we turn her over to the police?"

Gary sighed. "I'd say we leave that up to Dr. Knochenmus here." He glanced at Kenya. "What do you say? Do we turn her over when there may not be a link to the rest of the group so far as the police are concerned and subject ourselves to scrutiny when two-thirds of us don't have pulses?"

Kenya shook her head.

The woman at Jim's feet began to stir. Kenya reached back and shocked her with the Taser again. This time she did scream, although limply. Jim finally pushed Kenya's hand away.

"I think that might be good for now. We don't want to cause any permanent damages. At least for now."

"We need to know everything about them. No holding back. I don't care how bad we need to hurt her," said Gary.

"How would we manage that?" Jim asked.

"If I'm picking up on the good doctor's vibe, she's suggested we go chemical on her."

"Chemical. Yes, with the right cocktail we can get her to talk." Kenya said. "Any ideas?"

"What's in truth serum?" Gary asked.

"Sodium thiopental," Kenya said.

"I thought it was sodium pentothol."

"That's just a brand name. If we had hospital access, I could get some."

"What's in it?" Gary asked.

"It's a barbiturate, so it depresses the central nervous system. It makes the subject sleepy, feel less pain, less inhibition. The idea is to make you so calm you'll say anything top of mind. Do you know how to get some?"

"No, but I can get something like it."

They were stopped at a light, and Gary turned all the way around and smiled at Jim.

"No," Jim said, and Gary nodded. "*No*."

Chapter 27

Jim hadn't been here in years. He would have guessed the place had been busted and closed several times over by now, but here the house was, just where he'd left it last. He had been fifteen, looking to get high on something he had never tried before.

Elias, the little man who squatted in this house and was the proprietor of the illegal business within, had grown to be something akin to a friend. Other than occasional advice, nothing free ever passed between them. Elias had always been looking to make a sale, Jim had almost always been looking to score weed.

He didn't like needles, but on his last visit here, Jim had gotten a crash course on how to inject heroin. He had the tie off on his upper arm, making the squiggly vein in the bend of his arm pop out, and the needle poised in his hand like a reverse pencil as Elias coached him on exactly how to do it.

The older man could have just done it for Jim, but he took his own sort of pleasure from merely watching and giving pointers. It was a low point in Jim's life, and he had put it so far into the back of his mind that for long stretches of time, he could pretend he had only dreamed of nearly shooting up. If Gary had not been there, had he not shown up, Jim's life would have taken a whole different turn.

"All right," Gary said, parking at the curb across the street, "I'll go in first, smooth things over, then I'll bring a tarp or something so we can carry her inside." He turned to Jim and pointed at him. "Be ready to apologize, Jim. Elias is still upset with you."

"With me? But I didn't do anything. You punched him!"

"That's not quite true. I knocked out his front teeth. And I did that to protect you."

"From him!"

"These are very good points, Jim, but it doesn't change the fact—Elias is pissed with *you*."

Gary looked at Kenya. "You gonna be all right?"

She nodded, and Jim could tell from the expression on her face she was lying as best she could. She was a long-distance throw from all right, and he knew just how she felt.

"Be right back." Gary left the engine running, and Kenya reached for the ignition.

"Leave it running," Jim said. "We might need to get out of here in a hurry." He looked around nervously. Who and what was going on in that house wasn't the only thing to be worried about.

They watched Gary cross the street and skip up the stairs of the porch two at a time. He stood directly in front of the door of the screened-in porch. Gary knocked twice, paused, then knocked twice more. Then the door opened, and he disappeared inside.

"So," Jim began, looking down at the woman tied up on the floor, "you really gonna make us do this the hard way?"

She was breathing hard and sweating, causing Jim a minor amount of alarm. He finally decided she was hyperventilating by choice considering the hatred burning in her eyes. Even if that weren't the case, he wasn't about to untie her to find out.

"Help!" she screamed. Jim reeled back, putting his hands to his ears. Then he realized her shrill voice hadn't actually hurt at all. "Help!"

"You can do that all you want around here." He smiled at her. "It doesn't matter. This city has a police force of about six cops. By the time they got around to responding to the call someone *might* make, we would be long done with you."

She kept her hateful stare on him, but went silent.

Rather than have an eyeball match with her, Jim turned to Kenya. "So, what's your story?"

"I'm a doctor," she said after a long pause. "I work in the medical examiner's office. Worked. Work." She let her head drop and shook it as if not wanting to think about what had happened at the medical examiner's office. "My dad may be dead, but to me he's been gone for a long time."

"Why's that?"

Her eyes rolled up to him. "That's a little personal, wouldn't you say?"

"Yeah, but you want to study me."

She pursed her lips. "How are you feeling, by the way?"

"About the same. I ate garbage a little bit ago."

"Is that your first time craving anything out of the ordinary?"

"No. I almost ate garbage yesterday. Gary ate some too."

"Any other cravings or anything else out of the ordinary?"

He thought a moment. "Yeah. When I close my eyes, I get these weird visions. Well, one really. I see this large mass of rotting meat, all kinds of maggots coming out of it. Then I hear somebody eating."

"Eating the meat?"

"I don't know. I don't see anyone. Just hear them."

"So it's auditory too. Hmm."

"Does that mean anything?"

"I have no clue." Kenya opened her phone, opened an app he didn't recognize, and thumbed something in.

A moment later, Gary came trotting out, a smile on his face. Jim leaned over the driver's seat and pressed the button to roll down the window.

"Come on in." Gary hitched his head toward the house.

"What about our special friend?" Kenya asked.

"Bring her too. Nobody's looking." He made a show of looking up and down the street.

"All things considered, I think it would be a better idea if we weren't seen taking a hogtied woman into a house."

Gary shrugged. "Okay, so find something to cover her up."

"There isn't a garage or anything we could go in?" Kenya asked.

"No. Nobody uses the garage."

"We can't drive through the alley and go in through the back?" she asked.

Gary shook his head.

"It's either the front door or no door."

"All right, let's look around here and see if we have something." Jim climbed over the second row seat and peered into the hatch. He dug around until he found a ratty old blanket half covering some road flares.

"Got something." They spent the next few minutes wrapping the woman up, and she was no help throughout the entire process. Finally they had what appeared to be a body wrapped in a blanket or a giant, wriggling worm.

"Let's make this fast," Jim said. Everyone nodded, and Gary threw open the big rear passenger door. Jim got out, and together they carried the woman across the street and up the stairs. The woman was small, yet strong, kicking against them the entire way. Her screams were muffled, and Gary made a habit of tapping the bulge where her head was every few steps until she quieted down.

An old woman, standing on the sidewalk in front of the house next door, stared at them with filmy eyes that looked like the brown was leaking out of her irises. She wasn't dressed for the chill air and was wasted-away skinny.

"Hey, Miss Carter," Gary said as they went up the stairs; Jim would have sworn she hadn't been there a moment ago. Come to think of it, wasn't Mrs. Carter dead? He thought he'd heard that ten years ago. He'd have to ask Gary later. Kenya followed closely behind, averting her face away from the old woman. The porch door was open, and the smell of no fewer than six drugs Jim could identify hit him. Yet again he was amazed how this place operated essentially out in the open, with apparently no scrutiny at all.

Gary stopped and turned to Kenya. "I understand if you feel like you need to wait in the car," he said. "I mean, technically what we're doing is illegal, and inside there is highly illegal."

Kenya straightened and looked right at him. "No. I'm documenting all this for scientific purposes. My coworkers were killed for a reason, and I want to make that reason as important as possible."

He nodded and led them inside.

There was a low, constant, bassy thump of music that he recognized as the bass line for the song "White Horse." The living room had six people in it in various stages of intoxication. Five men and one woman who could've all been anywhere in age from thirteen to fifty by their wide, baggy eyes and prematurely lined faces were sprinkled throughout the room. Two of the men were parked on the couch, playing a video game on the original Nintendo Entertainment System; the woman was sitting on a stool, her face aimed at the window with blank eyes; and the other three appeared to be trying to play craps on the brown shag carpet.

"Hey, I got nexties," Gary said into the room without stopping. None of them noticed him in any way Jim could see. But they seemed to have a wiry readiness just beneath the surface, even the three on the floor with the dice who looked like they would fall asleep any moment.

They passed through the doorway leading into the kitchen and saw two elderly women and one marginally younger old man sitting at a table, counting money. There was a television on, tuned to *Judge Judy*, and a giant of a man wearing an 8-ball jacket and holding a shotgun.

"Go on down in the basement," the big man said. "He waitin' for you there." The basement door was to their left, and they had to come all the way into the kitchen to open the door and angle the woman so they could go down.

Once the door was open, the music got louder, full of bass to the point Jim could feel his ears vibrating. They came to a landing that had an exit door to the driveway. Jim doubted it could have been opened; it looked like it had been painted over at least a hundred times.

It wouldn't have made a good escape route anyway; there was another guard equally big and equipped with a similar shotgun standing right outside.

They walked into a cloud of smoke once they were in the basement. On the far wall, the word "sky" was painted with what looked to have been an actual hand in neon green. Three large, black, green-eyed dogs sat on their haunches in a semicircle around a short, bushy-eyebrowed, bald-headed man sitting in a chair two sizes too big.

"Hey, Elias," Jim said, giving him a sheepish wave. The barrel of a shotgun emerged from the smoke to Jim's left and jammed into his chest, driving him back a step. Of the few times he'd been afraid over the last nearly twenty-four hours, now he felt it most intensely.

"Motherfucker," Elias replied. It wasn't in anger; it was a usual greeting for him. Elias had maintained that the context of greetings of human beings was arbitrary and thus the greetings could be interchanged with a multitude of other phrases and be equally nonsensical. He also believed spoken language was nearly useless and would subject the people around him to long periods of enduring silence, many times resulting in the eliciting of information he had not been looking for, like which one of his men had been talking to the police or who was making side deals and skimming off the top.

Gary dropped his end of the woman and stepped close to Jim. He elbowed him in the ribs.

"Sorry. I'm sorry, Elias."

A long pause, then, "Sorry for what?" Elias's eyebrows went up.

"You know, about how we left things that last time?"

"What about last time?" Elias's eyebrows lowered.

"Y'know. I'm sorry."

"For what?" Elias's eyebrows mushed together.

"For how we ended things."

"And how was that?"

Jim took a deep breath. Elias wasn't going to make this easy.

"The drugs. And me running away."

"The heron ain't a problem." Elias pronounced "heroin" like he was talking about the bird. "My fractured orbital bone is." He tapped the side of his head by his eye. Jim didn't know about that. He looked at Gary, who was intently not looking back.

"I didn't know about that. Honest. I apologize."

Another long pause, then, "You apologize . . . okay." The shotgun in Jim's chest withdrew. He never saw the person holding it.

It was Jim's turn to pause. "So we're good then? We okay?"

"*Hell* naw. All I did was accept your apology. Now you gotta do right." Elias pointed a stubby finger at him. And pointed with his eyebrows too.

"What's that mean?"

Elias leaned to the side long enough to give Kenya a thorough up and down. "Who the bitch?"

Kenya gasped and was about to say something just as Gary took a small step back and gave her an elbow to the ribs.

"She's cool, Elias," Jim said. "She's a doctor."

"A doctor!" He sounded excited and suspicious at the same time. "I ain't had a doctor here since 1997. Muhfuggah went deep on some crystal. Went in on me like Black Friday. What can I getchoo, sweetness?"

"Barbiturates. Benzodiazepine or phenobarbital. Liquid marijuana if you have it."

"*Daaaaaaaaaaaaaaaaamn*, girl. You jump in with both feet, don't you?" He looked at Jim and waved a hand. "To be continued with yo ass."

"You have it or no?" Kenya asked.

He chuckled. "Slow down. I didn't say I didn't have it. You just orderin' from a brother's *special* menu. She a higher class, if y'all take my meanin'."

"Not for me. For our friend here." Kenya nodded at the woman on the floor. She'd thrown the ratty blanket off herself, but hadn't moved once she saw the dogs.

"Oh, you lookin' to go hard-core on a bitch? I got some ice cold that'll leave her as wiped clean as baby ass."

"No. We need to know what she knows. For her to spill everything."

Elias cocked an eyebrow and half smirked. "That it?"

"Yes," Jim, Gary, and Kenya said together.

"You need some of that Talktume," he said. "I got shitloads of it on hand. G, you know where my favorite chemist is? I ain't heard from him for a day or two."

"Not sure," Gary said. "The people our friend here is with might have something to do with what happened to him."

"And what happened to him?"

"He might be dead."

"Ooo!" Elias said, and "Uh-uhh!" He said it like he was watching one of those *Housewives* shows, and someone had just said something scandalous. He turned sideways in his seat and deposited a leg over the armrest. His body language said, "Go on."

"What's in this Talktume?" Kenya asked.

His eyes rolled over to her and, for a brief flash, narrowed. "Barbiturates of a special blend: liquid marijuana, spearmint, eleven herbs and spices—all that shit."

"Sounds nice. How much?"

"Depends. How about we administer some to li'l sis and see what she has to say?"

"So long as you don't try to go too deep in my pocket."

"Nah. Not like that. If'n her kith disappeared my favorite chemist, this is a hundred percent discounted transaction. I don't like money involuntarily leaving my bankroll. Ebony!"

A man nobody had seen stepped forward to stand next to Elias's seat. He wore a suit with a black shirt and black tie and was as dark as a shadow. The only things visible on him were his eyeballs and his lower lip, which was as red as the skin of an apple.

He handed Elias a small, plastic-wrapped package, and the pudgy man dropped it onto his lap. The dogs hadn't reacted if they even noticed Ebony at all. Elias raised a hand and, with a small amount of flair, snapped his fingers twice. A man dressed in white similarly as Ebony was dressed in black stepped between Jim, Gary, and Kenya. They all started but managed to keep their composure at the sight of the albino man.

"Let me guess, you're Ivory?" Gary asked.

"That is some in*sen*sitive shit!" Elias said. "You cold, man. You cold."

"I'm sorry for my associate," Jim said, looking at the albino. "He's got a Tourette's thing."

"Associate," Gary said, smiling. "That's a start."

Without acknowledging that anyone had spoken or that they were anything beyond vertical masses for him to step around, the man who had responded to Elias snapping his fingers produced a small knife, took the package from Elias's lap, and neatly sliced it open.

Ebony stepped over and gently helped the woman up. She looked around, a half-astonished expression on her face.

"Right this way, madam." Ebony's voice was a rich tenor. Jim wasn't expecting him to sound so . . . normal. He wrapped her arm around his, and she looked unsure, but still went along. "May I ask your name?"

"Mary." She sounded contrite, as if she had been the one doing something wrong and not the person who had just been kidnapped.

Snap-snap followed closely behind, all three disappearing into another room. The two men, even though they had been mostly quiet, had left an immense vacancy in the room. The four of them plus the three dogs seemed somehow inadequate.

"So . . ." Jim began.

"Where was I?" Elias said. "Oh yeah. Motherfucker." He really let the word roll off his tongue. Jim would have swallowed audibly if he'd had more than a thin film of saliva in his mouth. "Jim, how we gon' make this right? Whatchoo got for me?"

"Elias, I am very sorry for what happened to you. I was at an extremely low period in my life, and I regret ever coming here that day. I apologize for wasting your time, and I apologize for wasting your . . . product."

"All that shit is fine and dandy, but what about my eye?"

"I'm offering you my apology. If there is something more I can do . . ."

"I'm glad you offered! There is something you can do." Elias reached into his pocket or a fold of flesh—he was wearing a vest the same color as his skin, so Jim couldn't be sure. He produced two tickets and held them out. "You goin' to the Eddie party tonight."

"Elias, we are a little busy at the moment."

"You want to make this shit up to me, right?" He pointed at his cheek, all humor drained from his face.

"You know I do."

"Then go to a party for me. I'll give you somethin' to walk around with. I'm not lookin' for somethin' for nothin'." Jim doubted that. Elias wasn't exactly the giving type. Either he was making so much money off this party that the change he intended to throw at them was nothing, or paying them was somehow putting Jim and Gary into the little man's pocket.

"Why can't you go?"

Two of the dogs growled, their large teeth, which appeared to have been capped in gold, gleaming in their mouths.

"I'm not at liberty to discuss that particular aspect of my business. Will you go?"

Jim sighed heavily, feeling the weight of more than just declining an invitation hanging in the air between them. "Yes."

"Yes!" Gary literally fist-pumped.

"Now there's a very select clientele who will be there. A veritable who's who among the celebrity elite and choice celebriphiles. Considering the party isn't being held at a known location, you can exchange with anyone quite freely." Jim noted Elias's change in tone and demeanor. He'd even sat up straighter and was making eye contact with him.

"Exchange?" Gary said. "How much money are you giving us? And what if we need to make change?"

Elias waved a hand. "I'm the exclusive provider. Everything is prepackaged. All you have to do is take the ticket and pass a packet."

"What's the stuff?"

"Something new. I call it Viagra 2."

"Why?"

"Because it gets you *hard*."

Gary shrugged like he didn't get it. Neither did Jim.

"What do you mean? Like an erection? Doesn't Viagra already do that? Do people want to walk around with full boners at a party?"

Elias shook his head. "I'm not talkin' about no boners, man. It gets your whole body hard. Like a rock."

Jim didn't think he could understand in a way Elias could explain. "So we just exchange one packet for one ticket? One for one, like that?" Jim was surprised to realize he was feeling just self-destructive enough to agree to be a drug mule. He felt like the old him was resurfacing, the Jim he had already half buried when Mel had come along.

"Just like that." Elias steepled his fingers.

Ebony appeared again. "We are ready for you." He stood in front of Elias and turned around. The chubby man got into a crouch and leapt onto his back before they all went into the room where Snap-snap and Mary were waiting.

Jim had just assumed this room would have been filled with drugs. Every room in the house, for that matter. Instead, it was surprisingly clean, bare, and painted white. There was nothing ornate about it; the walls were composite wood, the floor concrete with a drain, the ceiling open so the pipes and ducts were visible.

Mary was tied to a dining chair with arms, surprisingly not struggling. She looked nervous, though, her eyes flitting to every person coming into the room. Jim felt his resolve waver; the initial heat after capturing one of the Adjacent had faded, and she was just one against . . . two, three, four, five—six people, and there was an extreme inherent unfairness to the whole thing.

He wondered if he was being sexist. No, he was being sexist. The right thing to do here was to get her high as a kite and torture the shit out of her until they found out every drop of information they could.

Jim wondered how experienced Elias and his crew were at this. Mary was already hooked up to an IV, a clear plastic bag filled with liquid suspended from a stand next to her. Snap-snap—he was going to have to ask his name; Jim couldn't go on thinking of him as that—was adjusting the flow and checking her pulse. Jim bent and saw her pupils were huge.

"You can start anytime," Elias said from Ebony's back. Kenya wasted no time, sitting in front of Mary Indian-style.

"I'd be careful if I were you," Gary said. "Her feet aren't tied down."

"I'm not worried about that," Kenya said, a strange tone to her voice. "Because this isn't the absolute worst I could do to her. I've done autopsies, many of them, and I know the worst places to cut. I could cut her in at least a hundred different places, and she would hardly bleed. I could make an incision smaller than a millimeter that she would die from in seconds. I could cut out her intestines and set them in her lap, and she would die from exposure or an infection or maybe even shock. So if Mary decides to kick me, then she'll receive the full focus of my creativity."

Jim felt a chill from the base of his neck all the way down to the heels of his feet that had nothing to do with his current state of being.

Gary and Jim had filled her in as much as possible while they had been riding around.

"What do you need the Bloom for, exactly?"

"To set us free," Mary said.

"To set you free from what?"

"Life."

"So you want to die?"

"No. Yes. I'm not sure how to say it."

"Say it however you like. Make me understand."

Mary went over the story of the Adjacent, including the Ancient One, who had allegedly bestowed the Testimony to Fyukis decades before. She explained the story of Brother and the spirit that was his other half, which had also begun life on Earth, even though it was not in all living things.

"Bullshit," Gary said under his breath.

"So then there should be six of you, right?" Kenya said.

"No." Mary's speech was slurred, and the albino made more tweaks.

"Excuse me, but what is your name?" Jim asked the albino.

"Fiel," Mary said.

"Fiel?" Kenya looked at Gary. "Who's that?"

"That's the other lady," Gary said. "The tall, hot blonde."

"You really think she's hot?" Jim asked. She'd been cute, but he wasn't so sure about hot.

"Well, yeah. Just because she's trying to kill me doesn't erase all that. In fact, that kind of makes her hotter."

"That's true, that's true."

Kenya turned back to Mary, annoyed. "Why did you call yourself Fiel?"

Mary made a show of concentrating, her brow knitting as she stared at Kenya.

"I am . . . Mary."

"Are you only Mary?"

Mary blinked several times, as if she were trying to shrug off the effect of the cocktail.

"We're all somebody else."

"But you," Kenya insisted. "Are you somebody else?"

"I am Adjacent."

"Is Fiel Adjacent?"

Mary lifted her chin defiantly. "Yes."

Kenya thought a moment. "Is Fiel human?"

"Fiel is life."

"Are you human?

A pause. "Yes . . . no."

"What do you intend to do to the human race?" Jim asked.

Mary shook her head. "Nothing."

"If the Adjacent succeeds, what will happen to the human race?" Kenya asked.

Mary's face turned red, then she blanched. "You will cease to exist."

"What the fuck kinda shit you people into?" Elias asked.

"I'll explain later," Gary said.

"Is this an intended side effect?"

"No, but it can hardly be avoided. Human beings—life—was not meant to be."

"And the only way to stop this is to keep your people from getting the Bloom?"

"Yes. That's what the Testimony tells us."

"That's their bullshit-ass Bible," Gary added.

"How is the Bloom administered? You have to consume it, right?"

"We had a doctor manufacture it for us. For decades we have scoured for the raw materials, and once we utilized the skill of a chemist to culminate them into the Bloom."

Jim noticed how her tone had become robotic. He looked into her eyes and was creeped out by how large her pupils were. His mother had had an eye test when he was a teenager and couldn't drive because she was sensitive to the light. He'd seen her eyes just before she put on her sunglasses, and even though it was his mother, the sight had given him a chill.

"Would you like to know how you will die?" Mary asked.

"I thought we would just wink out or something after you had taken the Bloom," Kenya said hesitantly.

"No. Not you. All life shall be extinguished like a flame, but you will die before that. We will find you. We . . . already know where you are. You cannot harm us because we already crave death."

"Okay, I'll bite. How will I die?" Gary folded his arms and smiled.

"We don't need to wait for the Bloom to pass through your body. We can kill you and extract it. We will crush your head under the tire of a car."

"Sounds gory. Looking forward to it."

"How about me?" Jim asked.

"We will take hot pokers and put them through your eyes. We will boil your brains."

"Sounds like a raw deal. Gary, you wanna trade?"

"Gouged eyeballs for crushed head? Throw in that sweet stereo of yours, and you got it."

She looked at Kenya and then Elias, Ebony, and the albino. "Would the rest of you like to know how you will die?"

"No thanks on that one, crazy lady," Elias said. "Look, is this going to take much longer? I got places I need to be." Jim knew that to not be true. Elias was an extreme agoraphobe to the point he couldn't even look outside and would probably die in here, melded to a couch.

"No," Kenya said. "I think we're almost done. Mary here is about to tell us how to kill the Adjacent."

"You cannot kill us. We recycle."

"I didn't know ten cent refunds were the key to immortality," Gary added helpfully.

"Sure you can die. If I were to open this IV valve, you would overdose and die in a matter of minutes."

"No. Brother would not allow my death. Not this close to our ascension. Two years ago, maybe a year, you might have been able to kill us, but the spirit would simply cycle into another body."

"Reincarnation?"

"Not reincarnation. That's a new life in a new body. I would simply continue my current life in an already existing body."

"Have you done this before?"

"Yes."

Kenya stood and got really close. Jim noted her looking Mary up and down. "I notice your clothes. They aren't exactly fashion forward. When were you born, Mary?"

"1943."

"And you're how old?"

"Thirty-seven."

Kenya folded her arms. Jim watched her think, her tongue rolling across her front teeth, pooching out her closed mouth.

"Did you die in 1980, Mary?"

The woman's eyes went wide and began dancing around in her head. She looked around her as if for the first time. "Who . . . who . . ."

"Mary, did you die in 1980?"

"I don't know." Tears streamed from the woman's eyes. "She isn't telling me what to say. She's not talking to me!"

"Mary"—Kenya laid a gentle hand on her forearm as Mary struggled against her bonds—"how did you die?"

Mary began yanking violently at her bonds, not trying to get away necessarily, rather looking as if she were having a seizure. Her body twisted in unnatural ways, one shoulder stretching high until it was parallel with the top of her head, the fingers of both hands bent backward like the second knuckle would slip and she could hold a cup with the back of her hand. Her face was a mask of fear and pain, pupils dilated, despite the cocktail of drugs stewing in her blood.

"I . . . I . . . fell," she said. Kenya was about to say something when she continued, "He . . . *pushed* me."

"Who pushed you, Mary?"

Instead of answering, she began whipping her head back and forth so violently her neck cracked. Snap-snap stood behind her and forcefully held her head still.

Mary's eyes moved independently of one another.

Jim was about to say maybe enough was enough when Kenya asked, "Why did he murder you, Mary?"

She went rigidly still, eyes perfectly focused on Kenya, and said, "Because he hates me. He hates us all." Then she slumped in the chair, her face mushing in the albino's grasp.

Chapter 28

"First things first. You two gotta get cleaned up," Elias said. "You stink."

Gary made a show of sniffing one of his pits and made a face like he was nonplussed with his smell. Jim still felt wired from what he'd seen and was nodding almost unconsciously.

"Yeah," he said. "Where's the shower?"

Elias made a face. "Do I run a YMCA up in this bitch? Ideally, the shower is in *your* house, along with a suit and tie for yo' ass."

"Right—right. Okay. What time should we be back?"

"The party goes from *dark* until *light*," he said, twirling one of the invitations between his fat fingers. "So I say get back here at six; then we'll take you down."

"So what are you going to do when we get back to my place?" Gary asked Kenya.

"Actually, I'm not going. I'm going to stay here and monitor Mary."

"Oh." He looked at Elias. "You cool with that?"

"My man, a beautiful woman has just said she would like to stay at my home for a prolonged period of time of her own volition. I will cherish the shit out of each moment."

Gary nodded, an unhappy look on his face. But he brightened considerably when Ebony produced a white paper bag and handed it to him.

"To take the shine off your nose."

"Hey, could you give me something?" Jim asked Elias. The smaller, pudgier man raised his eyebrows at him. "Liquid marijuana."

Elias smiled. "I still sold that hit you didn't take all those years ago. I guess I've owed you a refund all this time. With the rate of inflation factored in, I can get that to you."

Chapter 29

As they left Elias's house, Jim looked around. Something was different, like there was a palpable new ingredient in the air. He had looked around before they'd gone in but had been looking for people. There was something wrong around them, and Jim could not tell what it was.

"Something feel off to you?" he asked Gary.

"I haven't had a pulse in almost twenty-four hours. I'm rotting. Yes, something feels off."

"I'm serious. Something feels different out here. I don't know how to describe it."

"Okay, I'm with you. What do you think it is?"

"I don't know."

They climbed in the minivan, and Gary started the engine.

"Where are we going?" Jim asked.

"My place. We can get cleaned up and borrow a couple of my father's suits."

Jim nodded. Gary's father was about their size and shape, and he couldn't stand the idea of going back to his apartment in case Mel was still there.

Jim hoped Gary's father's suits looked good. He hadn't worn his own in about five years, right around the time he had interviewed for his current job. It had been a ratty, off-the-rack-looking thing back then and wouldn't be in danger of impressing anyone if he put that on tonight.

"Is it weird I'm kind of excited to go to this party?" Jim said. He was half talking to himself, although Gary nodded in agreement.

"I know, right? We are going to an Eddie party. I'm stoked! This will be excellent right before I die."

That was a bummer.

"Uh, yeah." Jim wasn't quite ready to deal with Gary being dead. Death was second only to personal nudity in things that made him feel ooky. "So, what are we going to do about these Adjacent people?"

"Don't even worry about them," Gary said. "They're dangerous like a wild dog is. Sure, it'll bite you. But if you get a big enough stick, you can whack it over the head and run like hell."

Jim was almost on board with that statement, but it kind of fell off at the end. He nodded and smiled, and quickly the atmosphere between them dissolved into silence.

They crossed Brush, then John R, and made a right onto Woodward.

"They sell fish there now?" Jim said, pointing to a squat gray building just off the corner. "That used to be a Picway. *Uck.*" Picway had been a chain of shoe stores, known for cheap, low-quality shoes. It had gone out of business when they were teenagers. They passed a series of single-story buildings, many of them surprisingly new. They drove past the MacGregor Public Library, now closed and abandoned, a newly erected black wrought iron fence surrounding the front. They passed the Henry Ford plant that had been closed since forever, and Highland Park Community High School, which had just recently closed.

Outside the city on the other side of Six Mile was the Palmer Park section of Detroit. They made a Michigan left and turned into a neighborhood behind a nest of apartments. These few blocks were a diamond in the rough—beautiful old houses located in an area that had been worn down by decades of apathy, poverty, and abandonment. Gary still lived with his father, who'd moved into this four-thousand-square-foot house with settlement money he'd been paid after Gary had been injured from a plastic child's spoon that had come in a cereal box.

There was a little boy in the front yard, wearing a big puffy coat and playing in a pile of leaves. Gary parked in the semicircular driveway, and they got out.

"Gary!" the boy said and ran in their direction. Gary caught the boy and whipped him around, high in the air.

"What's up, Will?"

"I got two today, Gary."

"For real? Where were they?" Gary made a show of looking at all points of the property, an intense look on his face.

"One was in the backyard. I got him right between the eyes. His brain exploded all over." His smile was broad, as if he were immensely proud of his accomplishment. Jim guessed he was talking about a rat or something.

"And the other?"

"That one was pounding on the door, and I opened it so he could get inside. Well, not a he; it was kind of a girl, but she was really messy."

"Full goo?"

"Yeah, full goo. She didn't even have eyeballs."

Okay, now Jim was lost.

"She crawled in the house like a snake. I thought she would've been standing; that's why I missed her. Then my gun jammed, and I had to retreat. She must have heard me because she followed me up the stairs. She left this long, slimy-black trail behind her, and she stunk too."

"Really?" Gary made an exaggerated expression, as if he were glued to every word.

"Yeah. I tried to barricade myself in my room, but she wedged into the door before I could get it shut. I had more ammo under my bed, and she was *right* on my heels. I barely jammed in another clip before she was on top of me."

Will shook his head, and Gary's eyes bugged out.

"And? And? Don't just leave me hangin', man. What happened?"

"Brains. All over my room. I got it all cleaned up, but it's going to be a month before it airs out."

"Where are they now?"

"I just finished burying both of them." He pointed to a huge pile of leaves. "Under there."

"Well, good work, buddy." Gary sat him down and scratched the corner of his head. "But you know you can't keep them there. Those leaves will blow away, and even if they don't, come summer next year, we have to mow the lawn."

"But they'll be just bones by then. Can't the mower just run them over and grind them up into dust?"

"No, no. I'm not buying corpse-grinding blades. Those things are expensive. You're going to have to uncover them and bury them properly."

Will hung his head. "Okay."

"Hey, you don't have to do it right now, all right?"

The boy looked up at him. "Will you help me?"

"Yeah." Gary's eyes got a little distant, then he nodded. "Yeah. I'll help you with it tomorrow."

Jim had always been the fifth wheel when Gary's little brother was around. Will worshipped his older brother, and Gary basked in it. Gary's mother had died at a young age, leaving him to fend for himself because his father had virtually no rules and abdicated his responsibility.

Which was why Gary lived a life of few rules and was irresponsible. Except when it came to Will. Gary made sure everything around him was structured and that he lived in an environment surrounded by love. Will's mother was nonexistent, and were it not for Gary, the boy might have easily been dead or a ward of the state. It was as if Gary was trying to give his little brother the life he should have had.

"How you doing, Will?" Jim asked.

"Fine." Jim had a suspicion the boy didn't like him. As if *he* were the bad influence. He wanted to ask Gary why Will's reception of him was always chilly at best, but then he realized this was an eight-year-old boy, which made Jim seem whiny in a way that made him uncomfortable.

"Is Daddy home?"

Jim shuddered. Maybe it was because his own father had died at such a young age, but the thought of calling a grown man "Daddy" when he himself was a grown man struck him as infinitely awkward. Gary had no such hang-up, even though it was only by default that his father was not as big an absentee as Jim's.

"No. He had to go see someone about a car," Will said. Which meant he'd be gone at least two days. Gary's father always had a hustle going on but had no idea how to hold on to his money. There was always the next get-rich scheme around the corner, some inside investment a janitor at some investment firm had, or some invention a cousin or some distant relative had who needed to hold just a couple of bucks until it paid off.

They had received more than $2 million in settlement money after the plastic spoon had cut the inside of Gary's mouth to shreds. Outside of reconstructive surgery and this house, there was hardly anything left to show for it after Gary's father's mismanagement.

Jim noticed the annoyed reaction of his friend. But Gary quickly recovered and smiled.

"Are you okay?" Will asked. "You look weird." He looked at Jim. "Both of you."

"Us?" Gary looked over his shoulder at Jim, a big smile on his face. The message was clear: not a word of any of this to Will. Jim kept his face neutral. "Nah, we're fine. Hey, you hungry? How about I make some lunch?"

They went inside, and Will hung up his coat in the long hall leading to the living room and kitchen. It always sounded hollow in here to Jim's ears, like there wasn't enough stuff or people to fill it. Which was probably true considering the scarcity of the furnishings.

They went into the kitchen, where Gary and Will washed their hands. Jim hung back behind the island, leaned against it, and folded his arms.

"Are you going to wash your hands?" Will asked.

"Nah, I'm not hungry."

"Mary Ellis says you can't be in the kitchen if your hands are dirty."

"Who's Mary Ellis?"

"She's my nana."

"Your grandmother?"

"Nanny," Gary said. "She's his nanny." He turned to Will. "Where is she, by the way?"

"That's what I said. She's upstairs resting. I think she said she had a headache. I took her some water an hour ago."

"Hm," Gary said. "Maybe I should check on her." That was another anti-Garyism. He wasn't a good checker-upper of the sick. Jim had had his appendix removed when he was twelve and had developed sepsis. That was a long stretch of time where he had not seen or heard from his best friend.

And when had Gary hired a nanny?

It was like he had a whole other life outside of Jim. He was surprised at the sudden pang of jealousy, although he wasn't sure what he was jealous of.

"Grilled cheese sandwiches okay?" Gary asked.

"With bacon?" Will asked expectantly.

"That wouldn't be a grilled cheese sandwich, kiddo, would it?" He put his hands on his hips and put on a stern face, but Will must have seen through the ruse, a big grin spreading across his mug. Gary leaned forward and wagged an index finger in his brother's face. "Where did you hear about sandwiches like that?"

Will stuck out his lower lip and shouted, "I learned it from you, okay?" before whirling on his heel and folding his arms. Jim was relieved, then saddened, to realize this was an inside joke between the two of them, much like he and Gary had had once upon a time. He realized his jealousy was for a longing of things lost between him and his best friend, and there was no one to blame. Jim had been the one to pull away, and that had begun happening long before Mel had come along.

"You guys get the stuff together, and I'll be right back." Gary dusted the top of Will's head and dashed out of the room.

"So," Jim said once Gary was gone, "grilled cheese. With bacon." He'd never had a sibling and wasn't sure of the protocol. Was he supposed to speak down to him or talk to him like an adult? What was the stance on swear words? Should he try to be really cool and toss out an occasional "fuck" as he spoke? Did he let Will turn on the stove himself?

"Wash your hands," the boy said. Jim nodded and approached the sink as Will opened the refrigerator.

Once his hands were clean, he turned around and saw Will carefully not looking at him. His instinct was to ask what was going on, something casual and noncommittal, but what came out was, "You're not about to cry, are you?" Jim didn't know why he'd said that and immediately regretted it. Will's face crumpled, and he charged Jim with his bent wrists tucked into the corners of his eyes. Jim put his hands up just in time to catch the boy in a half hug.

"I don't want Gary to die!" Will whimpered. The boy's voice was low, as if he didn't want his big brother to hear.

"Whoa—whoa—whoa, what made you say that?" Jim put his hand to the back of the boy's head, cradling it.

"He's sick. I can tell."

"He's not . . . he's not . . . *that* sick."

"Yes, he is. I can smell it on him. You smell too, but not as bad as him."

Jim couldn't smell anything, but he did remember Gary telling him once that his little brother had a superhuman sense of smell. At the time he'd thought it was one of those bragging things people said about the children in their own family. Someone who had a six-month-old who already knew how to walk or a two-year-old who could read a book—something like that. They were both technically dead and had the smell of rot on them, but that should have been covered up by the smell of weed. That Jim *could* smell.

"Oh no, buddy. That's just a skunk. We ran over one on our way here."

Will ground his head into Jim's stomach, shaking it left and right. He pitched his head back and looked into Jim's eyes. "I know what pot smells like. My brother is a pothead."

"Oh." Jim felt like he should have followed that up with something profound and convincing, but the boy was damn smart. He figured another lie and there'd be no hope of them ever getting along.

He knelt. "You want to know the truth?" Will nodded. "Okay, so I can't tell you everything, but here goes. I just found out my girlfriend is an assassin." Will's mouth fell open, and his eyes went wide. "Yeah. And yesterday, Gary took me to this place where this guy made these magical pills that we took. They are the reason why we smell funny."

The boy made a face at him. "Are you talking about Dr. K?"

"You know about him?"

"I know he's a scientist. He and my brother work together a lot."

"Right. Work."

"And anyway, what Dr. K does isn't magic. There's no such thing. It's *science*." He said it like Jim should have known better, like a nonbeliever to one who still believes in S-A-N-T-A C-L-A-U-S.

That stung Jim, and he regretted the next words he said immediately: "Well if it isn't magic, then how come the pill he gave us turned us into zombies?"

Jim instantly knew he'd screwed up but didn't appreciate to what degree until a few seconds later after Will smiled.

"Did you just play me, little man?"

Before Will could answer, they heard Gary at the bottom of the stairs, and a moment later he and Mary Ellis came around the corner.

She was gorgeous.

That wasn't even close to the right word, but it was all the vocabulary Jim had. She was easily five foot nine, although she was hunched and leaning on Gary. Her black hair hung in thick, heavy curls, framing a perfectly oval face. She had big dashes for eyebrows that kept her face from being too soft, yet enhanced her beauty even more. Her eyes were like two pools of black, and she had full, pouty lips.

Jim couldn't see too well underneath the oversize T-shirt and skirt that went down to her ankles, but what he could make out was pretty shapely. It was obvious why Gary had hired her.

He noticed belatedly that Will was watching him. He was certain his eyes had danced up and down the woman several times and wondered if the boy had seen all of that. Jim couldn't read the expression on his face, but he felt self-conscious all the same.

He gave Will a half smile and looked back to Gary and Mary Ellis as he helped her sit.

"Orange juice," Gary said.

Jim didn't know what that meant. "Apple juice," he said. Gary didn't say anything else, and Will stepped quickly to the refrigerator. He took out the orange juice, set it on the island, and looked at Jim.

"Cup," he said.

Jim really didn't get this game, but okay. "Glass."

"No, Mary Ellis has low blood sugar. I need a cup for the orange juice, and I can't reach them." He pointed to the cabinets overhead.

"Ohhhh!" Jim said, a little too loud for his own ears. He reached into the cabinet and grabbed a cup; Will snatched it from his hand and filled it before quick-walking it to Gary and Mary Ellis on the couch.

Gary held it up to her lips, and she took several long gulps, breathing heavily by the time she pushed it away.

"Gracias," she said.

"De nada," Gary replied.

Oh, so she was Italian? Jim found himself curling an imaginary mustache. Then he realized what he was doing and felt like a complete predator. Here the woman was near death's door or whatever, and he was more concerned about his penis.

He wondered if his penis even worked. Gary had said he'd gotten several boners. Jim hadn't gotten any boners.

Gary has five boners. If Mary gives Jim eight boners, how many more boners does he have than Gary?

Stop it!

To get his mind off himself and his possibly nonexistent libido, he walked over to the three of them. He felt as useless as shoes on a duck, more harmful because he was in the way as Gary and Will flitted about Mary Ellis. He'd never been any good around women who were in pain physically or emotionally; he simply froze and didn't know what to do or say.

He constantly stopped himself from saying, "You okay?" as Will picked up a magazine and began fanning her. After a few minutes, Will fetched her purse and fished out a small black pouch, unzipped it, and produced a slender machine that looked like an MP3 player. He also took out a cylindrical device and put something in it. Will's little hands were moving so fast Jim couldn't tell all of what he was seeing.

"Could you get me that dish towel?" Gary asked him. Jim didn't know what dish towel but assumed it was in the kitchen, somewhere near the sink. He headed that way, and Gary called to him, "Make it damp too."

Mary Ellis was sitting up by the time he returned, and she took the towel from him and pressed it to her forehead, then her cheeks, then the base of her throat.

"Thank you so much," she said. Her voice was actually husky and not a byproduct of whatever had just happened to her.

"No problem," Jim said.

"Do we need to take you to the hospital?" Gary asked. "Can you eat?"

"No, I'm feeling much better." Even her accent was sexy. Jim didn't entirely know what was going on. She was Will's nanny, but here they were taking care of her. He wondered if Gary had known about her illness and hired her anyway because she was so attractive.

Really attractive. Really, really attractive.

"I guess I'm still adjusting to the diabetes," she said. "I had a headache and thought I would just close my eyes a moment. I didn't know my sugar blood was low."

Sugar blood. Jim smiled. The way she said it made it sound like some sort of snack.

She did look tasty, though.

Jim found himself looking at her in a new way. His attraction pulled in a different direction as he began to wonder exactly how her flesh would taste. Without intending to, he took a step closer and was in the process of reaching. He came back to himself when Gary put the cup in his hand.

"Thanks," Gary said.

No, thank you, he thought. *What in the world was I about to do?*

Jim shuffled back to the kitchen and deposited the cup into the sink. He felt numb. Not numb like he was slowly becoming physically, but disconnected from himself. This had to have been what Kenya was talking about. Synapses slowly dying, and animal instincts rising to the fore. He had at least a full twenty-four hours before the effects of the Bloom wore off. How much worse would it get?

Will sat with Mary Ellis while Jim and Gary cooked. It had been a long time since he made grilled cheese sandwiches, and reminiscing took his mind off his errant appetite.

Chapter 30

Gary was managing the bacon while Jim toasted bread in a pan. Jim noticed his friend stealing small glances at him, and he could almost read his thoughts. A lot had happened since yesterday that had nothing to do with people trying to kill them. He hated confrontation, and Jim felt that butterfly feeling coming on in his stomach.

He'd already had one confrontation with Gary, but that had been in the heat of emotion. Now that he was cooled off, it was like he was naked or unarmed and didn't have the fuel of anger to shuttle him along. He had nothing but dread to pass the time and just wished he could take everything he'd said back, regardless of whether or not he'd been wrong.

"Smells good," Jim said, nodding toward the bacon. It didn't really. It smelled like bacon, which had always smelled good before, only now it had all the olfactory appeal of wet cement.

"Yeah," Gary said.

They finished cooking in silence, put everything on plates, and brought it to the table. Gary had wanted to bring the food to Mary Ellis, but she'd insisted on eating at the table, saying that eating on a couch was something slobs did.

Gary and Jim sat at the table even though they weren't eating, again at Mary Ellis's insistence. She didn't mention it, but it was impossible not to notice that only half the people were eating.

Will ate hungrily, like food was a new discovery and he liked it. Gary had made an extra half sandwich for him, and the boy tore through all three halves in minutes. He pushed his plate away and waited patiently for Mary Ellis to finish before the three men cleared the table while she reset it.

Gary washed, Will rinsed, and Jim put away, and they were done in less than two minutes.

"How's your homework, kid?" Gary asked.

"All done. I have a test Monday."

"Ready for it?"

"Yeah." Will sounded unsure.

"Are you?"

"No, but Mary Ellis said she'll show me some tricks."

"I don't want tricks. I want you to *know*."

"I told him I would teach him a few mnemonic devices," Mary Ellis said from the table.

"Demonic devices?" Gary said exaggeratedly.

Mary Ellis shook her head. Apparently she was familiar with his sense of humor too. He came over and sat with her at the table. She allowed him to take her hand, and he checked her blood sugar again.

"You feeling okay?"

"Yes, Gary. I am fine." She sounded mildly exasperated, but Jim sensed there was a part of her that enjoyed the attention. "Look!" She stood up from the table and did a silly little dance in a circle that involved a lot of hip. Jim's eyes practically fell out of his head. She was trying to hold in a smile when she sat back down.

"I just want to be sure," he said. "You gonna be fine to watch Will for the rest of the day?"

"Oh, of course. He is no trouble."

"All right. Jim and I have to go out tonight. Order a pizza or something for dinner, okay?"

"Yay!" Will shouted. Mary Ellis rolled her eyes. Jim thought she looked like a home-cooked meal kind of person.

"I told you I am fine. I promise to stay on top of my sugar blood. I check." She picked up the little machine and waved it. "Promise."

Gary nodded. "Will, you're the man of the house until Daddy gets home." He rested his hands on his little brother's shoulders and looked him in the eyes. "Will Riker Tate, I expect you to conduct yourself like a big boy. Be helpful and make sure you keep an eye on Mary Ellis."

"You're coming back, aren't you?"

"Of course I am." Gary knelt in front of his little brother. "No matter what happens, you'll see me tomorrow."

Will put a hand on Gary's shoulder. "Power down, nerd. I was just asking if you'd be back before I go to bed."

"Oh!" Gary seemed mildly embarrassed. That was a new one; Jim didn't even know that he had the gene. "No, uh, Jim and I are going to a party. We probably won't be back until well after you've gone to sleep."

"All right. That's all I wanted to know."

Jim followed Gary to the back door. Gary hadn't actually said goodbye, and Jim felt like someone should.

"See you later."

"It was nice to meet you," Mary Ellis said. She hadn't actually spoken to him before, and he felt a thrill down his spine at being addressed by such a beautiful woman. As they walked to the garage, her words rang in his head. He thought he would remember them for the rest of his life.

Chapter 31

Gary had moved into the detached garage so he could smoke his weed in peace. It wasn't because his father hassled him about it; his old man often came calling whenever he toked or outright stole it for his own use. Gary had a complicated relationship with his dad. It was obvious they loved each other by the way they always interacted, but Jim could see Gary held deep resentment for him as well, and that wasn't just transference on Jim's part. Gary's father *wasn't* a father. It had been completely cool when they were twelve when Gary had no bedtimes, could eat whatever he wanted, go to school if he felt like it, and swear, but that complete lack of structure had bitten him on the ass as he'd gotten older. Gary's poor grades had led to him not being able to go to the prom; because he didn't do homework and didn't know how to study, he'd failed Driver's Ed twice (he'd subsequently gotten a fake learner's permit from his cousin and somehow aced the test at the Secretary of State); and he was effectively banned from field trips after his teachers discovered he'd been forging his father's signature.

And ultimately, don't children just crave a parental figure deep down inside?

They were walking up the dirt driveway, which had long ago been overgrown by weeds and grass. Two ruts remained from tires driving in and out over the decades, and they walked side by side in them, silent.

When they were about a dozen feet away, the front of the garage began to silently lift. Jim realized it was the garage door, and Gary must have had the control in his pocket. It was odd to see a bedroom so completely exposed to the outside, and it was probably a bad idea because mice and other critters could probably get in without him seeing.

"Pretty cool, huh?" Gary asked.

"Yeah."

"It's a Craftsman 3/4 horsepower Ultra-Quiet. I installed it three months ago. It makes all the difference now."

"All the difference?"

"Yeah. The ladies don't wake up when I open the door to go get something from the house."

The door slid shut behind them, and Jim had to blink several times before his eyes adjusted to the dark. He found his eyes didn't react to changes in light anywhere near as fast as he was used to.

Jim had seen Gary with a fair share of women, but he'd struck out many, many times. Gary's theory was volume. The more women he approached, the more he could bed. His problem was he wasn't selective on any level. Gary appreciated a good-looking woman, but he would hit on virtually any woman—fat, rail-thin, ugly, sickly, sometimes elderly. Jim had saved his friend from many a sexual disaster, and considering he couldn't be around twenty-four seven, he wondered who his friend had wound up bringing home on the nights he hadn't been around.

The bed was neatly made, and the furniture didn't look like he'd looted a house fire. It was antiquey, almost as if he'd been going after a theme of some kind. Maybe New Orleans or France with the off-white dressers and canopied bed. There were burgundy patterned window treatments, a pile of pillows atop the comforter, and even a bed skirt.

This was not the Gary Jim knew.

"Nice," he said, turning in a slow semicircle. Gary had said he was taking his time with the decorations, and the last time Jim had been here, he'd assumed it would never be done. "Show me the rest."

They walked into a small bathroom with a standing shower, a sink that matched the style of the bedroom, and a toilet that could just as easily have flown itself from Mars. It was black with flame decals on the bottom. It was strange-looking beyond that, with no obvious tank and a compact, more oval than normal bowl and what looked like a row of lights to either side.

"It's one of those Japanese toilets," Gary said. "Expensive as hell. I let Will pick it out. It was the only way I could get him to agree with me moving out here. I'm thinking of bumping out the bathroom next year so I can put in a urinal."

"Let me guess," Jim said, pointing to the toilet, "you knew a guy?"

"Shit yeah. I wasn't gonna spend four thousand bones on a toilet."

They went into the small kitchen/TV room, and Jim was impressed with what he'd done with the modest amount of space he had. The biggest room by far was the bedroom, but the kitchen really had everything packed in it without seeming cramped. On the left a refrigerator and stove, both an industrial silver. The countertops were probably that faux marble that you couldn't tell from the real thing. The cabinets were a dark cherry, and the two-compartment sink had one of those detachable-head faucets that could spray anywhere.

On the right was a small black loveseat, with a pile of multicolored pillows on it. A triangular glass coffee table was set in front of it, and a large flat-screen television was built into the wall. Five years ago Gary had had an impressive DVD collection, and he had always been into the latest tech. That meant all his movies and TV shows had to be in the cloud.

Jim was just about to compliment him on the renovations when he turned and saw Gary had lit up a fat joint. He sucked on it hard, his face lined with concentration. Seeing him like that, Jim noticed for the first time he had sort of a gray complexion.

"Damn," Gary said. "I still can't feel this."

"Let me see that; I have a theory." Jim held out his hand. Gary gave him the joint, and Jim took a toke. "Yeah. I got nothing too."

"So, what's your theory?"

"Dead lungs. We don't need to breathe, so oxygen isn't flowing to our brains. So smoking won't do anything for us."

"I think I have some coke."

"Don't bother. That won't do anything either. Our bodies are drying up. Putting a powder up our noses won't do anything."

"So we can't get high?" Gary looked crestfallen.

"I didn't say that." Jim pulled the two vials of liquid marijuana out of his pocket. Gary's eyes went wide.

"What's that?"

"Liquid marijuana. I got it from Elias." Gary snatched one out of his palm, snapped it open, then sniffed the entire thing. "I'm not sure how much we're supposed to take."

"Who cares? We're dead. Let's just get high."

Jim was feeling self-destructive enough to not find fault in Gary's logic and snapped open the remaining vial. He brought it up to the tip of his nose, flaring his nostril and tipping his head back. Other than a joint, he'd never become comfortable with drugs the way Gary had been. He'd seen him do cocaine, meth, ecstasy, GHB, and a whole host of other injectables, sniffables, and smokables. It was like he was trying to see how far he could push his body.

Jim was able to stop his mind from thinking about what he was doing and snorted one really good time. It felt like he'd just shot alcohol up his nose, and he blinked several times, his eyes actually watering.

"Close your eyes. Close your eyes," Gary said. "It's leaking out." Jim clamped his lids shut and rolled his eyeballs left and right in the bath of highly concentrated THC.

At first it didn't feel like anything. Then . . . his skull began to lift off his head. The chewing sound that had accompanied the dark whenever he closed his eyes had company. It was a symphony of groans and chattering teeth, a chorus of tearing skin like thousands of thick wet towels being torn in half over and over and all at once, like marrow-filled bones cracking beneath the muffling wrap of muscle.

Jim thought he felt his heart beat a few times before stopping again. He opened his eyes and saw Gary, but in that moment cared nothing for the man standing before him. He wanted—*needed*—flesh. The air around him was cold and tearing him apart. He had to have the cohesive heat of life to keep him wound together. Jim hugged himself, his fingers foreign claws hanging off the end of his hands.

"I have to eat," he tried to say, but what actually came out didn't sound anything like words.

Gary's eyes rolled open and fastened on him for a moment. "Buhhreeeeeaugh," he said, foam pouring out of his mouth. Jim caught a trail of something on the air. It was sweet and hot at the same time, like an apple pie set out on a windowsill to cool. Jim had never seen such a thing actually done, but it had happened on TV often enough when he was a kid.

He turned in the direction of the bedroom, his body moving on instinct. Gary was close behind. His gait was choppy, shambling from foot to foot like he would fall over at any moment. Both their footsteps were as unpracticed as a toddler's as they bumped their way through the bathroom, into the bedroom, and they bounced off the outer wall, which would have gently lifted up and out of their way if only Gary would hit the button in his pocket.

The smell was even stronger here, though. Two independent smells, one young and particularly sweet, the other older, with the mild bitterness of an illness to it. Jim didn't care; he would take either one. Gary hammered the wall with one hand, and he did the same. A moment later, they had begun an arrhythmic beat that rattled the garage door in its tracks.

Picture frames fell off the wall, and they peeled the paneling away in sections. The cold ache at the center of Jim began to spread and squeeze at the same time. He had to have something—*anything*—to make it stop.

In frustration he turned to Gary and bit him on the shoulder. The taste was awful, more cold that made his mouth hurt. Gary didn't seem to notice, his palms flat on the door as he shook with his whole upper body. They were trapped in here. Jim understood that on a level just functionally above instinct. It pained him to move away from the wall, but he did so in search of another exit. He wandered back through the kitchen and into the TV room. His head swiveled back and forth, and then he saw a door.

He . . . remembered those. Jim made his way over, arms outstretched. He pawed at it, then pushed, then recalled there was something specific he had to do to the door to get it to open. He looked down at a silver handle and let one hand fall to it. His fingers wrapped around it, and he felt a thrill of excitement that this was what he was supposed to do. He pushed it down, then pulled on the door.

Nothing happened.

Jim groaned in frustration and tried again. Nothing.

Slightly above the handle was a *thing*. He didn't know what it was, but he was supposed to do something to that in relation to the handle. One, then the other. Jim slapped at it, and the thing that had been pointing left turned right. He pulled on the handle again, and the door sprang open.

It took a couple of tries for him to figure out that he had to move back from the door to swing it open. Jim stumbled out into the horribly cool air. The smells were stronger now, pulling him toward the house. He heard Gary behind him and realized they could go together. They could eat together. The two of them together. Like always. He wanted that.

Jim paused long enough for Gary to catch up, but his friend stepped on the back of his shoe, and they both went down.

They both began to climb to their feet, which meant climbing over each other, resulting in them not getting anywhere. When they clashed heads, Jim saw stars, and when his eyes stopped rolling, he looked at his friend.

"Gary?" His voice still didn't sound right, and Gary continued trying to climb over him. Jim took a knee to the head before he wrapped an arm over Gary's back and pulled him down. His limbs kept moving even though Jim had him pinned, and he straddled Gary's back.

"Gary. Gary, wake up." He wasn't sure what they had just experienced could have been described as sleep— maybe a drug-induced stupor of some kind—but he had to snap Gary out of it someway.

There was a squirrel not more than two feet away from Gary's face. It was still frozen in front of him, as if its stillness would make it invisible. Jim could still feel the pull of the two warm bodies inside the house and wondered if he could resist what instinct was telling him to do, let alone stop Gary.

Then Gary's groans became muffled, as if he'd stuffed a bag of cotton balls in his mouth. The squirrel had disappeared, and Gary's hands were shoving something brown and red into his mouth.

Jim's sensibilities were still too full for him to be shocked. He still felt the pull of flesh and blood and almost reached for Gary's mouth to get his share too.

It took significant effort merely to sit still as the feeling of reverse nausea passed. Jim kept champing his teeth, wanting to eat the various warm-blooded creatures he could sense nearby. Gradually, his higher senses returned, and he felt placed back in the driver's seat of his own body.

Gary rolled over and sat up. He raised a red-tipped hand to his head and rubbed it over his close-cropped scalp.

"Why do I feel like I've just been licking a dog's asshole?"

Gary was back to himself too, it seemed.

Jim was on his knees, and he slowly turned to look at Gary.

"You ate . . ." he began, "a squirrel."

Gary's eyes bugged out. "Quit shittin'. For real?"

"Yes."

"Damn. I just went vegan three months ago."

Jim made a face. "Really?" It was something else about his friend he didn't know.

"Yeah." Gary began rolling his tongue around in his mouth and spitting. "I gotta get some water to rinse the squirrel hair out of my mouth." He retched, then hacked and managed up a big glob of pinkish-whitish phlegm that he spat into the high grass before rising and starting toward the house.

Jim caught up to him and grabbed his shoulder. "I don't think you—*we*—should go in there."

"Why? What's wrong?"

Jim shook his head, not sure how to say it.

"I'm . . . hungry."

"So, that's good. I can get a glass of water, and you can fry up a burger or something."

"No." Jim squeezed harder. "I think I might eat somebody. Like Mary Ellis or Will. I think you might too."

"What? Hell no. Stop talking crazy."

Gary tried to pull away, but everything turned to slushy slow motion.

"What the hell is this?" Jim said and giggled at how deep his voice had gotten.

"Huh?" Gary asked and giggled too.

"Oh, man. I think we're high."

"High? You sound pretty low."

Jim held up a hand and waved it in front of his face. His fingers left trails before his eyes as images lagged in his vision.

"Let's go back to your place and wait this out."

"Good idea." Gary nodded and went on doing it for way too long. Jim laughed because Gary's eyeballs looked like two long columns in a rectangular face. Gary followed suit, and Jim could only imagine what he saw.

They shambled back to the garage, Gary remembering belatedly to open the garage door once they had bumped into it a few times.

They both marveled as the door slid up and tucked itself away. They were amazed by the bedroom and the mess they had just made, at the sink in the bathroom, at the floor tile, at the grout.

They took turns tracing shapes in the vertical and horizontal lines, both keenly interested in what the other would come up with next.

"Listen, Gary, I want to apologize."

Gary wiped squirrel drool off his chin. "Why should you apologize to me? You were right—if it weren't for me, you wouldn't be involved in any of this. I fucked up. Royally. And if it's the last thing I do—well, I guess it will be—I'm going to make sure you get out of this unscathed."

"No, man. No. This is about more than that, and seriously, let me finish. You've been there for me for a long time. A long time. And you've always had my back. Always. The first time you said something I didn't like, I just threw it all away. I abandoned you, and that, you know, that wasn't cool."

Gary nodded. "You did. You know what? You're a jerk." He barked laughter, and Jim joined in.

"Unscathed," Jim said. "That's a good word." Jim repeated it several times, and Gary joined in, repeating it even more until it lost its meaning.

They lay on the floor, half in, half out of the bathroom, Jim's legs poking into the kitchen, Gary's dangling into the bedroom.

Then they talked.

It felt like Jim hadn't done that in a long time.

Chapter 32

"Okay, so here's what we'll do. They're in the garage, but they left the boy and the woman in the house. We storm the house and grab them, then we send someone to the garage to tell them we have their loved ones hostage." Fyukis was pretty proud of himself for coming up with the plan. They could kill two birds with one stone this way: collect the two men and make them tell where they'd put Mary. He'd pondered this for a significant amount of time and had not been given her location.

"Won't work," Tim said.

Fyukis turned and looked at him in the backseat. The man looked very uncomfortable crammed in back there, which pleased Fyukis to no end. "And why not?"

"We don't know who those two are inside the house. They could be the help. We tell 'em we have hostages, and they come out guns blazin'. 'Sides, we split off in twos, who's gonna do the fightin', and who's gonna do the killin'?"

Fyukis understood what he meant and his deeper meaning. He'd nearly shit himself when the two men began shooting people at the medical examiner's office. Seven were dead according to the news. He was pretty certain that had been a smile on Ed's face as they'd listened. Even though Fyukis was technically not in charge, he still felt a certain amount of leadership had been bestowed upon him simply because of his advanced knowledge of Brother and the Testimony. His opinion should be valued; they should want to take cues from him.

"Then we surround the garage, storm it, and either flush them out or capture them."

"Again," Tim said, "won't work."

"And why *not*?" Fyukis was getting pissed.

"Who's gonna do the stormin'? Who's gonna do the waitin'? Ed and I could infiltrate, but if they get outside before we get 'em . . ."

"I know a few guys we could pay," Ed said.

"Abso*lute*ly not!" Fyukis refused to lower himself and the Adjacent to utilizing hired help. It had been bad enough they hadn't been able to manufacture the Bloom themselves, and look how that had worked out.

"I know," Fiel said, her voice perky as if they hadn't been up all night.

"*What?*"

"Nothing. We don't do anything at all."

"And how does that *help* us?"

"It allows us to reposition. The worst possible thing that could happen is for us to get into some sort of shootout with them, the police are called, and either we or they get arrested. We have to wait for an opportunity when they will be unaware and out in the open."

"Fat chance, that. As soon as they leave that garage, their heads will be on a swivel."

"Sure, they will. That's why we kidnap the woman and the child."

Fyukis's stomach dipped. He'd suggested that only as a means of getting to the two men, and then his idea would have been to let them go. But if Fiel was suggesting it—he'd seen the way she'd looked when those people were being killed. He would have guessed she was enjoying it. He didn't know if he could stomach another person dying on account of the Adjacent.

"I don't want anyone hurt."

Everyone in the compact car looked at him.

"I mean it. We are the chosen few, not savages."

"But what happens to them doesn't matter," Ed said.

Try telling that to my mother. In the seven decades since he'd become Adjacent, Fyukis had assumed his mother would eventually succumb. But she had hung on; she'd sunk her claws into life and held on with a rabid tenacity. She was 112 years old, and even though her body had decayed, she was still as sharp as a fourteen-inch gas concrete saw. He'd been avoiding her for the last twenty years considering he no longer aged. She'd made mention of it and very nearly extricated his deepest secret. She would have wanted to join him, and thankfully, he didn't have the ability to select congregants.

Nothing would have stopped her from pestering him to death.

"I mean it. It isn't necessary. If you cannot promise me now they won't be harmed, I will not allow it. Besides, it's not about them; it's about us. What we stand for."

"Well, we just went through a half dozen bodies to try and get to those two in the garage. I don't care how many people we have to kill, but they won't get away." Ed jabbed a finger toward the house, underscoring exactly who he meant by "they." Tim was looking at him with a blank expression, but Fiel had her head canted to the side like a curious puppy.

She was a weird one. He'd grown to like her less and less over the last few hours; he had found that Mary was the only one he cared for anymore. And she was not here.

"Do we need to put it to a vote?" Fiel asked.

"No." He didn't like it, but he had to accept it for the time being.

"So we wait for them to leave and catch them later," Ed said. "Using the woman and boy as bait."

"But how do you know where they'll go?" Fyukis still wasn't settled with this plan. "Or how to contact them? Like Tim said, they could just be the help; they may not know how to reach them."

"Ed's mother was a maid," Fiel said. "The help always has the emergency contact number."

Fyukis looked at Ed. "Your mother was a maid? You never told me that."

"You never asked about *my* mother." Fyukis heard the stress on "my." Was Ed trying to say Fyukis was self-involved? Fyukis decided not to push; he didn't want to lose the crowd any more than he already had. It was time to get out in front of this thing before he found himself being run over by it.

"So we go with a modified version of *my* plan," he said. "We get the woman and the boy. We keep them *alive* so we have a bargaining chip. We get Gary and Jim to come to an isolated location, we get two more pieces of the Bloom. Maybe we can torture out of them where the rest is." He turned all the way around and faced Fiel. "But like Tim said, if they don't respond to us taking hostages, what then? What's *your* plan to find them since *you* think it's such a great idea to just let them walk away?"

"I can see them. I am the Intercessor," Fiel said with a beaming smile. Fyukis's mouth fell open. The Intercessor was second only to Brother himself. No one would dare to just declare herself as the Intercessor. That was an honor the Adjacent as a whole decided. Fyukis had naturally assumed it was him; he was closest to Brother after the Ancestor had recycled.

"Wh—when?" he stammered.

"Just now." She smiled so widely he could see her back teeth.

She was a liar. He decided right then he was going to kill her.

Chapter 33

"I designed these vests myself," Elias said. The chubby little man was back in his throne, one leg thrown over an arm. "Still a Thrill" by Jody Watley was thumping through the ceiling.

Jim had been surprised to see Gary had suits of his own in his closet. He'd seen him wear exactly one suit, back in their junior year in high school after their principal had been murdered at a dry cleaner's. It hadn't been the chemicals, though; he'd been shot multiple times.

The suit had fit Jim surprisingly well, even with the tightness around his stomach. They'd cinched each other's middles by winding long strips of bedsheets around themselves after pressing and expelling as much gas as they could. Jim wasn't surprised, though, that despite the lack of a pulse and nerve endings that were hit or miss at best, he was uncomfortable.

"What are you wearing, some kind of girdle?" Elias poked at Jim's gut with a pudgy finger. "You got to take care of yourself. You guys are too young to be out of shape." He slapped Jim's tightly packed tummy and smiled at him.

Elias explained the vests in great detail. From the fancy Italian leather and cotton woven together in an intricate design to the minor chutes to either side of the wearer's belt buckle that would discharge palm-size packages of V2 when they pressed an elbow into their sides.

"It's the twenty-first century," Elias said. "You got to go high-tech, or you ain't doin' it right."

Elias had gone into tailor mode, primping and picking at them, making sure they looked ready. He didn't like Gary's shirt and insisted he change it.

Jim and Gary looked at each other. He was wearing a T-shirt underneath, but his wounds had wept some. Ebony, Malachi (formerly known as Snap-snap), and all three dogs had looked on dispassionately, as if it were a foregone conclusion that Gary would take off the shirt.

Jim had no idea what the man's reaction would be, but neither of them was in a position to do anything about it.

Gary protested lamely, all the while taking off his shirt. They had bandaged the bullet holes, but twice the wounds had oozed through as Gary's insides were turning to mush.

But the T-shirt remained clean, thankfully, and Elias hadn't insisted he take it off, although he did make note of Gary's girdle too.

Once they were outfitted with their vests, Elias made one last examination. "You couldn't look better if I'd designed you myself!" he declared. The vests, though trim, were stiff and as heavy as a backpack filled with bricks. As the night went on and they distributed their wares, the vests were supposed to loosen up.

"Hey, what do these tickets look like, Elias?" Gary asked. The chubby little man flashed perfectly white teeth and produced a ticket that had a number on one side and the name "Eddy" on the other.

"Six-digit number, and Eddie is spelled wrong on purpose. Don't worry about frauds; nobody has time enough to make 'em. Everyone gets their tickets at the party."

"Okay." Gary spread his arms, presenting himself before Elias one final time. "How do I look?"

"Passable at best," Kenya said, walking into the kitchen. Jim had completely forgotten about her.

"Hey, are you okay?" he asked, touching her forearm.

She blinked at him as if he'd just appeared out of thin air.

"Of *course* she's okay," Elias said. "What do you think I am, a savage? I sell drugs; I ain't a rapist."

"I guess I just assumed you went home at some point. You've been here the whole time? Doing what?"

She smirked. "Interesting you'd ask. I've been interrogating our friend Mary."

"What else did she say?"

She half winked. "Not so much what she's said, but she told me a whole lot."

Elias jabbed Jim in the side and gave him a sideward glance. "Let me tell you 'bout this one, son. She cold."

Jim looked from her to him and back again.

"I was thinking about what you said about their leader. About how he jumped out the window of a high-rise apartment building, and there was no body on the ground." Kenya took a bunch of loose-leaf papers out of the pocket of the lab coat she was wearing. He wondered if she'd even taken it off in the time she'd been here. She began shuffling through what he guessed were her notes. "At the very least, Fookis—"

"Close enough," Gary said.

"At the very least, he would have been critically injured, unable to get up and walk away under his own power. There's always the chance *someone* could have taken his body before the police got there, but considering the risk, I believe there may have been something more at play here than we were considering."

"Okay, now what that mean?" Elias said. "Because an hour ago you was talkin'—"

"What that means is I conducted a few tests. We already had Mary sedated, and by chance I got the idea to make a small incision on her forearm." Now Kenya was positively beaming.

"And the bitch's arm just healed up. Can you believe that shit?" Elias clapped his hands together. Kenya's face fell. Obviously he'd just stolen her thunder.

"Serious?" Gary asked.

She nodded. "There's more, though. I made several more incisions, each one approximately an inch longer than the last, until the last one was healing even before I finished. And each time, the wound healed faster than before."

"Like muhfuggin' Wolverine!"

"I tried to remove a section of skin, but the incision would always heal faster than I could cut."

"Then the bitch went Medieval 2.0!"

"Elias, I thought we talked about that word."

"What, medieval? I looked it up. I used that shit right, baby."

"Baby?" Gary asked.

Elias looked at him. He made a show of putting his arm around her waist and cinching his body next to hers.

"That's right," Elias said, a sneer on his face. "The lady chose me."

Kenya blushed. "After you left, Elias and I began talking. I realized I recognized him. He went to school with my uncle, and I had a crush on him back when I was eight."

"But you're not eight anymore, and he's old and fat, Gary said.

"Motherfucker!"

"Okay, okay." Gary threw up his hands. "Let's keep it professional, okay? We're just going to distribute some drugs, and you're going to tell us about how you tortured somebody."

Kenya composed herself while Elias went on eyeballing Gary. "As I was saying, or I guess Elias was, I went medieval a little. But it *was* for science."

"What did you do?" Jim asked, praying for this awkward moment to pass.

"I cut off her middle finger with a pair of pruning shears," she said quickly. Her tone was flat, like she just wanted to get it out in the open. "I wanted to see if her body would regenerate another."

"And?" Gary and Jim asked.

She shook her head. Then her smile returned. "But when I put the finger back near the stump, it . . . reattached."

"*Ewwww*," Gary said. Jim agreed.

"I might have been tempted to cut off more, but the idea was a little more gruesome than I was prepared for. No matter what she and her people did."

"So . . . where is she now?" Jim said.

"She died," Elias said. Jim's mouth fell open. "No, it wasn't us, man. Swear. The bitch just—the *lady* just keeled." He shrugged. "We took her off that stuff after Kenya was done, and she was talkin' and everything. She even checked her out."

"She seemed . . . normal," Kenya said.

"Obviously not," Jim said. "She could have been allergic to any of those drugs, or maybe even shock—"

"I'm a doctor. I know what both those things look like. Her vital signs had all returned to normal. She was conversational. Even appeared to be like a new person. She didn't die of anything we put in her. Her heart just . . . stopped."

"Why don't you seem more broken up about this?" Jim asked.

"Man!" Elias said, and Kenya shot him a look. "Sorry, bae. Go 'head."

"Mary dissolved," Kenya said. "You ever see that scene in *Fright Night* when Billy Cole gets shot on the stairs and he turns to goo?"

"Billy?" Gary asked. "You mean the vampire guy's ghoul?"

"I thought that was Jerry," Jim said.

"No. His name was Billy," Kenya said.

"I'm sure you're wrong," Gary said. "Billy Cole was the dude from—"

"*The Last Boy Scout*," Jim added. "Yeah—yeah, the football player with the gun who shot everybody—"

"And then he dropped the ball right at the goal line and said—"

"'Ain't life a bitch!' and blew his brains out!" Elias jumped in. "That shit was *cold*!"

The three men took a moment to chuckle and high-five each other while Kenya stared at them as if she was infinitely disappointed in the male gender of her species.

"Whatever the ghoul's name was," she continued, "he melted after Peter Vincent shot him."

Gary raised a finger. "I don't think—"

Kenya stared at him.

"No—no, you're right. Go 'head."

"That's what Mary did after she died. She turned into goo."

Gary nodded, and Jim shifted from one foot to the other.

"What?"

"I know that's a big thing and all," Gary said, "but it kind of lost all of its oomph after the segue."

Kenya sucked her teeth and rolled her eyes.

"Bae, go on and finish. They need to know," Elias said.

"Do you want to hear the rest?" she said, fixing an eye on Gary and then Jim.

"Yes. I'm sorry," Jim said. "Please."

"My theory," she continued after a long moment, "is that the Adjacent are connected by more than just being a small religious cult. I think there is some sort of metaphysical connection between them."

Gary made a face. "Isn't that a big leap? I mean, you're a scientist. Aren't you supposed to make theories based on facts?"

"Yes, under normal circumstances. But look at what we know. One of their members displayed extraordinary healing capabilities. Then she dies for virtually no reason, and not only that, her body completely decomposes in seconds. Remember when I asked how old she was? She said she was thirty-seven and that she was born in 1943. She was confused, but I don't think she was lying."

"So what do you mean?" Jim asked.

"I think whatever force or presence there is between them kept her alive after she thought she'd died. That it was using her to some unknown end."

"And what, it just discarded her after it was done with her?"

"Exactly."

"So whatever it is, if we take out Fyukis, then we stop it, I'm guessing." Jim crossed his arms.

"It's the simplest answer," Kenya said.

Gary looked bored. "Okay, can we go sell some drugs now?"

Chapter 34

They made it to Midtown by seven thirty. There was still no official location, just a general area where people were expected to mill about until they were texted an address. The city had any number of abandoned buildings in various stages of discomposure, although some were merely boarded up. Jim went through in his mind the areas he would have chosen to put on an event like this. He really was amazed at how Eddie was able to play it so close to the vest a mere few hours before the party began.

Eddie's parties always created a mini–financial boom in the cities where they were held. He also provided elite security so the celebs weren't in danger. Crime didn't increase during the party, the buildings weren't left a mess, and residential complaints were kept to a minimum, so it behooved the cities where they were held to not *not* put a stop to them, but to unofficially look the other way.

Right now there were celebrities from all tiers dressed in designer jeans, wearing jewelry from various gold and diamond importers, whose attire in their entirety was greater than the GDP of more than a dozen third-world nations combined. If Eddie had not also struck deals with the underworld to supply drugs, alcohol, and other contraband, some nefarious organization might have been tempted to rob them once the location had been determined.

But many of these underworld bosses were also on the invite list, and it would have been an embarrassment for them to have been robbed. Crime of opportunity was a bare minimum of a possibility. Crime in the immediate vicinity, if anything, dropped. Someone with a gun or knife would

see security floating around the building like bees around a
hive. And in the rare case that some drive-by shooter upset
with Brad Stone's last movie passed by, the entrance of the
dead-end street had a security detail. Since there was only
one occupied house, they were actually assigned as security
for the house, not the abandoned building where the party
was being held. Eddie had graciously paid for a weekend
stay at a five-star hotel in Bloomfield Hills for the two
residents, so they wouldn't have any guests anyway.

He had been throwing these parties for a decade and
had developed a tight ship.

Jim checked his phone around eight thirty. It was
dark, and they still had not been given the location. Gary
and Jim were in the back of a town car, the driver and his
companion silent in the front. Gary was unusually quiet,
and Jim knew that was because his friend was excited. He
always had reactions opposite to most people in situations.
Even though he had not needed sleep since he had taken
that pill, Jim felt the desire to close his eyes and put his
head back. He didn't dare, knowing something awful
lurked behind his eyes. He didn't know if Elias had put
something extra in that liquid marijuana or if it had reacted
in an unexpected manner to his body's new physical
chemistry, but he was afraid of losing control like that
again.

Gary's cell phone rang.

"No phones when you go in," the driver said.
"You'll have to hand them over."

"It's just my nanny," Gary said. "I'll only be a
moment." Jim wondered for the first time how Gary could

even afford a nanny. That settlement money was long gone, and he wasn't exactly the most employed person Jim knew.

"Hey, Mary Ellis," Gary said. Jim watched as his eyes widened and he sat up. "Gary. Yes." He sat frozen and a moment later began nodding.

"I understand," he said after several minutes of listening.

"What?" Jim asked, and Gary's head slowly rotated in his direction.

"Nothing. Talk about it later." He gave a whimpering smile and faced forward. Jim knew enough to know that it wasn't nothing. Something was wrong with Mary Ellis or Will. Maybe she had had another of those low blood sugar things. Jim wasn't a diabetic, but it didn't take a doctor to see that she had been thrown for a loop.

He wanted to press Gary, but when his friend didn't want to talk about something, it just didn't happen.

Whatever it was, Jim hoped he told him soon.

Chapter 35

"You're a maniac. A maniac." Fyukis threw his hands up in the air. He didn't know how, but somehow Fiel had seized control of the Adjacent, and she was calling all the shots. She had driven them here to Midtown as if of all the places the two men could have gone, *this* was where they'd be. What the hell was here other than hospitals and Whole Foods?

The Adjacent had waited for those two to leave and then gone for the woman and the boy. She had been ready for them, though. Fyukis thought he could catch her with her guard down by appearing at the door alone. He had concocted a full story about how he was a Jehovah's Witness and wanted to talk to her about the kingdom of God. Whether she let him in or not didn't matter; her eyes would be on him, and that's when Tim and Ed could spring out of the bushes and force their way in.

Instead, no sooner had he opened his mouth than she Tasered him. Fyukis went down in a shuddering heap, and she zapped him again. Tim and Ed had to spring to his defense, and Ed had been raked across the eyes. Tim grabbed an arm, and then she'd stabbed him with the needle.

A needle for Chrissake.

Anything could have been in there. Even though they were in a constant state of protection by Brother, that made the notion of getting jabbed with a needle filled with who knew what no less discomforting.

He had seen it in her hand but had been powerless to do anything about it. Tim had appeared, taking up the width of his vision and blocking his view of the woman. Even the massive Tim stumbled back when she'd stabbed him with that needle and plunged its contents into him.

But the two men wrestled her to the ground, dragging her inside, while Fiel stepped over them and into the house. It had taken the two big men several minutes to finally restrain her, both of them being wounded several times in the ensuing scuffle.

Fiel had to get the boy; Fyukis knew that. But there had been something about how she had casually passed him without so much as a backward glance. It burned him that she hadn't even paused to consider helping him. And then she came back.

Fyukis's blood ran cold.

She had the boy with her. He wasn't fighting, wasn't struggling at all. He glanced down at the woman Tim and Ed had pinned to the floor. Fyukis had already crawled in and pushed the door closed, still shaky. Fyukis could have accepted that fear or shock were what kept the boy docile, but the way she was stroking his hair and the side of his face . . .

It had been the same way she'd held that corpse at the medical examiner's office.

He considered calling her a maniac again, but there was no point. They had the woman in the trunk and the boy sitting between Tim and Ed. Tim had been sweating for the last half hour, but had said nothing.

Fyukis wanted to look at the boy. For some reason it was important that he see him, to know the child was all right. Maybe he could disguise his concern, make it seem like he was checking on him for no purpose other than to glean information they could use. Jim and Gary were obviously tenants if they were living in the garage. Perhaps something could be learned from the child of the landlord and his girlfriend—Fyukis supposed she was that. She was very attractive. He'd noticed that, but he wasn't sure Tim and Ed had. The two men had a surprising lack of emotion and were two of the flattest people he had ever met. It was when it came to violence that the two came to life.

He decided to stay put. Why help the so-called Intercessor? The balance of power had obviously shifted away from him. Let her lead for now, and when she failed miserably—he didn't know how, but he was certain he would aid in any way he could—they would see the blunder in trusting one who had not had enough years to live beyond a single generation.

She held up the cell phone they had found in the woman's purse so everyone in the car could see it.

"How do I unlock this cellular device?" she asked.

Fyukis thought that was a weird way to say it.

The boy stayed quiet.

"Remember what I told you." Fiel turned around and stared at him. The boy gave her the code, and she faced forward again. She prodded at the cell, then snarled and tossed it into Fyukis's lap.

"Open that *thing*," she said.

He shook his head, not understanding. Fiel was a twenty-something woman in America. How could she *not* know how to work a cell phone? As old as he was, Fyukis could.

He picked up the cell and used the code. He was about to search through the contacts when he stopped himself.

Let her ask.

She was looking at him. Her eyes rolled to the phone, then back to his eyes.

"Do it," she said. "Do the phone. Talk to them."

Do the phone?

It sounded like something someone his mother's age would have said, except the last time he had seen her, his mother had had a cell phone. And she'd known how to "do it."

"What do you mean?" he asked.

She pointed to the phone.

"That," she said. "Make it work so I can speak with them."

He wasn't expecting her plan to come apart so soon, but he was enjoying this. "Do you want me to make a phone call?" he asked.

"Yes. Make a phone call."

Fyukis realized he had never seen her with a cell phone before. He wasn't even certain if he'd seen her carry a purse. What modern-age woman didn't carry a purse?

"Which number?"

She made a confused face, and he found himself more intrigued than ever. Perhaps along with the responsibilities and powers of being Intercessor, there were some drawbacks. Like autistics who could count a box of dropped toothpicks instantly. Or maybe she had OCD of some kind.

"Boy," she said, "how do we contact the two men who were in the garage?"

"I don't . . ." he stammered.

Fyukis's heart broke a little. This was not what the Adjacent were about, terrorizing children. He twisted in his seat to face the child.

"What's your name, son?" He tried not to pay attention to Tim, who was sweating profusely now.

"W—Will."

"Okay, Will. Nice to meet you. My name is Sebastian." He'd thought better of offering a hand to shake and introducing himself by his last name. He didn't want to come off as too formal. "You know Gary and Jim, right?"

Will nodded.

"Well, we need to talk to them really badly. They have something that belongs to us, and we want to get it back. So why don't you give me a phone number so I can call them?"

"You want to hurt them."

"*I* don't," Fyukis said. "But my friends . . . they're a lot more mad than I am. They may do something harsh if we can't get out property back soon."

"My brother doesn't steal."

"Your brother?" Fyukis raised his eyebrows. He blanked his expression as best he could, not wanting to give the impression the boy had just given a significant piece of information. Whichever one it was, the boy would gladly deliver the other to see his big brother safe.

There weren't many contacts in this phone, and they were all entered by last name. "What's your last name, Will?"

"Tate." He swiped at his nose.

Fyukis smirked and turned back around. He casually thumbed through the contacts until he found Mr. Tate and laughed casually. Had he bothered looking to begin with, it would have been easy to deduce. Tate was the only name that didn't end with a *z* or have a rolling *r* in it.

He hit the name, and the phone called the number. Fyukis handed it back to Fiel and said, "Talk into the bottom part."

She snatched it away and narrowed her eyes at him. He supposed if she really were the Intercessor there would be some sort of reckoning; however, that didn't change the fact she couldn't get to heaven without him, just like he couldn't go without the rest of them.

Speaking of which, if they were getting close to wrapping this whole thing up, they were going to have to find Mary. Maybe Fiel could intercede and divulge her whereabouts.

Fyukis's blood chilled at the notion that she might *and* might not be able to.

"Hello?" Fiel said. "This isn't her. She's in the trunk. Is this Jim, or is this Gary?" That wicked smile spread across her face again. "Good. Is Jim there too? I need you to listen very carefully . . ."

Chapter 36

The driver dropped them at a boarded-up movie theater on West Grand Boulevard. Jim and Gary walked to the door, eyeing the place as if it would fall over at any moment. Across the street there was a gas station that looked on the verge of collapse and a liquor store that was half caved in. Jim didn't know what he was imagining the place would look like, but it wasn't this.

They stood on the sidewalk a moment, looking both ways as if they were about to cross the street. The driver had given them instructions on how to get inside, although it didn't look like such a good idea now. It looked as though they had just been delivered to the site of their future homicides.

"It's either now or never," Gary said and stepped forward. He raised his arm and knocked, double-knocked, then knocked again and stepped back. One of Detroit's finest rounded the corner just then, giving a single chirp of his siren before accelerating and leaving them behind.

By the time the cruiser had disappeared over the horizon line and they had turned back, a man was standing in the open doorway. It was dark behind him, and Jim could only make out parts. He had glasses over a pair of coal-black eyes, a grim line of a mouth, a narrow vertical column of shirt, a long, greasy-looking black beard, and two hands somewhere around the level where Jim's hands would have been if he didn't have them half-raised in the beginning of a defensive posture. The man stood fewer than five feet away, but in there it was so dark. Those physical parts of him could have spread apart and scrambled, eyes going down to where his feet were, mouth turning vertical and disappearing overhead, hands twirling clockwise and counter in a boiling, nefarious, clandestine soup of black.

"Come in," he said with an even, practiced voice, almost as if he'd had an eternity to learn those two words and practice, practice, practice for the day two idiots would walk into his domain and be devoured for troubling him.

Jim was about to say never mind when Gary stepped past him and inside. The man had barely moved, like he was a curtain Gary had parted and passed through, eyes affixed on Jim, waiting for him to follow his friend.

"What the hell?" Jim said, ignoring every ringing alarm in his brain. He wanted to catch up to Gary to find out what the phone call had been, but in the dark he only managed to fumble around and trip over whatever this place was filled with.

Jim followed in the general direction of the sound he heard Gary making. After a minute there came a light ahead that he saw Gary heading toward, and he followed as well. Once they had reached the source, a single, naked bulb hanging from a wire, they met another man, who happened to be made of a complete set of connected parts. He was standing beside a rectangular hole like someone had taken a sledgehammer to a wall—there was no door to be spoken of—and waved them inside.

Jim turned back before they went through. The man who had let them in, the ghost, the wraith, was gone. Hopefully returned to his post, waiting for someone else to knock on his door.

They walked into a smaller room, light coming from around a closed door in the far wall. The room looked like it had been under construction at some point. Drywall had been hung but not taped or painted. Baseboards were still uncovered by carpeting or tile, and fixtures were still waiting for switch covers or lights.

Gary pushed open the door, and they stepped into an alley. They joined a group of several people in various states of dress.

"Drugs, yes?" A bald man in a burgundy vest snapped his fingers at them. He had an earpiece microphone attached to his head and a clipboard pressed to his chest.

Gary nodded, and the man rattled off a series of numbers to no one in particular, and four men dug into giant cardboard boxes and descended on Greg and Jim, stripping off their clothes.

Jim had a brief flash that they would continue, stripping the flesh off their bones like vultures until they were nothing but skeletons.

"Hey, we have to keep the vests," Jim said. "We have to keep the vests!" he shouted to the man with the clipboard.

The man lifted the earpiece from his ear and nodded in their direction. "Let's make that happen!" he said before rushing over to a small cluster of women to resolve some other issue.

"I think we're all service people," Gary said. Jim nodded in agreement. Everyone was either dressed or getting dressed in burgundy vests, black pants or skirts, and white shirts. They were also getting armbands with different colors. There were several burly men with black armbands Jim guessed were for security, and gold armbands were for the women in skirts, who might have been passing out drinks or hors d'oeuvres. The men dressing Jim and Gary put red armbands on them, obviously for nightcaps of a different sort.

Once everyone was dressed and had undergone a final inspection by the bald man, he went over the ground rules and expectations with them. No one was to engage the guests in conversation. If they were asked a question, they could answer. If they were given a tip, they were free to keep it, but they were not to linger as if expecting a tip after they had provided their service. They were not allowed to take pictures or make phone calls. He had no intention of confiscating cell phones, but if any of them were seen even holding one, they would be immediately escorted from the premises and would forfeit their pay.

Finally, a back door opened, and a giant of a man with a black armband wedged through. He pulled out with him a cart filled with nondisclosure agreements attached to clipboards like the bald man held. Everyone formed a line to enter, and the big security guard handed each person a pen and a clipboard to sign his or her name before going into the party, affixing his own signature as witness after they were done.

Jim didn't know what the building had been before, but the interior looked fantastic now. They entered beneath a mezzanine into one gigantic room. The walls were exposed brick in patches throughout under a black, cosmos-looking paint that simultaneously reflected and absorbed light. Paintings from several artists decorated the walls, some well known, some from local artists. Jim knew this from a story he'd seen on an Eddie party covered on *Entertainment Tonight*. No money was exchanged at his parties, and absolutely nothing was for sale, but that didn't mean they weren't profitable for Eddie.

The known artists or their backers paid to have placement at his party. Each painting or sculpture had a QR code people could scan and either be taken to an online auction where the starting bid was an astronomical sum or they could commission to have work done themselves.

The parties weren't just venues to pump money out of celebrities, though. The famous themselves also used them as a means of putting two people in a room who might otherwise not ever have interacted. Since invitations were always in demand, agents would pay Eddie to get on a list for their clients to be invited to the same parties as other celebs. When Jackie Hale had wanted to get a part in a Philip Dochan movie, she brokered it by blowing him in a closet room of an Eddie party. When Legacy Grace wanted to play pro ball in the States again, he blew Arnold Aglet in the back of a limousine in the parking lot of an Eddie party. Writers pitched directors, but the right writers, not assholes who had really cool ideas that would be perfect for a Spielberg or a Soderbergh. Producers plucked relative unknowns from Eddie party attendees, well-to-do underworld types invested in legitimate businesses after making connections at Eddie parties, and old relationships were renewed at Eddie parties. Virtually anything that could happen in the celebrisphere did happen at an Eddie party.

Jim felt giddy when he spotted his first actor. He was from an eighties sitcom Jim couldn't remember the name of. He couldn't remember the actor's name either. He was probably just the type of celebrity who didn't belong here except that he'd been in an action flick with Ryan Gosling, and many thought he'd been snubbed by the Oscars last year.

He was probably here to stoke the flames of his rekindled career. The man was standing with a drink in hand. Apparently there was already waitstaff here, and the group Jim and Gary had come in with was a second wave.

Before he'd realized it, Jim was standing in front of the man, saying, "I think I gotta go!" The man flinched and turned on him.

"I'm sorry?" he said.

Jim realized instantly his mistake. This wasn't that guy. This was that other actor, the one Jim always had thought looked like the one from the eighties sitcom. He'd looked them both up on IMDB to see if they were related and could only find a quote from one of them acknowledging their resemblance.

"You enjoying yourself tonight?" Gary asked, coming up alongside Jim and seizing him by the elbow. He smiled at the actor and nodded.

"Actually, yes," the man said, sliding a ticket out of his sleeve apparently, and holding it low between his index and middle fingers. Gary took two long strides, stepping just past him, and when he turned around, the man took a step in a different direction, away from Jim and Gary as he was putting something in his pocket.

"You gotta be a little bit smooth," Gary said to Jim. "We're not like the rest of the staff; we're expected to make a little casual conversation. Chitchat. People don't want to feel like they're coming up to dealers for drugs. We have to make them feel like it wasn't exactly their idea. Like they were coming up to us for something else entirely."

Jim finally caught up to what had just happened. "You just did it? Just like that, you just did it?"

Gary nodded. "Yeah."

"But how did you know? How did he know?"

"Casual conversation. Pretty much any casual conversation would do, really. I'm a stranger, he's a stranger—what reason would we have to talk to each other otherwise?"

"Ohhhhhh." Jim felt as green as he really was. "So just chitchat?"

"Chitchat." Gary nodded again. "Try not to be too green; be natural, be cool. Don't try to sell the drugs; they'll do that on their own. Just sell conversation. Find something interesting about them—not about a movie or a TV show—and say something about that." He wandered away a few feet and turned back to Jim. "There's a little pocket in the front." He tapped his vest and melted into the sea of famous faces.

Chapter 37

"Who the hell is this guy?" Fyukis said. He was familiar, but Fyukis couldn't place him.

"Mary has cycled," Fiel said. "Into him."

"But that's not how . . ." His voice trailed off. He suddenly couldn't trust his own voice. Everything about the religion he'd been following for more than half a century was being turned on its ear. Things were happening without their usual process and ceremony.

He looked at the new man—bald-headed, Asian, dressed like he'd rummaged through the lost and found at a YMCA. He looked young and old at the same time and had the sallow complexion of a corpse—

Fyukis turned to Fiel, his heart hammering in his chest. "Who *is* this man?" he asked. He could tell by the look in her eyes that she was reading his mind.

"Yes, he was dead until this morning," she said, examining Fyukis with a curious eye. "I gave him life."

"You *what*?" he asked, gesturing with his whole body at the man.

Instead of answering, she smiled wider. "It's time for us to go. You all remember your cues?"

Cues? he thought. *What is she talking about? Are we about to go onstage?*

Fyukis's mind reeled. There was absolutely no precedent for resurrecting the dead in the Testimony. It was almost as if she'd just . . . made it up. Except there the man was, dead but alive.

There was an angry gash at the base of his neck, just above the clavicle, poorly obscured by the collar of his shirt. Fyukis couldn't believe he hadn't seen it before, but then again, he'd never thought to check people he'd seen walking around for mortal wounds.

"What is your name?" he asked the man.

"Steve," Steve said, his eyes pointing down at Fyukis where he sat in the car.

"Steve," Fyukis rolled the name around in his head. It just didn't sit right with him somehow. Probably because he shouldn't *still* be a Steve; he should have just been Steve's *body*.

He shook himself out of his reverie and looked to Tim and Ed. "You two seriously can't be in agreement with this. If Mary is dead, there are rights that must be honored, sacraments that must—"

"Mary is dead," Tim said, dashing his hand through the air. "Which means the Spirit must have cycled into another. The part of her we know, that *we* love, is still with us. So therefore she may never die."

"But how do we know that *this* is her?" Fyukis's voice went high and cracked.

"That isn't Mary," Ed said. "That's Steve."

"You know what I mean!"

"We feel what was in her that is in him now." Ed turned his face upward and spread his arms where he stood on the sidewalk. "Can you not feel Brother's hand in this?"

Fyukis's eyes went wide. The mere suggestion that he could not feel the presence of Brother while this imbecile so boldly claimed that *he* did . . . it was offensive. Even if Fyukis truly felt nothing.

He threw open the door and jumped out, slamming it behind him. "Of course *I* feel him! What took *you* so long? Let's go already!" Fyukis's hands were shaking violently, and he closed his eyes to center himself. He could feel Fiel smiling, gloating, as she lorded her power over him. He couldn't let this stand, but what could he do? Fyukis felt as though he were on a runaway train, headed for a destination he no longer knew.

They left Tim in the car with the boy and the woman in the trunk at the top level of a parking garage about a mile away from this "party" Fiel had told them about. Just another shit crumb atop the growing pile. They had to walk briskly to keep up with the woman, her blonde ponytail bobbing back and forth. Her pale skin practically glowed in the growing dark.

She stopped in front of a dress shop and peered into the darkened space. Before Fyukis could speak, she punched through the glass, which sounded the alarm.

"Be right back," she said to them.

He turned to the others. "She's crazy. I don't know what she is—maybe she is the Intercessor—but we can't just blindly follow her. Ours is a religion of knowledge, not flying-by-the-seat-of-our-pants-made-up-as-we-go-along hooey!"

Ed and Steve just looked at him.

"What is . . . what is wrong with you?" He heard the pleading in his voice, but couldn't help it. Tears sprang to his eyes. The religion he had loved for so many years was being bastardized, and no one was doing anything about it.

He had to kill her. As soon as possible.

Chapter 38

Jim thought he was getting pretty good at this. In less than a half hour, he'd passed out at least a half dozen of the V2 packets and was striking up a pretty good conversation with just about everyone he was rubbing elbows with.

Part of the trick for him was to always have something in his hands—a drink or an hors d'oeuvre so that he didn't look like some loser coming up to people. Tom Sizemore ran into him—literally, headfirst—and began verbally accosting him.

To his credit, the man didn't ask for drugs, and knowing his history from that celebrity rehab show (Jim couldn't remember the name), he felt guilty about considering giving him anything.

"Hey, buddy, how you doin', man?" Sizemore said. He had a drink of some kind in his hand, and Jim didn't want to *believe* he was drunk, but . . . he seized Jim's hand and pulled him into a one-armed black man hug. The guy was strong, a lot stronger than he looked, and his intense, narrow stare seemed to burrow right into Jim like he knew who he was because he'd read it off his soul.

"I'm good, I'm good," Jim said, recovering quickly. "How you doin'?"

"I'm maintained!" Sizemore was speaking a lot more loudly than necessary to be heard above the music. Jim refused to take it as a sign when he heard "White Horse" begin to play again. "I just want to see what Eddie's going to use *that* thing for!"

He wandered away to seize Coleman Young Jr. as Jim looked up at the giant disco ball suspended from the ceiling.

Chapter 39

They arrived at an abandoned movie theater on the Boulevard. Fyukis allowed himself a small smirk. If there were a party in there, then it was the quietest one ever thrown because he couldn't hear a thing.

She was carrying that infernal green dress over her arm and had given the shoes to Ed to carry. He had them hooked on his fingers by the inside of the heels, slung over his shoulder.

They had encountered very few people as they had walked, including a couple of teenagers with bulky jeans, construction boots, and hats that weren't set right on their heads. There were two sets of frail, elderly people who didn't look suited for any environment below seventy degrees, and a tall, bald-headed man with bug eyes.

"Open it for me?" Fiel said to Ed, taking her shoes and handing them to Steve.

For me, Fyukis thought. *She said open it for* me.

He didn't know how far this would go before he'd had as much as he could take.

Ed examined the boarded-up door before wedging his fingers beneath one corner of the particleboard and wrenching it away with two powerful tugs. A ratty door stood behind it, and it was all but destroyed with one kick. He stood aside so she could go ahead of him.

It was dark inside. Not that it mattered much. Fyukis had slipped in right behind her, and it was as if her skin cast off its own, creepy light. He thought about smashing her head open but doubted that he could strike her enough times to kill her before the other two men stopped him.

But he had to do something. She was too much of a liability. She was leading the Adjacent astray. The fact she was leading at all was the biggest problem. They had always been as one mind, always working together in the furtherance of one action—ascension for them all. She seemed to have some other agenda, some other goal that might not include the rest of them.

Fyukis knew coming along had been the right decision. An opportunity would come along for him to stop her. He just had to wait for it.

Chapter 40

Jim sucked at this. He hadn't moved any packets in half an hour. People kept giving him the eye. Tim Meadows had even told him to fuck off. He'd always seemed so nice on TV, and when Jim had sidled up to him and a couple of women, the man had just turned on him and said it.

Jim hadn't even spoken to Meadows yet. It was like the man knew what he was peddling and wanted no part of it. Thinking about it too much made Jim feel bad, and when he crawled in his head, he got quiet. Quiet meant no product being pushed. But then why did he even care about that? These weren't his drugs, and he wasn't getting paid. He was just the dummy who'd agreed to come here because—oh, yeah, his best friend was about to die and had wanted to come to an Eddie party as a last wish. Jim had almost forgotten about that.

He spotted Gary in a cluster of people, talking up a storm. He said something, and they all laughed, including a tall, heavyset blonde who literally pitched her head back and did something Jim could only describe as a guffaw.

They all not-so-discreetly handed him a ticket apiece, and he touched each person—a shoulder, a hand, the back of a neck, two fingers to someone's suprasternal notch (Jim had looked that one up on Google while looking for porn once) before he gave a curt bow and stepped away from them. Several had watched him go, although at least three seemed preoccupied with popping the pills and swallowing them with a sip of Krug Private Cuvée. When a waiter had told him how much a bottle of that stuff cost, he put it down on principle.

Gary had glanced over long enough to give a slight nod before giving Jon Bon Jovi an introductory pat on the back and shaking Jim Leyland's hand. Gary was really in his element, and Jim wondered not for the first time how they could have wound up so different when they had grown up so close.

He was still shaking his head when he spotted her. It was the briefest of glimpses, and his first instinct was that he'd been mistaken. Mel was certainly good-looking enough to fit in here. She was an accountant, though. She couldn't have—oh, wait, she was a government assassin or something like that.

Could she have a target here? Could she be about to kill someone? Shoot him or poison his drink? Or shoot her or poison her drink?

Jim was already walking in the direction he'd seen her go before he'd thought about it. He didn't know how this stuff worked or whatever the hell the justification was, and he was definitely not about to let her kill anybody.

Chapter 41

"Either you're late or you're early." A bald-headed man with glasses and one of those ear speaker things attached to his head glared at them from just inside a doorway. He seemed to have no fear of four complete strangers rummaging through boxes in an alley.

This was a man used to having his orders obeyed.

The petite man folded his arms across his narrow chest and shifted his weight on one leg. From the look on his face, Fyukis guessed the man was waiting on an answer.

"We are late," Fiel said. "Fashionably so."

"Not on my watch you're not." He marched over to them and put his hands on his hips. "Who do you people think you are? Do you not know this is not how an Eddie party is conducted?"

He went on to explain the significance of an Eddie party. How it was more than just a collection of celebrities gathered to have "fun." He did air quotes with his fingers. He explained that there was a definite social economic impact, that it had historical value, that it changed pathways in business, sports, and entertainment in general. Fyukis looked over at Ed, expecting the man to extract a gun and shoot him or just to seize him by the throat and crush his windpipe.

Ed did not move. As far as Fyukis could tell, he hadn't even registered that there was a human being speaking right now.

"The way you speak," Fiel said, stepping forward. She smiled as she grazed the backs of her fingers against the side of the man's face. "Stop."

The man's eyes fluttered. He hit the ground softly, his legs folding underneath him. Fyukis thought he had simply fainted, but he was so still. He watched Fiel staring at his body like she was waiting for something to happen.

Then he opened his eyes and got up.

His demeanor had changed, though. His posture was less rigid, his face slack. His eyes rolled around to each person, finally settling on Fiel.

There was something familiar and utterly alien about him, and a moment later Fyukis realized what it was.

He was dead. Or rather, he had been and had just returned to life. As he turned to look at Steve and then Ed, Fyukis realized this wasn't the first or even the second time he'd seen this.

Ed was dead too. Which meant Tim was too, and that made total sense. With Mary gone as well, that meant he was all alone.

The man moved to the boxes and began digging into them. He pulled out vests, shirts, and pants, handing them out to the three men.

Fiel began stripping off her jeans and shirt. Once again Fyukis stood in shock. He still had the sensibilities of a man of his generation, and a woman taking off her clothes in public, especially in mixed company, set him ill at ease.

He averted his gaze, but not before catching a little more than a glimpse of her body. She was well proportioned, full-hipped, with a firm, round buttocks and full, supple breasts that swayed in their amplitude as she leaned over, taking off one sock, then the other. He found himself peeking as she made a show of stretching her hands toward the night sky and giving a mighty yawn.

She reminded him of the beauties of his day—Ava Gardner, Veronica Lake, Olivia de Havilland. Her skin glowed in the harsh light from the building. Or was it actually glowing? Fyukis would not have been surprised.

He finally cast his glance at her feet, too ashamed of himself to look at her body any longer no matter how beautiful she was. He didn't know why he had never noticed it before; she was attractive, but it had always come off as a reserved kind of beauty.

Fyukis looked at the other two men and saw they still had the same half-blank expressions as before. Were they still in there? Or had they been suffused with something else that allowed them to walk and talk like human beings without actually being one?

Fyukis was finally able to look at her again once she had shimmied into the dress she had stolen. He watched as she plucked and pulled it properly into place, cupping her breasts occasionally until she had teased out a wealth of cleavage.

"Now we may go," she said. Fyukis looked around and counted. With Tim back at the car, there were now six of them.

Chapter 42

"What are you doing here?" Jim asked through gritted teeth.

Mel smiled at him, although she had that just-been-caught expression. "I'm here for the party," she said.

"Bullshit." Dean Rockwell tapped him on the shoulder. Jim looked up at the six-foot-six wide receiver and turned away.

"Ay, man, ay," Rockwell said, shaking his long dreads out of his face. "I know the deal. I got my ticket. Come up off some of that V2."

Jim frowned, pressed his elbow into the side of the vest, and cupped the small packet when it fell into his hand.

"Big fan, big fan," Jim said, pulling him into a one-armed hug. He slipped the packet to the man with their inside hands, deftly taking the ticket and sliding it into his pouch before breaking contact.

"What was that?" Mel asked.

"What was what?"

"Did you just sell drugs to that . . . that footballer?"

"Huh?"

"Drugs. You just gave him drugs, didn't you?"

"What was that?"

"You heard me. Answer my question."

"Come again?"

She growled in frustration and folded her arms, affixing Jim with her harshest stare.

"Is that why you came to this party?"

"Believe it or not, I was given a ticket."

"By who—Gary? I know he's here too, isn't he?"

Jim cocked his head. "Wait a minute. Waiiiiit a minute. Is that why you're here? Have you been following me?"

"I am *not* here for you," Mel said. "I'm here working. I have to . . . assassinate somebody tonight. A very important movie star. I have to shoot him before he makes his next movie."

"Who?" Jim narrowed his eyes at her.

"That's none of your business. Eyes only, top secret stuff."

"Where's your gun, then?"

"On my inner thigh."

"Then go kill him. Right now."

"Maybe I will." She took a couple of steps and whirled on him. "Or maybe not yet. It's a time-sensitive mission. It's very time-specific. I can't kill him before ten o'clock. You know, you . . ." She wagged a finger in his face. "Don't you try to turn this around on me. You're the one selling drugs. And that is illegal."

"And shooting people to death is cool?"

"It is when you do it for the government."

"What are you? CIA? FBI?"

"You're short a letter. Neither of those."

"Hey, man, thanks for comin' out," a man said with dreads pulled into a pony that trailed down his back. They gave each other one up high, and Jim pouched another ticket.

"Boss!" a sixtyish man with a buzzcut said. A woman he could only assume was his wife came along his other side and put her hand in his vest pocket.

"Peace," she said, making a V with her index and middle fingers. Then to his horror, she put her mouth to the base of the V and began licking, her eyes on Mel.

Jim hit both sides of his vest with his elbows. He grabbed the woman's hands and kissed both sets of knuckles. "It is *so* good to *see* you," he said before they moved along.

"Are you selling drugs while I'm talking to you?" Mel asked.

"*No.*"

"My man, did you drop a ticket?" A scrawny man Jim recognized as a music producer pointed, and he looked down. Jim bent, hit his vest again, and stood with another packet tucked between his middle fingers.

"*Thank you*," Jim said and shook his hand.

Mel swatted him. "You stop selling drugs while I'm yelling at you for selling drugs!"

"Bet you don't like being lied to," he said. "Bet it makes you feel stupid. Like you're trying to hang your coat on a hook that was never there, and then it falls in a puddle you didn't see, and that completely bums you out because you just got that coat and it's really boss and it's dry-clean only and the dry cleaner you use isn't really that good anymore and they may or may not be able to get the stain out."

"Can't you just go to another dry cleaner?" she asked.

"That would be so easy for you, wouldn't it? To just leave me there in that puddle while you go off to Royal Clean."

"Wait. If you're the jacket, then who's the dry cleaner?"

"What difference does it make, Mel? You're the customer, and you're always right." He took a step closer. "You're always right."

"Oh my God, Jim!"

"Don't try to change the subj—"

"Jim, your face is leaking!"

"Oh." Jim clapped both hands over his face and turned away. Even though he was facing them, he didn't see Fiel enter the room and the four men who came in behind her.

Chapter 43

"Hey, what's goin' on? Nice to meet you." The man offered Fiel his hand. They shook, and he gave her hand a gentle pump and lingered. "Tom Sizemore. Do I know you?"

In her brief time as a human, Fiel had learned she was attractive by their arbitrary and ever-changing standards. She had not chosen her own form only to have a form. Her gender was obvious; the female of the species was the giver of life. That this man would have "hit" on her, as she had learned this was called, was no surprise. This man standing before her was both intriguing and puzzling. There was something about him as unique as or even more so than the men for which she had come. She allowed him to continue speaking, curious what mild inanity would pour next from his lips.

Fiel didn't focus on the words—rather his tone and body language. He didn't move the way most of the others did. She could see her energy within him, changed somehow.

Finally, she put her hands on either side of his face. Nothing happened.

Well, not nothing. He put his hands on either side of her face too.

"I promise not to get offended if you put your hands on my chest," he said.

"This man is beyond the reaches of death," she said in utter awe.

"It's interesting you should say that," Tom Sizemore said. "There were three times in my life that I shouldda died. I couldn't even begin to tell you how I'm standing here right now. I'd love to tell you all about it over bacon and eggs." He raised his eyebrows. "Know what I'm sayin'?"

"Give me your phone number. I will call you later." Fiel had no intention of calling him or anyone else. Once her plan had come to fruition, no one would be calling anyone. Ever.

She walked away from Tom Sizemore as he was talking. He continued speaking another moment, then wandered off. No one could hold her interest long, no matter how other they were.

She walked into a cluster of muscle-bound men and trailed her index finger across their backs. None of them complained, most of them smiled and looked at her, and a few tried to engage her in conversation.

"Hey, baby, how many tickets for a suck job?" the tallest one said. Fiel cocked her head as if she didn't entirely understand. He wrapped a massive arm around her waist and pulled her in close. "Come on, you don't have to play dumb with T-man." He held up a wad of tickets above his head. "You want this or no?"

"You will do as a fine example." She smiled at him. His contact with her through their clothes was enough. It made the process take longer, which was perfect as realization dawned in his eyes as his lips turned blue.

"A passing of eons, saturating this planet in cosmic energy, to result in *you*." To say she sounded disappointed was an understatement. T-man's eyes bugged out before he slumped, and she caught him. His friends looked at her in surprise, probably because the man was more than a hundred pounds heavier than she.

T-man blinked and stood on his own. He took a step back from her so there was at least two feet between them.

"My apologies, madam." He lowered his eyes to the floor. The rest of his group began mumbling among themselves.

"T, you all right?"

T-man looked at the man who had spoken to him. "My entire life has been a waste. I am going to do something significant with it with the time I have left." He turned away from them and began walking.

"Hey, lady, what did you say to T-man?"

"I told him a secret," Fiel said, turning to him. "Would you like me to whisper it to you?"

Another thing she had learned watching human pair groups was that males tended not to be threatened by their typically smaller and weaker female counterparts. They tended to assume a woman couldn't or wouldn't be able to hurt them, and making an ominous statement such as she just had triggered no alarms for them.

"You would have allowed him to rape me right in the middle of this room, wouldn't you?" Fiel said to the man. He stiffened as life flowed out of him and back in less than a second. She smiled at him as he stepped away. The second was just as arrogant as T-man, and she wrenched him to her, dipping him like they were dancing partners and she was in the lead, pressing her lips to his and consuming the life inside him.

Fiel dropped him to the floor, alive again, and the man curled into a ball and began weeping. The last man took a step back, unsure of what was happening. Before he could turn to run away, she seized him.

"No! Help!" he said, and the people who turned to look either laughed or didn't react at all. Who would have taken seriously a massive man being unwillingly drawn into the grasp of a beautiful woman?

Chapter 44

"I need to find Gary," Jim said.

"So he *is* here?" Mel asked.

"Of course he is. I didn't come here for me. I—"

"You what?"

Jim realized how completely exhausted he was. Suddenly he didn't care anymore about keeping all this secret.

"Gary's dying. He'll probably be dead tomorrow. We took some drugs—"

"You *what*?"

"Hold it." Jim put his hands up. "It's not like that, and between the two of us, you kept the bigger secret. By far." He took a deep breath and wiped at the black goo spilling from his nose. "We went to see a guy Gary knew who was making something called the Bloom for this crazy cult that call themselves the Adjacent. But he double-crossed them or something, and they killed him—I think."

Mel listened silently, nodding, the wrinkle of concern in the center of her forehead deepening with each second. He could tell from the look on her face she wasn't believing him, but he had to get it out anyway.

"We were there when it happened. Gary was shot. But he didn't die exactly. That drug we took, that he made me take, it did something to us. If you don't believe me, here." Jim grabbed her hand and put her index and middle fingers to his throat. Mel looked confused a moment, and then realization dawned on her face.

"Jim, you don't have a pulse."

"I haven't had one for over twenty-four hours. I haven't slept, and I haven't eaten."

"You did eat garbage out of our trash can."

"Yeah, well, you know, that's just snacking."

She accepted it a lot better than he was expecting. He was thinking she would run screaming from him, but she had a we're-going-to-get-you-the-help-you-need interventiony look on her face.

"What happens when you come down from this . . . drug?"

Jim shook his head. "I *should* be fine. It's supposed to just wear off unless I suffer a fatal wound."

"Like Gary?"

He nodded.

"So all I have to do is keep you alive for twenty-four hours, and you'll be fine?"

"Yeah, but what about Gary?"

"We'll make him comfortable. Did the guy who made this Bloom thing leave any notes we could use to help him?"

"Not that we could find."

"In the meantime, we need to get you to a secured location to wait for this to pass."

"What do you mean?"

"If the Bloom is supposed to wear off in a day, then we just play a game of keep-away until they don't have any use for you."

"These people are dangerous, Mel. That's a tall order."

She gave him a look that was both far away and intense. "You don't know me very well."

He looked at her and just couldn't reconcile this beautiful woman with what he had just learned. Could she really be a killer?

A massive hand clamped down on his arm.

"I have him! He's here!"

Jim and Mel looked at the man. Jim was pretty sure he was on the Tigers, but he couldn't place the name.

"What are you doing?" Jim asked. The man continued shouting. Mel got into a stance, hiked her dress to midcalf, and thrust her hand into his solar plexus. A plosive of air escaped his lungs, and he stepped back but held onto Jim's arm. Jim tried to wrench his arm free, and the man grabbed on with his other hand. Mel kicked him in the groin from behind, and he fell to his knees, his hands releasing and cupping his balls.

"He's here!" someone shouted from the other side of the room. "I have him!"

"Gary!" Jim said and started pushing through the crowd in the direction of the voice he'd heard. He didn't know if Mel was behind him, but he couldn't let his friend fight alone.

He stepped on Harper Pearl's foot as he pushed his way through the crowd, and the newsman shouted, "Film at eleven!"

Jim reached a break in the crowd and saw two men holding onto Gary's arms, both pulling him like they were in a tug-of-war.

"For the last damn time," Gary said, struggling against them, "I have nothing but respect for your lifestyle, but I'm not letting either of you suck my dick!" The crowd had given them a ten-foot berth, and Jim was leaping into the fray when he saw *her* come out of the crowd on the other side.

Chapter 45

Fyukis had stuck with Fiel while the other three had surged into the crowd, looking for Jim and Gary. He almost didn't want her to find them. One, because it would mean she wasn't full of shit and actually had some connection to Brother greater than his. And two, because if she were right, then the knowledge he had spent the greater part of his long life absorbing was worthless—rules, laws, and tenets that could just be tossed out the window on a whim. The Adjacent were supposed to be peaceful. They were supposed to simply bide their time until such time came along as they could rejoin Him.

While he hadn't been entirely opposed to violence, he'd wanted to keep it to a minimum. In the last twenty-four hours, he'd been associated with and even witnessed the deaths of many people.

It had to stop.

Fiel was the reason, but could he actually do something about her, he wondered.

"Wait a minute," he said, tapping her shoulder as they came out of the crowd. "What's the point in doing *that* to all these people?"

"So we can be done faster." A massive man appeared with a black armband on. He easily peeled the four men into two groups of two, grabbing and holding two men by their shirts. He looked like a father who was about to punish two disobedient sons. "I thought *you* would appreciate that."

"No. Whatever that is that you keep doing, it's like you're turning people into half zombies."

She looked at him finally. "What do you care about people?"

"This kind of thing isn't in the Testimony. This isn't what Brother teaches us."

"Brother isn't real." Fiel rolled her eyes. She turned back in time to see three more security men come over and grab a man each.

"What do you mean, *Brother isn't real*?" Now he knew she was nuts. Fiel didn't look older than twenty-five. She'd just joined the Adjacent recently. What made her think she could say something so asinine and not think he would call her out on it?

"Because it's true," Fiel said.

Had she just read his mind?

"I don't need to read your mind. I'm responsible for every thought in your head. I allow you to be you."

Fyukis's mouth worked up and down, but he couldn't speak. Didn't have the strength to push words out, even if he could have formed coherent thoughts.

She looked at him again. "Who do you think healed you last night? Brother?" She shook her head. "It was me. *I'm* the one who has filled you with life all these years. You remained young because *I* knew I would have purpose for you."

"No." Fyukis shook his head. "It's because Brother is with me. He is guiding my hand. He didn't let me die because we are so close to joining Him in His Room."

"Oh no," she said, watching as security led the men away. The crowd had begun chanting "Fight! Fight! Fight!"

and groaned when they were gone. A tall blonde with an explosive amount of cleavage was standing nearby, and they began chanting "Tits! Tits! Tits!" "Now I'm going to have to go get them out of some closet. I really wanted everyone to see as I tore them limb from limb."

She sighed, and Fyukis felt something teetering inside him finally tip. This party was why she had waited. She wanted to be seen. They might have been able to get what they were after hours before now, but instead, she had intentionally dragged it out so she could hobnob with the rich and famous.

"You . . . want an *audience*!" Fyukis's voice sounded wrong in his ears, and when he leapt on her, it was as if his body had a will of its own.

She turned around just as his hands latched onto her neck. He began squeezing and fell on top of her. Fyukis couldn't tell if he was speaking or if he was just grunting like an animal as his fingers sank deeper, his thumbs crushing her throat.

"He's choking the *shit* out of her," he heard someone say.

She pounded at his shoulders, which only emboldened him. Fyukis could feel the cords of his arms bulging and his hands going numb as he leaned over her to put his weight on her neck. Fiel's eyes bulged open, and her tongue lolled out of her mouth, flopping around like a fish out of water.

"This looks really real," someone whispered.

"Nah. It's fake. Your eyes don't really bug out that way. That's just on TV. Trust me, I've strangled a few people on my show. It's a nice performance, though."

"*Shhh!*"

Fiel's feet drummed on the floor, and she dug her nails into the backs of his hands, raking up to his wrists over and over.

Fyukis held on a moment longer after she had gone still. He finally stood, looking at her body to make sure she didn't take another breath. He wiped his chin and looked around. Everyone was watching him.

He would go to prison for this. Even if he ran, it couldn't be avoided. There were over a hundred witnesses. But it had been worth it. If he had to wade through another seventy years to put the Adjacent back together, he could do that. Brother would be with him, as He had always been.

Someone began clapping. It started off slow and gradually built, several others joining shortly after until it had risen into full-blown applause. Fyukis was confused. Shouldn't someone have jumped on him? Tackled him and wrestled him to the ground? Where were the other security guards? There had to have been more than four.

Rather than standing there in shock, he chose to make an exit. Fyukis took a bow, still waiting for someone to stop him at any second. When someone began whistling, he chose not to wait around. He turned to head for an exit.

And walked right into Fiel. With fresh bruises rising on her neck, she grabbed him by the hand and forced him into another bow.

Chapter 46

"I need to get in there," Jim said. The massive wall of a man with his arms folded peered down at him. Wherever Eddie found these guys, they sure made them big. The man looked straight ahead again as if he had already forgotten he was there. Jim had to get in there. And since punching the guy would probably have no more effect than a kitten snuggling against his leg, Jim decided to reason with him one more time.

"Please. You just dragged my friend in there. Two guys were attacking him."

Still nothing. The guy didn't even respect him enough to tell Jim to move away.

"Let me try," Mel said, coming up behind him. He turned to her, surprised. She had made her position known regarding his best friend—that she didn't care for him. "Tolerated" was the word she had used. "The sooner we can get him out of there, the sooner I can get you out of here."

On the off chance she knew some official government lingo he would respond to, Jim stepped aside so Mel could speak to the guard.

She dug something out of her little purse and stood on tiptoe to hold it up in his face. His eyes rolled slowly over the ID or whatever it was, and he unfolded his massive arms.

"What can I do for you, ma'am?" His voice was as deep as a bottomless pit.

"I need to take one of the men in there into custody."

He turned his head slightly back, probably as far as it would go, then back and down to her. "Which one?"

"Gary Tate."

"No. Not that one."

"This is official business. I must insist."

"Sorry." He didn't sound like he was sorry. "He's not going anywhere until after Eddie is done with him."

"Eddie?" Jim said. "I know Eddie. I went to high school with him."

The guard smirked like he knew a secret Jim didn't.

"Then how about you let us in?" Mel asked. "When Eddie is done, then we'll go."

"Depends," the guard said.

"On what?"

"On whether or not you pass the test."

Jim couldn't see her face but could tell by Mel's body language she was getting pissed. Her bare shoulders hunched, and she dropped her head. Her feet spread apart, and he could tell she was getting ready to hit the guard. She'd done this very thing before. In hindsight, Jim realized there were signs that she was more than what she had told him.

"Last chance," Mel said. "You're interfering with an official investigation."

"Two things," the man said before refolding his logs for arms. "It is such a cliché when the teeny tiny woman beats up on the big guy in movies. Almost as if she's establishing her bona fides. And the guard is always some dumb lunkhead. In fact, his intelligence is in indirect proportion to his size. You could hit me in the groin or the solar plexus or some other soft, relatively easy target. I could break both your arms and legs and throw you in the middle of Woodward Avenue. Then I could turn into the chiropractor from hell and break every vertebra in your boyfriend's back. Then where would you be?"

Mel's back straightened, and her hands relaxed. She turned so Jim could see her face in profile. He didn't know that look and didn't all the way trust that she wasn't still going to try something.

The guard continued, "I'm not unwilling to allow you to save some face. My job isn't to beat people up. My job is to stop people from getting hurt, which sometimes means I have to hurt other people. I don't like doing that." He sounded like he really meant that last sentence. "Don't make us both do something neither of us wants to do."

"Paper, rock, scissors."

"What?" The guard laughed.

"You heard me," Mel said. "Paper, rock, scissors. I'm getting in that room whether you like it or not, and if you don't want to be forced to do something you don't want to do, then let's hash this out another way. I don't really need the exercise and have already filled my ass-kicking quotient for the week."

The guard laughed again, this time regarding her in a way he hadn't before.

"What's your name?"

"Mel. Yours?"

"Paul. Here's the deal, Mel. You're asking me to put my professional reputation at risk for a children's game. Mel, I think I should get something out of it if I win."

"What do you propose?"

He changed his posture so he was looking at her from a different angle. Even though they were officially broken up, Jim felt the twang of propriety, wanting to tell the man "hands off" after he had taken off his riding gloves and slapped the man briskly across the cheek with them.

"A date," Paul said. He smiled, showing off a complete set of perfectly white choppers all nestled properly in his head without overlapping. "I don't mean one of those dates you do because you're forced to; I mean I show up at your place with flowers, and we go do something enjoyable and get to know one another."

"I'm surprised you weren't more . . . up-front."

He shook his head, and his expression changed as though she'd said something offensive. "I used to play ball. For five years in just about every city I was in, I could get all the attention I wanted. I'll spare you the hairy details, but I was young and I enjoyed myself on *and* off the field. Maybe it's because I've matured, but I like it this way better."

Mel was her own woman entirely now. Even if they had still been together, she wouldn't have tolerated Jim "peeing on her shoes," as she liked to put it. She was a big girl and reserved the right to say no to any man she wished herself.

"Okay. Let's do it." Her fist over her open palm was like a stake pounding through Jim's heart.

They oriented themselves so their hands were less than a foot apart, while their bodies were about three. By their body language, they could just as easily have been pulling the pin on a grenade and about to run in opposite directions. Jim looked from her to him before settling on their hands.

"Best of three, okay?" Mel said. Paul nodded.

They tapped their open palms with the sides of their fists as she counted, "One, two, three—*shoot!*"

The big guy shot paper, and so did Mel. Jim would have guessed he would have shot rock too, and maybe that was what the man had been counting on—being underestimated. But this guy was no hammer, and he didn't see every problem as a nail. He actually thought, and in a thinking game like this, that made Jim worry. But Mel was a fierce competitor and excellent at games of chance. She would win by the skin of her teeth if it came down to it. He just knew she would.

They shot again, and this time she lost, Paul's rock to her scissors. Jim's gut clenched. Just one more, and she was the next Mrs. Paul. The guy was good-looking in a rugged sort of way, bald-headed, with eyebrows that gave character to an otherwise unremarkable face.

The last time they shot, she went paper and he went rock. Paul had tried the old double-down trick, and it hadn't worked.

"That's a tie," Paul said. "Walk away, or double or nothing?"

"Double or nothing?" Mel asked. "What more do you have to offer?"

"Safe passage." Paul grinned. "I know you're not with any alphabet outfit. Maybe you're a something. But not here. Not tonight."

"Maybe I'm an undercover cop."

He shook his head. "No. You don't look like an undercover cop."

She blushed and turned her eyes away. "I think that's kind of the point. What more would you expect?"

"I don't know. A little .22 in your purse, maybe one of those microscopic buds in your ear."

"That's not what I meant. Besides, you wouldn't be able to see either of those things. If you win . . . what do you want?"

She laid a hand against his upper stomach.

"Two dates."

"Two implies you want something. I'm more of a three-plus kind of girl."

"I can accrue enough charm over the course of two dates to get a dividend of a third."

"So do you apply financial terms to all the girls in your love life?"

"Only when it works. You ready?"

Jim was steaming. This was bothering him a lot more than it should have. He'd been nursing a headache for the better part of an hour, and now it was beginning to bloom. He blinked several times as they began to shoot. He couldn't concentrate all of a sudden. He felt weak, like if his knees buckled he would fall and wouldn't have the strength to get up again.

Nausea overcame him. Jim was pretty certain Paul had just won because Mel swore, but in that moment, he didn't care. All Jim wanted was to not throw up.

A thrumming began in his ears, and when he was able to lift his heavy eyes from the floor, they focused on two people, one who looked kind of familiar, the other just like a . . . a . . .

A what?

Something to eat?

Yes!

Jim took a step and almost fell over. The woman was closer, but the man had more . . . meat. Jim was so *hungry*. He had to . . . to . . . eat!

The door opened behind the man.

A slender hand reached up and tapped him on the shoulder. Paul turned, his hand still shooting scissors as he spoke to whoever was behind him.

"Yes, ma'am," he said after a moment and stepped aside, bringing his arm even closer to Jim's mouth. If he'd had functioning salivary glands, he would have been drooling. The woman stepped forward and spoke to another woman, who was much taller.

Jim looked her over, judging if she would be good to eat too. Tall, brown, tight clothes revealing curves and a nice line of cleavage. But the face confused him.

He knew that face.

"Jim, come on!" The shorter woman seized him by the hand and practically yanked him off his feet. He was able to keep his balance and craned his neck to snap at the big man as they passed by.

"If you don't take care of her, someone will," the man said before shutting the door.

Chapter 47

They found Gary handcuffed to a chair along with the two men who'd been attacking him. Gary seemed relatively calm, looking all around the room. The two men were extremely sedate. If not for the steady up and down of their chests, they might have been mistaken for dead.

Whatever Jim had been feeling a moment before had passed for the most part, but it had a lingering effect like a hangover. He needed to get out of here and someplace safe. If this was like what had happened to him and Gary at the garage, then neither one of them was safe to be around people.

Two security guards were still in the room. Mel quickly looked to all four corners of the ceiling, then the floor, then to each person.

She smiled at the one leaning against the lone desk pushed against a wall.

"I'd like to speak to whoever is in charge."

"How do you know it's not me?" one guard asked, his arms folded across his broad chest. He was smacking away at a piece of gum, and the sound set Jim on edge. He needed to reduce his agitation right now.

"Let's just say you don't have the right look." She made a show of looking around again, dismissing him.

"Hey, little lady, maybe you ought to get back to the party."

"Nice comeback," Mel said. "Do you want a round two, or are you going to get the person in charge?"

He smiled, but Jim could tell by the look in his eyes he was angry.

"You can talk to me, and I'll make sure whoever needs to know knows."

"I have this sinking sensation that you suck at the telephone game. If you don't mind, I prefer to just . . . talk directly to the person in charge." And with that Mel turned her back on him, settling a hand on Gary's shoulder.

"You okay?"

"Yeah, I'm good." Gary squirmed in his chair a little. "A little hungry, though."

The guard quickly stood up, raising his hand as if he were about to throw a punch. "Hey, don't you turn your back on me!" He actually didn't get the last three words out because as he extended his arm, Mel whirled on him, grabbing his forearm in both hands and wrenching around so fast Jim wasn't able to follow what she'd done. She kicked the back of his knee, and an instant later the guard was on the floor, gasping for air, and Mel was in a wide-legged stance, hunched over like she was about to give him a curb job.

"Mel!" Jim said, calling her attention.

She gradually looked away, composing herself. "Yes, dear?"

"We need to get out of here. Quickly."

She nodded. "You." She snapped her fingers at the other guard. "Get the boss."

"There's no need," the tall woman said. Jim was surprised. Her voice was very deep. And very familiar too. Shave off a little of the bass, and he would've sworn he was listening to . . .

"Eddie?"

"In the magnificent flesh, handsome." He—*she*—offered her hand to him, held high to be kissed, not shook. Without thinking, Jim took her fingers delicately and applied his sandpaper-dry lips to her well-moisturized fingers. She smelled nice, and it wasn't just the blood-sweetened flesh. "Although you're probably thinking of it as D-I-E, and I assure you, Eddy will last forever."

Jim just looked at Eddy.

"Sweetie, if you're done with that?" She wiggled her hand in his grasp.

"Oh. Yes." Jim let go of her hand. "Eddie? Like Eddie-Eddie?"

She rolled her eyes. "Vince, give us a minute." The other guard headed for the door. "Take the trash out with you?"

"Yes, ma'am." He helped up the other guard, who was still wheezing for air, and they left.

"Tell Paul nobody gets in, mkay?" she said over her shoulder.

After the door shut behind her, she turned a brilliant smile on.

"So, how have you guys *been*?"

"Good," Jim said. "I just made manager at the shop where I work."

"Fascinating." Eddy's eyes went wide, like every word out of his mouth was more interesting than the last. "And you, Gary?"

"I've been running a gay sex chat service for the last couple years."

"Ooo. And how's that going?"

"Paid off the house, and I'm socking away for retirement and my brother's college."

Jim had known about the gay sex chat thing, but he'd just assumed it had fallen off like everything else Gary had done before. It was difficult to believe he was actually having success with that.

"You make the calls yourself?"

"No. Used to. Well, sometimes I do still. Mostly I outsource."

"India?"

"Nah. Accents turn off most horny American males. The wrong accents, at least. I have a call farm in Norway. Slight accent, but just enough to intrigue."

"Mm, I'll have to get your number." She sat and crossed her legs. "As a matter of fact . . ." She reached into her deep cleavage and produced a small black cell phone. She quickly pressed several buttons, and moment later, Jim's, Gary's, and Mel's cell phones chirruped, and Eddy tucked her cell away again.

They all took out their cell phones, and Jim saw that Eddy's number had been added into his contacts. They looked at her in surprise.

"It's an app I have," Eddy said, looking mildly taken aback by the looks on their faces. "Won't be available for another six months, and even then not to the general public."

"Oh," Jim said.

"And what about you, sweet thing?" Eddy made a show of pointing at Mel with a well-manicured index finger. Eddy's hair was a matching shade of unnatural black, shaved down on the sides and back and teased up high on the top.

"I'm in accounting."

"Sweetie, there is nothing about what's going on here that has anything to do with books. I have a team of accountants, and if you were walking around the office, I'd have you fired so some work could get done." Eddy spread her hands and made a wide circle in Mel's direction.

"Um, thanks?"

"Now, what brings you two to my party?"

"Wha . . . what about me?" Nile Lent said, finally roused from his stupor. He was a real-estate broker who had made millions out of working in Birmingham and Bloomfield Hills alone.

"Shut up, Nile. You tried to beat up someone I went to school with. I ought to have you gutted and stuffed with concrete and dropped in the Detroit River." Her posture loosened, and she tossed up her hands. "Where are my manners? Gary, let me get you out of that chair." She stood, crossed the room, cracked open the door, and whispered to Paul again. He handed her a handcuff key, and she took three long strides back to Gary.

When Gary was free, he rubbed his wrists, probably out of instinct rather than actual discomfort.

"Eddy?" Jim said again. It was as if his brain was processing the person before him a hemisphere at a time. This was the person he had gone to high school with. This was also the person who was throwing this party. This was also the person who could get them out of here.

"Eddy," Mel said, "you have to get us out of here. There are some people after us, and they will ruin your party in the worst way if we don't leave as soon as possible."

Eddy folded her arms and cocked an eyebrow. Jim blinked as if seeing her for the first time again.

"You're pretty," he said.

"Well, thank you, darling. You're kind of cute yourself."

"No. I mean you. You're really pretty. You were ugly in high school. I don't mean that as an insult. You . . . blossomed."

"Oh, I . . . I think that's my first front-handed compliment." She laughed nervously, and Jim could tell from the expression on her face that it had been a long time since she had had anyone say something like that to her.

What was going on with his mouth? It wasn't working right; things were coming out of it that he wasn't conscious of. He also made the sudden intuitive leap that Gary and Dr. Kay had met through the gay sex chat line.

"Well, I can't have crashers at my party. I see you two have got the treats for my guests." Eddy produced four tickets. "Mind if I have some?"

Jim looked to Mel, who nodded and twirled her hand as if to say hurry up. He tapped both elbows into the vest and handed over the packets.

"Elias said this is some quality shit. I don't usually, but why the hell not?" Eddy stuffed two of the packets between her ample breasts and ripped open the other two. She poured them out onto the desk and quickly edged up two long lines with one of the packets. Before Jim could think to ask who the extra one was for, she half covered one ear with her hand as if pushing her nonexistent hair aside, bent neatly, and snorted one, then the other.

Eddy stood and closed her eyes, letting them roll around her head like she was in REM sleep. She nodded several times and said, "Mm-hm," as if listening to someone talking on a telephone.

Nobody spoke. Nobody moved.

Finally, she opened her eyes. "These things are best dealt with when the mind is divorced from the moors of sobriety."

"Yeah," Gary said. "I say that all the time."

Eddy bent her head. "Paul, is everything all right out there?"

"No. There's trouble heading this way. The guys are managing it, but it looks like they are on the verge of being overwhelmed."

"This is disappointing." Eddy sighed. "Oh well. No point worrying about it." She picked up her phone, pressed a button, and said, "Call Larry."

She pressed the phone to her ear and put a loose fist to one ample hip. Jim had seen transsexuals before, and they never had hips like that. If he hadn't known otherwise, he would've believed Eddy had been born a woman.

"Anybody got some gum? That shit must've had cocaine in it, and cocaine always puts a sour taste in my mouth," Eddy said.

Mel dug around in her clutch and produced a beaten-up stick of gum.

"Ooo, Doublemint!" Eddy said and popped the whole thing in her mouth, foil and all. Even though the nerve endings in his mouth were on strike, Jim felt sympathetic pains with each chew. He remembered Eddy doing that in high school after lunch every day.

"Hi, Larry!" Eddy smiled big like she was excited to be speaking with him. "Yes. Uh-huh. Right now." Her cell went by the way of the V2 packets. And she looked at everyone in the room.

"Well, as hostess I think it's time I made my appearance officially. Paul will see you out." She turned and grabbed up a long, thin cane resting against the wall. The top half was red, the bottom black.

"I don't think you should go out there," Mel said.

"I can't just abandon my guests. It'll be fine." She spun around, one finger raised. "Trust."

Eddy opened the door and, without looking back again, said, "It was good seeing you guys again. We'll have to meet up again soon and catch up."

Then she was gone.

Except for the two men handcuffed to their chairs, they all just stood around. Gary looked at Jim. Jim looked at Mel. Mel looked at Jim.

"So what exactly are we supposed to do?" Gary asked. "And is this supposed to be a rescue or more hostages?"

The door opened, and Paul half wedged himself inside.

"We should go. Now."

"What's going on out there?"

"Nothing the guys can't keep a lid on until plan B happens."

"Plan B?" Gary asked.

Paul grinned. "Eddy's been putting these parties on for a while now. You don't get as good as she is at it without knowing how to keep people safe. Those wristbands you have on are a kind of biowearable that tracks activity and position."

Gary shrugged as if he didn't understand.

Paul continued, "We already can tell that several of the guests have changed somehow. Heart rate, sweat, body temperature. Plus the fact they're all gathered together." He gestured with all four fingers for them to come on, and they followed him out. Eddy was standing on a small stage elevating her above the crowd. The majority of the people were watching her, but Jim could tell there was a tension flowing through the crowd.

"If I could direct everyone toward the bay at the rear of the building," she said. "We don't just go to the party—we take it with us!"

Jim held on to Mel's hand and Gary held onto his shoulder as Mel held Paul's hand, and they made a beeline toward the front doors.

"Everyone who is unaffected by whatever it is is going to be loaded onto a bus and moved to a secondary location," Paul said. "This will limit reputational loss and maximize the number of people kept safe."

"You sound very practiced," Mel said.

"It's only fun for the attendees. It's how I earn my living."

Chapter 48

Paul changed direction suddenly, almost wrenching Jim's arm out of the socket. They passed by Liam Neeson, who looked very concerned, but that could have just been his normal face. After several more twists and turns, Paul came to a stop.

"We're surrounded," he said, putting a hand to his ear.

"What?" Jim asked. "What do you mean?"

"Weird-looking people." Paul didn't turn around. His big voice naturally boomed over the music. "They all look the same, like there's somebody else behind their eyes."

"What's happening? What's wrong?" Mel asked.

"They're here," Jim said. "The people I told you about. Except there must be more of them because I don't recognize any of these guys." He couldn't read her expression, but he was afraid. There was more than him and Gary to consider. He had Mel, Eddy, and the stars of about a third of the action movies he loved to worry about. If the three of them could get outside and away, he thought everyone might be safe.

"We have to go through them," Jim said. "Right?"

"No. Too much bloodshed. Besides, you might not make it."

"Hold on, let me up there," Gary said, shouldering his way up to the front. He looked really bad. He examined the people staring back at them. Football and baseball players, bankers, mayors. There was a wall of people about two dozen thick.

"Nah. We can make it." He took a step forward.

"Hold it." Jim grabbed him. "Gary, you can't take on all those people by yourself."

"I don't have to beat all of them up. Just enough."

"Shit, why are you trying to play hero now?"

"They have my brother and Mary Ellis," he said. "They were going to try to make me turn on you."

"No."

"I don't want to think about what they've already done to them, but they're not going to win." His voice shook.

"I'm coming with you," Jim said. "We'll fight them together."

"That makes zero sense. It's reckless. They'll take me down eventually. If you come, they'll have us both."

"Tory Green," Jim said. "You could have left me then. It would've been easier for you."

Gary's eyes narrowed.

"Dude, why do you always say I got Tory Green off you? I whacked him with a stick, and he kicked my ass. *You* beat the shit out of him. With your broken leg and all."

"Me? No, it was you—"

"Guys," Paul said, "I don't care who gets into the fray at this point; they're closing ranks."

Gary nodded and charged. Jim wanted to scream for him to wait, but that would've been useless. He ran after him, and Gary dived for the legs of the man closest, who just so happened to be Andrew Ball, a defensive lineman for the Lions. He easily had 150 pounds on Gary, but the sudden attack had caught him off guard, pushing him back a few feet.

By the time the man had begun shaking him off, Jim was coming in with a flying kick to the head. Ball rocked backward but didn't fall, allowing Gary to drive him backward a few more feet. Jim could feel the others crowding around them; he felt hands and arms beginning to encircle him. He threw a haymaker and crushed Dave Coulier's nose to the side of his face. The man stumbled away, and Jeff Daniels filled his empty spot. He tried to throw another punch, but someone caught his arm. He couldn't turn to make out who it was, but Sam Raimi's face swam into view. Jim didn't know if he could punch him even if he'd wanted to. If it had been Ted Raimi, that would've been another story entirely.

He'd lost sight of Gary and knew all hope was lost. Fyukis and his group would take them away and do whatever they'd intended to do, and then it would be all over. Bad guys win. But at least they'd put up a figh—oh hell, this sucked.

Jim was being pushed to the ground. It was especially odd how quiet these guys were. They all had the same dead eyes and expressionless faces, giving him the distinct impression they were puppets being manipulated by someone else.

"Hey! They're beating up the drug dealers!" a British voice said. "Let's get 'em!"

There was an uproar of voices, and a moment later people began peeling off him.

Liam Neeson stared into his eyes and said, "Don't worry, son. You'll sell the rest of your drugs yet."

The two groups began fighting one another, and Jim found himself alone on the floor.

Nothing hurt and everything moved the way it was supposed to, so he got up. Jim had bitten someone and still had the taste of copper in his mouth. He wiped his chin and looked around for Gary. Jim spotted him straddled on top of Uwe Boll, savagely pounding his face.

He finally got up, covered in blood and teeth.

"Well, that's at least one down," Jim said.

"Yeah," Gary said slowly. "Wait, was he one of them?"

Liam Neeson had two men seized by the throat, while Paul was swinging a member of D12 by the leg and arm like a battering ram into a mass of people.

"Let's go!" Mel said, grabbing Jim's hand and tugging him to the door. Paul tossed the man in his arms like dirty clothes, while Neeson began ball kicking somebody else. A white-haired man stood between them and the door.

"Stop," he said, holding out his hands. They kept coming. He held his position until Paul grabbed one of his wrists and yanked, sending the man sprawling several feet behind them.

"It's okay," Paul said. "He's only done commercial work." They all nodded and kept going, pushing through the door to the vestibule.

They were blasted with warm air, and Jim felt like his joints had been lubricated. He felt a hand slip into his. Mel smiled at him, and he smiled back.

"We are going to make it," she said.

"Yeah."

They pushed the doors open to the outside, and Jim's jaw dropped. There had to have been more than thirty people out here. All of them were watching the four of them.

Chapter 49

"Paul," Gary said, "go left?"

The big man nodded, and Gary shoved Jim into him and broke to the right.

"Gary!" Jim shouted as Paul's arms folded over him.

"I love you, man!" Gary shouted as he leapt over a bush.

The crowd seemed momentarily stunned. Paul didn't bother speaking, instead hurling a trash receptacle in their general direction as he turned down a narrow walkway.

"Let me go!" Jim shouted. "I'm not leaving him."

"Keep moving," Mel said. "I'm going to give us a little breathing room."

Jim didn't know what that meant, and he didn't care. This was the first time in a long time that Gary needed him, and he had no intention of not being there for him.

But Paul moved fast. In less than thirty seconds, he was past the rear of the building and leaping a fence. Even in his distress, Jim marveled at how fast he moved, especially carrying an additional 190 pounds.

They ran for another minute before Paul sat him down and said, "You can't help your friend now. But your girl is fighting her ass off to keep you safe. Either you can help too, or you can walk back into their arms."

Jim looked over his shoulder once. Mel was about twenty feet away, her dress hiked up to her knees and her shoes gone. Not far behind her were several people quickly gaining ground.

"Okay." Jim nodded. "But we wait for Mel. They'll try to grab her to get to me."

"You get a head start. I don't think she's going to be a problem."

Jim turned and saw she was full-on sprinting in their direction. There was a man in an all-black suit with a build like a track runner who was gobbling up the space between her and him. Jim picked up a rock and fastballed it, peening it off the man's head. His feet kept moving even though it was obvious he was unconscious as he slumped to the ground, his legs scissoring him in a semicircle before coming to a stop. The rest weren't far behind, most trampling the man as they came on.

The three of them ran together, Paul bringing up the rear, tossing things randomly behind them. At some point they must have turned west because they wound up on Woodward. Traffic was much lighter at this time of night but still steady enough that they couldn't count on not being run over if they haphazardly crossed the intersection.

"We need to cross as many streets as possible," Paul said, charging into traffic. A yellow Volkswagen Beetle immediately clipped him, and he went into the air, seemingly hovering and somersaulting at the same time before coming down in a heap. The driver's brake lights flashed on a moment before he continued his run of the red light.

"Damn!" He rolled around on the ground in agony. Mel bent by his side. "No—no. Keep going. They don't want me; they want him, right?" She nodded. "Then get him somewhere safe." He gritted his teeth, holding one leg. He got up on the other and crawled the rest of the way across.

"There's a police ministation not far from here. Head to the hospital." Paul changed direction, grunting as he crawled. Jim and Mel looked at one another and continued running down the Boulevard. This section of Midtown had tall buildings that they might have been able to get lost in if they were open.

Jim chanced a look over his shoulder and saw no one. At least not a throng of people. His cell phone rang. He ignored it as they crossed the section of the Boulevard that bridged the Lodge Freeway and saw Henry Ford Hospital on their right.

"I need to stop," Mel said. She doubled over and gasped for air, and Jim watched her. He could have kept running; he wasn't winded at all.

"Oh, that's right," he said, "I'm dead."

"What?" Mel asked, still catching her breath.

"Let's walk." Jim took her by the arm, glancing behind them again. His mind went back to Gary and one of the last things they'd talked about. He didn't remember beating Tory Green; that had been Gary. Tory had broken Jim's leg, and then Gary had been there, saving him.

But then why could he remember the feel of a branch in his tightly clenched fists?

"I have to find Gary," Jim said.

"You have to get someplace safe. Somewhere they can't find you."

"I don't know if that is possible. They found us somehow at the party. And there are even more of them now."

"I found you at the party. I'd been following you."

"Yeah, but they wouldn't just follow. They've been trying to catch us. I think . . . I think they can see us."

"You sound crazy."

"Yeah. *That's* the crazy-sounding part of all this."

His cell rang again. Jim knew who it was and stopped walking. He took his cell out and saw "Gary" on the display.

"We don't have time for a call," Mel said.

He swiped his phone to answer and put the cell to his ear.

"I was beginning to think you didn't like me," a woman said.

"Who is it?" Mel asked, tugging on his arm to keep him moving.

"Where are you?"

"You've been content to drag this out so far. Don't rush."

"You have Gary, right? Otherwise I'm hanging up."

"You really don't like to let a girl have her fun. Yes, I have him."

Jim noticed she said "I" instead of "we." The mass of people that had been chasing them minutes ago had certainly seemed like a group effort.

"And he's alive?"

"Not alive, but you know."

"What do you want?"

"A matching set."

"Where?"

"Home. And bring the rest of those party favors."

Before he could speak again, the line went dead. Jim looked at Mel.

"No way," she said. "No way you're going to just walk back into their hands."

"I have to. They have Gary, and I can't abandon him."

"What are you going to do? How are you going to save him? There were too many of them, and Jim, you're not a fighter."

"I'm not a lot of things. It's time I started."

He turned to go, and she said, "I'm coming with you."

"You still haven't gotten your wind back. I don't want you coming. I couldn't stand it if they got you too."

She set her face into one of her displeased configurations. Jim was surprised to feel it still bothered him, but not as much as it once had.

He took a step back from her.

"Wait!" She ran up to him and threw her arms around his neck. "I love you, James. I know I fucked up, really stepped in it big-time and smushed my foot around. But loving you wasn't—isn't part of an assignment." She pushed back from him and held his face in her hands. "I would kill all of them for you. I mean that."

He could see the seriousness in her eyes. Jim nodded.

"Let me walk you to the hospital. You can find a phone or something and call a cab." He realized she probably had her cell phone, but it was a means of leaving her without feeling too guilty. They walked quickly, and when they were at the entrance, she hugged him again.

"Be careful."

"I will. If there's any way out of this, if there's any way for me to get away with Gary, I won't hesitate."

Mel nodded and stepped closer to the entrance doors until they slid open.

"I love you, Melanie."

A tall, rotund guard stepped out, his thumbs hooked into his straining belt. Jim didn't wait, sprinting off back the way he had come. He could feel Mel staring at him. It was the easiest and most difficult thing he had ever done.

So she wanted the drugs. Jim knew someone else who would be interested in getting his hands on them too.

Chapter 50

"So, what's the plan?"

Gary had tried playing it cool, but that cute blonde had just gone on staring at him for a really long time. He had been around his share of weirdoes, and this one had finally taken the cake.

Hot chicks were never supposed to be weird. Maybe dumb, odd, or perhaps a little racist, but strange? She was his first.

So rather than just squirming in his chair for who knew how much longer, he figured he'd just flat-out ask what the game plan was. The bad guys always liked to tell their plans, and that was how the hero unraveled them.

He had thought that Mucous guy was the leader. It was obvious now that Gary was looking at her.

"You don't have to wait until everybody gets back to give me a blow job." Gary regretted saying that. The last thing you wanted was the weirdo chick on your knob. His stomach groaned. He hadn't eaten since that squirrel Jim had told him he'd had.

"You guys making a food run? I could use a Double Quarter Pounder right now."

Still nothing. She wasn't even blinking. *Damn.* Maybe she wasn't the leader.

Gary decided. If she was going to do her catatonic thing, let her. He'd escape right in front of her. He gave the zip ties around his wrists a preliminary tug. They weren't on too tight. He could get them up to the base of his thumbs. He went for it and pulled hard.

There was no pain, and perhaps that allowed him to pull longer than he otherwise would have, but it just *felt* like he was hurting himself. Gary stopped and looked at the woman. She still hadn't budged. If she wasn't going to try to stop him, he thought he might as well really try to escape.

"Okay," he said. "Here goes. I'm really gonna bust out this time. Maybe I'll take off your clothes and ravage you after. Only if you beg me, though."

He didn't know what her story was, but he wasn't going to sit around and wait for someone to explain it to him. Gary took a deep breath, steeling himself. He didn't want to do this—it went against human nature—but he had no choice.

Gary closed his eyes but yanked on the restraint even harder than last time. At first nothing happened, and then a moment later there was a snap in his left hand and then another in his right. There was no pain, and Gary found that not feeling the pain was as awesome as he'd originally thought it would be.

His hands slid out easily, and when he looked at them, his thumbs looked way too long. He flexed all his fingers and was shocked as they snapped back in place. Hm, maybe this total lack of pain thing wasn't so bad.

He looked at the woman again. She still hadn't moved. Gary was almost concerned. She was the bad guy. Bad guys weren't supposed to just let the good guys walk out. The metal chair he'd been strapped in was bolted to the floor, which had prevented him from just standing up and waddling away, so he still had the problem of his ankles being zip-tied to the legs of the chair.

"I don't suppose you have a knife or a pair of scissors?"

She didn't move.

He tried lifting one of his legs to see how much play the chair gave. It wiggled very slightly. Maybe he could work it loose. Well, there was no time like the present.

Gary began lifting one foot, then the other, pulling the restraints as hard as possible and rocking the whole thing left and right. Since his legs didn't tire, he figured it couldn't hurt to go as fast as possible.

After a few minutes, the screws began to whine as they gave, and then came a metallic *plink* as the front legs of the chair came free. The back legs were still bolted, and he realized he'd just gotten through a half dozen problems and had six more to go.

Then he noticed a seventh. Probably.

The woman hadn't moved, so far as distance, but her mouth had opened. Her eyes were still aimed straight ahead, and she was stiff as a mannequin, and yes, Gary could definitely see a perfect set of all-white teeth. He didn't want to wait around to see what that was going to mean for him, and he sat back in the chair.

Gary pitched himself backward, and the chair legs screeched before tearing free from their moorings. As he picked himself up off the floor, he realized he could have slipped his feet off the legs of the chair had he just shimmied off it.

He looked at the woman again and saw her mouth was open even wider. He took a couple of steps to the left so he was out of her direct line of sight. Maybe a missile was about to shoot out of her mouth; maybe it wasn't. Gary figured he was safe either way.

Now to figure out how to get out of this room. He figured it was about twelve by fourteen. The woman was standing in front of the only door, and there were no windows. She had come in and closed the door behind her right before opening all the packets of V2 he'd had and downing the contents. Gary guessed it was some variation of a speedball with pepper or something thrown in and had been planning on taking one for himself at the end of the night. He figured Elias would be so ecstatic about what he'd earned that he would be forgiving about being one short. Besides, Gary was about to die anyway.

Thinking about that bummed him out. Not that Gary was afraid to die. No, he'd taken ill really bad when he was in high school and had almost died then. Gary had wound up losing about a dozen feet of large intestine. He had reconciled himself to the absolute fact of death and had been totally clearheaded about life ever since.

That was why he wasn't scared now. At least for himself. Gary was worried about the people around him. His little brother, Mary Ellis, Jim, and even his father. The old man just didn't know how to handle things, and money flowed through his hands like water. Once Gary was gone, his business would fall apart, which meant no income, which meant they would lose the house. Sure, it was paid for, but there were things like taxes and utilities that he had taken over from his father because he would always "forget."

He had to make sure Jim survived this whole mess. Jim had always been dependable, and he would make sure his brother was taken care of. Jim would've thought of things like setting up trust accounts, a will, or a college savings plan. Gary was just no good with that sort of stuff.

He pulled in a deep breath and let it go. Gary figured he was going to have to get past this woman. It was odd, but she was the first hot chick he didn't want to lay a hand on.

Her mouth was halfway open now. Gary didn't know what this particular endgame was, and he didn't like that he was the only other living thing in this room. Well, kinda. She was either getting ready to drop some heavy knowledge on him or start eating, and he had the sensation she'd said everything she was going to.

"Now or never, right?" He quickly walked over to her, thought about it, and went back for the chair. Gary picked it up and approached her like a lion tamer without the whip. Should he poke her with it? Maybe smash her over the head? Coming into direct physical contact with her seemed like a bad idea.

He finally settled on working the legs around either side of her body and pushing the bottom of the seat against her chest. Then Gary pushed the chair to the side, intending to make her step out of his way. At first she didn't budge, but then she took one step and then a second.

When he had finally moved her about five feet from the door, he figured he had enough space and set the chair down. Then he turned to the door and saw there was no knob.

"Shit," he said. If there was no knob, that meant they were holding him in here until they let him out. Obviously, this woman was supposed to be doing something to or with him. They hadn't planned on him escaping, though. Or her overdosing and turning into a zombie.

He wasn't about to give up yet. Just because there wasn't a knob didn't mean the door couldn't be opened. Maybe there was a secret knock code or something to let someone outside know she was done with him. They had some sort of process to extract the Bloom from his body or thought they did, and maybe that was what she was supposed to have been doing in here with him. Since he had no idea if there was a knock or what it would have been, he had to figure something else to get out of here. Gary put his ear to the door and listened. He couldn't hear anything on the other side, but that could easily have been because the door was solid and the room soundproof. You built a room with no windows and no doorknob on the door for a reason.

Maybe he could pry it open. It occurred to him that he hadn't used his card yet. He dug his wallet out of his pocket and fished it out. This baby could pick several types of locks. It had to work.

Gary slid the card between the door and the frame, sliding it around where he guessed the jamb should have been. The card didn't catch on anything, and since there was no knob, he figured the latch could just as easily been at the top or bottom of the door. He went all the way up and all the way down with the card, and still it didn't hit anything.

"What kind of door is this?" he said aloud. He was no door expert, but he didn't figure there could be anything too complex about it. On the off chance it wasn't locked at all, Gary pushed at the door, and it didn't budge.

Okay, what next?

Gary put his hands on his hips, looking at the door, and took a step back. He thought he felt something behind him and looked.

The woman was standing right behind him, her eyes wide, her mouth all the way open.

Gary screamed and leapt toward the door, pinning his back against it. The woman's eyes were still dilated, and she appeared to be stiff, even though she had to have moved almost halfway across the room to get to him. She reminded him of Chocolate Chip Charlie from the movie *The Stuff.*

"Oh, I've seen things," Garrett Morris had said before opening his mouth wider than any human mouth should have been capable of. A couple of cutaway shots later, and his whole jaw had torn off before a thousand gallons of white goo had tried to consume Andrea Marcovicci. Thankfully, Paul Sorvino had been there with soldiers who just happened to have had a flamethrower with them.

Gary didn't see any indication that white goo was about to shoot out of this woman's mouth.

He slowly stood up straight, composing himself. He turned the woman to the side so her open mouth wasn't aimed at him. Maybe she wasn't going to eat him, but after all the drugs she'd taken, the odds were good she would vomit soon.

Gary looked at her again. If he couldn't open the door, maybe he could make them let him out. He smeared his hands down his shirt, wiping off imaginary sweat. He didn't want to touch her—she still creeped him out—but it had to be done.

Gary stepped behind her, wrapped his arm around her neck, and placed his other hand atop her head.

Chapter 51

"Okay! Whoever is out there, you better let me out now. I have your . . . your person here, and I'll break her neck if you don't let me go." He listened a moment and didn't hear anything. This room could easily have been soundproofed—Gary had no way of telling. "You hear me out there? I mean it!"

He stood still, waiting simply because he had nothing better to do. The woman's body was soft and pliant, except for her neck and face; those muscles were bulging and hard.

Gary was really starting to worry about her. Had she had a stroke?

There was some sound from outside the door, then metal scratching on metal as someone began unlocking the door.

It swung inward, and he realized he hadn't tried the hinges. Gary mentally kicked himself and dismissed it because he had to focus on the next few minutes.

One man stepped in. Gary didn't recognize him but felt as though he should have. He was tall, classically handsome, with a long, straight nose, full lips, and sea-green eyes. His blond hair was cut short and trailed into a stubbly beard of the same length.

He stopped in the center of the room and put his hands behind his back. His black suit would have been perfect except for the lapel, which had been ripped to the shoulder.

Gary had unintentionally backed up to the wall. He readjusted his grip on the woman's neck, pulling her head at an angle to make his point.

"I mean it. I want out of here, and I want my brother too."

"Don't worry; it will all be over soon." The man's voice was a rich tenor, and Gary realized he did recognize him.

"Hey, don't you do gay porn?"

He couldn't help needling people—even at the most inopportune moments, like now. But it had somewhat of an effect. The man's perfect smile slipped a moment, and a crease of anger folded his brow.

"I am Dovesilk. I'm a singer. Have you not heard of me?"

"No. Sorry."

The man frowned, turned around, and left. A second later someone else came in the room. The man was chiseled and towering; even in his custom tailored suit, his muscles bulged, threatening to explode out of his clothing with one miscalculated flex.

Arson Speight had been in just about every action movie for the last twenty years. He'd blasted more aliens, eviscerated more underground mutants, decapitated more terrorists, and convicted more greedy investment bankers than anyone. Gary definitely knew who this was.

"So, are you here to break me out or what?"

"It's not so simple as that," the six-foot-eight-inch-tall man said. "We have no problem letting you go. After you give us the Bloom."

"Aw, shit. You too? I have to say I'm disappointed."

"Then you won't be disappointed for long. You won't be anything in a short amount of time."

"So you guys are going to kill me?"

Arson smirked. "What we are going to do isn't so direct as that. Killing you is . . . superfluous."

Gary had never heard his hero use a word like that in any of his movies. "What's that mean?"

Arson laced his massive hands together, twiddling his thumbs. "Unnecessary," he said.

"Oh. Then why didn't you just say that? I hate when people use big words just because they know big words."

"Technically, 'unnecessary' is a bigger word then 'superfluous.' The former has five syllables, the latter four."

Gary's geek boner was totally being destroyed. He rolled his eyes.

"What's wrong with you? Why are you talking like that?"

Arson sighed. "Is it always your response to waste time? Must you dally even in the face of entropy?"

"All right, I think I got most of that." Gary chewed his upper lip a moment. "You're saying the world is about to end?"

"No. I'm not saying that at all. Only life is about to end. Everything else remains."

"Whose life?"

Arson spread both his hands. "All life."

"What! Are you cool with that? Unless I'm mistaken, you're a card-carrying member of the living."

"I am. And I have recognized my folly. Excuse me, my mistake."

"Your mistake? What do you mean, like you're a mistake being alive?"

"Essentially, yes. Life, particularly the sliver of it we understand, was never meant to be. The person you have in a chokehold there is the epicenter of all life."

"So she's supposed to be Eve?"

"You're thinking is too small. *All* life."

Gary thought about that. "So like dogs and cats too?"

"Go bigger."

"Wolves and lions?"

"Think about living things that don't have a heartbeat."

"Trees?" Gary said after a moment.

"If it is alive, then it is due to her."

"Evan Carson who ate his boogers in fifth grade?"

Arson nodded.

"My pet turtle?"

Again, he nodded.

"Water bears?"

"I don't know what those are, but if they are alive, then yes."

"My second-grade teacher, Mrs. Malfroid?"

"*Yes.* Would you like to move on now?"

"It's cool, it's cool. I'm just trying to understand. One last question?"

Arson rolled his eyes. "Go ahead."

"I know he's dead now, but what about Burl Ives?"

Arson's expression went dark. "*No*. Not *him*. Accursed creature!"

Gary smirked and nodded. "That's what I've been saying. He was supposed to be so beloved. I knew there was something off about that guy. You can ask Jim. I always said so."

They stood in silence a moment. Gary looked into the doorway. He could hear people out there, but they stayed out of sight. His hopes of getting out of here were dwindling by the second.

"So, where do we go from here?"

The big man's expression brightened again. "You have options here. This close to Fiel's ascent, we have chosen a more . . . enlightened means of accomplishing our goal."

"Your goal is to kill everybody. Including yourselves. Don't you know suicide is a sin?"

"No. We are simply assisting in returning property to its rightful owner. Suicide and sin are both man-made concepts. They hold no validity here. Especially not now."

"Are you trying to say God is made up?"

"No. I'm simply saying we have no concept of him. In the entirety of our existence, we have never met him. We have her."

"What's all this 'we' business? I thought you said this life creature is her?"

"We are her. She is us."

"Because we're imbued with her . . . life force?"

"Yes, but I'm not talking about you or what you're assuming. The life you were given was stolen. That has manifested itself in you as free will, as you would describe it. She gifted us with life anew, making us a part of her in a much more intimate way."

"So you're saying you've been reborn?"

"Your words, not mine."

Gary narrowed his eyes but held his rebuke in check.

"Where's that other guy? The leader. Mucous-something."

"Fyukis?"

"Yeah. Him. Bring him in here."

Arson shrugged his blocklike shoulders. "As you wish." He about-faced and left.

Several minutes later, two men escorted a bedraggled-looking man to the doorway. He was old and withered, his back as straight as the letter Q. They let go of his arms, and one man gave him a light shove, propelling him into the room.

Chapter 52

The old man shuffled his feet quickly, yet somehow managed an agonizingly slow pace. His arms were bent at the elbows as if they were still being held by his escorts. His head was down, his eyes aimed at some indistinct point in front of him.

Gary didn't think this was a trap, but he still wasn't chancing it. "That's far enough right there, old man."

The other man shuffled a few more steps, then halted. His mouth began working up and down, and Gary listened but couldn't hear him speak. He noticed the old man had no teeth; his mouth was wrinkled and folded in like a rolled-up sock.

"Who are you?" Gary asked. "I asked for the leader, that Fyukis guy. Where is he?"

The old man cleared his throat several times, making a pronounced effort to straighten his back somewhat, and faced Gary directly. "You're looking at him."

Gary didn't recognize this person by the way he looked; however, the voice was like that of the Fyukis guy.

"I swear if you guys don't stop screwing with me—"

"Go ahead. Break her neck. I wish you all the luck in the world." The old man sighed, then drew in air, his breath hitching as he inhaled. "I doubt it will work, though. I thought I'd choked her to death a few hours ago. She all but laughed in my face."

"What the hell happened to you? How did you get so *old*?"

"I suspect when I began to reject her, she began to withdraw her protection of me. She didn't make me old; I am old. I'm one hundred and ten years old. But her energy, her power—*her whatever*—kept me young. All these years . . ." The old man shook his head. "I thought I was strong in the Knowledge. I knew Brother was with me." He sounded angry—lied to. He finally raised his eyes to meet Gary's. Both were filmed over with cataracts. "I was a Christian once. I don't know if it even matters anymore, but would you pray with me?"

"Is this another game?" Gary was always suspicious of people who suddenly turned their lives over to Jesus after they had done their dirt. He had no intention of being this man's get-out-of-hell-free card.

"I suppose it doesn't matter." The old man sighed and waved a hand as if flicking something off. "Wherever I go after this, I deserve it, right?" His head sank down again as if the effort to keep it upright had been too much. "You should let her go." He sounded like a little puff of air had been let out of him.

"Uh-uh. She's the only thing keeping the rest of you away from me."

"No, she's not. Her proximity to you is helping to draw the Bloom from your body. The two are attracted to each other."

"What?" Gary had noticed his skin had started feeling prickly over the last few minutes. He removed his hand from the top of her head and almost screamed when he looked. His hand appeared to have a hundred inch-long pins pushing their way out of his skin all the way up to his wrist, where it disappeared up his suit jacket sleeve. "What the hell is this?"

"Everything in the Testimony states that the Bloom is poison to those who are not meant to ascend." Fyukis was looking up at him again and appeared to have a slight smirk on his face. "I suspect once it is pulled out of you, you really will die." He stretched a withered arm out to his side and brought it in swiftly, slapping the catatonic woman. Then he spat on her and was in the process of balling up his fist when three men hurriedly entered the room and grabbed him. They dragged him away as he screamed and struggled as much as his feeble body would allow.

Arson stood in the doorway again. "Are you ready now?"

"No." Gary let the woman go and shoved her. "Dammit." The front side of him felt tingly, and he imagined more pinpricks reaching for her.

"You may like to know that your friend is here."

"My friend?" Gary's mind raced. Not Jim, no! He had the Bloom in him too. If she got it from the both of them, then it was all over for everybody.

He kept his expression confused. The woman was about midway between them. Gary quickly stepped up behind her again, grasped either side of her head in his hands, and *wrenched* it side to side.

Arson smiled, watching as she fell.

Chapter 53

Getting Elias and crew to come pick him up wasn't a problem. Convincing them not to kill him on the spot was.

"*Motherfucker*," the little man said, the long barrel of some sort of rifle or shotgun sliding out of the rear window to train on Jim. Elias added his own .22, looking large, and his tiny hand. It looked impressive in his hand, or maybe that was because he was aiming it at Jim's head, along with three other men with shotguns. "Gimme two good reasons I shouldn't cap yo ass right now."

"Because I have all my tickets for the drugs I sold." Jim put his hands up on instinct.

"And number-motherfuckin' two?"

"Because you can get the rest from the people who took Gary."

Elias narrowed his eyes. "How do I know you ain't pullin' some shit?"

"Because if I were pulling some shit, I would've wanted as big of a head start as possible; I definitely wouldn't have called and told you exactly where I was."

"Oh." Elias withdrew his gun and looked around at the other men in the SUV. "That shit sound pretty reasonable, don't y'all think?"

"Yeah, boss. I could believe that."

"Rhetorical fuckin' question!" Elias tapped the man who had spoken on the head with the butt of his little gun. The man winced and turned back to Jim, lacing one arm over the other as they dangled out the window. "So it's 'if I were,' not 'if I was'? That shit don't sound right."

Jim thought about his grade-school English. "It's subjunctive." He couldn't remember what "subjunctive" meant, though.

"Right—right—riiiiight. That shit subjunctive."

They stared at Jim for a long moment.

"Don't just stand there lookin' stupid and shit. We gotta go get my boy. Get the fuck in!"

They took off once Jim gave them an address. He'd assumed that by "home" Fiel had meant Gary's home. It was the one place that was reasonable for them to both know about.

They rode in silence save for Elias's occasional muttered threats of what he was going to do to the people who had dared to steal from him. Jim had seen enough of his ruthless side not to doubt that he could and would do everything he was saying.

Jim was squeezed in between two modestly huge human beings; the shotguns they had resting on the floor between their feet looking like peashooters next to their massive frames. Ebony was driving, and Elias was riding shotgun, while a sixth man was seated in the seat at the back.

There was room enough that Jim could have sat back there. The guy was smaller than him even. But there was a vibe about him that came off as extraordinarily lethal, and Jim chose to say nothing and stay put. The guy had no gun, in fact, no weapon of any kind that Jim could see, and he had an almost serene air about him. The man hadn't acknowledged Jim in any way, and he faced front again.

This guy was the most dangerous of them all. Guaranteed.

"So, how's Kenya?" Jim asked, breaking the awkward silence.

"She good," the little man said. There was something odd about his tone, but Jim didn't want to press.

"You didn't want her to come?"

"She didn't want to come. She got her own mind."

Jim sensed there was something more to it, but let it go.

His confidence in their success began to climb considerably, and when they rounded the corner of Gary's street, the vehicle pulled up to the curb.

"Take this," Elias said, thrusting a cell phone in his face. "That's a burner, but it's still gotta lotta minutes on it." Jim turned to get out after one of the men opened the door and slid out, but Elias grabbed his forearm. "Make sure you don't fuck me."

"Elias, I'm not."

"That's right. You not." The pudgy man held up a finger as if he were actually warning Jim away from stealing from him or something else ill-advised. Jim refrained from pointing out that they'd given him a car ride, and had he been up to something, he simply would have gone on his way without alerting them. "And gimme my vest too."

Jim took off his suit jacket, then began fumbling with the buckles that harnessed the vest to him. The man who had stepped out first helped him and sat back in the SUV with it.

"Now go assess the situation, hit the button on the text, and we come blastin'."

Jim nodded, again not willing to point out that that had essentially been his plan that Elias had repeated to him, save for the blasting part. There was every likelihood Gary, Will, Mary Ellis, and Mr. Tate were here.

"Put some music on," Jim heard Elias say before he turned away. Immediately a rap song began blaring, and Elias shouted, "No! Not that shit. Put on some Bach. I'm stressed enough as it is." The song cut off, and classical music began pouring out of the speakers.

The game plan was to ring the doorbell, his hand on the phone the entire time, ready to push the button. The text message was simple: hi mom, I made it home. And then he would toss the phone into a bush after he had seen what was inside. The others would come rushing and storm the house, ideally killing Fyukis and his people, although that seemed like a bad idea that worsened with each step. The man had survived falling out of a multistory building. What if they were all like that?

Jim couldn't chance Elias and his goons barging in and shotgunning everyone and only the good guys die. He tossed the burner cell into a gated yard, hoping it was too dark and he was too far away for Elias to see. Jim had to think of something else.

He cut across the lawn of the house next door to Gary's and jogged up to the porch. He was scared to knock and scared not to. The people on the other side intended a grizzly end for him and Gary and had done who knew what to his best friend's loved ones. It seemed surreal, but he reached for the doorbell and pressed it.

A moment later the door swung in, and Jim's jaw dropped.

"Ma?" he said.

Chapter 54

"Boy, where the hell is my car, and where is your jacket?"

Jim seized his mother by the arms and pulled her outside. He leapt into a bush with her and forced her head down.

"What the hell is wrong with you? Let me go!"

"How many of them are in there? Ten? Twenty?"

"How many of whom?"

"The kidnappers."

"I knew it! I knew you were involved in something bad."

Jim's stomach lurched as he realized he had said too much. "What?" he said. "No, I'm not."

"James Stephens, you talk to me, and you tell me what's going on right now."

"I—"

"No."

"What had happened was—"

"The truth."

She stared into his eyes, giving him the full "look." Jim could feel his will waning as he was boiled down to an eight-year-old boy with a broken leg. He remembered her asking how it had happened all these years ago.

All Jim could think about was his father, who had just killed himself the month prior. In her hurt and anger, his mother had spared no detail of the torture he was languishing in in hell. Jim had beaten the school bully in a blind rage. He hadn't just tried to hurt him; he'd wanted to kill him. Afterward, he was saturated with regret and knew if he confessed to anyone he would go to prison. And then hell, effectively leaving his mother alone.

But he couldn't just lie to his mother. Whatever he said he had to believe. It had to be the truth.

"Gary did it," he said, still in his memory from long ago. "Tory was hitting me, and he saved me."

"Gary did what?" his mother asked. "He kidnapped somebody? I knew it. I knew he was up to no good. That's why I came here. I knew I'd catch up to you if I waited here long enough. He's such a bad boy."

Jim didn't like how she had said that last sentence so wistfully. "No, Ma. Gary didn't kidnap anyone. Gary has been kidnapped. They're not here?"

"What? Of course not. What would I look like hanging around a bunch of kidnappers? It's just his cute little brother and Mary Ellis."

"You know her?"

"Of course I do. I met her at the family reunion. You know, the family reunion you always skip?"

"Okay, fine. But why was she there?"

"You know I love Gary like a son. Ever since his mother died, I've always taken a special interest in him. His family is my family as far as I'm concerned. I invited her."

She stood and brushed herself down. Gary noticed what she was wearing—all black pants, her hair done up in a tight bun. She had on gloves too.

"Why are you dressed like that?" Jim asked, rising.

"What? This? I wear this all the time."

Jim knew that was a lie. He didn't believe he had seen his mother wear the same outfit more than twice. And she wasn't dressed for style per her usual; she was dressed like . . . like she didn't want to be seen.

"Ma, you're all dressed up like a spy." He'd said it half in jest, thinking about what he had just found out about his fiancée—or ex fiancée, whatever she was.

"What? No." She looked confused, then her face blanked the same way Mel's had in their apartment, and Jim wasn't entirely certain if her response was legit or if she was just that good.

"Why are you in the bushes with your mother?" Will asked.

Jim looked up and saw the boy on the porch.

"We're just talking," he said, brushing off his knees. Will was giving him a look as he helped his mother back onto the porch and joined her. "What are you doing here?"

"*I* live here," Will said. "Why do you need to talk to your mother in our bushes?"

Jim could see this conversation descending into something he couldn't dig himself out of. "Because," he said, brushing past the boy and going inside the house.

Chapter 55

"Okay, can anyone tell me why you two aren't currently kidnapped?"

Mary Ellis looked nervously at Will, her arms folded over her chest. "I don't know how to describe it," she began.

"The guy *melted*," Will said. "It was so cool."

"Melted?"

"That's what he told me." Jim's mother put her hands on her hips, and the boy sat down in the chair behind him. He looked uncomfortable for some reason. Jim looked at his mother and saw the top few buttons of her shirt were undone, revealing a few inches of cleavage.

Oh.

Apparently both the Tate boys had a thing for his mother.

Jim stepped between them, pulling up a chair and sitting across from Will. "What do you mean, he melted? Like he got really sweaty?"

Will rolled his eyes.

"No. I *know* the difference between sweating and melting. This guy turned into a green, viscous fluid like Billy Cole in *Fright Night*."

"Well, that's pretty descriptive."

His mother slapped him across the back of the head. "Don't tell me you're believing this foolishness!"

"Ow, Ma!"

"Don't "Ow, Ma" me. A child just told you a grown man melted in front of him, and you accept it like he's telling you the time. What is wrong with you? And where the hell is my car?"

"Southfield," Jim said. "Ma, there's a lot here you don't understand. I can't explain it all to you. Why aren't you two at a police station?"

"What are we supposed to tell them?" Mary Ellis said. "We were kidnapped by a man who . . . who *derretido*? Plus, my work visa isn't exactly current."

"So the people who took you aren't here?"

"What kind of fool would I be to walk into a house full of kidnappers?" Jim's mother said. "I don't know why you haven't called 911 yet."

"Before the guy melted, did he say anything?"

Will's eyes were wide. "He gave me an address. I said it over and over until I memorized it."

Will gave him the address. Jim didn't need to write it down because he was familiar with the area.

"That's near the mall," Jim said. "But it's in an industrial area. Why would she describe that as 'home'?"

"No," his mother said.

"No what?" Jim looked at her.

"I know what you're thinking, and the answer is no."

"Well, I'm a grown man, and I don't think I need to ask the question."

"You can be a grown man all you want to, but the answer, whether you ask or not, is no."

Jim made a face as she folded her arms, as if putting an exclamation point on the end of her statement. He couldn't believe he was actually having this conversation. After his father had killed himself, she had turned into one giant blanket, covering every aspect of his life. All the field trips he couldn't go on, all the parties he couldn't go to, all the sports he couldn't play, and every time he rode his bike, she was there. It was a miracle he'd even had Gary as a friend growing up.

Jim realized there was something he was forgetting. It had to do with rescuing Gary, and it was somehow related to drugs. Was he supposed to call someone?

"Crap—Elias!"

Jim leapt out of his chair and charged the front door. He ran outside, waving his arms and screaming just as a big SUV was passing in front of the house.

To Jim's horror, their guns were pointed out the SUV's windows.

Chapter 56

Jim dived, hitting the ground and rolling. It was all over for real this time. He would be just as dead as Gary when his forty-eight hours were up. He heard shouting and recognized Elias's voice, telling his men to put their weapons away. Jim got up, running back toward the house and waving behind him for Elias's men to stay back. He knew his mother carried a gun, and she was bound to come out shooting.

"Wait! Wait!" Before he shouted a third time, there was a pop, and Jim felt the impact catch his hand like he had just caught a line drive with no glove. His mother was in a forward shooting stance, shoulders hunched and arms straight, the smoke still trailing from her Glock.

Jim instinctively cradled his hand to his chest, turning to hide it as much as possible.

His mother dropped the gun, running toward him and screaming. "James! Oh no!"

"I'm okay. I'm okay." He held out his other hand for her to stop, but she swatted it aside and began pawing at him as they came back inside.

"Let me see it! Let me see it!" she said over and over again, checking him for bullet wounds. Jim let his hand fall to his side and held it tight against his leg.

"You missed me. I told you I'm all right."

"Oh no, not you too. Not you too!" she moaned.

What the hell was she talking about? His father?

Jim's mother raced her hands down his arms, and just before she got to his hand, he clenched it, telling her exactly where he'd been hit. He balled his fist and held it firmly at his side.

"Come on, James. You have to let me see it."

"Ma, it's fine. I'm fine. Seriously."

"James Aloysius Stephens, if you don't open your hand and let me see, I'll break your arm."

He had no choice but to let go.

"You're shot!" his mother said. "I shot you."

"Yeah, but it's only my hand. I have two."

He tried to disarm her with a smile. She gave him a grim look and folded his hand against her bosom. Of course, that was when Will appeared in the hallway and saw.

"Everybody okay in there?" Elias called from outside.

"Yeah, Elias. Come on in."

A moment later the small man came in with one of his men. Jim felt a touch of disappointment it wasn't the guy in the backseat.

"Uhh, everything all right?" he said once he was in the hallway.

"They're not here," Jim said. "But I know where they are."

"You're not leaving." Jim's mother locked eyes with him. He stared back and felt his will pushing against hers. He didn't say anything, but he could feel the shift in his favor. "Fine. I'm coming with you. And you can explain on the way why you're not bleeding."

"This your bitch or somethin'?" Elias said, looking her up and down. "I don't usually go over thirty-five, but damn, you make a brother wanna revise his policies, you know what I'm sayin'?"

Jim turned on him, ready to boot the diminutive asshole back to his SUV. "She's my mother!" he said through gritted teeth.

"Then why you grippin' her titties?" He shook his head and looked at Jim's mother. "Madam, my apologies for referring to you in the pejorative. Please forgive me."

"My name is Carol," Jim's mother said. "If we might be killing people tonight, we should be on a first-name basis, don't you think?"

Chapter 57

Jim's mother had made the guy in the back squeeze over so that she, Will, and Mary Ellis could get in too. Already Jim was impressed, despite the stakes having risen considerably with her along. Jim had no doubt he could continue to act if Elias or one of his men went down. But what if his mother was shot? Jim didn't know if he could maintain his nerve.

Along the way his mother talked to Mary Ellis and discovered her name was actually Marielis. She was from Bolivia and had immigrated here to go to medical school. She had met Gary, who quickly informed her he was in need of a housekeeper and nanny. Jim still didn't understand how he could afford such a luxury and how in the world the horniest guy he knew seemed to have no interest in the hottest woman Jim had ever seen. He even had the passing sensation that she might have a crush on Gary. She didn't mind them calling her Mary Ellis; it was actually sort of cute to her.

They dropped Mary Ellis and Will off at a square gray building called the Hotel Royal Oak along the way. It was a lot more impressive inside than he would have guessed, with a fresh modern look with dark wood paneling and exposed brick and backlighting that made it look more like a nightclub than a sixty-nine-dollar-a-night motel.

Once they were checked in to the hotel, Jim sat in the back with his mother, and she began to fuss over his hand in earnest.

"I didn't want to scare the boy," she said, giving him a flat look. "Tell me why your hand looks like this."

"I, uhhh." Jim looked at the silent man in the back with them.

"Don't worry about Stacy. He'll keep quiet."

"Stacy?" Jim said, and the man looked at him. "I mean, that's a fine, fine name. I'm just surprised he actually spoke." He looked at the man again. "Not that you *can't* speak; you just look like you're in a zone and don't want to be disturbed."

They bumped down Eleven Mile Road until they eventually merged onto I-75. Jim's mother elbowed him in the ribs to get his attention again.

"It's this thing we're involved in . . ." he started. He gave her the abbreviated version, hesitating to tell her the more unbelievable parts but diving in with even those in the end.

When he was finally done, he felt his muscles sag, surprised to know he'd been as tense as he was. It actually felt good to let it all out, even though he had already told Mel. There was something different about telling his mother, though. Like he was telling the person who was supposed to make it all better.

He stared at her, wondering if she had believed a word of it. She didn't seem to be blinking, and she sat still so long he wondered if she had fallen asleep with her eyes open.

"All right," she said.

"All right?" he asked, unsure. "What does that mean?"

"It mean we here," Elias said from the front.

Jim watched his mother as he slid out of the SUV, her eyes still unreadable. He realized that in the years since his father's death, she hadn't just swaddled him from the world; she had also hidden herself away. He had no idea the things she was capable of or whatever she had done in the time before, although he had always felt she was somehow wasting herself by simply being a secretary at Wayne State.

"Try not to lose it again," Elias said, handing him the burner phone.

"Yeah. Try not to blow my head off this time."

"Ay, I'm hurt," Elias said. "I'm gonna circle the building. Give me ten minutes before you do anything."

Chapter 58

Jim's mind scrambled as he tried to think of a way to resolve this before his mother could get inside. There were who knew how many people in there, they knew he was coming, and a good chunk of them were athletes.

This plan was looking worse by the second.

The more he thought about it, the more he realized Elias and his crew had no cause to be careful. It's not like drug dealers played nice with people who stole from them. He and Gary would just be collateral damage. They wouldn't mind taking the vest off Gary's bullet-riddled body, and Jim had just done them a favor by handing his over.

Yeah. This was a really bad idea.

He thought about turning back but realized Elias playing honest was his best hope. He certainly couldn't get in there and make them do anything on his own. Maybe he could call 911. That would scare Elias off, but that didn't sit right with him either. Even if the police did somehow manage to arrest everyone and recover Gary, they would quickly realize something was wrong with him, and he'd be in their custody until the pill wore off and he died. Jim was sure his best friend didn't want that either.

He found himself wishing he'd asked for a gun, then looked for a stick. Jim was around the corner of the building, out of sight from the SUV, foraging around for something he could wield.

Then two pairs of hands clamped down on him.

"Don't struggle," a voice said. "We don't need to hurt you."

Jim nodded, feeling the breathing of someone close behind. He threw his head back and heard the sharp crunch of a nose breaking. But whoever it was didn't cry out and didn't release him. A third pair of hands grabbed him by the ankles, and he was lifted off his feet.

Jim was freaked out both from no longer being under his own power and by how he was captured so quickly by people he still hadn't seen. They moved rapidly toward a side entrance, and he realized his hands were still free. Jim struck out underneath him, mostly missing, but occasionally making contact with a head or an arm as they carried him overhead. But their progress never slowed, and right before they came to the door, it swung open, a short, bald man letting them inside.

They took him through a narrow hallway, brought him to a small office area, and stood him up. Jim was about to start throwing punches at the man in front of him until he realized he was looking at Arson Speight.

"Good evening," the man said once one of the others handed Jim's wallet to him. He flipped it open and looked at the driver's license behind its little plastic window. "Mr. Stephens." He smiled wide, showing two perfectly even, perfectly white rows of teeth. "You know who I am, don't you?"

Jim nodded, just like he would have when he was thirteen and he and Gary snuck in to see their first Arson Speight movie together. *Volcano Killer* didn't hold up on repeated viewings, but it was the first in an eight-year streak for them where they saw every single one of Arson's movies in the theater.

"Good. Now that we know each other, let me lay my cards on the table. We have your friend, and we want to let him go. As you know, the two of you have something that belongs to us."

"You're one of the Adjacent?"

Arson rolled his eyes. "We can dispatch with that term now. I think it's outlived its usefulness."

"I don't understand."

"Fiel. The Adjacent"—he made air quotes with his fingers—"were simply a front she used. A means to an end."

"I still don't get it."

"Ninety years or so ago, actually more, Life came to 'life.' She took on physical form to investigate personally what the living creatures had chosen to do with what they had taken from her. It took some time to gain control of her physical form, even longer to gain actual sentience and then understanding of us, and she quickly judged us unworthy of what we had taken. She's here to take herself back."

"Well, that's a lot to take in." Jim thought a moment. "Let's say I buy this. Why can't she just suck the life out of everybody and go back wherever?"

"She is the physical embodiment of life. You can't simply kill her. And she wants to take back *all* life. That means animals, plants, single-cell organisms—the whole shebang."

"And you're fine with this?"

Arson pursed his lips. It was a strange question to ask, but even stranger not to have an answer. The big man leaned back in his chair and stared at Jim.

Since no answer was forthcoming, Jim moved on.
"Why would I agree to help you—*her*?"

"Because she has a deal for you. She will allow you
and your friends to live out the rest of your lives."

"While the rest of the world turns to shit?"

"I didn't say it was perfect."

"I'm going to have to say no, I think, but I have to
ask the same question—why doesn't she just take it from
me?"

"Some indefinable occurrence. You actually have to
willingly give up the Bloom. The physical part will pass
from your body and you *will* die, but there is the essence of
it that you will take with you. She needs that."

Jim felt the odd twinge of a new sensation. Arson
had just lied to him. He didn't know what part or if the
whole thing was a lie, but there was no way Jim could
believe what he'd just been told.

"So if I agree and I imagine Gary does too, you just
let us and our friends and family walk off into the sunset?"

"Essentially, yes. And I know what you're going to
say. What guarantees do you have? Well, none. And that's
why you can trust her. Fiel has no reason to lie to you.
You're too insignificant. The world is going to come to an
end, you included. But there is no reason why you can't
have your time extended by what would be a very
considerable amount of time for you, but a blink of an eye
in the cosmos."

"Well, when you say it like that . . ."

"Take some time. Think about it. You have until
sunup."

"I want to see Gary."

"That's not possible."

"If you want me to really consider this, then it starts with me seeing my friend. Otherwise, no deal."

Arson frowned and pursed his lips. He stood, towering over Jim. One of his cinderblock fists tightened, and Jim briefly wondered how much damage it would do to his face. But the man didn't approach him at all. Instead, his eyes rolled into his head, and he had a sudden beatific smile. Jim thought he was having a seizure, but it was over a moment later, and his eyes settled on Jim again.

"Let's go." Arson turned and stepped around Jim. The man walked fast, and Jim practically had to jog to keep up. Outside of the office was a giant open room. There were big holes in the floor; Jim guessed they must have been where huge dies had been to press out car parts. There was a mezzanine against a far wall that had been partially demolished. They didn't step out onto the floor; rather, they stayed close to the wall, turned through an open doorway, and went down a long flight of stairs.

There were many, many people milling about. There were men, women, and even some children—some familiar faces, a full rainbow of ethnicities, rich and poor, and even a few with physical handicaps.

If Martin Luther King saw this, he'd cream his jeans, Jim thought.

Once they were downstairs, they passed even more people. Jim changed his initial estimate from a few hundred to somewhere shy of a thousand. And that was just from the rooms he'd seen. There were other doors he'd seen that had remained shut and people coming in from outside through other doors.

Even if Elias and crew did have enough bullets to shoot all of them, did Jim really want that to happen? He had the feeling that even if they were here willingly, something had happened to change their will. The way Arson spoke was so different from any of his characters in movies, and while Jim had read and heard enough rumors to believe the man actually had a much higher than average IQ, his manner of speaking had always been relatable in interviews.

In short, Jim concluded that Arson's—and everyone else's—will had been co-opted by Fiel. Maybe if he could just get to her, he could stop this. How he would do that, he wasn't sure. If she was what Arson said, killing her would be killing all of humanity. No, not just humanity—all life everywhere. There had to be something else, something short of killing her, that could free all these people.

And what was that other thing Arson had said—that Jim was going to die too once the Bloom had passed through him? He hadn't been critically injured like Gary had. Dr. K had said they would simply return to life once they'd completely metabolized the pill. But then again, how much testing had the doctor done? And Fiel had actually been the one to give him the instructions. Which one of them knew more about how it actually worked?

They came to a big burnt-orange-colored door. Several dozen people stood around in all manner of dress. An old man in Crocs eyed him, and Jim thought he looked familiar, but he could have just as easily been another celebrity.

Arson didn't tell anyone to open the door, but one of them stepped forward, unlatched it, and swung it inward in time for the big man to step through without breaking stride. They both entered, and Jim saw Gary pressed against the far wall in a half crouch, looking like he was ready to run or fight, whichever came first.

"Gary, you're all right!" Jim said. He wanted to run and hug him, but held back. Something was wrong with his friend's skin. It looked like he had spiky acne all over his face and hands.

"Not exactly," Gary said. "Watch out; don't get close to her." His eyes flashed down to the body Jim hadn't noticed. Fiel lay on the floor, obviously dead, her head at a sharp angle to the rest of her body.

"But—" Jim said, but was cut off by the big door closing behind him. He was so distracted by seeing his friend alive and well—sort of—that he hadn't noticed the giant human being walk right past him and out of the room.

Gary shook his head and swore. "How'd they get you?"

"Coming in," Jim said. "We were trying to mount a rescue."

"We?"

"Elias brought me. My mom came too."

"Really?" Gary brightened. "I thought we were screwed." For a moment Jim thought he was joking. Gary must have understood the confused look on his face. "How much do you know about your mother?" He smiled. "Because I know a lot. A whole lot. About your mother."

"Wha—" Jim said just as an explosion rocked the whole building.

Chapter 59

They both picked themselves up. Jim eyed his friend, wondering about this new intimacy between him and his mother.

"What is this, Gary?" he asked. "What's going on?"

"I'll put it to you like this—I think your mother met Mel before you did. Stay away from the door." A couple of smaller explosions shook the room, and Jim grabbed onto Gary to keep from falling again.

"What happened to your skin?"

"It's her." Gary nodded at the body on the floor. "She's pulling the Bloom out of me. Out of you too."

Jim's skin had already started prickling. He didn't understand. How could she be doing anything if she were dead? And if she were dead, how come they all weren't?"

"V2 was made with a milder version of what we took. She took all my drugs at once. I think it fried her brain or something. She did them all in here, right in front of me, and then she just stood there, staring at me. I broke her neck, but I don't think she's completely dead."

As if summoned, Fiel sat up. Gary and Jim both jumped and clutched onto one another more tightly. Her hair was a yellow rat's nest atop her crooked head. She had her back to them, and Jim hoped she hadn't realized they were in the room.

Gary gave him a light shake and mouthed something, but Jim couldn't read lips for shit.

"What?" he said. Gary rolled his eyes and pointed at a spot closer to her. "No way; I'm not getting one step closer to her.

Gary bared his teeth at him and whispered, "You do realize we're already locked in the room with her, right?"

"Okay. Yeah."

"In a few seconds, one of these walls is going to come down. I don't want to be under it when it falls."

"How do you know—"

Another explosion, almost as big as the first, shook the building, dust and grit raining down on them. Jim could hear people yelling outside the room. They sounded panicked and disorganized. He looked in Fiel's direction and saw she was standing about three feet away from them, her back still turned.

It was all he could do not to leap into his friend's arms. Gary slowly led them to the center of the room. The latch on the big orange door was thrown, and it opened. Jim had time enough to see someone stepping in. There was a roar of an explosion, and a chunk of ceiling came down, taking off the front half of his flesh, clothes and all. The man disappeared in a cloud of dust, the air suddenly thick with it.

Two nylon lines dropped out of the hole, and there she was—Mel, in all black, wearing a pair of goggles and crouching with some sort of machine gun in her hands. It was a blunt-looking deal with a crazy-looking scope on top of it, and it appeared it would be really good at chopping people down. Jim found himself hoping she hadn't used it.

"Come on," she said.

Gary and Jim raced for the lines and began climbing.

"Get back here!" Jim could feel Arson beneath him. He grabbed Jim's line and shook it violently, almost throwing him off. Mel squatted, squinting one eye as she looked through her scope. Jim watched her as he clung to his rope, hoping she would take the shot, but praying she wouldn't kill him.

Jim barely noticed as Gary swung on his rope. He was almost shoulder to shoulder with Gary when he dropped, coming down feetfirst into Arson's chest. They both went down, but the big man came up quick. He struck Gary as he was getting up, then kicked him several feet away.

Jim was about to let go to help his friend when Mel and his mother pulled him the rest of the way up.

"I have to get him!" he said. "I have to save him!"

The two women looked at each other, and Mel propelled herself into the hole. Jim twisted around and saw her hit the floor and roll onto her feet. She held a knife underhanded, the blade gleaming against her wrist.

Arson was already halfway up the line, and she slashed him across the back. The big man grunted and fell, landing on his feet. He turned in time to be slashed twice across his torso but didn't seem to notice. He reached for Mel, and she ducked out of the way, plunging the knife into his side. He winced and tried to backhand her, and she was gone again.

She'd left her knife in his ribs, though, and Arson didn't bother pulling it out. He advanced on her, and Jim found himself wanting to shoot him.

Arson should have been on the ground in agony and bleeding to death. But there he was, bearing down on her. She still had that machine gun across her back, and Jim was simultaneously proud and terrified that she hadn't used it.

Mel took a few steps backward, edging closer to the wall. Arson finally pounced, and she stiff-armed him in the chest, stopping his forward momentum, and dropped and spun, sweeping his legs out from under him.

Arson might have been an action movie star, but that was a far cry from being a trained killer. Mel followed up with a backhanded blow to his jaw, dislocating it and drumming his head off the floor.

Gary rolled onto shaky legs. "I could've done that," he said, stumbling into her.

Mel got under him, wrapping his arm over her shoulders.

Jim yelped at the sound of gunfire a foot away from his head. His mother was shooting into the open doorway.

"We need to move if you want to get out of here," she said. Jim watched as they made it to the lines. Gary was sturdier on his feet and was able to begin pulling himself up. Mel gave him a light slap on the back, then grabbed the other line.

"No!" Jim yelled as Fiel appeared behind her. Mel whirled, deflecting the woman's hand with her elbow and striking her in the chest with the flat of her hand. Fiel stumbled backward and stepped forward again just in time for Jim's mother to rake her across the chest with her machine gun.

Mel was still frozen, her hand in front of her.

"Mel?" Jim said. "Mel, we have to go."

"No, *we* have to go," Jim's mother said, hauling Gary the rest of the way up. "She's been compromised."

"You don't know that," he said to his mother over his shoulder. "Mel, come on!"

Instead, Fiel stood again, shambled over to his girlfriend, and laced her hand into Mel's. She slumped, then straightened, then slowly turned and looked up at Jim. Mel's eyes were wrong.

"We have to get out of here now!" Gary and Jim's mother pulled him to his feet by his arms. Several people had flooded into the room. His mother cut the lines before they could climb and then put a harness over Jim's head. He paid no attention as she buckled it around his body, looking only at Mel, who was staring up at him.

It had to be her still. It had to be. If she were one of them, she would be trying to shoot at his mother, Gary, and Jim.

Jim's mother dropped what looked like a grenade into the hole. There was a loud bang, and then the room below them was filled with smoke.

"Hold on to me," she said to Gary. Jim came out of his stupor in time to see her fasten another line to the harness she had put on him. She gave it a hard tug and let go, and it began reeling up into another hole in the ceiling above them.

At the roof of the building, Elias waited with his men. They helped them over and cut the lines. Two men stood to either side of Elias, shotguns in hand. They hadn't freaked out, but their eyes were wild. Even Elias looked ready to cut and run.

"Hey," Gary said, placing a hand on Jim's shoulder, "we'll get her back. We will."

Jim thought about all those hundreds of faces he'd seen. No way could he have fought through all of them. And if they did find her, what then? Mel was one of them now. He thought about everything Arson had told him. Jim hadn't believed what he'd said at the time, but he wanted to believe now.

"How are we getting off this roof?" Gary asked. They were near the edge, and Jim's mother pointed to a vehicle in a lot across the street. It was small and could probably only hold five people at most. "So who are the lucky losers?"

"That's easy," Jim's mother said. "They want the two of you, not the rest of us." Her tone was flat, matter-of-fact. She walked over to Elias and began talking to him. The little man nodded as she bent over, her mouth to his ear. Jim turned his head and saw Gary staring. His mother's black outfit was very formfitting, and as disgusting as the thought was, Jim could acknowledge in a very, very distant manner that she was built well and amply proportioned.

"Cut that out, okay?" Jim slapped his shoulder.

"Huh?" Gary said, his eyes still locked on Jim's mother's ass.

"Stop lusting after my mom. That's a sin!"

"No. Lusting after my neighbor's wife is a sin. She's sixty-eight years old and weighs three hundred thirty pounds. I'm sorry you can't appreciate how hot your mom is. If you want to make it even, I can show you my dad's dick pics." Jim had been around Gary's father enough to have already seen the Bulge, and he wanted none of that anaconda.

His mother came back and said, "We're going to go in a minute. The three of us and one of those big boys."

Jim was impressed. "How did you get him to agree to let us have the car?"

"Simple." She pulled the tie out of her hair, whipping it around and letting it fall over her shoulders. Gary's mouth fell open. "He can't run. He'd prefer to make his last stand here if our plan doesn't work."

That still didn't explain how she had gotten him to agree to come up here to begin with, but he sensed that was much more than he wanted to know. It was well known that Elias was mildly agoraphobic, but the wild look of fright in his eyes went well beyond that. She had threatened or promised him something that surpassed the terror he was currently keeping in check. Jim didn't want to know what it had been that convinced a drug dealer to risk his own skin to save someone else.

Someone's cell rang, and Jim recognized it was the same ringtone Tony Soprano had on his cell in the old HBO TV show. Elias pulled his cell out and put it to his ear.

"Hey, baby, how's it goin'? I know, I know." He sounded conciliatory, like he didn't want to upset whoever was on the other end—Kenya, probably. "No, I'm sorry I forgot. We kinda got held up." He listened a moment. "What, now? Where exactly? I don't know the address. Oh, in the building? Actually, we on the roof."

Jim's mother narrowed her eyes.

"It's cool," Gary said. "Kenya works at the county medical examiner's. She snuck us out earlier."

"Snuck you *out*?"

"Oh, no, we were only pretending to be dead," Jim said.

"Does that have anything to do with all those people who were shot there?"

"Kind of." Gary nodded. "They were looking for us."

"Okay, baby, hold on." Elias stepped over and held the phone up to Jim. "She wanna talk to you."

Jim shrugged and took the cell. "Hello?"

"You don't have long, so listen. Only the three of you can go. I figure that woman with you has to be your mother or something, right? Once you get off the roof, head east once you get to Fourteen Mile—understand?"

"But—"

"No buts. East on Fourteen Mile, and make sure you pick her up when she falls. *Trust.* Go now."

The line went dead, and Jim looked at the cell before tossing it back to Elias. "We don't need your guy," Jim said.

One of the two big men frowned deeply.

"What?" Elias said. "Why?"

"I don't know."

The three of them went to the edge of the building. There were people down there, and several were trying to scale the building.

"Probably coming from all sides," Jim's mother said.

He quickly told her the game plan, and she made a face.

"Why am I going to fall?" She sounded offended.

"I don't know."

She whipped her hair up into a pony and tied it before sliding her machine gun off her shoulder. Gary looked like he needed to excuse himself. Jim opened his mouth, wanting to ask her not to shoot anyone, and she gave him a look.

"It's either them or the end of the world, right?"

That was an extremely effective, yet simplistic, way to think of it.

"Carry on," he said, hoping Mel wasn't down there. She took careful aim and began firing, sweeping quickly left and right, plucking people off the outer wall of the building and creating a wide space on the ground below. Nobody ran; everyone hit with a kill shot simply fell and died.

"There's more coming," she shouted behind her as she dropped the machine gun and climbed over the edge. "Cover us."

The two big men and Ebony came to the edge. She began rappelling, and Gary and Jim climbed over and followed her lead to the best of their ability. The men pumped rounds into the people below, who trickled along, but never seemed to stop coming.

When they were finally on the ground, a man grabbed Jim's mother by the shoulder. He was wounded but still strong as he wrapped his arms around her and tried dragging her away. Before Jim could do anything, she simply dropped out of his arms, coming up with a knife in either hand and began slicing at every vital part within reach—his throat, his stomach, his crotch. Gary and Jim both winced as the man finally fell.

"Come on," she said and dashed toward the street. A group of about a half dozen rushed toward them, and she headshot each one without losing stride. Gary and Jim hustled to catch up to her. Jim's view of his mother expanded with each step. She was a killer without hesitation or remorse, boiled down to simple survival. He had no clue how he'd never met this woman. As emotionally distant as she'd been when he was growing up and every other complaint he'd ever had about her was still far short of him believing her capable of anything like what she was doing now.

There were about thirty people ahead of them, and Jim was considering trying to run away from them like a giant game of tag. But his mother surged ahead, picking up steam. She dived into the crowd, her arms a blur as she slashed, hacked, and stabbed. The first half dozen fell before they had realized what hit them. Jim and Gary were just catching up as two more men fell and the crowd began to overwhelm her. There were about twenty of them now, and they divided, a few more than ten turning toward the two of them while the rest struggled with her.

Jim saw the man right before he smashed into the crowd. He didn't see who it was, but once again they had been caught off guard, several people falling as the man used every part of his body to strike, ram, kick, knee, elbow, or headbutt everyone in his path.

As his forward momentum halted, two tall men advanced on him. The man rolled into a ball right between them and sprang into one man's midsection, apparently plunging his fingers into the man's lower torso while the other grabbed him. He spun around, striking the second man with both his elbows, stunning him before neatly plucking out his eyeballs.

The group that had been advancing on Gary and Jim stopped, apparently confused by this new combatant. Gary used the opportunity to ball kick three men in succession, dropping them as Jim's mother and that lethal guy who'd been in the back of Elias's SUV pressed from the other side.

Jim was no fighter, but he threw himself into the scrum. He threw a haymaker, forgetting he was swinging with his injured hand, which bounced harmlessly off a bald-headed pudgy man's face. He grabbed Jim and headbutted him, making him see stars. Gary stepped behind him and ball kicked the man, who promptly dropped and began rolling around on the floor.

There were four people still standing when the lethal man spoke. "Keep running. I will take care of these." He had a strange accent Jim couldn't place, but the three of them began running. There was a truck parked in the city right-of-way on their right about eighty yards ahead. Someone climbed out of the flatbed, and he hoped that was Kenya. He looked over his shoulder and saw nothing but a giant mass of bodies advancing on them. It was something out of a zombie movie, and Jim hoped Elias's man had gotten away.

The unsettling part was how quiet they were. Other than their footfalls, which were largely masked by his, Gary's, and his mother's, they made no noise.

The figure ahead of them stepped out into the street. The horde behind them had already blocked the meager amount of traffic on Fourteen Mile; no doubt the police had been called by people who had witnessed what had to have looked like a riot in progress.

"Woof," Jim thought he heard his mother say as she came to a sudden stop. She put her hands on her knees, lifted her head, dropped it again, and vomited. She tried to take another step, but began convulsing violently and fell to the ground.

"What the hell?" Jim said.

"Get her legs," Gary said, scooping her up by under the arms. Jim thought about just grabbing her and tossing her over his shoulder as he took hold of her calves. His mother was very petite; she couldn't have been that heavy. When his back almost gave out, he agreed with Gary. They both needed to carry her. It must have been her outfit or something in it because she was heavy.

Kenya waved for them to keep heading for the truck while she raised what looked to be a cartoonishly shaped and sized plastic laser cannon. If it weren't for its size, he would have guessed it was a child's toy. There were three cables that ran from the back of it into a pack she had strapped to her back. She had on dark glasses, which was weird considering that other than the streetlights it was pitch-black outside, and as they passed her, Jim noted her earplugs.

She was aiming the cannon at the mass of advancing people, rotating quickly from side to side. Jim chanced a look after they'd gotten his mother into the flatbed and saw the first row of people fall to the ground. As far as he could tell, that cannon wasn't doing anything except for a green light emitting from the end of its "barrel." Kenya began walking backward in their direction. She had on formfitting pants and boots with a thick heel, and he caught Gary staring. For some stupid reason he found himself feeling something akin to jealousy that Gary could so casually switch his lusty looks from his mother to another woman.

"One of you get in the front," she said, sitting on the tailgate and scooching back, aiming the whole time. The engine started.

"Who's up there?" Jim said.

Someone stuck a hand out the window and gave a peace sign.

"Dr. K?" Gary said.

"Let's ride, folks," the old man said.

Gary indicated with his eyes that Jim should go up, giving a sidelong glance at Kenya. Jim narrowed his eyes, but went. He got in beside the old man, who looked surprisingly healthy considering he had to have taken the Bloom as well.

"I know what you're thinkin', and I'll tell you aaaall about it when there isn't an angry mob ready to tear us apart."

Jim nodded as Dr. K put the truck in drive and pulled away.

Chapter 60

Sunday

"You guys are dead, man. And there ain't nothin' I can do about that."

"*What*?" Jim said. "But you said—"

"Hey, *wait*." Dr. K held up his hands, his unlit joint dangling from his lips. "You didn't gimme a chance to say 'unless.'" Gary and Jim were both quiet a moment, waiting for him to continue. "Unless you are willing to do what needs to be done, man." He gave them both the eye.

"What the hell does that mean?" Gary asked.

The doctor raised his eyebrows at him. He bent to Jim's mother, feeling the pulse in her wrist, and asked, "How you feelin', honey?"

"Better," she said, still looking green. Kenya had put a cool towel on her forehead and put her on a saline IV to rehydrate. "I still feel like I was thrown off an overpass onto I-75."

"Oh man, that is excellent. *Excellent*," Dr. K said.

She opened her eyes and gave him a murderous look, but still wasn't in any condition to back it up.

"I saw this thing on the news about this company that's developing a kind of flashlight for the police that's supposed to make anybody sick who has it shone in their face. I couldn't get my hands on one, but I found the specs for an earlier prototype by this company, IOS, right? Except theirs relies solely on light-emitting diodes, or LEDs, right? That was so simple to do I decided to challenge myself. Like what if the dude was wearing sunglasses or was blind or wasn't facing you? I came up with this baby that incorporates LED and several transitioning bands of light that go in and out of the visual spectrum. This will go *through* your eyelids—hell, it'll go through your skull. And it also uses sound waves that pretty much do the same thing. You probably hear just a little beep, but this thing is doing so much more than that—"

"We get it. It makes people nauseous when you shoot it at them," Jim said.

"Nauseated," Gary said, correcting him.

"Well, yeah," Dr. K said, eyeing Jim.

"You know what would've been even cooler?" Gary asked. "If it made people shit themselves too."

The doctor's face fell. "The first gen did that."

"For real? What happened with that? How come you didn't put that in this one?"

"She's supposed to be a nonlethal weapon. The first gen would have made people shit. To death."

"Whoa," Gary and Jim said.

"And you used that thing on me?" Jim's mother said. She sat up, glaring at the doctor. "Ow, my head." Dr. K and Kenya helped her settle back down.

"I kind of can't sell it as a military and police alternative if it's essentially just another gun." Dr. K shrugged.

Gary sat down heavily. Jim looked at him and saw he looked exhausted. For a walking corpse, he looked awful.

"Gary, you okay?"

"I'm . . . fine." He looked at Jim. "No, I'm not." His hands shook, and Jim came over. Jim put a hand on his friend's shoulder, and Gary covered it with his own.

"How about that unless, Doc?" Jim asked.

"Oh! Yeah. When you look at me, do I look like you?" Dr. K asked.

"I'm still prettier," Gary said. Even his voice sounded gray.

"Right." The doctor smirked. "Well, how do you feel about consuming human flesh?"

"Ew," Jim said.

"I don't know about that," Gary said. "I don't want to eat anybody."

"I'm surprised you'd say that," Dr. K said. "I mean, you're talking to me."

"I don't know what that means," Jim said.

"You have your wits about you, so to speak. By now you should be a pair of mindless creatures, no more mentally capable than rabid dogs. The fact you aren't says you have consumed living flesh."

"No, we haven't," Gary said.

"Well, you did eat that squirrel," Jim said.

"*One* squirrel. And that's not human flesh."

The doctor stroked his chin. "Did you bite anyone?"

"No," Jim said.

"Yeah, you did. That guy the first night. At LB's," said Gary.

"Okay, I bit him, but I didn't take a chunk out of him."

"Even a small amount initially carries a long way," the doctor said. "If you bit someone, you would have scraped off hundreds if not thousands of skin cells, and unless you immediately rinsed your mouth out, you eventually swallowed them."

"I guess I consumed human flesh," Jim said. "But that was just the once. I haven't bitten anybody else, and Gary only ate a squirrel."

"*Okay*, I ate a squirrel. That's been established."

"I mean, is that enough to have carried us through to now?" Jim asked.

"Based on your size and the amount of physical activity you've been engaging in, I'd say no. Have you gotten anyone's blood on you, particularly your face?"

Jim thought. They'd gotten into some scraps. He couldn't specifically recall. "Probably," he said.

"Blood is enough to do the trick. So long as it's from a living human being."

"I'm in," Gary said. "If that's what it takes, give me a twenty ounce O negative."

"Be right back." The doctor held up a finger and disappeared into a back room.

"So what is this, the backup lab?" Gary said to Kenya.

"I suppose," she said. "I didn't know about this place until tonight—last night." She leaned against a counter and folded her arms. "I didn't know my father was supposed to be dead either."

"Then how did you know to come rescue us?" Jim said.

"My mother. She told me my father had left specific instructions. What she didn't tell me was that my father had called himself and left those instructions. He's been following you two."

"What do you mean, following us?

"Literally. Just about everywhere you have been going, he has gone too, monitoring your progress."

Jim wondered if that feeling of being watched had been Dr. K. Whoever it had been, there was nothing to be done about it now.

"What about you and short stuff?" Gary asked.

"A means to an end." She waved her hand. "He had a pretty good lab setup that allowed me to do some experiments on Mary's remains."

Jim recalled the gooey mess that had been left of her.

"What were you able to figure out?"

"Not much about the Adjacent. But Mary had been dead for quite a long time."

"How long?"

"I can't say for sure. I'm not even a hundred percent on the reliability of my tests. And it isn't as if there is a scientific precedent for a human being melting."

Dr. K came back in the room holding two bags of blood.

"Gentlemen, I have our finest AB Rh-negative with a twist of anticoagulant citrate and a dash of a nutrient phosphate and dextrose."

"What?" Gary and Jim said together.

"It's blood. Drinky-drinky." The doctor put the heels of his hands together and lightly clapped after he had passed the bags to them.

Jim found it mildly gruesome that the bags had big straws sticking out of the tops of them, like pouches of Capri Sun. He wasn't as certain that he could do this as he had been a moment before.

"Shouldn't we . . . I don't know, shoot this up or something?" Jim asked.

His mother cracked open an eye and glared at him.

"You mean a transfusion? No, this is much more effective. If you had an intact vein, we would have to massage it up your arm and into your torso. You have no heartbeat, no means of circulating. Whereas if you consume it, the blood has a means of reaching several organs, much the same way as alcohol does."

They both nodded and clinked pouches before drinking. Jim was pretty certain Gary didn't understand either. Out of the corner of his eye, he saw Gary watching him and realized his best friend was racing him. Jim sucked harder, swallowing big mouthfuls of cold, coppery blood. He thought he detected just the tiniest bit of mint, but couldn't be sure.

Gary finished first and belched before wiping his mouth. "Hats off to the chef," he said.

Even before he finished, Jim could feel something. He felt warmer despite the cold of the blood. He felt his face flush, and he shivered. He stopped drinking, the taste suddenly repulsive to him, leaving a few ounces in the bottom of the bag.

"You'll need to drink all of that," the doctor said.

"I don't want to. I'm done. I'm . . . full."

"James, finish your blood." His mother's tone was quiet, but held all the firmness he'd ever heard from her.

"Yes, ma'am," he said and put the straw back to his lips. Air had gotten into the bag so that when he finished, it made the same slurping sound as a milkshake did at the end. He sucked at his teeth, feeling the coppery film and wondering if they were stained red.

He felt better. Almost like that time he'd been put on a glucose IV in the hospital and felt like he could have run a marathon after.

"I don't feel so good," Gary said. Jim saw he'd taken on a distinctive green hue, and Dr. K approached him, his brow wrinkled in concern.

"What are you—"

The doctor was cut off by explosive, projectile vomit, all red, hitting him like that scene from that horror movie with the girl in it. It covered Dr. K from his glasses down, and he removed them, gently placing them on the table next to him and squeegeeing the lower half of his face with his hand.

"That's not supposed to happen," the doctor said.

"Dad, are you all right?" Kenya said, stepping over.

He held up a hand, and she stopped.

"My bad." Gary's eyes rolled. Jim grabbed him by the shoulder again as he slumped forward. "I'm sorry, Jim. I'm sorry, man. Tell Will . . . tell Will I love . . ."

Gary's body went limp. His eyes didn't even close.

"Gary?" Jim said. He shook his shoulder. "Gary. Gary!"

"Oh no," he heard his mother say.

Kenya put an arm around his shoulders and put a hand on his wrist.

"He can't be," Jim said. "He . . . *can't*."

"I'm so sorry." Kenya gave him a gentle squeeze.

Jim allowed Kenya to pull him away, but he kept looking at his friend's body.

"I don't understand why this happened," Dr. K said. He started to check Gary's wrist for a pulse, appeared to think better of it, then checked it anyway.

"There has to be something different. Something that happened to him that didn't happen to John."

"Jim," Kenya said. "His name is Jim . . . Gary was shot."

"No, that's not it. I was shot too," Jim said.

Jim's mother finally turned his face away from Gary, tears in her own eyes, and she cradled him into her arms.

Jim wept.

Chapter 61

The explosion got everyone moving again.

"Mel," Jim's mother said.

"Who?" Dr. K said. She ignored him, settling Jim into a chair. Kenya had taken her lab coat off and covered Gary's body with it.

"Dammit, I don't have my knives." Jim's mother looked around, no doubt for something lethal. Jim still felt like he was in a cloud, high above this room, as if what was going on here didn't matter.

"We can take the back exit," Dr. K said. "We can slip out—"

"No, we can't." She placed her hands on the counter, looking around. "We have to fight. She already has the exits covered."

"Well, if we can extract the Bloom, then there really is no reason for them to bother with us."

"Except that if we give it to them, that's the end of the world, right?"

"Right." Dr. K finished wiping his glasses and put them back on his face.

"Does that ray gun thing still work?"

"Uh, yes. But it's hell on batteries. It probably won't last more than a few minutes."

"All right. You have anyplace where we can dig in? Somewhere it'll be harder for them to get to us?"

"This building used to be a bank!" Dr. K held up an index finger. "There's a vault in the back."

"Good. That's where we'll go. Can you lock it from the inside?"

"Yes. And the only way to open it is the combination. I don't know it, but we can unlock it from the inside."

"Can't we just call the police?" Kenya asked.

Jim's mother looked at her. "No. The phone lines would have been the first thing she cut."

"I'm not leaving Gary," Jim said.

"No, he's coming with us." Jim's mother handed the two doctors microscopes. "In case we need to fight, you can use these. They can crack a skull. Let's move!"

She and the doctor carried Gary's body by the arms and legs. Kenya led Jim along until they got to the vault.

"They're going to know we're in here, so I want to wait until the last moment to shut the vault door," said Dr. K.

They laid Gary's body down at the back of the vault. Jim stared out, numb to what was happening.

"Jim, this looks like it's coming down to us or the rest of the world," his mother said.

He looked at her, not understanding.

"Jim." She slapped him across the cheek a couple of times, and he looked down at a grenade in her hand. "I won't let them take us."

She still looked ill, and Jim guessed she might not have been able to get up if he pushed her down. He smiled at her.

"Thanks for saving me, Ma." He inclined his head toward where the noise was coming from. "I have to go fight Tory Green, though." He put his hand over hers, and she looked at him, confused. Then he tightened his fingers around the grenade and stiff-armed her, driving her back to the far wall of the vault. Before the doctors could say anything, Jim ran out.

"Don't let her out here," he said over his shoulder as he made his way back down the narrow hallway.

Chapter 62

Jim heard them pounding at the door. They'd be in here soon. He was relatively certain he understood how these things worked. He pulled the pin, and as long as he held on to the handle, it wouldn't explode. At least he thought so. As far as Jim knew, the thing would explode anyway. All his knowledge came from movies he'd seen.

There wasn't a moment to think about it anymore. The door burst in, bodies flooding through. Jim climbed on a table and held the grenade high over his head.

"Stop!" They continued flooding into the room. "Any of you come near me, and we all go. Back off. Way off!" He was channeling his inner R. J. MacReady. Jim was hoping to force them back and out of the building, where he would let the grenade go off, hopefully taking as many of them with him as he could. Jim didn't know if the bank vault door could withstand a blast, particularly with all the chemicals in here.

He saw the same expression in the sea of faces— uncertainty. They wanted him intact. He shook the grenade over his head, and they began backing up to the walls. The doorway cleared, and a moment later, Mel came in, followed not long after by Fiel.

Mel was as beautiful as ever, but Jim could see the same blank look in her eyes. Fiel looked awful. Jim recalled how beautiful she was the other night with her long blonde hair, bright green eyes, and bare midriff. Now her hair was a tangled nest, her neck and jaw appeared broken, and she had bloody holes that had soaked her shirt from the chest down.

Mel's eyes focused, and she keyed in on him.

"James, come down from there. Give me that grenade." She raised her arms like a toddler wanting to be picked up.

"No. And don't you come any closer either. I swear I'll blow us all up." Jim said it with as much conviction as he could, but he didn't really believe it. Now that Mel was here, he had no clue what he would do. "I know you're not you."

"I'm me, James. I am. But I am Fiel too. I am Life."

He finally got it. The letters of her name could be rearranged to spell "life." "I don't believe you." She took a single step forward. "Stay back!"

"You don't want to kill me, James. You don't want to hurt anyone."

"No, I don't. I also don't want the world to come to an end. I can't let you do what you want to do."

She put her hands on her hips. "Now, James, what am I supposed to do with that?" She sounded more herself now, personality showing more in her eyes. "You can't just stand up there forever, and the police are going to come at some point."

"I—I don't know," he said, realizing he didn't really have a plan. He was just trying to keep his mother, Dr. K, and Kenya from being killed or turned into one of these zombies. "Why can't you just leave? Why do you have to *do* this?"

"Life as we have utilized it has been a waste," Mel said. "Human beings are the highest life-forms on the planet—the ambassadors of life—and look what we've done."

"What are you talking about? War?"

"Yes and no. It's much simpler than that. Living things live by killing. We consume the things we kill. Every time we kill, it's like we're *stabbing* her. Her awareness came through pain." Mel shook her head, putting a hand on Fiel's shoulder. "She only wants back what is rightfully hers."

"It doesn't work like that. Once you give something that significant, you can't just . . . just Indian give. We're alive now. We're *here*. Maybe we can talk it out, come to some compromise. What if we all become vegetarians or something?"

She shook her head again. "Same problem, James. We still have to kill plants and other living things to eat. There is no distinction for her. It's all pain."

"There has to be another way, Mel! You can't just wipe out, what—*trillions* of life-forms—because it makes one entity uncomfortable."

"The number is irrelevant. James, in one thousand years, every living thing on this planet now will have died. Each replaced in its own generation by a successor that will go on consuming other living things so it will survive. Humans, animals, plants, insects, bacteria, single-cell organisms—all consume or end life so they may live. It's a circular reference—it doesn't make sense. We should all be put out of our misery."

The grenade was snatched from his hand, and Jim almost fell off the table. His arms pinwheeled, and someone grabbed him by the shirt until he'd balanced again. He looked at Gary, who looked worse than ever, smiling at him.

"Gary!" Jim said.

"In the rotten flesh!" He smiled, his front teeth gone.

Chapter 63

"How did you—" Jim began.

"I dunno. I just woke up."

"Give me that grenade back."

"Nuh-uh. I gotta better plan." He turned to the crowd, which had surged forward. "Hey, all you stupids. Back off. *Way* off."

"I already did the MacReady thing," Jim said.

"Oh. Okay. Here's the deal. Me versus *you*." Gary pointed at Fiel. "In a battle to the undeath. Winner take all."

Mel made a face. "What?" she said. "That's stupid."

"*You're* stupid," he said. "That's why you lied to your fiancé about being a government killer, and he dumped your ass." She looked wounded by his words, and Jim was slightly uncomfortable. By the same token, she actually looked more like herself than one of them.

"I don't think this is a good plan," Jim said. "Give me the grenade back. I think I can reason with them."

"No—no—no—no. The only thing these stupids get is blunt force. And since even *I* don't have enough dick to slap all of them around, I'll just skip straight to Boss Stage. Challenge, or do we go boom-boom?" He pulled a second grenade out of his pocket and clinked the two together.

Fiel stepped forward. Her mouth yawned open, and she hissed, "Challenge accepted."

Chapter 64

"All right then." Gary turned around and tossed one of the grenades. Jim gasped, turning in time to see his mother catch it.

"Gary! Ma!" He looked at both of them in turn in frustration. "I had this."

"Honey, let's be honest. That was when everybody thought Gary was dead. And you pushed me down. I could've handled it."

"Ma, it's Gary. Do you seriously think he has a plan?"

"No. But it is Gary. He gets very lucky. I've seen it."

"That's right, Jim. Your mother has seen me get lucky." Dr. K and his daughter had joined them. "Anyone want to give me a deep, passionate kiss with some under-the-bra action before I battle for the fate of all mankind?"

Kenya folded her arms. "Who exactly are you supposed to be flirting with?"

Gary hopped off the table and smirked at her. When he turned back to Fiel, she grabbed him by the arm and wrenched it out of the socket.

"Hold it!" he shouted, holding up the grenade. "I guess I should have mentioned the ground rules first. First off, nobody does anything until *both* of us are ready." He walked over to Kenya, limply holding up his arm. "Can you fix this for me?" Kenya cocked an eyebrow at him, took his hand in both of hers, and slowly raised his arm. It popped audibly. "Better. Thank you."

Jim wondered what exactly his friend's endgame was. Of course they weren't going to play fair. Did he intend to?

"I beat you, we all go free, and you go back to wherever you came from without ending all life on Earth."

"How about her letting all these people go too?" Jim said.

"Oh yeah. You let these people go too. You beat me—which ain't likely today—and Jim and I surrender to you. You do whatever the hell it is you need to do. And we'll go willingly."

Jim wasn't so sure he agreed with that, but stayed silent.

"Winning is determined by whoever knocks the other one down three times. A knockdown can be completed with a punch, a kick, any physical striking, or by physically picking up and throwing down. No chairs— that's pro-wrestling bullshit."

"What about eye-gouging?" Fiel said.

"I . . . I guess. Any maneuver is legal so long as it's done with the body."

"What about the ripping out of intestines?"

"Sure."

"If a spine is torn out and the opponent is unable to rise again, does that constitute winning?"

"Uhhh . . ." Gary looked around. Kenya, Dr. K, and Jim's mother all mumbled in agreement. "Okay. Do you have any rules?"

"No hairpulling."

"Fine. Do we have a deal?"

"Yes," she said.

Chapter 65

Fiel smiled. This man had not yet seen even a tenth of her power. The aspect of her that allowed her to reanimate the so-called living was waning, but there was so much more she could do. She was all life, not just human, and could devour him with the bacteria inside his own body. But that would be boring. That would be . . . brief.

If she were about to end her life and all of existence, then she wanted these last few moments to last. She wanted to spread her wings and show her power in a way everyone present could appreciate. An opponent who was physically gifted, strong in appearance, would have been preferable, but she would take what she could get.

"All right, let's do this!" Gary said.

She had allowed her body to deteriorate from these meager attacks in anticipation of her transition. Now she simply reversed the deterioration. It was as simple as what she had done for Fyukis after he had thrown himself out of the apartment building. Now she was enjoying watching him rot with the old age she had exempted him from for all these decades.

The bones of her neck crackled as they realigned and knitted back together almost instantaneously. She lifted her head up, smiling as his eyes went wide in surprise.

"All right. Let's do this," he said again weakly. In the brief time she had been observing this planet, she had seen a scrum or two. Tim and Ed were quite proficient at murder. She had never engaged in such acts with her own two hands; she had always directed others. This would be . . . interesting. Perhaps she would start with—

He punched her.

Fiel pitched backward and crashed to the floor. She blinked and looked around, disoriented. A hand reached out, and she stared at it, not immediately knowing what it was for.

Fiel finally took it, and Mel pulled her up to her feet. She gave her a look of concern.

"Go for the ears. Blunt force to the chin. You'll disorient him, and he'll fall. He's almost dead. It's a miracle he's on his feet now."

"Hey, enough of that over there," Gary said. "Let's get this done with."

Fiel brushed past Mel. She clawed at his face, but he was surprisingly fast for a man who was mostly dead, dodging backward and peppering her face with three quick punches. She swiped at his head again, and he was gone. A second later his fist bonked her on the top of the head, sending her careening.

Fiel didn't understand. She was trying to hit him, but he kept moving! It was so frustrating. This was a unique feeling for her, even among the several quadrillion life-forms she had awareness of. She actually hated this particular being—this *man*.

The damage he inflicted was actually useless; she healed instantaneously. It required her to withdraw her presence from a great many life-forms, and for them it would be like waking from a strange dream. She wouldn't need them in a short while anyway, and her victory would be all the sweeter as they perished as well. All of them had been healed from their own wounds as at the time, her external influence was stronger. Now it was virtually nil; she probably couldn't reanimate a blade of grass. These last fifteen or so in this room with them were all she had influence over, and if they died, they would stay dead.

But her internal influence over her own body had grown exponentially. She allowed herself a moment to explore, realizing she had much more than human DNA she could draw upon. Fiel wanted victory via a display of power, and now was her opportunity.

As the man named Gary moved in closer to attack, she could feel her hand burning feverishly as flesh and bone began reknitting.

Chapter 66

Gary moved in to attack. Fiel was hunched over, like she was injured on her left side. Gary and Jim had both been big fans of boxing growing up, to the point they actually had gone down to a gym to train. Both of them had been cured of this desire after seeing a boy their age get knocked out cold. He had been fine, sitting up a moment later. But when they had taken out his mouthpiece, the two of them saw the empty black row where his upper teeth should have been.

It didn't stop them from fantasizing, though. And watching every boxing match that came on TV. Gary had gotten into the Philly Crabshell defense, where he could easily shoulder roll away from any right hands Fiel might throw and counter with a straight right. It looked strange watching his best friend beat up a girl, but considering the stakes, Jim rooted for him.

And then everything went to hell.

Gary was in the wrong stance for the Philly Crabshell to be most effective. He was standing right handed, while she was in a semisouthpaw stance. When she struck, it was fast, and Gary barely got his head out of the way in time. But something about that hand was different. It was bigger.

Fiel tucked it away behind her hip again, but it was big enough to where she couldn't completely hide it. Jim saw hair or fur going up her forearm and stupidly did something that was the reverse of helpful.

"Gary, look out!" Jim pointed at her, but it had the opposite effect. Gary turned and looked at Jim, allowing a precious few seconds for her to get closer and strike.

He stumbled back a couple of steps but didn't fall. That was good, at least. Then he slowly turned, revealing the cavernous hole in his chest as he did a slow-motion fall.

Chapter 67

"Gary?" Jim said. "Gary, get up."

"If he is unable to rise, we win, correct?"

"Just give him a minute. You cheated."

"I have done no such thing."

"You tore his heart out!"

"And that violated no rule. It was intended as a deathblow."

"Let me see your hand. Yeah, you *changed* it!"

"There was also no rule against body modification. If he doesn't rise before the count of ten, I expect the both of you to surrender."

Gary listened to them argue. His good buddy, Jim, always a friend to the end. He'd kind of screwed him by distracting him at a crucial moment, but no friendship was all roses. Gary felt himself drift again, like before. He'd told them he'd just fallen asleep, but it had really been much more than that. He found himself in an empty room. It felt as though nothing but him moved, as if he were the only thing exempt from the crush of time standing still. Gary could feel a presence, could sense it somewhere inside this room, but no matter where he looked, he could find no one. It was like a radio station that came in as half static.

As he explored the room now, he saw a table in the center of the room. On top of the table was a glass bowl, filled with what appeared to be water. Gary realized he had an intense thirst and went to the bowl. He put his hands to either side of it to lift it to his lips and drink, but it was either too heavy to be picked up or glued to the table. Instead, he tried to dip his hand into the bowl, hunching over it in anticipation. But his fingers bounced off what he thought was water.

Gary turned, feeling the presence in the room moving closer.

"Hello?" he said to the room. His voice sounded tinny, as if it were coming from far away instead of from his own mouth. He felt the hairs on his neck and forearms stand and turned around. This was so . . . Gary didn't know the word for it when something seemed real but couldn't be. Maybe something French.

He looked at the bowl of water again and thought about how thirsty he was. He hadn't had anything to drink in *forever*. Something in the back of his mind said if he could get this bowl out of the room, the water would be like water again, cool and refreshing. Gary put his face in the bowl and tried to lap it up like a dog. It was like he was licking a smooth block of concrete.

A voice whispered something, and his ears pricked up. It was familiar and foreign. Gary held still a moment, listening. He couldn't understand what was being said, but there was something repetitious about it that unnerved him. Gary ignored it and grabbed the table by a leg. Maybe if he could drag the whole works out of the room—

"Why do you struggle?" a voice said.

Gary jumped. He looked all over to see no one there.

"Are you afraid?" To his right sat a wizened little man, a few tufts of gray hair on his head.

This wasn't the presence he'd felt before. This was someone new. Ish.

"I'm not afraid of anything. I'm just thirsty as hell."

The old man pointed. "What would happen if you were to never drink from that bowl? You know this place isn't real, right?"

"Shah." Gary waved a hand. "Of course I do." He hadn't known that, but didn't feel the need to admit it to this complete stranger. Was this some sort of dream state?

"Yes and no."

"Yes and no what?"

"It is and it isn't a dream. It is the dream of the dying."

"Why am I here and not . . ."

"In heaven or hell?" The old man gave a mighty shrug. "You came here because this place is a source of immense gravity. To you."

"But I don't even know where this is. How can this place be important to me?"

Another shrug. This guy was already getting annoying.

"You are not the first."

"To die? Duh."

The old man smirked, and Gary got the impression that he wasn't just old, but *really* old.

"I mean to come to a place not the final destination. It usually means something."

"What, so I'm in purgatory? I don't believe in that."

"Not purgatory." The old man waved a hand. "Eh, Adjacent to that."

"What does that mean?"

"You are not done."

Gary *hated* the way this guy spoke. Like in half sentences or something, waiting for Gary to fill in the rest.

"And *why* am I not done?"

"Because there is more to do."

Gary narrowed his eyes. "Could you cut the crap? Just out with it already. What are you trying to say?"

The old man shook his head. "You are listening?" He held up a finger. Gary was about to say something else when he heard the steady rhythm of a voice. It sounded like . . .

Counting.

And then he remembered.

"I have to get back up . . . down . . . I have to get back! How do I—"

"Take the bowl out of the room."

"But I can't! That thing is glued down or something."

"It will pain me to say it, but listen. When what is obvious and apparent is impossible, make what is obscure and incapable happen."

"Hey, look, I'm a Christian. I don't get all into—"

"The bowl cannot be moved. Move the room instead."

"Move the room? What the hell does that mean?"

"Grab the handle and push!"

Gary didn't know what that meant either. But as if his arm were powered on instinct, it lifted and began grasping at air. His hand wrapped around something just to the side of his face. He could feel it despite not seeing anything there. He looked at the old man, who gestured toward the wall. Gary saw that there was a door now that hadn't been there a moment ago.

He "pulled" the room and was surprised when it actually began to move. He paused and checked to see the table was now several feet closer to the far wall, the opposite direction from the door. He pushed the other way, and it appeared as though the table was sliding toward him, but his brain retranslated it so that he saw the whole room as moving and the table as remaining still.

Gary had to turn his eyes away. It was disorienting, giving him a feeling akin to seasickness. When the table bumped into his legs, he climbed over it as he continued to push, and a moment later, the table had slid completely out of the room.

He let go of the handle and rushed out of the room. The table was there, but the bowl and the water were both gone.

"Hey, where'd it go?" he asked, popping his head back into the room.

"What?" the old man said.

"The bowl. Where did it go?"

"Where it has always been."

Gary was giving serious thought to beating the shit out of him.

"Are you . . . God?"

"I've no idea who you're talking about."

"That wasn't a no."

"No. I haven't met God." The old man made air quotes for some reason. "I couldn't pick him out of a lineup."

It wasn't a denial of God's existence exactly, but neither was it a confirmation. Gary had a feeling the old man was significant to the cosmos somehow. Despite his religious affiliation, he did believe in aliens and higher beings. The Bible was simply a part of God's story, and God had done things both before and after it.

"Who created this place?"

"You did. You needed rest."

Gary could feel himself fading as he was being pulled back to that other place. There was so much more he wanted to know. He opened his mouth to speak, but no sound came out.

"Don't worry," the old man said. "You can come back anytime you want. The answers will all wait."

Chapter 68

Gary stirred. Jim was never religious, but he said a small prayer as Gary slowly got up. He had convinced Fiel that a thirty-second count was proper. He'd taken it as slowly as possible, gradually coming to the conclusion that Gary really was dead this time.

Gary looked around. That hole in his chest looked awful. He smiled at Jim and waved before Fiel rushed over and hit him again, knocking him down a second time.

"Hey, no fair!" Jim screamed. Fiel shrugged, holding up two fingers to signify she had almost won. Gary got up again. It was obvious he was in no shape for a fight. Fiel cocked her head, obviously sensing the end was near.

"In one move I will clear the entire chessboard with my first move," she said.

"You said 'move' twice," Gary said.

"I know," Fiel said. She looked annoyed.

"It's just when you're redundant like that, the listener tends to focus in on the second word rather than the meaning of the entire sentence."

She stepped forward and kicked out his knee, bones cracking like dry branches over someone's knee. Gary hobbled backward, teetered, and stayed upright. Jim saw Fiel's foot had turned into a giant hoof.

Gary backed up a little more, adopting the crane style like Daniel did in *The Karate Kid*. To Jim's knowledge, Gary didn't know karate.

She tore his arm off. Jim and everyone else gasped. Even Mel had a horrified look on her face.

"Wow. You're a celestial being, and this is the best you could do?" Gary asked.

"Gary, are you okay?" Jim's mother asked.

"What the hell are you doing?" Jim asked.

"Poking the bear." He turned back to Fiel. "Who would've thought that the personification of life itself could be so ugly?"

"What?" Fiel looked at him curiously. "I constructed this body to be the epitome of beauty. All men desire me."

"And I don't mind a little extra in the trunk, but you gotta wide, flabby ass."

"I do *not*."

"Sure you do. Jim and I were talking about that the first night we saw you. Weren't we, Jim?"

"Look at the blonde with the floppy donkey booty, that's what we said." Jim didn't know the play, but he could go along.

Fiel's eyes went wide.

"You *monster*!"

Jim was about to make some clever quip when she flung herself at Gary. He got his arm up at the last moment, putting his bad foot down and yanking, pulling her off her feet, ankles over ass, and spilling her across the floor. Fiel immediately got up, her eyes wild, ready to tear him apart. All eight of her fingers elongated and fell like loose strings. They darkened, and Jim noted the talonlike tips. She began flailing her arms around, her whip fingers whistling through the air. Jim had recognized her hand had turned into a big cat's paw and her other foot into a hoof of a large animal, but he had never seen anything like this.

Gary hobbled away from her as quickly as he could. She swung and missed, those claws embedding themselves into a table and ripping a chunk off. There was a beaker filled with clear liquid next to him, and Gary grabbed it and flung it at her head. Fiel screamed as it smashed into her face, her skin reddening, blistering, and healing within seconds. She hadn't tried to get out of the way. She hadn't even blinked.

Her transformation continued, her arms changing to match her fingers, darkening and going boneless until she had two purple-gray noodley appendages.

She screeched, and the sound was earsplitting. It sounded like the mating cry of a giant bird. An appendage flailed in Gary's direction, and he dived out of the way. It seemed as if she had gone beyond anger; Gary's continued existence seemed to offend her.

He had backed up nearly to the wall, where several of her followers stood. She swiped, and he tucked and rolled out of the way again, her talons burying into the flesh of three men. They cried out in pain and grabbed at the cords, but even they must have had barbs because the men pulled their hands away, bloody gashes in their palms from where they'd touched her.

She yanked, and the talons ripped free, the men either dying instantly or fainting from the pain. Others began backing away in fear. Even Mel, although she wasn't backing into the entranceway.

Fiel threw her head back and howled, the sound throaty and floor shaking. Two more followers dropped dead, and their bodies shriveled like they'd been sucked dry by an invisible straw. She was bigger suddenly, and bony protrusions came out of every exposed area of skin. No way could Gary knock her down now even if he'd had two good arms and legs.

Fiel continued to grow, no part of her recognizable as human now. Her face had split down the middle, and the two halves sagged, a wedge of white bone forcing its way out. Four fist-size, gaping black holes were to either side of the wedge, and Jim had the distinct impression these were her eyes.

Her mouth yawned open, her jaw extending all the way down to the middle of her chest. Her breasts had withered and hung off the bulbous torso, her shirt shredded and hanging onto what had been full, curvaceous hips mere moments before.

Another man screamed and fell to the floor. He reached for Jim in his last few seconds, realization dawning in his blue eyes as the life drained out of him. It took only seconds, and his flesh looked like the same texture as beef jerky.

There were fewer than a dozen of Fiel's people left, one of them Mel. Jim looked at her.

"Honey," he said, "look at what she's doing. You have to break free, or she'll drag you down with her."

Mel thrust her chin out. "My life for her. None of us would have lived if not for her. Every second is a blessing I don't deserve."

"So you're cool with being sucked dry like a can of pop?"

She blinked. "I. . ." Her voice trailed off.

Jim wanted to press the attack. It seemed as if the others could make some independent decisions if placed in a stressful enough situation. Her master had just turned into a thing and was draining her followers to underwrite its transformation. "Mel, she wants to do this to the rest of the world. That means your family too."

She pulled a look of disgust. "I have no family."

He thought for a panicked moment. "Your brother. What about your brother? Doesn't he matter to you? He'll die too." She made another face like she wasn't sure. "What about me? I know we took a hard left, but are you telling me there isn't a part of you that wasn't hopeful we'd work through it? That we'd get back together?" Another hesitation after she took a step toward him. He raised his hand. "Come on, Mel. I *need* you. I *love* you."

Fiel's reshaped body hunched to avoid the ceiling. What she'd gained in mass, she'd more than lost in speed and mobility. Even with a bad leg, Gary was able to get away from her. There were only two of her minions left, not including Mel, the men holding onto one another in terror.

"For her," one of them said, his voice trembling. His body shriveled so fast his eyes exploded from his head, reddish-grayish goo hitting the other man in the face.

"For her," he said weakly.

"You don't want that, Mel. You want a life. No matter how we came to be, here we are. We're *people*. We're alive."

"For . . . her," she said, and his heart ached for the woman he loved. She had edged forward, and he took two big steps to meet her, clasping her hands in his.

"For *us*."

Pools of tears were standing in her eyes. Jim would have been crying too if he'd had tear ducts that worked.

Fiel had just about destroyed the far wall with one swipe. Gary was getting away pretty handily, but she appeared to have him cornered and was closing in. She now had five appendages, those whiplike cords with talons on the ends. Her mouth was the size of a door and hung open wide enough for him to step into. She lashed out with one of her talons, and Gary caught it with his remaining hand.

He jumped backward, pulling faster than she could follow. She must have been front heavy, because she began to topple. But there was nowhere for him to go. Nowhere for him to go as those taut cords wrapped around his arm kept him where he was. She fell on him, a mighty grunt escaping her as she hit the floor.

Chapter 69

When she finally rose and turned around, Jim could see that she was also worse for wear. Gary had kept her at bay with various instruments, impaling her with pieces of jagged glass, scalpels, scissors, and other makeshift weapons. The head she'd had had been shed for a massive, pulsing purple sponge thing without eyes.

She slid back to Jim's group, throwing her talons in the air in what he guessed must've been a declaration of victory. She roared, and this time her horrible voice did shake the room.

"You think you won?" Jim asked.

The roar stopped short, and the pulsing thing atop her massive body narrowed.

"I'm sorry, but it looks entirely different to me. I saw Gary pull you over. I saw you lose."

She pulled off his remaining arm, which had been stuck to her body, holding it aloft as if evidence of her victory.

"So what? It's an arm, not a trophy. You . . . lost."

The creature roared again and pointed as best she could with a ropy appendage at Gary's inert form a couple of dozen feet away. Jim steeled himself, not wanting to think about Gary.

"You remember the rules. Downed by the other person. You didn't knock him down. He pulled you down on top of him. You—*lose.*"

The purple spongy thing rotated left and right. Was that her shaking her head? Mel put her hands to either side of her head and groaned in agony.

"She says . . . she fell on top of him," Mel said. She knocked him down with her body. She wins."

"And the only reason she fell was because he pulled her over."

"And when she fell . . . she fell on top of Gary."

This conversation was going nowhere. Jim wasn't about to budge and concede the end of the world.

"I have a suggestion," Dr. K said. They both looked at him. "Sudden death," he said. "It doesn't appear as though Gary is in any condition to continue, so why not allow Jim as an alternate?"

"Me?" Jim pointed stupidly at himself.

"Why not? You're both approximately the same size, the same build. You're a viable sub."

"She accepts," Mel said.

"Wait a minute!" Jim's mother said. "He can't. I'll go."

"She does not accept. Only him."

"He's my baby, dammit. James, *no*. I forbid it!"

Jim closed his eyes a moment. "One condition," he said. "Mel and the others take my mother out of here. It's the only way to keep her from interfering."

Mel moved toward his mother. She got into a stance, but before she could do anything, Dr. K popped the cap off a syringe and injected her in the neck. Jim's mother turned and slapped his hand away, but the damage was done.

"You promised," she said to Jim before her eyes rolled up in her head.

Kenya caught her slumping body.

Chapter 70

It took a moment for the three of them to collect Jim's mother and carry her to the door. Fiel's last follower stayed behind, a wild look in the man's eyes. He was clearly afraid, but seemed to accept his life was "for her."

The Fiel-creature vibrated, the sensation coming up through Jim's feet. She was almost as wide as she was tall, several more tentacles having sprouted from her body. Jim was more able-bodied than Gary, but this thing was a lot more menacing than what he'd faced.

Gary.

Jim didn't know if he'd survived—he couldn't see how, but held out hope. There was too much junk around Gary for Jim to get a good look. He had to focus now on the impossible task at hand.

Who was he kidding? There was no way he could knock her down. Not without getting his arms ripped off. He didn't know how Gary had managed not to freak out when that had happened. Jim had an idea. He'd run into the vault and lock himself in. If Fiel couldn't get in, she couldn't get what she needed to transition or whatever and end all life on Earth. Someone would eventually have to come along, and they would kill her or something.

He nodded that he was ready. Before he could move, one of the tentacles whipped out, snatching a chair off the floor and flinging it at him. Jim ducked on instinct, feeling the chair pass overhead as he hit the floor, recalling that that had been against the rules, but to panicked to call it out. He heard Fiel's giant body slithering closer and rolled over and began crawling in another direction, hopefully away from her.

Jim rounded a corner and climbed to his feet, peeking around to see her still coming his way. The purple spongy thing had sprouted what looked like three bright red antennae, swiveling around like they were honing in on his location. In the other direction was a straight shot to the corner where Gary had been, but there were so many broken-up tables and chairs over there, he couldn't really make out anything.

Jim looked down and saw a deep pan of some clear liquid. It could have been water; it could have been acid. He picked it up and hefted it at her. A tentacle whipped at it and shattered it midair, liquid and glass fragments splashing her and the floor. As she slithered over where most of the water had fallen, she teetered. For a second, Jim thought she was about to fall, and then he realized—even if she did fall, she wouldn't stop. She was too close to winning, too close to what she wanted.

He grabbed a chair by its legs and hurled it at her. The chair bounced off harmlessly as she continued advancing on his position. He looked over his shoulder at the vault door as he backed up. This was it: either he ran in there now and prayed for someone else to save him, or he stayed out here and found a way.

"Dammit," he mumbled and turned toward the mess of chairs and tables, climbing over and tossing things aside, trying to put more space between them. Jim's leg caught on something, and he looked to see a metal shard sticking out of the floor that had hooked through the leg of his pants.

"*Dammit*," he said again. He didn't wait, unbuttoning and unzipping his pants right away to get them off. Jim wasn't thinking all the way through, though. He had his feet jammed halfway up the pant legs when he realized he should have taken off his shoes.

Fiel had wedged herself mostly through the narrow walkway, already lashing out at him with her long, barbarous tentacles. Thick goo flicked off them, sprinkling Jim in the face and neck she was so close. He managed to get his feet out of the shoes and slid the rest of the way out of his pants. Jim fell on his ass and crab-walked backward until he was right on top of Gary.

Or at least where he should have been.

Jim slid his hands over the floor, trying to confirm what he was seeing. Despite his situation, he found himself smiling. Gary was alive! Sort of. He had to have been horribly mangled in the fall, and he would be for real dead in short order, but not just yet.

Fiel squeezed through and began inching toward him. Jim could go around the other corner, but he was going to have to climb over a pile of broken chairs.

Jim would have to dive in and swim through those chairs in order to have a chance. The first tentacle slapped the floor inches away from him, ripping away tile in its wake. He scrambled to his feet, pressing his back into the corner where the adjacent walls met. She had to have known she had him trapped.

Fiel drew closer. Her tentacles raised; any one of them poised to strike could probably break every bone in his body. Jim would have swallowed nervously had he saliva.

In what he thought were the closing seconds of his life, a tentacle or a tail wrapped around his ankles. Jim was yanked off his feet, and with a tiny plosive of air, his back hit the floor.

"*I* win." Fiel's voice, wherever it had come from, was sultry and feminine. The giant thing before him ceased moving, the tentacles dropping off and liquefying. The rest of it calcified in seconds, shrinking in on itself and beginning to crack at the top.

Seconds later tiny fingers peeked out of its center, and it was opened. Out stepped Fiel from the desiccated husk in all her feminine perfection completely naked.

"I must say I did not expect you to be as enjoyable as the other one. And you are not physically repulsive to me." She waggled her hand. "Entirely." She came closer and stooped in front of him, her full breasts swinging in his direction. "Would you like to have sex? I am still a virgin. The males of your species value this, yes?"

His eyes drifted to the thick blonde bush between her legs. Even though he was terrified, Jim did feel himself responding.

"No?" he eventually said.

She cocked her head and smiled at him. "You're lying. You desire me. Even now. At the end. You should consider the point of remaining chaste for the affections of a woman you spurned. And the fact you're all about to die anyway. I have seen several movies that indicate the act is quite pleasurable." She made air quotes around the word "movies," and Jim guessed she was either using them wrong or was talking about porn.

Jim didn't ask how she knew about Mel. He didn't think it mattered. He pondered reconsidering a moment, not out of desire but to prolong all of existence for a few minutes more. "Doin' it for mankind," he could almost hear Gary say.

Hell, who was he kidding? A woman built like her, the world would meet its doom in seconds.

Her curly blonde hair spilled over one shoulder, and she stared at him with those big violet eyes. Jim had to snap himself out of her entrancing stare by reminding himself that she had just turned into a giant, man-drinking monster not long before.

She smiled, her full lips parting to reveal perfectly straight white teeth. "Time's up." She had her forearms draped across shapely thighs and held her hands out in front of Jim. At first he thought she was about to touch him, but she went up and down his body, a buffer of space between them until she stopped, one hand poised over his ribs.

"There it is," she said.

"There *what* is?" he wanted to ask, but a second later, pain lanced his entire body. Jim shook violently as she looked at him with intense curiosity. He wished he could have blacked out or at least screamed. The pain was too much to bear in silence. His nerve endings were alive and on fire as every part of him jerked and bucked, Fiel curiously watching him with her hands held out as if she were warming her hands by a campfire.

Jim's spine bowed as he began seizing. She leaned back on the balls of her feet and began roaming her hands over her face, breasts, and stomach, and between her thighs. Fiel seemed to have gone into the deepest of ecstasies as she began panting heavily, biting the edges of her hands, pinching her nipples, and sliding her fingers over the cleft of her vagina.

Jim felt something suffusing throughout his body. He felt full to bursting, beneath the agony a familiar sensation his mind couldn't comprehend. His arms and legs were totally out of his control, kicking and scratching at anything around him. Fiel was touching herself, still on the balls of her feet, and bouncing like she was riding him. He was certain his skin was about to come off when his whole body went rigid as *something* left his body.

He collapsed, exhausted, breathing heavily. Jim had no idea what that had been, but the sudden lack of pain was a pleasure all unto itself. His heart hammered in his chest, and he realized—his heart was hammering in his chest!

Was he alive? Jim couldn't help but smile as he looked around. His skin had mostly returned to its normal color, and his mouth flooded with saliva to the point he began drooling uncontrollably. He began sweating, and if he weren't so exhausted, he would have wiped his arm across his forehead.

He finally looked at Fiel. God, she was *beautiful*. He should have hated her, but in that moment, he would have given her anything she wanted. It had to be the afterglow of whatever had just happened. Jim felt the warm damp against him in his underwear and knew it definitely wasn't pee this time.

She held something between her thumb and forefinger, though. He forced his eyes to focus on it, and yes, it was one of those black pills. Had she pulled *that* out of him?

"No," he said weakly just before she popped in into her mouth.

"Ahhhh," she said and smiled. "Just one more to go. Where is the other one's body? He has to be around here somewhere."

As if on cue, something dropped out of the ceiling and fell on her. Fiel lay sprawled on the floor, her head between Jim's thighs as a pulverized and dismembered Gary began savagely biting at her neck. Jim couldn't believe that his friend was still alive. Well, sort of.

His legs were completely shattered, hanging off him at odd angles. Gary tore long strips of flesh off her neck and back, swallowing them and diving back in until he could get to muscle. If Fiel had been knocked unconscious, she quickly woke up and began screaming. Her eyes were wild, frightened, as she tried to push herself off the floor, and between mouthfuls, Gary headbutted the back of her skull several times until she went back down.

Gary shimmied up her body and tore her ear off, taking a strip of cheek with it. She moaned loudly on the floor, her arms fumbling as if they had an uncoordinated mind of their own as she made a weak attempt to move. He headbutted the side of her face twice, and she went still. Gary had torn away all the skin beneath one eye all the way to her nose and down to her jaw. He went back to her neck, savaging free ropes of muscle, blood spraying Jim and slowly pooling around him.

When Gary's teeth finally clicked against bone, he moved to another section of neck, chewing away flesh until the bones were fully exposed.

From Jim's angle, he could see skin and muscle begin to regenerate and attempt to knit together. Gary attacked this new flesh, consuming it just as feverishly as before. There was already more blood on the floor than Jim could believe one human body could hold. It soaked into his underwear and socks, both already dark with filth.

Gary headbutted the back of Fiel's head several more times, and she twitched even more. A giant mound of flesh formed at the base of her skull, and Gary chewed through it. Finally, he reared back and shoved the bone of his upper arm into the wound, fished around, and her head came off.

Jim could do nothing but sit in horror as her body finally began to succumb to the damage Gary was inflicting. Strings of some kind extended from her neck to her head, but Gary shredded those and gave her head a last few headbutts for good measure.

Her head had spilled over Jim's thigh, attached by only a thick strip of flesh. After all he'd seen tonight alone, Jim shouldn't have been surprised when she spoke, but he was.

"I've read your Bible," she said. That made Gary pause. "In my brief period of consciousness, I have never met him, but I know it could have been none other than him. He stole from me to make you. You are supposed to strive to be like his son, but you will always fail. Not because he is 'perfect.' Because he *knows*. You are expected to survive on faith, while he has definitive knowledge." She laughed softly. "Do you know how infinite the gap is between certainty and even the most miniscule doubt? You will strive to know him, and he will pass you by. All I wished was to spare you a grand embarrassment."

Fiel laughed again, louder this time. Jim could hear her mocking him, mocking all of mankind with that laugh. They may have stopped her, but ultimately she hadn't lost because surviving had never been her measure of victory.

Gary reared his head back and, with a strangled cry, smashed into her skull. He did it over and over again until Jim heard the thick crack of bone breaking. He closed his eyes as Gary clenched bone between his teeth and lifted a section away. Jim couldn't close his ears, though, as his best friend ate her brain.

It went on for what felt like forever, until Gary finally slumped onto Jim's side. They lay like that for a while.

Chapter 71

Nobody came in. Jim figured they had to have been suspicious or even curious. Maybe they were certain the two of them had died and were waiting on the end of everything else. He kept expecting her body to fizzle and dissolve, but it stayed there like a real dead body. Fiel's brainless head lay a few feet away from them, and her headless body was just about in his lap.

He felt Gary moving and looked at him.

"Gary?" he said. "That you?"

"Yeah," Gary said after a long moment. His voice was drunken and . . . thick. "I blanked out there a moment. Did I . . . did I just do something weird?"

Jim thought a moment. The answer was yes if he was asking about eating another human being. The answer was no if the question was if he had just saved the world.

"Not really."

"Good." He was silent awhile, and Jim kept thinking any minute his friend was about to die. "I'm so *tired*."

"You should be. You just saved the world. The whole universe!"

"For really real?"

"Yeah."

Gary raised the nubbin that was the remains of one arm. He began wagging it back and forth slowly, then faster.

"What's that?"

"I'm giving myself a hand. Nobody else around to do it."

Jim stood. The movement was slow, and just about every bone in his body crackled. He punted the head, and a wave of goose bumps passed over him. Jim took a deep breath—it felt good to breathe, even with the rank husk of that thing Fiel had emerged from a few feet away. He put his hands together once, twice, building a pace until he was applauding his friend.

Once again he was expecting Gary to pass, and once again he was still here. It couldn't have been comfortable to be in the state he was. Legs pulverized, one arm completely ripped off, and the other arm half missing. Jim wanted him to stay, even now, even like this.

"You okay, Gary?"

"Yeah. I'm pretty good." He let his head drop back against the wall. "No, I'm not. I don't feel so good, Jim. I feel like I need to hurl."

Then he leaned forward, opened his mouth, and left.

Jim put his hands to his mouth. That was really it this time. Gary was gone.

Jim wept.

Again.

For really real.

Chapter 72

They eventually came back, Jim's mother included. Dr. K couldn't keep his eyes off her for some reason. Jim hoped it wasn't another schoolboy crush on her.

"She has a remarkable metabolism," Dr. K said, taking her in. "She should have been out for another four hours at least."

"You're lucky my son isn't dead." She smiled at the doctor, cradling Jim's head to her chest. Jim got the threat and decided not to point out that had he been dead, the rest of the world would have followed shortly after.

"What happened to her head?" Mel asked. "And your pants? And her clothes?"

Jim was numb. Not for what they had narrowly avoided, at least he hoped so, but for Gary. His friend of more than twenty years really was gone. Jim had to have spent at least fifteen minutes straight crying.

"It's okay, baby, it's okay." His mother was holding on really tight, and he couldn't have been closer to her boobs unless she was feeding him.

"So what does this all mean?" Kenya said.

"I don't know," Dr. K said. "I really don't know. If she was who she said, then we shouldn't be here anymore." He put a crooked index finger to his chin and then leaned over to examine the headless body.

"I found the head!" Mel announced happily. She was over by a far wall. "The brain's gone. Jim, where's her brain?"

A smoke detector went off. They all looked around until Jim could smell smoke.

"Fire," Dr. K said, pointing out the obvious. Jim's mother got to her feet and dragged Jim up too. Jim didn't want to go. He kept expecting Gary to lift his head and say he was all right. That it was just a scratch or something else smart-assy. He imagined them as old men, Gary just a torso and a head, sitting on a porch.

Gary just kept not moving, though.

And then Jim saw it on the floor, just below his mouth like he'd spat it up. And then Jim lost it all over again.

The pill.

He pointed and screamed, having to be dragged away by all of them until Dr. K pulled out another syringe and popped it into Jim's neck.

Chapter 73

They watched it burn. Sure, Police and Fire eventually came, but by then the best anyone could do was control the blaze enough that it didn't burn down any other buildings, not that that would necessarily be a bad thing in this neighborhood.

Despite it being a secondary base of operations, Dr. K didn't own the place in any legal sense, and thus there was nothing to connect him with anything that had gone on inside. They had put Jim in the passenger seat of Dr. K's truck and hadn't stood out in the least as they watched along with fifty-plus other onlookers watching as the burning building nearly singed its adjacent neighbors.

They had reason to stick around. The creature inside had definitely appeared dead, but had it still had any of the power it had shown before, they had to be sure. The early morning was cold, and the fire warmed them some, although they were all kept back a fair distance.

"I'm getting tired," Mel said. "And I'd like to get Jim home."

"I think I'd like to sleep on the couch if you don't mind," Jim's mother said. "Just so I can know he's safe."

"Take my truck," Dr. K said. "And, Kenya, you should go home and get rest too."

"You're staying?" his daughter asked.

"Just for a little while longer."

"Anybody holding?" She narrowed her eyes at the crowd.

"That nice young man with the thick gold chain over there, I think."

Kenya shook her head and smiled. "Just give Mom a call, okay? I know you guys are a little weird right now, but she thinks you're dead."

"Sure—sure. I'll call her in a few hours."

Dr. K made his way over to the man and enjoyed a joint or two while the fire eventually died down and the crowd gradually petered out.

He didn't know why he stayed. It wasn't on the suspicion that that thing posing as a beautiful woman was still alive. He just . . . stayed.

So when something did emerge from the mudlike ash, he actually was surprised. He had a few items with him, but nothing that could destroy something that could have survived a several-hour-long fire.

He approached cautiously. It was more than just the curious scientist in him; it was also the morbid voyeur. Whatever it was had to have been hideously deformed. Temperatures inside the building had to have risen several hundred degrees. Whatever semblance of life this thing had clung to was hardy and painfully earned.

It was still digging itself out when he got within a few feet of it. Dr. K could make out milky white limbs in the moonlight and the bulbous mass of something that might have been a head. It was difficult to tell what was what in the poorly lit filth.

"It's you," he said a moment later when it finally flipped over and stared at him.

Chapter 74

Jim woke an hour before sunrise. He didn't know how he'd made it home and where Mel had come from, but he lay there just a little while longer with her body draped across his.

He felt refreshed. His mind was clear, although a little foggy on the events leading up to him going to sleep. He remembered running away from *something*. What, he couldn't have said. He remembered Gary had been hurt, but it couldn't have been too bad if he'd gone home and to bed.

Jim eased himself from underneath Mel an inch at a time. There was something about her too. He stood over her, naked but not really caring that he had no clothes on for the first time he could remember. It was as if that awkwardness had been an old version of himself, and he had shed it. Like he'd been through something that made the everyday things that always bothered him trivial. He shrugged and went into the living room.

There was someone on the couch. Whoever it was was covered in a blanket, which made Jim think he or she was an invited guest. Too small to be Gary, maybe it was a friend of Mel's.

Jim crept over and peeled the blanket back from his mother's face. Then he remembered he was still naked. He felt his cheeks go hot, but it was a normal kind of embarrassment, not his usual, panicky, sweaty, have-to-be-talked-out-of-his-bedroom version. He smiled at his mother and covered her face.

In this moment he felt like he could have gone outside and done ball-flapping jumping jacks in the parking lot. Save for a small sore spot on his neck, Jim felt *really* good. The only thing disconcerting was exactly *why* he felt this way.

He was typically in good health, despite his usual deprecating sense of self. Jim went over to the refrigerator and poured himself a glass of milk while he contemplated where this new buoyant feeling was coming from.

It had to do with the blank period in his memory. As he sat at the table, sipping his milk, he began to recall brief snippets. There was a doctor he'd met with Gary and . . .

"Oh shit!" he said. His mother stirred, and he covered his mouth belatedly. He remembered the pill and the people shooting. *Gary* being shot. Eating *garbage*. All of it came back to him in a flood, and he felt like yelling at someone to make it stop. He couldn't contain himself and had to step outside.

He was careful not to shut the door and lock himself out. It was one thing to be out here with no clothes on; it was another to have to knock on the door for his mother to let him back in. Jim wasn't worried about neighbors; he and Mel had the only apartment on the second floor. Besides, today was Sunday.

That made him smile wide despite all the crap flooding back to him.

"Dammit!" he said when the door closed. Oh well, he may as well enjoy it out here for a little while. The sun was coming up soon; the horizon was a nice mauve. He sat down on a concrete step and enjoyed the boys dangling in a light breeze. The only thing that would have made this even nicer was a nice fatty. It had been a long time since he'd partaken. Maybe he would later.

But what to do about Gary? Jim scratched his ear. What had happened had been beyond awful. But somehow, he wasn't even worried about that. It was almost as if that was going to be all right too. He was concerned about Will, though.

Just as he felt himself settling in, he got a pee-boner. Usually he woke up with one, but whatever. He stood and walked to the rail, estimating how far away the bushes were, and let fly between the spindles. His arc was fantastic, like he'd never peed before. As he was finishing up, he thought he heard something below him. Now this would be embarrassing. He was the only one up here and had no place to go. Hopefully, it wasn't a cop. and he prayed he hadn't just urinated on somebody's head. Jim would have to move posthaste.

As whoever it was started up the stairs, he thought about calling out. Maybe he could talk the person out of coming upstairs. The floodlights on this part of the building were out, so he couldn't see the landing below him clearly, but a bulky shadow appeared a moment later and rounded up his stairs.

Jim stepped back, hoping it wasn't Deepdick. He felt awkward around that guy every time he saw him. There was something about seeing another guy's shaft and knowing he was packing a cannon when you were moderate at best that was a little intimidating.

"I am so glad you're naked," the person at the bottom of the stairs said to him. Panic seized Jim, stronger than he had ever felt in his life before. It was one thing for someone to think he was gay; it was another thing entirely if that person was about to actively do something about it. He didn't want to fight, and he especially didn't want to do it naked.

When Gary emerged from the shadows, whole and intact, Jim was shocked into relief. He ran to his friend and threw his arms around him.

"Uh, Jim?" Gary said. "The streams shall not cross."

Jim took a step back, still holding his friend by the shoulders. "But how?" he asked, searching his eyes. Not only was Gary alive, but he had arms and legs and pallor.

Gary was *alive.*

"Fiel." He shook his head and smiled. "I don't know why, and I don't know how."

"How do you feel?"

"*Great.*" Gary shrugged. "Elias is going to be pissed, though."

"Oh yeah. I forgot about him. Will's okay. My mom and Mel too."

"For real?" Gary searched Jim's eyes, and for a moment both men teared up. It would have been an awesome moment for a hug, but they'd already done that, and, well . . . they were naked still.

"Mel?" Gary raised an eyebrow.

"Yeah, I think so."

Jim couldn't resist touching his friend and threw an arm around his shoulders. The sun had just peeked over the horizon, and the minor amount of warmth in the chill air felt good, but it was time to go in. They both gazed at the sun a moment, and to Jim it was like the birth of a whole new life for him. For the first time, he didn't know all the answers and was perfectly okay with that. Maybe he would feel differently in a few hours or days, but he was okay with that too.

"Hey, what's the deal with that?" Gary asked, thumbing over his shoulder toward the parking lot. Jim looked and saw his Ford Fiesta haphazardly backed into two spots in the parking lot. A rear tire was up on the curb. His car was covered in filth and bashed in on the passenger side, and the windshield was severely cracked on the left. It looked like there was a note pinned beneath a wiper.

Jim shook his head and shrugged, not really caring enough about his car to get upset right now. Instead, he gripped Gary around the shoulders even tighter, raised his hand, and knocked on the door.

"My mom's on the couch." Jim smiled, knowing some comment or other was coming.

"Nothing out here she hasn't seen before."

"Good morning."

They both turned at the voice behind them. The tall, onyx-skinned neighbor from downstairs was wearing a powder blue and white silk robe. He had Jim's Tupperware container in his hands and a half smile on his face. "I brought this back. You guys partying in there?"

He took a step forward, his smile broadening.

Jim could feel his mother leaning against the other side of the door as she looked through the peephole. The doorknob turned in his hand.

"No!" he and Gary screamed together.

Epilogue

Jim was dead. He lay there, at the end of his life, listening to a fly or something buzzing around and reflecting on how exactly he'd gotten here, on the carpet of his living room.

"I'm dead. Am I . . . dead?" he said several times, the voice coming out of him sounding like a stranger's. He heard laughter cut through the air and wondered why Gary and Mel had poisoned him.

"Baby," Mel said, spooning against him on the floor, "you're going to be fine. Just . . . go with it."

"Why did you let me do that?" Jim asked. "This is *terrible*." He rolled over on his side, hugging himself.

Even though it hadn't been that long since he'd toked, the sensation was infinitely worse than he recalled. Even with the vertigo dissipating, it still felt like the walls were tilting in and on the verge of collapsing on him. His whole body felt ten times heavier, and it was all he could do to lift his head even slightly off the floor.

"Maybe she was right," Gary said. "Maybe this isn't for you anymore." Jim could see him on the couch as Mel took another spliff. Gary hadn't even smoked any this time, instead just watching the two of them pass it back and forth until Jim felt the pull of gravity like a high-powered, industrial magnet and fell to the floor. Mel began stroking his belly until gradually he felt somewhat normal again.

"Let's go for a walk," Mel said. "That okay?"

Gary had already lost interest in them, the remote in his hand like he was about to turn the TV on.

They stepped outside, and the fresh, cool air was like a dialysis machine. Jim could already feel his head clearing. Mel laced her fingers through his and tucked her body into him. He felt even better. He didn't care that it was getting cold out; being next to Mel always felt good.

"I don't want to have a talk-talk, Jim," she began, and he felt a slight dread creep into his guts. No man wanted to have "the talk," and this certainly sounded like it even if she was saying it wasn't. It had been a week since all the craziness had ended with the Adjacent and Gary dying and magically returning to life.

Well, not magic-magic, but something.

"Jim," Mel said, interrupting his thoughts.

"Yeah—yeah. Just a little . . . cloudy still." He was, but he also didn't want to have this conversation. He'd been bold with her in the heat of anger all those days ago, but now he was just a little boy not wanting anything but love and approval. "Sorry, you were saying?"

"I don't wanna lose you," she said. His heart filled.

"I . . . don't want to lose you either, Mel. I love you." He recalled that something had happened to Mel too, although he didn't understand entirely what it had been.

"We got off on the wrong foot." She stopped on the walkway near the basketball hoop at the rear of the parking lot. He looked at her and contained his smile as she bit the corner of her lower lip. She was sexy when she did that. Hell, Mel was sexy no matter what she did. "I've done some things I'm not proud of. For a while I didn't really think about it. I suppose I never wanted to." Neither of them needed to say what those things were. Mel was some sort of contract killer for one government agency or another. And apparently, his mother had been too. "I didn't tell you because I couldn't. I couldn't tell anyone. And, well, it was easier if I didn't have a past."

"Your parents?"

"Retired teachers. They live in Arizona."

He nodded. "And your brother?"

She rolled her eyes. It had been because of him that some of this had been brought to a head. "Let's just say he . . . washed out of the business. But he's always been able to find me."

He turned to hug her, and she put a palm to his chest. "What?"

Mel forced a smile, and her eyes rose to meet his.

"I'm kind of . . . not done."

"Kind of not done? What does that mean?"

She huffed. "I can't exactly put in a letter of resignation. I have to fulfill a contract."

"What does that mean?" he asked again.

"Three," Mel said, holding up fingers. "I have three more."

Jim opened his mouth to speak, but nothing came out. He honestly didn't know what he could've said.

Mel nodded, turned, and began walking again. Jim quickly caught up with her. She'd folded her arms against the cold, and he wrapped his arms around her as best he could.

"This feels awkward. Would you let me go?"

Jim slid an arm around her shoulders, and they walked around the dumpster. Mel took a deep breath. "I want to start over," she said. "With you, Jim. I want to do it right. With nothing between us. No lies."

"Okay, that sounds great."

Except for the part where you go and kill three people.

"I'm moving out."

He put a step between them. Looked down at her. "But I thought you said—"

"Yeah, but I need to do it this way. I need to make it right for us. After I'm done . . . if you want me still, I'll come back." She looked up at him with tears in her eyes.

Jim felt his own tears brewing and felt one spill over before he thought about holding them back. They stood silently watching one another, their faces working automatically to stem the tides of emotion.

"James, if you love me and you want us to be together, you'll say, 'Hurry back.'" She shook her head and looked at him again, her eyes watery, but clearer. "That's all I need right now."

Had Jim ever doubted this woman loved him, he'd been a fool. He knew that now. He knew it just as surely as he knew he was about to put a dagger in his own chest. The words spilled out of him without thought.

"Hurry back."

"I'm still your skyflower?"

He nodded, close enough to breathe in the sweet smell of her.

She nodded, sniffed, and then turned them around, and they began shuffling back to the apartment.

"I'm cold, Jim."

Those three words warmed him more than the little furnace in the maintenance closet of his apartment would in a few minutes. She'd called him "Jim," which meant the immediate danger between them was over, and telling him she was cold was her way of having him draw nearer to warm her body with his own. That last part was a little iffy. It was his belief that the Bloom had had side effects. Jim couldn't describe them all with words, but one he attributed to it was his lowered body temperature. He'd checked every day since last Monday, and though it had risen steadily, he seemed to have topped out at ninety-three degrees.

"When?" he asked just before they got to the stairs.

"Tonight," she said. "After you go to bed."

"What makes you think I'll be able to go to sleep tonight?"

"Oh, I know how to put you to sleep." Mel turned to him and, before he could start feeling too sorry for himself, dragged his face down to hers and kissed him deeply. It was all wet and sloppy. Probably one of them drooled a bit.

"Oh," he said, his clenching guts easing.

"No reason we can't get this show on the road right now." Jim was about to say something about it only being six o'clock, but Mel proceeded to turn Jim around so she could rhythmically spank his ass. He'd quickly gotten used to the milder displays of affection because the way Mel did it could be cousin to utter embarrassment. Despite her play, he knew she was absolutely serious, and at some point in the night he would be struck on the buttocks in earnest, in addition to being bitten, scratched, and perhaps even choked. Although the last would be more of a surprise than actual displeasure.

"Are you two getting ready to have sex?" Gary asked on the balcony above them. This time Jim did feel his cheeks color. Mel had a big grin on her face, and Jim thought his head would explode. "Can I watch?"

"I'm going upstairs to light the candles." Mel skipped up the stairs. "Meet me in five!"

Jim had forgotten about the stinging candle wax. Thankfully, that was only for her.

Gary quickly came downstairs and joined Jim. Today had been the first day the two had actually spent together in a week. Gary had been spending all his free time with Will and Mary Ellis.

"So, I'd better head back," Gary said, thumbing over his shoulder after he'd shrugged his jacket on.

"Hey, I meant to ask you," Jim said, "how come you don't talk to Mary Ellis?"

"I do. I see her every day."

"No, I mean *talk* to her. She's just your type. Y'know, breathing."

"Why would I talk to her?"

"Are you serious? I think she even likes you."

"Mary Ellis?" Gary said it like he didn't know who she was. He narrowed his eyes.

"Yeah. She's a lot better looking than what you usually go after. Plus, I think she likes you."

"Really?" Gary looked off in the distance. "I don't know." Gary looked boyish suddenly, and Jim saw why. He was unsure.

"Hey, you gonna be around tomorrow?" he asked, switching the subject. "Elias wants to see us."

Jim's knee-jerk response would have been no, but he stopped himself, suddenly reminded that Mel would be gone.

"I guess." He didn't really want to see the little man. Not ever again if he'd been the person Gary had gotten that godawful weed from.

"Then come by and scoop me after work." Gary looked up at him and put up a hand. "Nothing bad. As a matter of fact, he was happier than I've ever heard him. What did your mother do?"

Jim frowned. Not only had he just learned that his mother was in an industry related to his fiancée's, but she also had some sort of drug connection. She was making good on the promise that had gotten Elias and his men onto the roof of that building in Madison Heights. Jim kept trying to get hold of her, but she kept not being home or kept not answering her phone. She owed him a lot of answers, and he intended to get them soon.

Before he could respond, a horn sounded from his apartment. Jim was used to it, but Gary flinched and backed into the parking lot.

"Okay, I'll see you tomorrow, all right? Bye."

Jim's best friend in the world quickly walked around his apartment building and disappeared. Jim trudged up the stairs, in a sour mood about his mother, when he laid eyes on something he could appreciate: Mel in an all-white teddy, with those puff things trimmed around it.

She gave him a demure smile as he approached, and Jim leaned in for a kiss. He forgot about his troubles, as minor as they were, and stepped into their apartment, shutting the door behind them just as the hook from Bimbo Jet's song "El Bimbo" began to play.

Several miles away and hours from then, the ground began to stir. The sun had just buried itself beneath the tree line as the earth in a particular section of a municipal park began to heave. A mound of earth rose like a giant anthill as the tips of two fingers peeked out of the dirt. The mound contracted, widening until a pair of slender, muscular forearms extruded from the top.

The arms fanned out, palms planting on either side of the mound. With tremendous effort, the figure pushed, breaking roots that had been growing and interweaving for decades. The head came free, then shoulders, then a torso, all caked with dark soil. The body dragged completely out, kicking away clumps of clay and soil that had accumulated and entombed the body over the many years since its burial.

Finally, the body lay atop the earth. It was still a moment before it began retching and coughing violently, dislodging dirt and other detritus from its lungs. It continued long after it began gasping for air, like a drowning man breaking the surface.

At some point it became aware, and he curled into a ball as the coughing eased and he began breathing normally. He began shivering from the cold, his tattered clothing barely covering his body.

A skinny dog cautiously approached him.

"Where?" he asked, not recognizing the word he was speaking. "Where?" The dog came nearer, sniffing him. He held out his hand without knowing why, and the dog nuzzled it, then lapped his fingers, then finally pressed its head beneath the man's palm. He began scratching its scalp, and the dog came even closer, nestling its body against his.

It was so warm. So *alive.*

The man didn't know why, but the dog began licking his face, and he laughed, half turning away. He had never seen a dog before, at least that he could remember, but he liked it. He felt so happy, even though he didn't know where he was or even who he was.

"*Dog,*" he said, not knowing what the word meant.

Then there was a flash of light between him and the skinny dog. The mutt's whimper was cut off, and then it was gone.

No, not gone. It was somehow *inside* the man. He looked down at his chest and began digging his fingers into his skin. He could feel it there, but it was quickly receding, becoming a part of him.

The man felt a wave of sadness pass over him. And then he felt better.

He stood. He was still cold, but it didn't bother him as much. He didn't know where he was supposed to be, but he picked a direction and began walking.

"*Jim,*" the man said.

www.ingramcontent.com/pod-product-compliance
Lightning Source LLC
Chambersburg PA
CBHW030617250626
47154CB00006B/1815